The Sword of Bere'dn
A Story of Dyurndale

Dylan J. Marquis

Edited by: Caitlin Hopkins

Exterior Graphic Design by: Matthew Chu (www.mattchudesign.com)

eStore address (www.CreateSpace.com/6048634)

Available from Amazon.com, CreateSpace.com, & the Kindle app

Printed by CreateSpace, an Amazon.com Company

First Edition

ISBN: 1523964170
ISBN-13: 978-1523964178

DEDICATION

This book is dedicated to all the aspiring authors out there. You there, reading this book who has a story inside that is screaming to get out: open the cell door and free the fantasy within you.

A story untold is a spell worth casting.

CONTENTS

ACKNOWLEDGMENTS

First and foremost, I want to acknowledge my wife who has supported me from when I first had the idea that created this story all the way to its printing. She always listened to me while I expounded on what would happen next in the story, as I described scenes completely out of context, and fantasized about publication. As if she wasn't already amazing enough, she was a source of constant encouragement throughout the whole creation of this book. She is the inspiration of my life. Behind every successful man is an even more powerful woman who supported him to get there.

Without my mentor, Arylias Nova, I probably would still be waiting on an acceptance letter from a publisher. She provided both the information and surety to publish this book myself. She guided me towards my editor and my graphic designer, and she let me tag along at her table at a comic expo the first time I handed out samples of the book.

My editor, Caitlin Hopkins, was fundamental in helping polish this stone. She put up with my incessant questioning as I learned about the editing process and she saw weaknesses in the story that I was too jaded to see. A painted egg can still be rotten, and she ensured that I didn't have spoiled goods.

The artwork on the book is beyond my expectations, and to Matthew Chu, that admiration belongs. He, too, put up with a million questions that I berated him with. I had a rough idea for what I wanted, and he created a masterpiece with minimal instruction. To entice and allure with but a glance is a cornerstone of publication.

There are so many friends and family members that also helped me with information, suggestions, contacts, and support that I could fill a novel with their names alone. For your sake, the reader, I will simply tell you that whatever you do in life, never do it alone because the best fortitudes are those of companionship, loyalty, and love.

1 The Arrival

After he died, the emptiness of the dark began to fill with life and was replaced by the feeling of awakening. His senses began to develop as if he was coming out of a dream, but his life and final thoughts before his end were still fresh in his memory. He remembered his wife's red eyes as they brimmed with tears; his adoring children that sat around his deathbed as they consoled the grandchildren who barely understood that tomorrow he would be gone. He replayed the memories in his mind. He missed his family, but he eerily embraced the reality of his death. However, he was surprised that there was no bright light at the end of the tunnel, and he was afraid of whatever reality he had awoken to.

He kept his eyes firmly shut for fear of his new surroundings. The self-inflicted darkness made him feel uneasy, but the thought of opening his eyes to find some damned nightmare was terrifying. He kept calm, but what he heard around him did not meet the expectations of the celestial afterlife he had harbored throughout his existence before. Although he was apprehensive and bewildered, he was positive this could not be a punishment based on the way he had lived in morality. As he thought it over, an anxious knot formed in his stomach. How could he be so sure? Beyond his confusion, he simply hoped that the forthcoming events would be an adventure, and not the prologue to eternal condemnation.

He had been firm in his beliefs and sure of the convictions that directed his mortal morality. Yet, this new beginning was beyond his certainties; this was something else entirely. He lived under the assumption that his passing would be accompanied by choirs of angels who would receive him into a city in the clouds. Majestic beings should have been playing harps and lyres as they floated through the air on mighty wings, but no winged creatures sang in the silence.

Physically, he felt refreshed and inhaled a deep breath that he had not had the strength to do in ages. A cool breeze rolled tenderly over his skin. He could feel the weight of clothing on his body. That gave him more surety of life; or, at least, some form of corporeal existence. The sound of gulls broke through the quiet. It was a sharp and pure melody that, together with the smell of saltwater, told him an ocean was nearby. There was a recurrent crash of waves that seemed close, yet far enough away to remove the theory that he might have been laying on a beach.

He thought to himself that maybe this wasn't the next life; maybe death was the doorway to perpetual reincarnation. Had he been birthed as some new creature, or person, burdened with memories from his previous life? That possibility was unfathomable. Despite the perplexity of the afterlife, one truth had been resolved; death was not an end for him but another beginning. No reasonable answers could be developed until he opened his eyes.

His eyes fluttered open. Lying on his back, he stared up at a decrepit, stone ceiling. There was minimal illumination provided by sunlight that found its way through cracks in the walls around him like light from behind a curtain, left slightly amiss in the waxing hours of the dawn. He propped himself on one elbow and looked down a long arched tunnel, which gradually turned away. He leaned his back up against the undamaged wall behind him. Oddly, it was unaffected by age like the other walls that entombed him; the stones were smooth and the mortar in between them was fresh.

The question of what should be done next was only superseded by the curiosity of his location. As he lifted himself off the cool ground and brushed the dirt from his clothes, he found his lean body more able than it had been before his death. He was young and revived. His bones didn't ache or creak with age. Years had passed since he felt well, so it all struck him as odd, but it was immeasurably satisfying.

The daily dress of his former life was undershirts and well-worn jeans, but he found those had been replaced by garb that was foreign and interesting. His pants and shirt were a sturdy but comfortable material made of dark browns and beige; they reminded him of clothes from a time before technology. His shirt collar was open, and from it hung horned, toggle buttons. When fastened, they would inhibit the weather from cooling his neck. Perched across his shoulders, he wore a long hooded coat made of some animal's hide that felt thick enough to soften a blow but not so insulating to make him sweat. The pelt was a mottled, patterned, myriad of colors that his mortal eyes had never seen. Encompassing his waist was a belt, adorned with various pouches that bulged with possessions yet to be explored. His boots were a sturdy design that he found to be strange but seemingly appropriate; the tops of them were folded over like a buccaneer's.

Excitement overcame him as he opened the first snap on the pouch closest to his ornate belt buckle. Whatever this new life was that he had been given, it came with gifts. He was distracted by his shiny brass belt buckle that was covered with notches and inscriptions. The indentations made him think of cryptic markings on an ancient map; holding a secret yet to be deciphered. He wanted to stare at them long enough to understand them, but there was no obvious answer to the cipher.

Rumbling clamored up from the earth beneath his feet. Dust fell in curtains from the arched ceiling above him and onto his head of chestnut brown, shoulder-length hair. As he found his footing, he shook the debris out of his mane and was surprised by its fullness. Before he arrived in this new world, his scalp had been barren.

As he brushed out the rest of the grime from his locks, another tremor sent more dust into it from the ceiling. He reached up again but stopped as he noticed his hands. There were no spots of age or marks on fragile skin; his fingers were straight, plump, and strong like decades before his death. He longed for a mirror, but as he searched for something reflective in his many pouches, yet another turbulent quake interrupted him. His heartbeat quickened. He was instinctively fearful of his rising pulse and worried that his heart would fail him again. He clutched his chest and recalled his newly discovered strong hands and limbs; death from a failing heart was no longer on his list of things to fear. His heart pumped even faster as he realized that he could have excitement again.

The tumultuous convulsing crescendoed. This disturbance was much greater than the ones before, and it shook him off his feet and hurled him to the ground. The roar of crumbling rocks and cracking stones filled the tunnel. A loud crash echoed down it as a cloud of sand rushed towards him.

Once the cloud settled, he moved towards the bend in the tunnel ahead of him. Light seeped through the broken and missing pieces of the walls, but the holes were too small to see anything of worth. The sun's rays were visible in the dusty haze like solid spears, and he ran his hand through them in continued admiration of his new body. Every few moments there was another shudder with no apparent pattern. After the dust storm that rushed him, he gave up on removing any dirt from his hair or clothes. As he turned the corner in the burrow, he was surprised to see that it led to nothing. He expected a longer stretch or a light in the distance but, instead, the tunnel had collapsed. Panic swallowed and replaced his exhilaration with something more familiar. Thoughts of despair washed over his mind. He pondered which of his life's sins made him deserving of this entrapment; tormented by some agitating, unending quake.

He pushed on the walls around him, hoping that he could cause them to give way, but they would not move. He pressed his face against one thin rupture to peer through it, but he only saw the ocean. Far away in the distant horizon, where the edge of the world seemed to start, he could see a tempestuous storm swirl. He went from gap to gap in the broken stone as he tried to see what was outside. He pushed on the areas that were surely weak from the frequent shaking, but the walls were as solid as a singular piece of stone; not a grain of earth was moved by all his toil. His cheekbones burned with frustration. He reared back with one fist, charging the sinews of youthful muscles. Ignoring every mental warning bell, he swung his clenched fist at the impenetrable slab.

His motion was interrupted by a thunderous vibration. The constant tremors had become a disastrous earthquake that caused him to stumble backwards the way he had come. He tripped over a stone and fell to his back. His faith in the afterlife was shaken like the turbulent ground all around him. He inescapably worried that there had been a mistake in his sentence.

No more questions came to mind as he resigned himself to whatever fate came next. Whether he was crushed by rubble or entombed within the tunnel, he felt hopeless to control it. The ceiling began to crumble away. His beliefs never mentioned getting buried alive…unless this was hell.

The earthquake vibrated the loose stones around him and the sand levitated above the floor. Cracks splintered through the walls and the chatter of crumbling mortar joined the cacophony. The grinding of sliding stones sharpened his senses and he looked to the bend in the tunnel ahead of him that split with one thunderous vibration. Sunlight erupted through and poured on to the floor like water from a cracked vase, but the new weakness in the stone was not so big as to allow his escape.

Stones continued to fall and roll across the floor. The once tiny holes that allowed slivers of sunbeams through were now visible patches of sunlight, sky, and a world beyond. He picked up pieces of stone around him and lobbed them at the disintegrating wall. His desire to be free of those confines outweighed his fear of the tunnel collapsing down on top of him. More of the structure began to slough away with each stone he threw. His arms ached and the muscles burned, but it was invigorating. He could see more of the world outside: a bright beach in the distance with foliage-covered cliffs in the dark blue horizon beyond.

His terror turned into enthusiasm again. The rush of adrenaline was so intense that he thoughtlessly jumped up and ran towards the freshly made opening. He sprinted with a foolhardy fervor that could not foresee the outcome of his actions. He leapt at the weakened wall, shoulder first, hoping to dislodge the remainder of it. His plan worked and the wall exploded outward into open air. He could see the crashing waves far below him. He immediately realized how foolish he had been as he started to fall.

* * *

4

Darkness enveloped him, and he thought he was dead again. His eyes snapped open. He felt the solid surface of ground underneath him and the warmth of the sun on his back. He was lying on the edge of a crag that had barely caught him. He pushed himself up and touched a warm liquid on his face. There was blood on his hand and his head throbbed, but he was glad to have survived.

He easily climbed up the slate gray cliff face he had fallen from. It had enough cracks to make the short ascent possible. It was warm and held in the heat of the day. After his short climb, he discovered he was on a lonely spire, and he was able to see that the whole island tower had many small ledges that jutted out from the sides. There was a mainland to his right, but it was too far to swim to, and the cliff's edge he stood on was far too high to descend. The mainland was impregnable except for one narrow ravine that was directly across from where he stood.

He walked around the circumference of the island to each place where there was a smaller protuberance like the one that caught him. Each place where there was a ledge, he thought there might be a subsequent path down, but when he looked over the edge, his hopes were dashed like the waves on the rocks far below. He saw no sure way to escape and returned to the caved-in channel to see if there was anything there that might help him. He approached the entrance from the opposite side from where he emerged.

The crypt started below the surface of the lonely stone pillar, and it rose out of the ground like a bulging rib that ended in an elaborate archway. It was filled with debris from the collapse. There was a small patio area outside that was covered with gravel and semi-encircled with stones. Broken pieces from the decorated archway were strewn about in the gravel. The structure was obviously important enough to have been decorated in the way that it was, and although he had no attachment to the entryway, he couldn't help being slightly upset by whoever had destroyed something so intriguing.

Complicated statues stood on either side of the entrance and were no taller than he was: about two barrels tall but no longer as rotund. On a pedestal to the left, a feminine, half-serpent naga figure wrestled with a larger rugged, bulky one. The larger of the two looked almost as if it had not been completed in that it was made from the same stones on the ground around it, whereas the other statue was smooth and looked like glass. Despite the disparity in size, the naga seemed to be forcing the stone creature down to one knee as if she had an inordinate amount of strength in her slender form. The pedestal to the right of the crumbled entryway had a place where two other statues were similarly wrestling. There was only one whole statue who wrestled the broken remnants of where its opponent once was. It was a masculine, nearly human creature that had flowing robes around its waist and wings on its back. Its humanoid hands were slender claws like that of a bird and its arms were equally proportionate, yet more muscular than any avian appendage. Its muscles were lean and toned like a leopard ready to pounce. Even in the stillness, the creature looked alive. The four figures were locked in a stationary battle for dominance where not one of them had the clear advantage. No matter what their purpose, their possible significance to the tunnel was alluring to him; most especially the naga statue.

He felt drawn to her as if a siren's song was pulling him in a trance, but he heard no music; only felt the ballad in his core. His hand involuntarily stretched for her as if to awaken the glass with his touch. With each step he took, the song in his head grew louder; intoxicating and lovely. Before he touched her, his hand grazed the naga's opponent. The ground once again shook and severed the spell he was under.

It was dissimilar to the tremors and earthquakes of before and was a more intentional vibration in the ground; like the beat of a distant drum. Directly across from the hole in the tunnel wall, the ground near the edge of the cliff split away from the spire. It fell into the ocean below and darted away into the waves as if it was pulled on a line.

An enormous mountain rose out of the waters. The piece that had fallen from the cliff tower conjoined to the whole mass as it began to change shape. It moved and turned towards the man who stood with a shocked, gaping mouth. The land mass lethargically lifted what appeared to be its head from behind the mountain top.

The man glanced at the statues and realized that this mountain was the craggy creature entangled with the naga. The enormity of the gigantic creature was alarming enough to paralyze him. He felt compelled to flee, but his only options were to bury his face in his hands or find a place to hide.

The tunnel, he nearly said aloud and slapped his hands over his mouth to prevent the accidental escape of an utterance. He cringed at the suffocating place and its inescapable walls, but it was still more appealing than the threat of the mountainous giant. Without further hesitation, he sprinted towards the gaping hole and haphazardly flung himself through it to scramble into the darkness.

The ground continued to quake as the stone giant slowly reached the pinnacle of its elevation. Overcome with compelling curiosity, the man leaned his head around the edge of the broken tunnel wall. Waterfalls fell from the giant's back to include all manner of sea life that had been unfortunate enough to get caught in its rising. The giant was shaped like a man formed from a forested mountain. Where a head of hair would be, the giant had trees and vines that draped down its back. The foliage that covered its shoulders looked like a hide of armor. Underneath it, the outlines of gargantuan scaly slate could be seen. It wore a kilt made of constantly undulating molten rock that erupted from its belt as soon as its waist was above the water. The sea came up to the edge of its volcanic clothing and the crashing waves splashed against it, creating a cloud of steam above the water.

It slowly turned its head to where the man crouched, but instead of waiting to see the giant's face, he retreated farther into the tunnel. The ground shook again but in rapid and successive explosions like an athlete's sprint. The giant had seen him! He scrambled as far back into the tunnel as he could and found his back against the perfect stone wall again. The hole in the wall was plunged into darkness as the shadow of the giant approached the cliff tower. The thundering explosions stopped and through the hole, he could see the giant's fiery kilt. The pulsating garment bubbled and popped yet never splashed on the ground around it. The man held his breath in some vain hope that the giant had not realized he was there. A sudden grinding stone echoed through the tunnel as the kilt moved away, and the hole in the wall was blocked by a cavity where one of the giant's eyes might reside.

The empty socket was big enough to serve as a large tub. The blackness of the crater was darker than a shadow where light refused to go. The two tremendous plates that formed its eyelids slammed together silently. When they slowly opened again, the blackness filled with a fiery torrent of lava and smelted metals. Its iris was filled with a roiling gold that was speckled with slag, and its pupil was obsidian with cloudy swirls of gray.

"No use hiding!" the giant boomed. His slow deliberate voice was a resonant tremble that made the dust on the walls fall to the ground. His voice didn't sound malicious, but a towering creature hardly seemed gentle.

"Well, come out of your hole, little mouse. I could just as easily remove you from it," he said as he backed away from the hole. "Your time has come and I have waited for long enough. Indeed, I fell under the heavy mantle of slumber and have destructively suspired here for more time than I can fathom," he said with no diminishment in volume, even standing high above the gap. "Forgive me, I have neglected my introductions. I, child, am the maestro of mountains! I swirl the streams of planetary blood, rebuild the shores decimated from crashing waves; form mountains from plains, divide them to create ravines, and redirect rivers with stone…but my duties pale in comparison to what you are meant to do. You were summoned to save the world!"

2 The World

"That thing almost killed me!" he said quietly to himself, so as to not be heard.

The stone giant started to laugh. It was a deep chortle that sounded like boulders crashing into a quarry; the sounds echoed off the water and into the tunnel. "You're already dead!" He said in between laughing. "I fear that my restless slumber may have caused the tunnel to collapse; my most sincere apologies. You are small for a promise so great," he said, his voice reducing to a low growl as he stopped laughing. His eye filled the hole in the wall again. "You're the first one to ever come here this way."

The man said nothing.

"You're rude too. I thought you would be bigger or stronger maybe."

The uncomfortable silence between them continued. The man shifted where he sat in the darkest corner of the tunnel, trying to somehow back into it even further.

"My name is Kapell dun Shan but you may call me Kapell."

A brief silence followed where only the crash of waves far below could be heard.

"I have told you my name," he continued, "It is usually customary to return the gesture."

"Simon," he said quietly. "My name is Simon...or, it was anyway."

"He speaks!" the giant said to no one in particular. "Tell me, did you expect something else after your death? I have always wondered what so many of your kind expected to see. The disappointment on your faces is...interesting. Did you imagine chubby baby angels playing harps, flying on tiny wings? Or did you hope for handmaidens sitting on clouds, waiting to feed you bowls of grapes? One man expected a rickety gold fence hinged on clouds with some old man at a podium waiting to read his name off a list. That one made me laugh."

Simon had envisioned similar things for his afterlife but remained quiet in the corner. He was fearful of the world—excited but timid from his first encounter with a giant.

"Or were you afraid there would be more fire?" Kapell continued. When he said the last word, his iris changed from a roiling gold to a bubbling burning metal so bright that it caused Simon to squint. "If it's a game of waiting you want to play, you will lose. I have waited here a long time for someone to come through this gate. I would not like to see you fail, but if you stay here, I fear that you will. There is one who comes for you, and if you linger, she may see to it." Kapell's voice changed to a growl at the mention of this other person.

Simon was still unsure of Kapell's intentions, but he realized that this afterlife would be better spent outside than in a suffocating tunnel. And whatever threat the giant was referencing was enough to motivate him instead of waiting to discover the particulars. With that, he picked himself up, straightened his clothes, and shook out his dusty hair one last time. The giant backed away from the hole again and Simon stepped out of the tunnel, into the light, and onto the grassy cliff tower top.

"You have arrived!" the giant yelled. The gust of wind that escaped his lips knocked Simon onto the ground. Amidst his laughter, the giant bent over holding his stomach. His face was rather close to where Simon fell.

"I'm terribly sorry, Simon," the giant said in between chuckles and wiped strange tears of laughter from his eyes. He flicked his finger and the sparkling stones clattered across the top of the lone spire where Simon still lay. He eyed the giant's tears as they skittered here and there, and he couldn't help but feel a desire to retain them for whatever value they might hold. The way light refracted through the tears made him recall the infinitesimal gem he had given his wife in a life before: the way his young hands shook as he professed his love. He reached up to wipe away his own tear that escaped at the thought of having lost her companionship.

"Welcome!" the giant said as he sat down in the water.

Huge plumes of steam rose from the place where his molten clothes vaporized the sea. His head was level with where Simon sat, still speechless.

"Where am I?" Simon asked as he stood back up. "And what are you?"

"You're dead!" the giant said with another laugh. "I am an author of all things in the ground. I was made to keep up this place; anything that touches the ground, I was assigned to be the 'gardener' for, of sorts."

Simon stared at him, unsatisfied with the answer, but still curious enough to probe for more answers. "And where is 'here'?"

"This, my small squishy friend, is Dyurndale: the place where all souls travel after they die."

"I'm in purgatory?"

"No," Kapell laughed. "Do you truly think your previous life can be expiated by some effort on your part? No, that's not what this place is, and it certainly wasn't created to cause suffering...but so it has become. This place is a journey; a short life after your life, however long, or short, that might have been. Well, it used to be a wonderful place to travel before the next stage of existence," Kapell spoke nostalgically. "People no longer come this way. Now they just pass it by." The giant pointed to a cloudy green aurora above the clouds that speckled the sky. "It used to be an opportunity for people to take a long walk through nature and see all the beautiful things that exist in the world; things that they never had a chance to see in their former lives. It is surprising and sad how many billions of people have passed through here who never ventured from the familiar. There are creatures, places, and scenic views in your world that could never be described but only appreciated by being seen. Did you ever stand on a high mountaintop and look out over a forest with nary a building in sight?" The giant put his hand on his chest and extended the other as if to emphasize his prose. "Have you ever been in a place of natural stone, not those cities of glass and fabrication, where there was no rush of people?"

"So, what happened to this place?" Simon asked, feeling a little anxious to understand.

"Excuse me; I do get a bit carried away sometimes. As I said, people used to enjoy this place. It is still beautiful, but the birds no longer sing the same way and the flowers have faded. Even the waters of the sea, the wind in the air, and the fires deep in the ground have become unnatural. Dyurndale changed as more corruption came into it. Your species are like livestock; you laze, and congregate like cattle- and often, you are just as stupid. All it takes is one bad shepherd to lead the whole flock scrambling off of a ledge or—even worse—into some congregate submission.

People kept coming here even though the beauty started to fade. Some would come and wander into the wilderness, thinking that this was the next life. They foolishly ignored the signs on the path."

"There's no guide, or map, or something?" Simon asked. "Didn't you tell people when they got here where to go?"

"Dyurndale wasn't made to be a processing center but...there did used to be a sign, actually," the giant said with a thoughtful expression. "That was a long time ago...I remember now! Even though I made a sign, the first few people that came through here just sat down; they waited for some form of epiphany to reveal where they were. It seemed that people did their best in pairs. Dyurndale was simply intended to be a short stop, and not every person who came through here understood that or appreciated it. People came through and then stayed. They built a hut, then a house, then a home, then a city! The more that came, the more that would stay; and collectively disregard their inner motivation to enjoy Dyurndale. People turned to the corruption and greed of their mortal ways. The more people that stayed, the more neglected the way out became.

Sojourners used to mind that path as they walked, but then people stopped noticing the way it had begun to rot. In the beginning, your kind was oddly mindful of it. They picked the weeds, straightened a stone out of place, moved fallen branches; that sort of thing. As time went on, and more people stayed, less people walked the path, and the less inclined I felt to manage it. Eventually people stopped walking the path at all. There was a rare one or two every couple decades, but they were the exceptions.

Realizing the opportunity that all these new 'residents' proposed, a darker power started to dominate this world like an oppressive regime. He is not from your life before and not quite from this one either. He came from the heart of the sun and possesses a fire so hot that even water cannot pacify him. He took the form of a man instead of the burning giant he used to be. He is called, 'Etnian de Aithna.' His dominion was not enforced without an army. He brought help in the form of creatures so dark and terrible that they even make me shutter. I have never seen him to be honest, although, I have heard enough stories to fill volumes. His regime became an empire that hunted down every foolish soul stupid enough to stay here, and there were plenty to find. The people who had not walked the path began to run down it. They tirelessly fled to the next life but could not escape Etnian's reach. Your people stood no chance against him. His thirst for a growing army was insatiable. Every time someone new showed up, they were hunted down, captured, and forced into submission. There were plenty of people who went willingly into his service, too; the very sea here before you swore her allegiance to him.

In the beginning, people started their walk in a beautiful garden that I made for them. It was full of life and plenty; people could try any fruit that ever hung from a tree, vine, or bush. Etnian razed it to the ground. All that remains is a scarred landscape full of black withered trees and salted earth.

Kapell's story both saddened and intrigued Simon.

"Why didn't people fight him?" Simon asked.

"They did! There were many great battles fought against him in the beginning. The forces of good waged a losing war. There are still those who resist, but I fear their efforts are lost. Even those brave warriors were captured, tortured, interrogated..." the giant trailed off in his dialogue as if he remembered something painful.

"I still don't understand why *I'm* here. Why would I want to come to a place like this? I was promised something, and trying to escape some evil tyrant was not it."

"You were brought here to help change things. You're the first person to come through Dyurndale in a century. People have stopped coming…they have forgotten…" the giant trailed off again, lost in thought.

"You're not seriously expecting *me* to kill this Etnian guy; are you? I'm a nobody; I sold life insurance before this—oddly enough," he said to himself. "And what about my family—will they come here, too? I can't stand to think they would be sent into this hell."

"This is far from hell, albeit an unpleasant place to be without hope. Killing Etnian might be the ideal way of ending his reign, but I am unsure of how to kill him."

"If I'm the hero of the story, shouldn't I at least have a sword? Is there a stone I can pull one from?"

"Story? This is no fantasy, child. If you die here…you will not simply wake up."

"Well, then why don't you just come along? You seem like a strapping young…whatever you are."

"To be honest, I—I do not know why you came," Kapell continued ignoring him. "They never told me that part; just asked me to wait for your arrival."

"Who? Who told you to wait? Did they tell you what I was supposed to do by any chance? Maybe we should just wait for a phone call…maybe a carrier pigeon? Do you have phones here?"

The giant looked away from Simon and continued as if he hadn't heard him, "Are you supposed to defeat Etnian? Is that why they sent you?" Kapell scratched his head, lost in thought. Birds flew from the trees on his scalp as he moved his fingers. "Maybe you should walk the path that has been neglected for so long," Kapell continued speaking to himself. "It will be difficult…but, yes, that must be it. The roads will be watched by Etnian now, so as to defend against those that still try to make their way out through the Gate of Naru—that's the gate to the next life," he said over his shoulder to Simon."

Kapell continued rambling without directly speaking to Simon again. "It has been a very long time since anyone has had an opportunity to walk the path and restore its purpose, otherwise I would have been woken. I remember the people that tried though," he said as he sadly shook his head. "I remember the hordes of people that tried, by force, to take Naru. Oh, I lost so many friends. Surely, not one person has been successful since Etnian came to rule. Everyone who tried was killed, or worse: captured."

He turned and looked at Simon again, "People have lost hope and no longer believe they have a better choice. I think you are the one to restore hope, but it will not be easy. The way will be difficult, maybe even lost, or covered by time.

My role was to wait here for someone who could help. I was hoping you could tell me why you have come."

"I have no idea," Simon said a bit indignantly. "I woke up expecting heaven, and I got death, fire giants, and demon creatures? I mean no disrespect—and your story is pretty interesting; sounds exciting, even—but I'm not sure I'm the right guy for this. My biggest accomplishment in life was being there for my kids. I was a family man. I worked a lot but I was always there for them. Now I'm gone," he said, mostly to himself. "I wonder if she'll be okay," he said as he thought about his wife again. "She was always my better half. I love a good adventure and I've read enough stories about the meek becoming the brave, but I'm pretty sure I'm not that kind of guy—I want to be but...I'm nobody."

"Everyone is somebody, and you are the person we need. You must be! This gate has always existed—since time began—always standing, never receiving a soul, and now you've come through it. I was told to wait here in the waters until your arrival, but it took so long that I eventually fell asleep. Come to think of it, there used to be a stone bridge that led to the main land, but I see that time has taken that too." He pointed towards the main land in confusion.

"Kapell, please; I am not a hero. I've never been in a fight let alone been told I had to kill some fiery giant."

"All you have to do is get to the other end of the path. I doubt there is more that is expected of you. Just show people it can be done, that should be enough."

"I'm to save the world on a supposition?" Simon asked. "How can I show other people the path to walk when I don't even know the way?"

"Sometimes a leader needs to be brave, even in uncertainty; faith bolsters the strength you lack."

Faith, Simon thought. The word warmed his chest, but he still felt forced. He didn't feel that he had a reasonable choice to make, and he couldn't resist his own frustration. His choices were to begin this indeterminate journey, fraught with peril, or stay stranded on a lone spire, talking with a mountain.

He sighed and reflected on his simple life before: but there was little time for that. This world needed help. He had never been one to pass up the opportunity to give kindness where he could. He was compelled by a sense of duty. If he had the power in him to help, he had to. *I'm no hero,* he thought, *but maybe he's right. Maybe I was sent here for a reason.*

"Our time is short, and I know you have more questions and must be afraid—"

"I'm not afraid!" Simon interrupted. "But you want me to face an army on my own. It's kind of a big decision."

"The town of Canton is just up the river and in it a small group still holds onto hope. It has been ages, but hopefully their name hasn't changed; they used to call themselves the Kalinaw. To find them, go towards the center of the city but be careful who you ask; their numbers are plenty, but their secrets are dangerous."

"I'll do what you ask, but—"

"That is sufficient for me! I know you were ordained whether you believe in it yourself, or are later convinced; your purpose is clear to me."

"You sure you won't come with me?"

"I cannot; your arrival has set things in motion which I must usher along, and there are tools of war I must retrieve."

"Do you think I could at least get a lift next door?" he asked. "Looks like there's a storm coming this way, and I'd rather not be stuck out here when it hits," he said as he pointed far out towards the sea.

"Oh no, I have talked for far too long! That is like no storm you have likely experienced," he said. "That 'storm' comes with a purpose. That storm comes for you. Her name is Veadus Naufrage, and she is not merciful, or kind."

"Me?" Simon said, panicked. "Maybe if you hadn't talked so much I wouldn't be stuck up here!"

"Yes; I am not very good at managing time; that is my brother's job. I cannot take you to the land and hide you by the time she gets here. I will, however, give you a push in the right direction. Look, there, below us."

Simon walked to the edge of the cliff. A boat bobbed in the foaming water. There were places in the rock that were carved out and meant to be used as hand holds that were smoothed and sculpted by the passage of years. Halfway down, the ladder had eroded from time and repeated abuse from the crashing waves.

"That boat was intended just for you, and it has been maintained by loyal artisans of mine who were tasked with its care. There might have been a legitimate path down the cliff face many years ago, but time has not been kind; a boat is easily replaced and repaired, but without my care, the sea has abused the shores. Veadus will be upon us before you attempt a descent, but I can get you to the boat and give you a push towards the Vareex," he said as he pointed towards a ravine in the cliff face. "That is the most I can do for you. I hope you live from the attack that I will do my best to thwart."

"Give him to me!" said a voice that sounded like a torrent of raging rivers. The roar reached them as if she sat by their side. The two turned to see Veadus erupt from the storm clouds that threatened to devour them. Her typhoon was only an arrow-shot away. She exploded from the black billows like a predator waiting for the opportune moment to overcome her prey. She was nearly as enormous as Kapell, but much less haphazardly assembled. The dark storm trailed behind her like a bride's train as she rushed at them with an outstretched hand that ended in slender fingers with sharpened nails.

"We are out of time," the giant said. "You will have to jump."

3 The Attack

"You want me to jump?!" Simon said.

"The witch approaches; we have no time. You have seconds to decide…jump to me. You may be able to hide in my trees."

The stone giant did not wait for him to reply and grabbed him off of the stone tower as he closed his hand around him. Through the cracks in Kapell's hand, in between his fingers, Simon could see the sea giant rush towards him. Even at the distance they were from each other, the two giants were able to converse.

"You cannot win this fight," she yelled.

"And you cannot kill me without killing him," Kapell said, "You need him alive to feed the ravenous armies of the Darkness. To what end does his destruction serve but yet another loss in your feeble war?"

"'Feeble'? You cantankerous old mountain! The vapidity of your existence is only confirmed by your annoying attempts to protect the irritating insects that enter this world."

"I don't even know what that means," Simon said to himself.

"Why do you care for them so much?" she asked. "They do nothing for you! You so desperately wish to keep his inevitable death prolonged—whether we kill him now in some manner reflective of your failures, or use him as fuel for the fires of your destruction, we shall kill him either way!"

Veadus was of softer and more feminine appearance than Kapell; beautiful even, for being half a sea serpent. She glided across the water with grace yet obvious ferocity. The light of the sun shone through her as it hung in the sky behind her body and was blurred by the water she was made up of. Inside the confines of her skin were schools of fish, whales, and even the silhouettes of sharks. She glided towards them on the tidal

15

wave Simon saw from the stone cliff tower. The bottom half of her body was a darker green and was covered in scales like that of a fish. Her hair was thick like coral and the spaces between were filled with seaweed.

She stretched out her hand towards where Simon hid inside the giant's hand. Kapell moved his body to block her watery grasp. Her hand crashed into his back and exploded like a tidal wave crashing onto a rocky shore. The salty spray of water quickly settled on the surface of Kapell's back. He could feel that the water carried Veadus' soldiers who now raced along the forested surface of his body.

"You must run," the giant said. "Her forces are coming for you."

Simon looked up towards Kapell through the gap where his fingertips touched the palm of his hand. There was just enough space to see figures that blocked out the sun behind his shoulder. They moved down his enormous chest and gravitated towards the giant's core. They were bright blue figures shaped like Veadus, but more masculine and less graceful. The bottom half of their bodies looked like that of a snake, but as wide as a tree trunk. There was a company of them, and they were all wielding weapons made from parts of the sea. Some of the hilts were made of coral and others were remnants of sunken treasures, or ships. Another company of creatures, more man than serpent, followed in their wake. They glided behind the naga-men, and their skin shimmered like that of a bala shark. Even at their distance, Simon could see that their eyes were black and their faces grim; further eliminating their humanity. On their backs, they had bows made of twisted drift wood that hung next to quivers packed full of arrows. They quickly pulled their weapons from their backs as they raced along, strung arrows, and loosed them towards Simon, who was still crouched inside Kapell's hand. Some of the arrows found their way through the cracks in between Kapell's fingers. The arrows harmlessly clattered onto the floor but began to change shape as they landed. The arrows writhed and morphed into slimy green eels. They twisted and turned and once they had finished their change, they started slithering to Simon, but he had nowhere to go.

He kicked the eels and crushed their heads as he danced around their attacks. He looked up towards Kapell, hoping to catch his attention long enough to signal him for help. Simon tried to push open his giant stone fingers, but it was a wasted effort. He shouted at the top of his lungs to try and get his attention, but the battle between the giants raged.

Veadus attacked Kapell with a spear she materialized from the sea. The waters crashed into her open hand and fell away, leaving behind the coral form of a weapon. She thrust it towards Kapell's face, but he blocked it and swung with his colossal fist. He punched her in the stomach, which exploded in a wave of water but solidified once his hand passed through. He slammed his shoulder into her, but she allowed his hulking form to pass through her body. He stumbled into a deeper part of the sea, and the water washed over him as if to swallow him. The salty water filled his closed hand where Simon was and threatened to drown him. The water level dropped as Kapell gained his footing. Through the space between his fingers, Simon thought he saw an ancient waterlogged ship in Kapell's other hand. The giant had grabbed whatever he could from the seafloor when he stood back up, and he hurled it at Veadus in an attempt to subdue her. The ship knocked her into the water and her form momentarily disappeared. Kapell was limited so long as Simon was in his hand, but he made as great a defense as he was able.

The melee worked to Simon's advantage. He was jostled and soaked in Kapell's hand, but the eels were as debilitated. He held onto the roots in the giant's palm and fingers and continued stomping the eels that came too close to him, or grabbed them by the tail and smashed their heads on the giant's rocky skin. He hoped for an alternative but, for the moment, he had no other choice.

Veadus leapt up from the sea in full form again. She thrust her hand towards the beast of stone as she recovered from the impact of the sunken vessel. Swordfish, stingrays, seaweed, and all manner of shards of sunken debris shot towards the face of Kapell. Many projectiles hit their target and he covered his eyes with his free hand. In that momentary victory, Veadus seized the opportunity and threw herself at the mountainous giant. The shape of her body disappeared as it became a tidal wave that covered Kapell. The water from Veadus' dissolved form filled the cracks and ravines of Kapell's body as it rushed along his stony skin like translucent veins of surging rapids. The foamy rush through the cracks of his skin seemed to slow him down like they were extensions of the Witch's clutch. He fought against it, but it appeared that Veadus had him in a grip even he could not escape. A geyser of water shot up from behind Kapell; it rose in a steady stream until it hit the back of his head. The water collected around his head in an enormous orb of water that trapped his hand on his face, where he was still holding his eyes. Simon was again soaked in the salty torrent.

He looked back to where Veadus' assailants raced towards him. As the water filled the crevices, the naga-men and archers were more enabled to move along the craggy surface. The archers continued to fire their arrows into the spaces between Kapell's fingers.

Simon looked back towards the encapsulated face of the giant and could see a bright fire behind his entrapped fist. He struggled to pull his hand off of his face, but the water held it firmly in place. Veadus had become the very force that kept Kapell's head submerged in the swirling globular sea; Simon was sure he saw her menacing smile in the sphere. The bright fire behind Kapell's hand became radiant, and the water around the edge of his hand started to bubble. The bubbles became a furious surge of boiling water. Simon could see his mouth moving, like he was trying to say something, but the water muffled the loudest of sounds to be heard.

He flung his head backwards and a volcanic eruption spewed from his eyes and then out around his hand. The streams of molten rock rocketed from the water orb and into the air. The sky above the giants darkened with ash, and a volcanic storm cloud began to form. Purple lightning bolts arched between the clouds, striking the water orb that encased the giant's head. He continually tried to pull his hand away from his face to no avail. With one final and tremendous effort, he ripped his hand away and destroyed the confines of the water orb. As he pulled his hand from his face and the water fell back towards the sea, he yelled so loudly that it hurt Simon's bones: "RUN!"

His other hand flung open and exposed Simon to Veadus' soldiers.

Another wave came from the sea far below and crashed into Kapell's shoulder. It rushed towards the sea witch's warriors so as to expedite their attack.

Simon had no idea what to do, or where to run. He felt a wave of emotions run through him: confusion, fear, and frustration; all of which exacerbated Simon's ignorance of how the new world worked.

As if in response to Simon's insecurities—but mainly his lack of action—the giant swung his hand downward, causing Simon to lose his footing and hover in the air. As the effects of gravity caught up with him, Simon reached towards twigs and roots that peppered the stony hand. In the same moment that Simon had a grip again, Kapell's hand moved towards his body with Simon feeling like a flag flapping in the wind. He could see the forest floor of the giant's torso rapidly approaching. He could see trees, bushes, and grass moving towards him.

"Jump!" the giant yelled. Simon reacted without fully addressing the fear that held him in place.

He jumped blindly. The branches of trees whipped and scratched his arms and face as he fell through the air. As he landed, he rolled onto a particularly spongy area of moss that would have been a nice place to sleep if he wasn't fleeing from sea bred nightmares intent on killing him. He gathered himself up and started to run. He was surprised that his body was drawn towards Kapell's skin as if the creature generated his own gravitational force. Simon tested his theory as he dove from one stone to another. As he ran, he quickly fell back to Kapell's body. He knew the sea was downward, but since his feet were firmly drawn to Kapell, it seemed to be forward instead. Either gravity had shifted, or Kapell truly was the master of geology. Either way, Simon ran as hard as his renewed legs would take him down towards the boat by the tower.

He bounded over boulders, leapt over logs, and wildly pounced to protruding precipices. Each time he did, his feet fell swiftly back to the surface of the giant. With his next leap, he landed in a puddle, which might not have been abnormal in any other forest he happened to find himself, but the water in this place had a master. He wondered if all the water was in her control. The momentary thought was brief enough where his heaving breaths and pounding steps didn't overwhelm his hearing. He heard something beyond the thunderous melee between the giants and braved a glance behind him, upward towards the titans' faces. A tidal wave was crashing towards him. On the very crests of the waves, Veadus' soldiers rode with a sportsman's ease. He pressed himself to run faster.

The boughs and trunks behind him began to bend under the duress of the crashing water, yet he never stopped sprinting. His lungs burned with numbing fire that he hadn't felt since before the hairs fell from his mortal scalp. He flew up an inclination in the surface of the giant's leg but realized too late that it was a small cliff. The water that pursued him surrounded the outcropping and he became trapped on a tiny peninsula.

He stopped at the very apex of the outcropping and could do no more than flinch as poorly aimed projectiles landed around his feet. The wave that carried his attackers was upon him, and he had no other choice but to leap in to the ocean below. He would have to hope that he was neither trampled by the warring giants, nor smashed against the stone cliff tower that had birthed him. He crouched down, charged his legs, and pushed off towards the water below with all the strength he had. He didn't know if he could break the gravity that rooted him to the stone golem.

Simon felt a disorienting change in equilibrium and fell down towards the sea. The water around the giants filled with steam from the constant vaporization that Kapell's kilt caused. Simon hoped the water below him was clear of any rocks he might land on. After a lengthy fall, Simon landed deep in the surging sea. He kept his eyes firmly closed as he swung his legs to emerge from the surface again. He broke the surface of the water with a gasp, but the frigid water forced him under again. Determination overtook his fear as he thought about being smashed against the rocks or trampled under a giant's foot. He swam hard against the current in an effort to gain a breath. Each time the light of the water above seemed to penetrate the darkness of the sea, he was pulled back underwater. Not for lack of Kapell's valor, Veadus had a slippery grip on Simon.

He struggled in the water again, and with each stroke he began to rise out of the sea. He broke the surface and sucked in the salty humid air with a tremendous breath. He glanced back up at the giants and saw Veadus hunched over from the strike of her enemy. Simon heard a splash of objects nearby and just caught the sight of a group of Veadus' lifeless minions falling from Kapell's crushing grip.

Treading water was difficult, but it seemed the sea had loosened her grip on him. He floated helplessly in the water and was sloshed back and forth.

Veadus' form began to take shape in the water around him. She quickly lashed out of the water like a snake to try and overcome Kapell. She grabbed him from behind, but he nimbly bucked her off of his back and rushed to strike before she landed in the water again. She pushed him back towards Simon and he worried that his position was the worst place to be. The giants above him struggled in an embrace much like the one by the stone entry way. The steam around them made the giants step in and out of vision in a red haze that was caused by the fire of Kapell's kilt.

Simon tried to swim towards the small boat, but the constantly changing waves prevented him from making any progress. The boat violently rocked against the stone tower, and he wondered if it would stay afloat much longer.

The vapor cloud began to diminish as if being beckoned, and the sea calmly swayed with intent. The volcanic kilt rose above Simon's head as the sea level rapidly dropped. Veadus had had her fill of the battle between earth and sea. She used her control of the water to call every drop of moisture in the vicinity to her aid. The water funneled towards her body as she grew in stature and diminished in beauty, breaking Kapell's grip. The water flooded her body unevenly, and bulging masses of water bubbled from every part of her. Her grim expression was a clear sign that her next attack would be a final effort.

Simon would not reach the boat and then the shore before her next attack. Veadus was not the only one whose patience with the battle had ended. Kapell could manipulate the earth as easily as she could use the water. The sea floor far below Simon's treading legs rose out of the tides, and he was forcefully lifted out of it on a flat smooth stone that jutted from Kapell's leg. The forest that grew on his skin parted for the rising crag.

The salty air chilled Simon quickly but competed for the warmth that the fiery kilt above him provided. He looked up towards Kapell's head and it seemed to be a day's walk away. Kapell looked down at him and winked.

Simon was grateful that the adventure didn't end in the dark, abusive torrents of the sea. The immediate benefit of this new situation was that the undulating mass of lava that composed the giant's kilt separated Simon from Veadus' minions. Despite the threat that his life was under, a momentary grin found its way across his lips. Being rescued by a creature of such legend beyond his wildest of dreams was indisputably exciting.

He rose on the platform to the giant's knee. "This is absurd," Simon thought out loud, "I must be dreaming."

"You're not dreaming." said a small voice behind him. A perfectly smooth black orb rolled from the surface of the giant's skin where the protuberance began. A figure, no bigger than his hand, emerged from the round orb. It looked like a pangolin made of stone. It walked on four legs and rose to two as it got closer. Its front legs ended in long, sharp claws, and it kept the appendages close together as if folding its hands. The hide of the stone beast was plated armor like reptilian scales that covered it all the way to the tip of its long, wide, and flat tail. "You need to get up," it said dryly. "Master Shan is slightly preoccupied. He sent me to relay the message."

Eel-arrows interrupted their conversation.

"You need to get up!" said the pangolin again, this time more aggressively. "You need to get to the boat," it said as it pointed down the leg of the stone giant.

Simon looked back towards the small boat which stayed in its place close to the stone tower. He could see that it was a simple vessel and barely big enough for two people. There was an oar in its belly, yet he had no idea how to sufficiently row, even when not fleeing for his life. "How am I supposed to get down there?"

"I can help." The small pangolin stamped its tiny foot on the rocky protuberance which then cracked straight across its width. The small ledge turned back towards the sea below. Simon crouched low against it and held onto whatever crack his fingers could find. There was a loud scrape and a wave of gravel carried the stone slab on its way. The pangolin's little hands waved around in the air like he was conducting a symphony, and Simon got the impression the small creature had abilities much like Kapell's. The "ground" of the giant's leg constantly disappeared and reappeared behind him; he was below the giant's knee and rapidly approaching the sea again.

The next steps of his journey were upon him without an opportunity to consider all the options. In his mortal life, Simon allowed himself time for consideration based on facts and data. There were never any real threats to his wellbeing, or projectiles, or heroic demands. He felt thrust into this position, but with each passing moment, he felt the captivation of adventure. He was beginning to think that he might actually want to be the hero.

His thoughts were interrupted as the time to decide was upon him. The sea was only a stone's throw away. "I can't swim that fast," Simon said to the small stone pangolin that stood upright.

The constant pitching and jumping of the stone slab didn't seem to affect it.

"Ah, but you don't need to!" said the creature.

As if Kapell was queued by the comment, he pulled his foot out of the water and kicked with enough force to send Simon and the platform into the air and straight towards the small boat.

The ledge flipped and launched Simon from it. He heard the angered shouts of Veadus' remaining brigands nearby. In the strange excitement of the last few moments, he had nearly forgotten about them. Simon landed in the boat and onto a leather seat that was surprisingly comfortable for a boat of indeterminate age. The momentum with which he landed caused the rope that kept the boat moored to snap. The boat floated towards the shore, but with insufficient momentum. He was still far from victory.

Simon picked up the oar and haplessly paddled towards the ravine in the sea cliffs. He looked back towards the warring giants and saw Veadus' army land in the water. He realized with frustrated exclamations that he had no hopes to escape them. He frantically struggled in his attempts to paddle away.

The ocean around Veadus shot towards her like inverted water spouts and caused her form to grow to twice her original size. She had even formed legs to better secure her victory. Her attractive visage became a demonic nightmare. She held Kapell by the neck as he repeatedly clobbered her thickened arm. She looked down from her new form and made eye contact with Simon. The battle seemed to freeze. She became formless as her countless quantities of water fell back towards the sea. The sea between the stone giant's feet began to swell as if a mountain was forcing its way through the surface. A face formed before him: *her* face.

"You will drown," she said with a maniacal laughter that caused Simon to drop the oar.

He felt that fear might be his unfortunate and frequent companion during his journey.

"Not if the Land can help it," Kapell replied.

He spread his arms wide and immediately flung his hands towards each other. Her forming head moved towards the small boat and she opened her mouth in an unnatural way as if to swallow it whole. Kapell's hands came together with a concussive force that made Veadus' head completely evaporate. The resulting swell lifted the boat onto the height of a wave, and Simon gripped the sides for what was going to be a thrilling ride.

Kapell filled the voids in his chest and blew gale force winds across Simon and his tiny ship. It launched the boat towards the openings in the face of the cliffs far away where Kapell said the Vareex began.

Simon was, once again, thrust into the seat, and as he bounced into the bottom, he struck his head on the hard keel. The world became momentarily dark again—the deep dark that coupled unconsciousness. He couldn't help but think—despite the fear of dying once more, and the aching in his head—that this adventure would be a fulfillment of his every juvenile wish to be a hero.

4 The River

He awoke inside the boat and looked up at a clear blue sky, bordered by boughs of green. The warm breeze carried a pleasant petrichor. Soft sloshing water against the side of the wood made the scenario nearly peaceful, if it weren't for his recollection of the past few moments. A smile crept its way onto his face; it hadn't all been a dream. He thought about Kapell and wondered if he had defeated Veadus. He was grateful for the giant's heroism, and wished he could have thanked him, but was glad there was some semblance of distance from the Witch. Had it not been for Kapell, he would have surely drowned at her hands or been pierced by her minions' weapons. The curiosity of the fantasy and the pleasant senses around him were relaxing but not so much that he didn't want to learn more about where he was now.

He sat up and climbed into the leather seat to see that he was floating down a river with dense forest on each side of him, with intermittent barren or pebbled beaches. Where the forest met the water, the ground sloped steeply upward onto banks that would have been foolish to try to ascend. The steep inclines were repeatedly interrupted by crevices, which seemed to be remnants, or beginnings, of other rivers. Some of them were barely wide enough to be considered a trickle, while others were broad enough to accommodate a ship.

The river that he floated along twisted and turned around bends that made its length impossible to ascertain. The current flowed smoothly with minimal turbulence or interruptions, accenting the comforts of his simple, gifted boat. The seat he was on was cushioned and sat low in the keel; the back of it was similarly fashioned and leaned against the stern of the small craft. It was the most luxurious of dinghies he had ever seen. The sides of the vessel were smooth and polished with a lacquer that reflected the sunlight above, but not quite as brilliantly as the gold trim that topped the edges of the sides. He grasped the polished edge of the boat and carefully leaned out over to peer into the dark water. He slumped back into the boat as he twisted his mouth in uncertainty.

"Where did that armadillo go? I hope he didn't fall in," Simon said aloud. "And now I'm just talking to myself."

Maybe I have a map or something, he thought as he started reaching for one of the pouches on his belt.

"You could talk to me," said a soft, female voice.

Simon jumped in surprise. A blue, stone ball rolled out from under a corner of the boat's prow. When a shape emerged, it was that of a small frog, instead of the pangolin that he had seen before.

"Weren't you black before?" Simon asked with a confused expression, relaxing back into his seat.

"No, that was Sid; such a brute he is. My name is Lazuli. I come from much finer stone than him."

Indeed, she was a more alluring material than the black of the pangolin's make; she was a lazurite stone so brilliantly azure that Simon was captivated by her beauty. Her skin was a royal blue, speckled with flecks of yellow and black, and warty like a toad. The rest of her was in keeping with the expected form of a frog. Despite her unique coloring, Simon might have thought nothing of it. Conversely, she looked like solid stone instead of soft flesh. It was as if she was unable to remove all traces of her former stillness, and, until she spoke again, Simon was unsure if she was petrified. Her voice was mixed with a warbled tone like she spoke through a pool of water in the back of her throat. "Technically, I should not even be helping you, but the world is a different place these days."

"I appreciate your help, but unless you can reach the oars, I'm not sure what you can do."

"So, you do know your destination? Good, I'll be on my way." She jumped up on the edge of the boat, preparing to jump into the river.

"Wait!" Simon said. "I meant no offense; this world is strange and I'm a little overwhelmed."

"All of a sudden I am of use to you?"

"Well, I am in great need of assistance," he said awkwardly. Offering a frog his manners felt strange, but he tried to maintain his civility. "I may not know *exactly* where I'm going," he said with a chuckle.

"I have a feeling you do not know at all."

"Yeah...that's true. Kapell wasn't exactly specific."

"He has been waiting for you longer than his memory can serve him. Many of us have been waiting for you."

"What makes me so special, though?"

"The smallest of leaves can have the most brilliant of colors. You were destined for great things, although your time and form were unknown to us."

"I hope to fulfill the expectations," he said more to reassure himself than Lazuli. "He told me to find the Kalinaw in Canton."

"Yes, but finding them may be difficult. At the moment, you simply need to let the river lead you; it will take you where you need to go. You will find Canton at its end."

"Well, that seems easy enough—"

"...yes but sometimes the easiest path only appears to be so."

An unnatural ripple in the water intersected the minor disturbance the boat made. It caught Simon's eye, and in the same moment, the evil expression of the Witch's sneer flashed in his mind with alarming clarity. He shut his eyes and shook his head to chase away the vision. As he opened his eyes again, he thought he saw a shadow dive deeper into the water. He grabbed the edge of boat and leaned outward to get a better look but assumed his paranoia was simply playing tricks on him. He saw nothing in the dark water.

"What did you see?" Lazuli said, hopping closer to him. She carried a note of urgency in her voice.

"There was something in the water...maybe it was nothing, but...I hope it wasn't—"

"Don't say it; that witch deserves no recognition," she said quickly as she hopped up on the edge of the boat, puffed out her throat, and emitted a bark that interrupted him.

She sat on her coiled amphibian legs and balanced on the outermost edge to peer into the water.

"She was once a mighty ally, but in the Battle of Torchdale she turned."

"The Battle of what?"

"Did Kapell tell you nothing? The Battle of Torchdale was the deciding victory that solidified the tyranny of Etnian de Aithna. Vea—she—that vile sorceress—was decimating his forces on the shores of his homeland far away to the east when she turned. I have heard stories that he now controls her somehow, and she is his slave, but the merciless way she turned on her own kind...on my kind..." she stopped talking like the pain of the memory was too great.

The silence made Simon empathetic. "I'm sorry for your loss." He let the words hang in the air like the palpable quiet that filled the space between the river walls. "I hope Kapell is okay; he was fighting...you know..."

Simon trailed off again as he saw another ripple interrupt the water's surface. He tried to ignore the danger that the ripples implied and convinced himself that it was just a fish.

"Can she reach us here?" Simon asked, keeping his eyes on the water looking for another shadow.

"Her power is limited, but her influence is not."

"I swear there's something down there."

"There are predators in the sea that wait for their prey to come within distance enough to strike; peacefully waiting for their victims until the right moment."

"If you're trying to be encouraging, you're not really helping. Is there a way we can get out of these ravines?"

"We may be able to drift by unnoticed, but a time may come when Her brood attack. If they do, I will defend you—with my life, if need be."

Simon looked at her skeptically.

"You must learn that presumptions are the guise of ignorance, and the downward slope to folly," she said turning her body as she looked up at him.

Before Simon had a chance to seek clarification, a geyser erupted next to them. The boat lurched far off onto the bank of the river under boughs that masked the embankment. More geysers erupted from the water, and rain from the river fell on the branches above.

"The trap is sprung," Lazuli said.

She began to grow and become an even brighter blue; a color bright enough that it seemed to emit its own light and make Simon squint. She started changing shape and continued growing rapidly to the size and shape of a woman, but much taller than any woman Simon had ever seen. She grew until her shoulders were above Simon's head and any former reptilian features had disappeared. Her shoulders were broad and the muscles he could see were thick and defined like that of an athlete's. There was no hair on her slick-skinned head.

When her metamorphosis seemed to have finished, armor began to form on her new body like scales growing from her skin. The plates of armor expanded until their edges met, melded, and became solid sheets. The metal was a reflective gold like on the edges of the boat, and it made Simon wonder if she was the boat's attendant that Kapell had spoken of. Her armaments had large stones on the shoulders that rose to geodic points, which stuck out in varying directions; the purple crystals looked like impenetrable armor and dangerous weapons. Below her chest plate, and from her waist, hung a segmented tasset with enough additional cloth to provide a modicum of decency. From her bare scalp, a helm formed like the armor that was on her skin. On the crest was a bright emerald fin, topped with spikes. It, too, looked as though it might serve as a weapon on its own.

She turned slightly to look over her shoulder at Simon, and he saw the gems mounted on the front of her helm were the same labradorite hue as her former skin. As she eyed him, her complexion changed to a mottled brown and green with flashes of the same blue she was fully colored with before. It gave her a more human appearance, but her eyes eliminated the similarity. They were a fiery orange with elongated pupils. Simon half-expected to see her shoot out a long reptilian tongue to moisten them. "Just stay on the river," she said quietly over her shoulder.

She jumped out of the boat and onto the surface of the water like it was solid ground. Despite her size and encumbered appearance, she ran across it as easily as if she were on flat stone. Her speed was so swift that her feet barely disturbed the surface of the water.

Beyond the boughs of the trees, Simon could see a serpent rise out of the river. Its head swiveled threateningly on a thick body and was accompanied by several spear-shaped tentacles. Simon had no desire to see the rest of what might be hiding under the water. Before he turned to flee, he saw Lazuli race towards the creature with a long spear in each hand. She had them both pointed backward, slightly dragging in the water, but as she drew closer to the creature, she quickly turned the blades up. She readied her stance to fend off the creature.

"Definitely not going back out there," Simon said as he stepped out onto the wooded shore.

Being on the shore was reassuring, instead of being at the mercy of the water's current and creatures. Simon's experience was enough to urge him away from any puddle or pool; he had no idea how far Veadus could reach.

He could hear the clash of the sea serpent against Lazuli's defenses. He took a step towards the water's edge to try and offer some form of assistance. He wanted to help but felt ill-equipped. He was too inexperienced to tell if she was gaining an upper hand, and he knew his efforts would be useless against the sea serpent. Still, he felt as if he was doing more harm by doing nothing. He hesitated and looked back again at the battle beyond the edge of the river. He moved to the boat to see if he could push it out and even provide a distraction to Lazuli's benefit.

The sea creature shook its head and fins flared from its crown; the startling whip of extending fins interrupted Simon's efforts as he tried to dislodge the boat from the shore. It roared a terrifying scream that shook the leaves off of the trees. Lazuli slashed and swung at the creature, leaving gaping wounds that irritated it more than slowed it down. It bellowed another roar and lunged at her. She crouched down against the water, preparing for the attack. As the serpent's gaping jaws rushed to meet her, she thrust her weapons up to pierce it. Simon felt a surge of heat burn across his face as he felt utterly useless to stop what was happening. The serpent slammed into her and forced her underwater; huge geysers of water exploded from the impact. The resultant rain on the leaves above Simon was a disturbing transition to the silence that soon followed. The serpent's tail whipped into the air as its body disappeared under the water.

A sickness overcame Simon, and he felt the need to vomit. He had never experienced someone else's death before, and to see something so violent and merciless happen only a dozen yards from him was sickening. With a sliver of hope, he wondered if there was any way she could have survived.

The tepid repercussions of the battle caused small waves to continuously push their way onto the shore where Simon stood. The water soon settled unnaturally and added to the strangeness. He stood there for a long time, unable and unwilling to move for fear of causing a sound. The silence in the air was enough to make his breaths sound like a whirlwind and his heart like that of a battle drum. Not even a bird made a noise in the trees around him.

Simon wondered what to do next. The river was a foolish path if the creature still lurked in it, and the silence made the idea of crashing through the woods just as hopeless. He stuck his hands in his pockets and hoped that an answer would develop. Instead, he just stood in that spot and watched the water settle for what felt like a lifetime. Lazuli was lost, and although he had only just met her, he felt responsible for her death; the thought made the sickness return to his gut and he clutched his stomach to force the discomfort away. He cursed his inaction and felt determined not to let her sacrifice have been in vain. He went over the short battle and wondered if there was anything that he could've done; any moment of advantage that he had let slip by.

"No, there was nothing," he thought out loud. "I don't even have a weapon."

"Well, that should make this easier," said a gruff, rocky voice that seemed to float down the hills behind him.

Simon turned around quickly to see...nothing. He looked on the ground for another ball of stone, but nothing was there. He looked into the shadow of the trees on the ridge on the other side of the river, but no shadows moved. He looked above him and behind in the woods, but no leaves rustled nor branches swayed.

"Fantastic; talking to myself wasn't bad enough, now I'm actually going crazy."

Simon turned back towards the river. The serpent's gaze bore down on him; its head only inches away. It looked fearsome in the river, but at this distance, it was much more terrifying; further exaggerated by the realization of its enormity.

"Where's Lazuli?" Simon was surprised to hear himself say.

"Bravery?" the serpent said, as it coiled its serpentine body backward slightly. "Only moments ago, you turned your back on her, but now you challenge the very thing you feared?" It swayed from side to side, assessing which direction to strike from.

Simon didn't move; certainly not faster than his mouth had. He felt foolish to not have simply run when he had the chance. Carefully, his eyes scanned his dilemma. He spotted a spear jutting from the side of the serpent's body and just beyond that, the small boat. There were many scars along the serpent's skin, and several other weapons stuck out of its hide, most of which appeared to have been broken off or scraped away. The spear he eyed was Lazuli's.

"You couldn't dream to move fast enough," said the serpent. "If she couldn't kill me, what makes you think your chances are any better?"

"I could never kill you…we haven't even been introduced." Before the banter could continue any longer, Simon ducked and ran past the serpent's head, grabbed the spear out of its side, jumped towards the boat, and used the spear to vault himself through the air. The serpent quickly slithered, but not fast enough to catch Simon in its mouth. Simon landed in the boat and the serpent's scrambled movements caused the water to push the boat farther away. It gave Simon the momentum to get a head start. He was out in the middle of the river before the serpent's ripples stopped having an effect on his movement.

He glanced back to see his enemy rise high into the air and laugh.

"This was your plan; to strand yourself in the water?"

"I was kinda hoping you'd think I wasn't worth the trouble." Simon said over his shoulder as he tried to paddle down the river.

"Your worth is the reason the trouble has found you out. You cannot escape the reach of Madame Naufrage!"

The serpent rushed towards him and the water surged from its displacement. The boat began to lift out of the water on the crest of a wave, but Simon quickly realized that it was another long part of the serpent's body. It lifted the small boat towards its gaping mouth. Although it only took seconds to be put in that hopeless position, it felt like time slowed as the severity of the situation impressed upon him.

The serpent tilted the boat towards its cavernous jaws in an attempt to swallow Simon like a clam out of its shell. Its teeth were thousands of curved, barbed spears which better served to take bites out of a mountainside rather than swallow one tiny man whole. The smell of foul, rotten flesh made Simon gag and the thought of being digested was more than he could cope with. Simon fumbled with his belt. He prayed for something to drop into the creature's mouth, to deter it from swallowing him, but not knowing what trinkets he had withered his hopes. He knew, despite the odds being heavily weighed against him, he had to fight. There was no more time for indecision.

Simon took the spear in both hands and, with the broad side of the weapon's head, slapped the serpent across the foremost part of its face. Despite the foolishness of the move, there was a satisfactory result. It made the creature rear backwards in surprise. It roared so ferociously that Simon lost his grip and nearly fell in to the water. Nevertheless, Simon felt a laugh work its way out of his chest at the thought of slapping a leviathan across the face. Chuckling all the while, he struggled to stay in the up-turned boat.

The serpent lunged towards Simon and, with little thought to what might happen next, or how unlikely success was, he lunged too. He pushed himself off with his legs as hard as he could muster. He thrust the spear forward, towards the serpent as it unhinged its jaws to swallow him. Adrenaline surged within Simon and his spine sparked as if it was electrified.

There was an unexpected satisfaction as the spearhead sank deep into the serpent's eye. He shouted and laughed in excitement, "That's for Lazuli!" Simon had expected the spear to clang harmlessly off the serpent's tough skin.

The sea snake reared back and flailed its head around as it tried to dislodge the weapon and Simon; who happened to still be holding onto the spear. Eventually, his grip gave way and he was flung far down the river, far enough to gain the illusion of safety. As he dropped in, the current changed from the placidity he was first introduced to. It was strong enough that Simon had little choice but to let it take him along. While being pulled downstream, he glanced back towards the defeated serpent and saw it frantically grabbing at the spear with its tentacles.

He found his spirits somewhat uplifted when he also saw the boat floating back down the river. It was overturned, but he was happy enough just to have something to hold on to. It moved down the river much faster than he, and with a little maneuvering, he caught the boat as it passed. He managed to crawl up the side of the small boat and right it at the same time. He fell in, completely soaked but pleased that he could add *leviathan slayer* to his recent list of accomplishments. He could only hope that the creature would die from the wound. Although he doubted it would, he lied to himself for the sake of a moment's peace. For even a moment, at least, he could breathe without the need to defend his life.

The cries of the sea serpent died out as he continued down the river. With each new turn and bend that separated him from the nightmarish beast, Simon became more at ease. He leaned back and listened. He had no other option but to let the river guide him. Even if he desired otherwise, there was no oar in the boat with which to change his course. For the time being, that seemed to be the least of his worries.

The sky grew dimmer and the darkness of night dripped down over the high ridges of the river. The crevices along the banks seemed to fill up with twilight faster than the sky around him. His anxiety returned as the shadows played around him. He felt the piercing gaze of unseen creatures, and he was unsure if it was simply his fear of the darkness that spied on him. His doubt waned with every rustle of leaves on the banks and distant howl of a beast calling to companions. His surroundings were surely full of unknown predators. He recalled Lazuli's warning about presumptions and his feeling of safety on the water disappeared along with the light. He was inclined to trust his instincts and tried to slouch down in the bottom of the boat as best he could.

Night was an impatient creature, and the world became a shadow that masked even his own body. He was blind with not even the light of a moon to provide solace. The crickets he expected to hear were absent. The sound of the boat gliding through the water was the only thing to pass his time. Sleep was a companion he did not have; strangely, he hardly felt fatigued. He knew he should feel exhausted, but his body buzzed with energy in the dark; he did not feel removed from the threat of the leviathan.

He longed for a light to see by or a sound to signal some semblance of safety. The blinding darkness and quiet was so unsettling that he almost would rather have faced the serpent again. Hours passed as he silently drifted on the water. He could feel the boat turn or bounce off of the shore but it was impossible to see what it hit.

A pale light cut through the darkness in the sky. Simon thought that enough time hadn't passed for the sun to rise but many of his assumptions were being corrected that day. The glow swept across the sky as he drifted closer. The water in the river bend ahead of him mirrored lights that were rippling reflections of something just beyond his vision. As he got closer to the turn, the glow of an unseen city eradicated the darkness of the river. He thought of Kapell's mention of Canton. He was grateful to think that he wouldn't have to continue alone in his journey, and that he could see the faces of other people.

As he drew nearer, he squinted from the lights that shined towards him. A building like a dam stretched across the width of the river and towered up each embankment all the way to the tops of the ravines that bordered the waterway. The continuity of its walls was interrupted by barred windows and slits that likely held soldiers behind them. At the base of the dam, an elevated dock stretched from one side of the river to the other and had a singular staircase that led down to the surface of the water. Beneath the port, even in the dim light, Simon could see the turbulent whites of water being disturbed by massive paddle wheels. The city beyond the dam was mostly obscured except for the tips of towers that rose above it.

The current quickened beneath him. The change in speed encouraged his hopes. He could be out of the river even sooner than he expected. However, the sight of the giant wheels made him wonder if he could resist the current enough to avoid being crushed. As the city became closer, he could see the shapes of people begin to emerge from doors along the dam and from each end of the dock; some were even walking along a bridge above the port that spanned the building's width. Simon smiled at the thought of finally meeting other people; not the creatures of stone, water, and amphibia that he had the privilege to meet so far.

Maybe they're expecting me, he thought. *Maybe Kapell told them I was coming.*

He sat up a little bit straighter. He was still too far to be heard with a shout, but the urge to be seen was enormous. Over the wind he heard the distant clanging of a bell.

They must be expecting me, he thought.

His excitement bloomed as his mind drifted to fantasies of being celebrated, lifted on shoulders, and thrown a feast. His reveries were interrupted by a quiet splash in the water by the boat. Although the lights from the bridge were bright, they mingled and made curtains of heavy shadows with the night all around. They weren't bright enough to illuminate what might have made the sound.

The bell was joined by several others on the wind. He heard several more quiet splashes around the boat; several of which were accompanied by a hissing sound, like a candle being snuffed by moistened fingers. His pleasant thoughts drifted to apprehension. He squinted at the bridge he was drifting closer to. He saw more people lined up across it, but he still could not see them enough to make a better assessment of the growing concern in his mind.

The people on the bridge ran from one side to the other; there was about twenty of them, equally spaced. An unintelligible shout drifted on the wind over the sound of the bells, and the shapes each unanimously lifted something into the air. Once he floated a few feet closer, he saw a familiar colored plume above each of their heads: fire.

Whatever they had lit all launched into the air. The small fires arched above the top of the dam and flew towards the small boat. Most of the fiery projectiles landed harmlessly in the water around Simon, but two of them struck the boat; one in the prow and the other in the stern. They were long arrows with flaming heads and black shafts that still vibrated from the impact.

Simon reached into the icy water, trying to splash enough onto the arrows to exhaust them before they caused any permanent damage to his vessel. Once the arrows were extinguished, he immediately plunged his arms down, and started paddling in order to escape the attack. His hands started to ache from redirecting his boat through the cold river's clutches.

He glanced back towards the archers and saw that another volley of flaming arrows were sailing towards him. How he longed for the dark again.

The dark, he thought as his eyes snapped up to the shore.

He furiously beat the water and ignored the numbness that seeped its way into his arms. He hoped that he could find some solace in the crevices that lined this river. More arrows landed in the water around him. One touched down frightening close to his body, between his outstretched legs. His pants were immediately singed and, as if the fire had a will of its own, it shot up his leg like hungry vines. Without thinking of the lasting repercussions, Simon swung his legs into the water and was baffled that his feet touched the ground below the surface. The water was still up to his neck and the cold pulled the very air from his lungs. He dug his feet hard into the ground below and ran as best as one can in frigid water. He held onto the edge of the boat, pulling it down to use it as some form of barrier. The next volley of arrows all hit their targets and the boat was rocked by their impact.

The ground rose to meet him as Simon moved closer to the shore. The light from the city lessened as it was blocked by the trees and boughs on the embankment. Even though plunging into the darkness again was not what Simon had hoped to do, being pierced by flaming arrows was even less desirable.

The water was up to his waist when he tried to stay hidden behind the small boat. More flaming arrow heads punctured the keel and singed Simon's skin. It made him drop the boat and his only hope was that the archers weren't wise enough to aim for him in the darkness. Perhaps they would think they had struck him long enough for him to escape. There was a crevice only twenty feet away. It was about six feet wide and only a trickle of water dribbled from its mouth. He would rather have been in there than exposed on the bank.

He reached into the boat and pulled several arrows out through the bottom and hoped that they would continue to burn with enough light for him to navigate the dangerously dark crevice.

The sound of rushing waves hammered down towards Simon. Either a swell of water had been released from the dam, or something worse was close behind. Although he was sure what it was, he braved a glance over his shoulder to see the dark outline of the sea serpent.

"I still have one good eye, boy!" roared the serpent. It lunged at him and the sickening smell of its rotten breath hit Simon in the face like a brick.

He turned back towards the crevice and ran as hard as he could for the safety of the narrow ravine. The serpent bellowed as several flaming arrows buried deep into its skin. Simon let out a shout of both fear and excitement. He expected to feel the serpent's massive jaws clamp down on him, but he continued to run. He could feel the serpent's hot breath on the back of his neck as he leapt for the crevice and scrambled down before braving another glance.

The serpent roared once more and the ground beneath Simon shook him to his knees. He turned around to see the serpent unable to fit in the narrow walls of the crevice. Realizing its loss, it retreated to the safety of the water to escape the archers' arrows. Simon had escaped, but he still didn't feel safe. He wasn't sure if anywhere was safe.

Simon had no hope of approaching the city from the river. He turned and went the only direction that he was able: forward. The walls of the crevice were smoothed by the once constant flow of water. The rushing sound of the river rapidly disappeared the further he walked, and he was left to his silent thoughts. He wondered if the city would be receptive to a stranger and worried that he would be quickly ousted. He no longer assumed he would be celebrated, and he started to feel a surety of imprisonment or execution.

His anxiety lessened as the canyon started to incline. It made him hopeful that scaling the walls wouldn't be a necessity, and that he might get a better view of the land while avoiding the watchful eyes of the city guards. He was eventually forced into a heavily wooded area as the crevice continued to climb up out of the labyrinthine river network. Up ahead was a small pond that connected to other wrinkles in the earth that splintered down in different directions. He climbed out of the basin and hoped that the trees would provide him with sufficient cover. He could see the light of the city seep through the trees and regretfully extinguished the dying flames of the arrows under his foot. The minuscule amount of heat that they were providing was also quickly missed; his clothes were still wet from his plunge into the water.

As he reached the top, he could see the enormity of the city of light. It filled the entirety of a massive canyon that reached around bends beyond his vision. The canyon was so wide that he thought even a well trained archer couldn't manage an arrow halfway across. He imagined a bright torch might appear as a tiny dot on the other side.

It was a city of stone with none of the modern buildings Simon had seen in his former life. It seemed like a moment taken from history. The upper most echelon was quite close to him and was only protected by a low wall meant to keep mindless livestock in, as opposed to keeping people out.

Simon worried about where he might hope to begin his search for answers. A city so large would be difficult to navigate, especially when looking for a secret group. Still, he was determined to move forward. He clambered over the low wall into the dirty confines of an animal's pen. He hoped that whatever creature lived in that stall was in the small barn close by and not lurking in the darkness. If it was sleeping, then it would mean his invasion might go unnoticed by any bleating animal. He looked around and saw nothing that raised alarm.

The inner walls of the pen were even lower than the outer city wall. He could see the lanterns of the city beyond and narrow walkways between the buildings; many of which had flickering lights that shone from within. He considered wandering the streets of the city then and there, but he thought better of it. For now, his best option was to wait for the daylight to return.

He skittered on freezing legs to the barn nearby and looked in through an open window to see a group of animals huddled in one corner. They were the size of cows and were covered in shaggy coats. They seemed harmless enough to ignore. He crept inside the barn, climbed up a ladder onto a hay loft, and tried to hide underneath the hay so as to be overlooked by any passerby. As comfortable as he made himself, he had no hopes that sleep would grant him an audience.

He sat in the hay and hoped that answers would find their way to him. There was nothing he could do but wish his clothes would dry faster. Shivering in the hay, he eventually fell asleep. His dreams were filled with the recent stimulus he had been exposed to, but the fear he felt was exacerbated, as nightmares tend to be. His mind replayed his encounter with the serpent but ended in his failure rather than his bravery. He dreamt of Lazuli and felt even more guilt in his imaginings than he had in reality. He felt confused and lost in a shifting place, throughout the dreams like he was searching for answers that were just out of reach at every turn, an endless, clicking, puzzle cube. Worse than them all, there was a sickening fear that preceded the ominous shape of a fiery, open-mouth grin, intent on consuming him. The evil that chased him was more sinister than the worst nightmare Simon had ever had in life. There was a heat to this new enemy's fire that was nearly palpable everywhere. The fire of Veadus' evil master chased Simon with a fervor that he felt powerless to escape.

5 The Chase

A warm morning breeze awoke him, and he was grateful to leave the nightmares behind. His grogginess faded quickly, and the daylight warmed him in the hayloft. There were voices in the air that made his muscles tense, and he hesitated to move at all beneath the hay for fear of being seen. He tried to look towards the voices amidst his camouflage, but eventually he had to ease his way out to get a better look.

He crawled over to the loft opening that overlooked a narrow street which wound back and forth towards the city center. Despite the lack of space in the avenue, it was filled with people. They were all dressed in clean clothes, which were decorated with little color. Thinking of his own richly painted calico coat, he looked down over himself. The clothes he had arrived in were dirty from the previous day's adventures. It might work against him if he walked among the people; he'd stand out far too much. He tried to pick the hay from his clothes and hair as best he could, but it seemed hopeless to successfully get rid of it all.

He climbed down out of the hay loft and hesitated at the gate of the pen wall. He glanced around to see if anyone was watching or had seen him climb down out of the barn. No one seemed to pay him any attention; even people who were only a few steps away.

He looked down at his coat as he ambled down the narrow street, trying to brush it off. Someone bumped into his shoulder as he walked and almost knocked him down. Where the person had collided with him, it looked as if mud had been smeared across Simon's coat. He tried to brush it away, but the more he swatted at the dirt, the filthier the fabric seemed to become. The dirt spread like beaded water over his coat.

Simon quickly stepped in to the shadows of a side alley. After a brief moment, the captivating colors that the coat once had were replaced. Each place where the color stopped, the dirt spread out, joining with the other spots that found their own places to reside. The entire coat began to change and mimic the drab brown and beige shades of the clothes around him. He let out a sigh of relief and felt a bit of confidence return; now, he was more inclined to move about the streets without fear of being noticed. With his camouflage secured, he stepped out into the street again and started to explore.

He continued moving towards the city center and occasionally asked people for directions. They gave him strange looks as if he should know where it was. Beyond that, he was paid no attention. The people of the city seemed to be completely engaged in their daily lives. He was directed across bridges, down sets of flagstone stairs, and back up others. The buildings had components that were obviously fabricated materials—huge squared stones with thick veins of mortar—but the roads and the majority of the structures were carved directly from the canyon. Speckled, red shingles uniformly roofed the homes, and wooden signs swung above doors with carvings of the stores' varying wares. Oxford green shutters framed the latticed windows, and Simon couldn't help but want to stay right there and postpone his quest. He empathized with why others might forget the appeal of the journey they were once destined to make. The city's natural formation was captivating along with the quaint architecture of its buildings.

There were parts of the city that opened to the unseen canyon depths far below, and Simon felt his stomach twist each time he looked over the edge. There were plenty of handrails to keep him from falling down the narrow, steep steps, or off the breathtaking cliffs that looked out onto other parts of the city that were built far against the other side of the canyon. He stopped at one such precipice just to appreciate the architectural feats around him. Several small rope bridges, and a couple wide stone ones, connected the opposing sides of the canyon. The stone bridge closest to him had a complex network of supports underneath it, holding it up. Amongst the spider's web of girders, small buildings had been assembled like birds' nests in the rafters of a neglected cathedral. He could just make out the shapes of people through the dirty windows and felt a flicker of juvenile excitement at the thought of finding his way to the dangerous hovels.

Roped pulleys stretched between the sides of the canyon and seemed to be constantly in motion, as they carried crates or bags between both sides. The whizzing sound of a dangling package as it slid down a taut line caught his attention, and he turned to catch sight of someone sending a parcel onto the network of lines. He wondered if there was a way he could send himself on a ride across just for the sport of it.

He broke away from the site and made his way to a higher part of the canyon, up onto one of the wide stone bridges. As he gazed back over the way he had come, he lost his breath at the sight of the rainbow caused by a massive waterfall that dumped into the canyon from the Vareex he had escaped the night before. There was a mission at hand, so he turned his eyes away to where he was heading.

He could see that he was near the city center, which was made up of a conglomeration of taller buildings that sat somewhat lower than the rest of the city. The buildings had been collected in the center of the canyon on a plateau that had many different roads and rope networks leading to and from it. He hesitated to go towards what seemed like the epicenter of the metropolis for fear of drawing unwanted attention, but the parts of Canton he had wandered through so far made getting lost more likely than finding the Kalinaw in the outlying boroughs.

He crossed the bridge without hurry. He did his best to mingle in the crowds that made their way across the bridge, and he avoided the horse drawn carts or carriages. Even though he still stole occasional, nervous peeks over his shoulder, he tried to enjoy that he was not currently being chased. The incredible views certainly didn't hurt. They absorbed the rampant questions and fears in his mind so that he could let his feet carry him swiftly.

He made his way onto the plateau but it could hardly be recognized as one once he was amidst the buildings. He passed through a set of gates in one wall of the streets that opened into a city market square. There were lines of booths that made up a sizable market. The market place was in front of a set of massive gates with gargantuan towers on either side. They formed an archway to a long, wide, road that could have held thousands of people along it and hundreds across it. Beyond that was a tower that could have served as a city on its own. It was as wide as any skyscraper Simon had ever seen and on its sides hung other towers that protruded like thick veins under the stone skin of the structure. The main roof of it seemed flat from where Simon stood, but it was so high into the air that it was hard to tell. The smaller protuberances had pointed green roofs that were each topped with various weathervanes that added to the beauty of the city as they reflected the daylight off of bronze and golden metals. It seemed like the other buildings in its make, except that the orange stone was interrupted by floors of the tower made of a dark, shiny, stone like marble. The walls were frequented by both balconies and windows. He stopped admiring the architectural feat to stare at the walls around the market place and the buildings that rose above them; awestricken by the artistic prowess of the city.

When he arrived in the aisles of market booths, he looked around at the various wares: weapons of inimitable design, clothes much like those around him, with a few booths selling more extravagant colors, steaming and dripping foods, and even a booth where small dragons were being sold in metal cages. The merchants could sense his newness, as if there was an involuntary pheromone that announced his ignorance of the city and his sudden arrival; he couldn't restrain his wonder of their goods either. They all crowded around him in an incoherent mass of voices, competing for his attention and, more importantly, his money—which he had none of. They pressed in on him and waved shirts and jewelry, shouting promises of satisfactory fulfillment only available through their merchandise. Simon tried to politely decline their offers and move away from their adamancy, but he was unable to break the wall they had created around him.

The crowd forcibly parted as a short, stocky fellow pushed his way through, yelling, "He doesn't want any!"

The merchants gave way to him and slowly they wandered back to their booths, waiting for their next potential customers.

"Fly away, you vultures!" he called after them. "Adger's the name," he said as he thrust his hand out to be shaken. Simon returned the gesture. Adger's hands were rough and strong, showing Simon that he was obviously a craftsman or worker of some kind. The man was a couple inches shorter than Simon and a few inches wider too. Two different types of glasses were perched on top of his balding head, and a pair of goggles hung from around his neck. He wore a dark orange jacket that had obvious signs of age; there was even a tan patch on one arm where the jacket had been repaired. Simon spied trinkets and tools sticking out from the inside pockets of the jacket and from the front pocket of the smock tied around his neck that hung down just below his waist. His boots were tighter and shorter than Simon's, and he had his patched pants tucked into them. They looked well maintained like they were polished often, but not to such a degree that they had any reflection. He beamed at Simon with a kind grin that was framed by smile-lines on his bare face.

Simon didn't have the opportunity to give Adger his name as the man immediately started talking again. "You must be new in town. Did you come from one of the other cities?"

"Well, I'm not exactly from—yeah, I'm not from around here," Simon started to say as he walked to a nearby booth. He aimlessly looked at the various swords and weapons. "Thanks for the help back there." He tried to sound casual to mask the fact that he had no idea what he was doing, or where he might say that he was from if the question arose again.

He nodded at the owner who's booth he had approached and then picked up a sword slightly longer than his arm, and just as wide as three fingers.

"Ah, the Dragonius; a mighty fine sword," Adger said, sidling up next to Simon like he had just found a new best friend.

"We call it a Gladius where I'm from," Simon said trying to sound casual while avoiding an arrogant tone. "Something like that anyway; I really don't know much about swords."

"Oh, then I'm just your man!" Adger said excitedly. "I see that you don't carry a sword; wise choice friend, best not to draw attention from the guards—but we live in dangerous times."

"May I make a suggestion, sir?" The salesman spoke as he overheard Simon's uncertainty. He stepped from behind the booth, carrying a tray of daggers.

"I'm really okay," Simon said as he held up a hand and stepped away from the booth. "I was just browsing, honestly."

Simon walked towards another table covered in jewelry; hoping to lose the attention of his admirer. Adger followed closely behind; quite interested in the stranger. Simon felt slightly uncomfortable for having gained anyone's attention but the short, round man seemed harmless.

"So, what's your name then?" Adger asked kindly.

Simon eyed him and felt even more skeptical of the way that Adger peered at him cheerfully. "I don't really have a lot of money, sorry," Simon said empathetically. It occurred to him that he had no money to pay for anything, namely food. He was glad, for the moment, that eating was not on his list of immediate needs.

"Oh, no; I don't—I'm not asking for money. I just want to extend the warm welcome of this wonderful city." He raised his hands to gesture at the market square. He looked back at Simon with a big grin. He couldn't tell if it was genuine.

A series of percussions interrupted Adger before he could continue.

"What was—?" Simon started to say.

A deep chorus of drums filled the market square and drowned out his question. Simon noticed that merchants hurriedly packed away their things and lowered the gates on their booths.

"We have to go," Adger said with an obvious urgency in his voice. His former cheeriness had disappeared.

Simon was hesitant to move. The stranger he had just met was a still a stranger, and if Simon's experiences had taught him anything, it was to be cautious.

"Trust me; you don't want be late to this gathering; not if you want to see tomorrow. We need to get there before the high trumpets," Adger said, walking away from him while trying to urge him along.

A single trumpet joined the drums.

"Okay, fine; do whatever you want. Good luck, friend."

Adger turned and ran towards the tall tower that was at the end of the wide road beyond the archway. The merchants and their customers all moved towards it with the same urgency Adger had. Most of them wore fearful expressions on their faces. Simon thought it was better to follow along than be the one left behind. People poured out of the gates that led into the market place and rushed to the tower, and Simon moved among them.

The drums and trumpets seemed to have reached their full chorus; people began to sprint instead of run. Some people even lost a hat or dropped a bag as they ran but didn't turn back for it. Others ran half-dressed out of buildings and homes, hurriedly buttoning a shirt, or fastening a jacket.

The drums became even louder. This made Simon more nervous, and he started jogging towards the large crowd along with everyone else. He was still unsure of what was happening and he didn't want to run towards a situation that there might not be a way out of. Simon hurried into the crowd and weaved his way a short distance into the back of the throng. The road was bordered by wide tiered seats all of which were more packed than the road full of people. He found a small amount of comfort in the knowledge that he was not the very last person in the crowd, but thought it might be better to have a seat off to the side.

The people around him all looked towards the city tower as if they were waiting for something to happen. The music continued to boom and it was apparent that it was coming to a close. A few people rushed into the crowd behind him. Simon saw a man sprint from one of the small gates that bordered the market. He was a poorly dressed man in little more than rags. There was a fear in his face much greater than those who had already corralled in the meeting place.

The brass instruments played the high note that Adger had warned of. The crowd erupted in vociferous cheers that made Simon turn away from the sprinting man. Halfway up the tower, a person stepped out onto the balcony, but Simon was too far to clearly see him. He could see the person raise their hands and the crowd became even louder in response. Simon felt obligated to participate but weakly applauded instead. The sound of the people was deafening, yet over the bellowing throng, he heard the beats of the drums and beyond that, he heard the faint sound of a pleading voice.

"Please! I'm here! Please—wait!"

Simon looked behind him again to see the ragged man wildly wave his arms.

"I'm here, please don't!—" his voice was lost in the noise of the crowd.

Simon still absently clapped while he watched the man dash towards the crowd. The drums stopped beating. Stones around the man erupted, sending rocks and dirt flying into the air. Simon stopped clapping in surprise but managed to maintain his composure enough not to fully turn. The man continued to run towards the crowd. He ducked and covered his head from the falling debris as he ran.

41

The raining earth began to collect and form into creatures. They ran alongside him but looked like nothing more than organized piles of stone.

"No! It's not my fault!" the man begged again.

The stone creatures bounded several steps beyond him and simultaneously each raised a foot into the air. They slammed their feet on the ground in front of his path and the road collapsed in a plume of dust. The man and the two creatures disappeared into the hole together. As they fell into the void in the ground, one of the creatures quickly turned its head towards Simon. Before they made eye contact, Simon felt his face forcibly turned away from the scene.

"Don't look," Adger said, and then he took his hand away from Simon's face. "Just keep clapping. You are new; aren't you? *That's* why you can't be late, and that's why we clap and cheer; even when we'd rather throw stones."

"What happened to him?" Simon asked as he glanced back at the street that was completely normal again; even the dust had settled already.

"He's was dragged down to the catacombs below the city," Adger said bluntly. "You'd be taken, too, if they saw you looking. The Steward thinks we don't know what happens to stragglers; that we don't believe the rumors of the oubliettes hidden throughout the city. I've been trying to find them for weeks, but if the golems see you looking, you disappear too."

"Wow, that's terrible," he said genuinely disturbed that the seemingly innocent man was just dragged down to some dungeon for nothing more than tardiness. "Who is the Steward?"

"…Really? The guy we're all cheering for. You don't know him? You must be from Portalswald, or somewhere out there, eh?" Adger asked with a chuckle.

Simon raised an eyebrow at Adger and continued absently clapping.

"Really; where are you from?" Adger persisted as he stopped clapping and turned towards Simon.

Simon still didn't answer. He became nervous about Adger's questions and turned back towards the Steward.

"You smell like a barn," Adger continued. "We haven't had any new people here in a long time. Did you crawl in over the wall?"

The clapping had stopped and still the people looked towards the tower. The Steward was speaking, but he was too far away to be heard.

Adger was still facing Simon as he waited for an answer.

People around them started to whisper things, "Shut up, Adger!" and "Pay attention," or, "You'll get us killed, or worse; be quiet!"

"Silence!" The Steward's voice boomed across the masses. Adger slowly turned back towards the tower, as if moving gradually would make it less apparent that he was causing the disturbance.

"Do you not find my words pleasant to hear? Am I not the provider of all that you have? Yet, you dishonor me with your inattention!"

The people around Simon and Adger all turned towards them and backed away just enough to isolate them. Before they stopped moving, someone pushed through the crowd towards Simon and tackled him into the other people. Simon fell amidst the crowd and the attacker disappeared. Adger was gone too.

"Guards!" the Steward bellowed.

Simon heard cries rise up from the crowd, but from where he was on the ground, he couldn't tell what was happening. He quickly stood up and could see several shifting crowds close to the stands. He looked out into the market where his attacker fled and caught a glimpse of a green cloak fluttering through one of the market gates.

One of the stones from the road flew into the air. Simon watched it soar above the stands where it stopped and hovered. Cries from the crowd made him look back down towards the shifting masses, and he could see the head and shoulders of an armored guard rise above them. Close to Simon, people scattered and another stone flew into the air. A guard climbed out of the crater where the stone had been.

The guard was shrouded by a hood and cape that covered armor made of metal scales. Its face was covered with a shapely, formed metallic mask that concealed all but small slits over the guard's eyes, which smoked like an ember in a dying fire. The armor it wore gave it a distinctly mechanical appearance, but its movements were fluid and seamless. The guard drew a sword that was nearly as tall as Simon and as wide as his two hands. The terrifying weapon was like the darkness left by the nearly set sun, except for a thin glowing line that ran along one serrated edge. The blade burned with the same intensity that its eyes did. Simon shuddered with fear. He was unsure if the guard was man or beast, but based on Kapell's tales and his own experience with Veadus' forces, he had no desire to wait to find out.

Many guards emerged from the street and pushed through the people with ease. A crack echoed above the shouts of the panicked townsfolk. The hovering stones broke apart into several long, slender pieces that looked like arrows.

Not more arrows, Simon thought.

The stony weapons hovered for a moment more and then unanimously flew towards where he stood. Several people were struck, and the rest of the arrows narrowly missed him. He looked down where one had pierced the hem of his coat. He noticed that one of the pouches on his belt was missing.

That guy must've taken it, he thought.

He had no idea what might have been in the pouch, but he still felt instinctively threatened by its absence; more so than by the arrows at his feet.

Without waiting for any additional encouragement to run, he scrambled to his feet but stumbled backwards over the fallen people around him. He thought of the Gladius he had handled at the booth before and wondered if he could manage to obtain a weapon in the confusion. He hated the idea of pilfering anything but felt justified that it would be for the sake of his own mortal defense.

He managed to find his footing again and pushed his way to the market booths. He saw the weapon Adger had called the Dragonius. It was at the far end of the row of vendor stands. As he made his way for it, he heard the sickening crunch of a wooden structure as it collapsed behind him. He dared a glance over his shoulder and saw one of the guards plow through a booth. Valuables and clothes went flying everywhere in the shockwave of a retail-loaded explosion. The guard raised his sword and threw the fiery, long weapon at Simon. He ducked as he ran and felt the airstream as the sailing weapon narrowly missed skewering him like a piece of meat. It impacted with the booth just to his left and immediately ignited it like a match in a vat of oil. He had to make it to the Dragonius.

The heat of the burning boutique was intense enough to divert Simon to another route. He careened towards the other side of the row but tripped on the uneven stones on the ground. He crashed into a row of tables nearby and flipped heels over head, bringing anything nearby down with him. Another sword was launched through an overturned table, nearly killing him again. He kicked his way out of the mess and dashed for the weapon booth again but when he turned towards it, it too was on fire. His heart sank and he decided it might be better to pursue the thief than hope to overcome the Canton guards.

He escaped back into the horde of frightened people as they ran through the market. The bedlam provided some protection to Simon, but it also slowed him down; an opportunity for the guards to quickly gain on him. He had to wade through the crowd, whereas they simply bowled them over with their humungous stature. Still, Simon ran, hoping that the narrower streets outside the market would give him enough cover to escape.

He kept expecting to be pierced by an arrow, or feel the crush of one of the guards' massive swords, but he managed to evade them. He urged himself to move faster, even though he could sprint no harder than he already was. He was relieved when he passed through one of the market gates.

The street he was on was more cluttered than the ones he had seen before. It was overgrown and seemingly abandoned. Vegetation had found its way through cracks in the stones, and boxes were piled against the walls of the buildings and strewn about in the street. Even with all the debris, the road was wide enough to accommodate a parade. The windows in the buildings were almost all broken or missing. Some doors hung on their hinges while others were knocked into the houses. Simon could see why the thief had chosen this particular exit as his escape.

The market gate archway behind him exploded as another guard's sword came flying through it. Simon ducked and stumbled to the side of the road. He realized he'd have to let the thief go for the sake of his own safety. He darted towards an open doorway to hide in one of the houses. Hopefully, if he hid well enough, the guards would also abandon their pursuit. He stepped around the door which looked like it was about to fall off of its hinges with the lightest breeze. He moved into the house as quickly and quietly as he could, hoping that the creaking floors would not call attention to him.

He heard the clatter of armor and hurried footsteps. He glanced around his surroundings in search of a place to hide, but the neglect inflicted upon the building made a better hiding place unrealistic. He was in what appeared to be an inn, or a small tavern. A lone remaining table and a few scattered chairs were to his right and a bar to his left; the open end of which pointed towards the window and would have made a poor choice for not being seen. There were stairways going up in the back and a set next to it going down in to shadowy depths below; neither of which seemed to be a better alternative than simply hiding behind the open door. As he heard the clanking grow closer, he started to regret voluntarily cornering himself.

He crouched down below the front windows of the small inn and pressed himself up against the wall. The sound of footsteps outside the inn continued getting louder and then stopped in front of it. One of the guards barked an order which was immediately followed by an invigorated gait. The sound of crunching wood and shattering glass in adjacent buildings told Simon that his hiding spot had been a poor choice. It sounded as if the guards were tearing the buildings to pieces.

Simon felt brave—or foolish—enough to glance out the window. He knew that inaction would be a worse choice. Hoping that the hood on his coat would lend him some level of imperceptibility, he pulled it over his head and slowly rose just beyond the corner edge of one of the front windows. The formation outside was four by ten guards deep, and they were directly in front of him. Additional groups were going into other buildings on the street and kicking down the doors, or charging in through the missing ones. Simon understood why everyone cheered so emphatically for the Steward that they would rather stone: they rightfully feared his guards.

Guards were smashing their way into buildings on the intersecting streets and they met no resistance besides one disheveled occupant. In one of the windows across the street from Simon, he saw the shape of a hooded head, and his heart jumped; hopefully, this person was the thief. The figure pulled away from the window as a guard approached the house. The guard pushed his way into the door, and had to stoop down to accommodate his unnatural size. Simon heard a muffled shout and saw a flash of light in the window. The guard was defenestrated and two more guards rushed in behind him. There were more sounds of struggle and another bright flash before the fight ceased. The two guards that had entered the house rushed back out onto the street with bewildered expressions on their faces.

The guards' leader went over to them, yelling. The guards shrugged their shoulders in confusion and the leader, in one motion, drew his blade and separated their heads from their bodies. He stood for a moment with his sword in the air. Simon noticed it was much larger than the guards' he had seen before, and his armor was unique too. His hood sat around his shoulders, and his galea helmet had a metal crest that looked like a battle axe instead of horse's plume. He wore a dark violet cape with golden embroidery that depicted two dragons chasing each other in circular combat.

The leader spun towards where Simon was hiding, and the stairwells he had avoided before immediately became a wiser choice than where he sat. The lead guard came back to the larger group and started talking to one of the other guards, and he pointed in the direction of Simon's refuge. Simon ducked back down below the window and noticed that the color of his coat began to change again. The color of the hood was turning gray like the dirty and darkened inn. He hoped that he would blend into his surroundings just enough that a glance might keep him unnoticed.

He headed for the stairwell going up. The stairwell was narrow, even for a regular sized person. If his pursuant chose the same path, they would get lodged in the narrow stairwell. At the very least, this could potentially buy him some time. Simon carefully stepped on the first stair. At first he was pleased to find that it didn't creak, but when he put his full weight on the step, it let out a long painful squeak, the alarm of which was intensified by his overwhelming desire to remain quiet.

Simon froze, afraid that any additional adjustment in his position would give him away. The air was still and cold; not even a subtle movement of the wind could be heard. The sound of his breath seemed like a raucous song amid the silence, so he drew a deep breath and held it. There were no sounds of guards smashing in through doors. There was no clank of their armor. For a moment, Simon wondered if they had all left.

His hopes were dashed as splintering wood and shattered glass filled the small common space of the inn. Simon bounded up the narrow stairwell, taking three or four steps at a time, using his hands as he scrambled up.

He got to the top of the stairs and quietly stepped around the stairwell wall. If a guard looked up the stairs, they would not have seen him. No guards bounded up the stairs after him. Either the guards had not heard him ascend, or they assumed he went to the basement. Simon kept his back to the wall of the stairs and could hear two guards below talking about the squeaking stair. They were arguing about going up or down. It would seem their hesitation stemmed from the last guards' failure.

Their discussion allowed Simon to assess his surroundings and plan his escape. The upstairs area of the building looked like it had once housed several very small rooms. Most of the walls were knocked down or demolished so that it was mostly an open, empty area. A window on the far wall faced the street below and another window to his right faced the roofs of close, adjacent buildings. The only reasonable escape he could make was onto the rooftops but the guards below would see him make for the window. He wondered if he'd even have time to open it…Simon had no way to know if age had sealed the windows closed. A moment could cost him everything.

Looks like I'm crashing through it, he thought.

He listened to the guards downstairs and waited for his opportunity. A shout from outside spurred the guards' into action, and it sounded as if they both started going downstairs.

He heard a scuffle, which he guessed came from a disagreement about who would be the one to squeeze in the ascending stairwell. Another shout came from outside, and the two immediately chose directions. Simon's time for action had arrived. He looked around him for some kind of weapon but saw nothing more than broken walls and scattered dishes. He grabbed a cup by his feet and threw it down the stairwell. The cup narrowly flew over the guard's head which he didn't notice due to his struggle to squeeze up the stairs. The cup harmlessly smashed against the hearth just beyond the stairwell and the guard tried to look over his shoulder. Simon seized the opportunity. He ran towards the window and jumped.

He covered his head and dove for the glass. He could see the buildings beyond the window but realized midair that he had no idea if they reached all the way to the wall of the inn. He smashed through the window. The guard shouted after him but was still stuck in the stairwell. Simon's stomach lurched as gravity caught up to him and he fell towards the roof below. He landed on the hard ceramic roof tiles and was grateful it was a brief fall. His hand gripped the roof as he slid down the incline towards an alley on the opposite side of the building on the main road.

Angered shouts came from inside the abandoned inn and up from the street below. Simon struggled to get to his feet, but he couldn't gain traction. He slipped on the smooth surface of the tiles as he descended towards the edge. While he frantically and hopelessly groped, Simon peeked back at the window he jumped through. A guard was standing at it with a bow drawn, and Simon was sure he heard a faint laugh come from behind the guard's mask. He released the arrow and Simon pushed off of the roof as hard as he could. It barely missed his face, and the fletching scratched him as it zipped by. He turned as he continued to slide down the roof, and he crouched down on his legs as best he could to maintain his balance. When he neared the edge, he jumped towards an adjacent building and hoped to land on its flat roof.

Elation filled him, and he felt strong and terrific, like an adept acrobat flying through the air. The edge of the roof was nearly under his feet. Arrows clattered around him, and the promise of escape was at the front of his mind. His toe caught the edge of the roof, and he tumbled as he landed. He rolled across the roof and over the opposite edge. The terrific feeling he had before completely shattered as he fell. He landed in a pile of boxes with a crashing symphony of debris.

Consciousness had not escaped him, despite the fall. He nearly laughed from his assumption that his agility was enough to perform such an escape. He quickly crawled from the confines of the debris and hoped to hide before the guards caught him. He noted a turn at each end of the alley that led away from the inn. He sprinted for one and took solace in the knowledge that there were two buildings between him and the guards.

He reached the corner and peered around it into a short alley that led to another street. It looked similar to the one he left behind, except narrower with even more overgrowth. A shiver ran up his spine that made him quickly turn, but there was nothing there. He spun wildly back towards the road expecting to face whatever his nerves warned him about. The alley was as empty as his stomach, which chose that opportune moment to let out an audible groan.

He crept towards the road and peered around the corner and then up and down the empty street. He had no inkling of what his next destination should be; he wasn't expecting any of this. He glanced over his shoulder again, still unable to shake the tingling sensation that ran up his neck. He thought it best to simply put as much distance between him and this city as he could, especially the guards. He could see the tall city center tower behind him and hoped he was on the opposite side of it than when he entered the market. His mind was made up: flee the city, and hope to find the Kalinaw somewhere else. He decided to make a straight line out of the city and hoped that the dilapidated streets would allow him to go unnoticed. He turned to run across the street to the safety of another dark alley, but as he buckled down to run, someone ran into the alley from the street and knocked him down.

"You!" Simon said, staring at the figure who had knocked him down before.

The thief wore a green cloak that was hemmed with an ornate paisley design that was sewn into place with golden thread. The cloth border shimmered like it was made of liquid, but he assumed it to be a trick of the light. He quickly realized the thief was a woman; evident by her dark, long eyelashes and piercing green eyes. So fierce was her gaze that his sense of her wrongdoing was uncontrollably diminished. Her face was covered by a triangular cloth mask that was made in the same fashion as her cloak but let the caramel skin above it be seen. The rest of her was also quite clearly feminine, and her svelte appearance made her intimidating; an even more capable thief. She wore a tight, leather, corset breastplate, connected to minimal pauldrons tucked under her cloak. Her pants were made of a hide not much different than Adger's jacket. Her boots were hidden underneath black leather greaves that had golden vines that crept up towards her knees.

"There's no time for blame!" she said in a commanding but melodious voice. "Come with me."

"No way! You stole my pouch. Why would I follow you?"

"They're coming! Here, take it back then." She tossed the small pouch back at him and it landed in his lap. The contents clattered onto the ground. "Do what you want; I don't care," she said as she quickly strode past him. She went down the alley, looking from side to side. She ran her hands along the stones as if trying to decipher them.

"There's nothing down there," Simon said as he picked up the contents of the pouch off the ground. There was a silver handle with a mixture of symbols, swirls, and letters on it; none of which Simon recognized or had the time to further examine. It was just long enough to accommodate the grip of both his hands, and it was no wider than two fingers across. It had a sinuous curve down its length with an elliptical shape across. The metal was warm in his hand and he felt pleased to have pursued its theft even though he didn't quite know what it was. He shoved the pouch in his coat, grabbed the silver handle, and followed after the thief.

"I'm telling you, this alley doesn't lead anywhere, lady."

She turned and narrowed her eyes and said, "I thought you weren't following me."

"Well, your friend proved that ignoring you won't help either."

"Who? Adger?" she said indignantly. "That fat toad is as much my friend as he is tall—" she stopped as if she had more insults to assign him. She looked beyond Simon towards the street.

"What?" Simon said, shrugging his shoulders.

She raised her hand to silence him. "Do you know how to use that thing?" she whispered and pointed at the silver handle in his hand.

"No, I don't even know what this thing is—"

She interrupted him again, "It was in your pocket and you don't know how to use it? It malfunctioned for me."

"So, that was you that killed that guard? But how did you get—"

"Forget it. Come on," she said as she grabbed his coat and pulled him down the alley.

"Whoa!" Simon stepped back from her and swung his arm to break her grasp. "I don't even know you, you stole my stuff, and you expect me to follow you down a dead-end alley?"

Footsteps echoed into the alley from the empty street.

"You ask more questions than Adger!"

"So you do know him! I guess I can add *liar* to your list of traits."

"I never said I didn't know him; there are few in this town who are not familiar with the ceaseless chatter that pours from his mouth."

"Well, I want nothing to do with either of you. Good luck." Simon turned and quickly walked away from her.

She grabbed Simon from behind and covered his mouth. He struggled to get away from him, but she slapped him against the side of the head.

"Shut up!" she yelled in a whisper.

The jogging guards were getting closer. Simon struggled and bucked his back hard enough to loosen her grip. He sprinted down the short alley towards the street, disregarding the threat that sounded even closer now. He ran blindly into the street and looked towards the sound of the footsteps. He immediately regretted his decision and wished he had stayed in the alley with the thief.

Walking towards him was a group of guards that, for a brief moment, didn't see him sprint across the street. Simon knew he had been made as soon as he turned the corner of the building across the street. The wall behind him disintegrated in an array of stone chunks. Simon stumbled towards the side of the narrow alley from the surprise of the attack and crashed into a pile of boxes and crates. The silver handle he grasped broke free from his hand and clattered across the stone ground. Simon scrambled to his feet and looked over his shoulder as several guards turned the corner.

The alley he was in wasn't very long, and he could see another street at its end. He ran down the alley, stooping to grab the mysterious metal object. He ran for the alley's end and could feel the wind from the other street flow into the alley.

Almost there, he thought.

He was only steps away from turning the corner into the next street when a guard crossed into his path; one that was even larger than the largest guards behind him. Simon instinctively thrust his hand towards the guard as if to stab him with the silver handle. He held his breath as he prepared to be crushed and slashed to pieces. Instead, he felt heat. In response to the stabbing motion, a blade of flame sprouted forth from the handle and pierced the guard's armor. The guard swayed on his knees and fell backwards from the force of the life leaving him. Simon tottered over with him, still holding on to the newly birthed weapon which stuck out of his breastplate. He stepped off the guard into the street and pulled the fiery blade out of the guard's chest. He was awestruck by the way it seemed to drip flames onto the ground yet still maintained its shape.

"This...is...awesome!" he said out loud.

Another group of guards stood in front of him and just stared. The other group from the alley stood behind him with the same bewildered expressions. He looked from group to group, waiting for someone to move. The only sound to break the tension was the dripping flames of Simon's sword as they sizzled on the road.

He looked back at the weapon in his hand with a new understanding of its importance. The blade beneath the flames was narrower near the handle than the end where it tapered and curved backwards. Although Simon had never held any blade sharper than a dinner knife, he instinctively put his hands together on the sword. He slightly bent his knees to lower his stance as he slowly backed away from the guards who hesitated to attack him while they stared at the flaming blade. He hoped that killing the largest of the guards would dissuade the rest of them from chasing him any farther.

"I had nothing to do with that loud guy at the tower or the thief who knocked me down!" Simon said.

One of the guards stepped towards Simon and in a deep guttural voice said, "We care not for petty squabble, but that sword is not something you should have. Give it to me."

Simon turned and ran. A unanimous roar sounded from the groups of guards, and the chase had begun again. The thief darted from the alley on the opposite side of the street where Simon had slain the guard and fell into step with him. Simon looked at her with surprise and disbelief.

"When you've been here as long as I have, you learn a few tricks," she said and looked at him with a grin that could only be perceived through her eyes. "We have to fight them. They won't tire, nor will they give up. Hiding will only prolong this endeavor."

"I don't know how to fight," Simon said in between breaths. "I've been lucky so far, but I'm not a fighter."

"You seemed to handle yourself well enough with that brute," she said with little exhaustion in her voice. "This way!"

She grabbed his sleeve, and they veered down an intersecting street. They ran towards another alley and Simon welcomed her help. At first, Simon had been grateful for the plethora of furtive opportunities that the alleys provided but now they seemed to be more of a hindrance.

"I think I've had enough of alleys," he said.

"Trust me," she said, looking directly at him as they ran.

They ran into the alley, and for a credulous moment, Simon hoped they had escaped the guards.

The thief ran her hands along the sides of the alley as before. "I know there's one here somewhere," she said, "Ah! Here!" She turned towards the wall with one hand against the stone. She swung her fist towards the wall with enough force that would have shattered every bone in her hand, but it went through the wall. The stone rippled like water. She pulled out her hand, and a low arch appeared that she stepped through.

She stuck her head back into the alley and said, "You coming?"

Simon let out an involuntarily, "Whoa."

She disappeared into the dark tunnel again which had widened from her initial punch to intersect one of the windows of the building. He saw her step through the tunnel and expected to see her inside through the window but when he looked, she wasn't inside the building. He glanced back towards the street and heard the clatter of the approaching guards. He looked at his flaming sword, and it flickered out with a sputter. He stepped in front of the dark tunnel.

"I am not the enemy," said the thief from the darkness within.

With a little fear, and a bit of excitement to match, Simon put the hilt into his pocket and stepped through the arch. The wall closed behind him and he was plunged into absolute darkness.

6 The Tunnel

The tunnel was dark and had the usual musty odor that was expected of a subterranean passage. Simon reached back to where the tunnel closed, but his hand swung into open air. He spun back around and felt forward, but there was nothing there either. He reached out to both sides and was able to touch the walls.

"What are you doing?" said the thief's voice in the dark.

"I can't see," he said.

"Get out your sword."

He heard steps walking towards him as he pulled the warm handle back out of his pocket. He felt a hand wrap around his. "Here, let me try," she said. She shook the handle in his hand. "I still don't know how I got that thing to work. How did *you* get it to work?" she said with a note of derision in her voice.

"I just kind of stabbed at that guard like this," he said and stepped forward, making a jabbing motion that broke her grip.

The tunnel filled with orange light but not from the fiery shape of the blade. The fire spilled from the handle onto the ground as if it were water being poured from a pitcher. Simon shook the handle to break the stream but instead it withdrew into the hilt and hovered above the end like the flame of a candle.

"I thought you didn't know how to use it," she said.

"I don't, so let's get out of here before it goes out again."

"You're going to need my help."

"Is that why you stole it from me; because I need your help?"

"I stole the pouch from you that looked the most burdened with coin, but this," she said gesturing to the handle, "I do not know what this is. If it

53

wasn't for Adger, it would have been easier."

"Was he in on this scheme of yours?"

She ignored the question. "You're lucky I knocked you down or those guards would have killed you, too."

"Why would I be happy you stole from me? You don't even know me."

"Did you ask him?" said a voice from beyond the light of the sword-made-candle. It burst to bright life again and formed into the saber. The flash of light in the tunnel was enough to reveal Adger standing just at the edge of the darkness.

"So, he is the one," he said.

The fiery sword's brilliance diminished again to the steady flicker of a long wick.

"Who's 'the one'," Simon said, feigning ignorance. Somehow, these two were referencing his unique arrival through the gate.

"I was about to tell him, Adger, and if you'd keep your mouth closed long enough to let me, maybe I can do this my own way."

Turning to Simon, Adger said, "Sorry about getting you in trouble back there, friend. I bet she hasn't even told you her name. Taken off her sneaky mask? No?" Adger shook his head and looked back at the thief. "We really need to work on your people skills. Filch is what we've come to call her; never told us her real name. I'm Adger, as you know, but what about you? 'Fraid I didn't get your name before."

"I'm Simon," he said. He was amused by Adger's personality, albeit slightly annoyed that he was almost killed for his persistent friendliness. Nevertheless, he was inclined to trust him, whereas Filch had yet to show her face after robbing him. Neither was she forthright about who she was or what her intentions were.

"Great! There's grumpy Filch, I'm Adger, and you're Simon. You know who we are; we certainly know who you are now. So, let's get to it then. We need your help, friend."

"I've heard," Simon said, "Save the world, kill the bad guy; I know."

"What?" Filch said. "No, we want you help us kill the Steward. Anyone with a sword like that and a coat like yours must be able enough to help. We need four, and you're the best fourth we've seen in a long time."

"Oh. Well, I'm not really here for that."

"Oh come on," Adger pleaded, "Filch is too moody, I'm too short, and—"

"And your brother is too stupid," Filch said to Adger.

"The problem still stands that you want me to trust you two; one of which is a thief and the other who abetted her."

"She's the thief; I had nothing to do with that," Adger said quickly. "Approaching you—not stealing from you—was my idea when Filch told me about that coat of yours."

Simon was glad for the mysterious coat but cursed it for having revealed its capabilities under the scrutiny of Filch's watchful eyes. "I have other things I'm supposed to do. I can't delay for a...what's it called—coup."

"We don't want to overthrow the Steward, we want to kill him," Filch said with an aggressive tone that made Simon eager to redirect the conversation. She made Simon wary, but Adger's personality helped to counteract it.

The growl of Simon's stomach echoed in the cave. "Can we at least talk about it over some food?" he said.

Simon wondered if they were members of the Kalinaw, and if they weren't, being trapped in a tunnel might not be the best time to ask them. Their plan of the Steward's abdication made Simon a little more at ease than the idea of asking them about the secret group.

"Great idea!" Adger said as he ushered him down the tunnel. "I'm hungry, too. We can get something on the way."

Filch lingered behind them and looked back down the tunnel as if she expected their pursuers to burst through the air.

"We're nearly there anyway," Adger said.

The tunnel was filled with light before Adger finished his sentence. The floor in the darkness behind them fell away and opened into bright caverns with massive geodes jutting from the walls in the crevice. The bottom of the cave was beyond sight and the light from the geodes never reached it. The geodes cast a spectrum of colors onto the tunnel walls. Through the brilliant rainbow, there was a fiery, red glow that climbed the tunnel wall like a lengthening shadow in a waning sunset. The three of them stopped to look at the lights that washed the walls, but the crevice before them was less comforting than being plunged back into darkness.

The wound in the floor was blocked by a dark mass of earth. It was speckled with protuberant, red stones, illuminated with whatever fire gave it life. It slowly began to take shape and separate into limbs and form a head. Despite the opportunity to flee that the creature's lethargy provided, the three of them stood watching this thing take form. Its head stretched into a long, wide jaw, like an alligator's, but its body was broad and stocky like a boar. Translucent red plates lined the ridge of its back, and in the darkness, a tail with sharp spikes could be seen. Although they would rather have been behind the creature so as to better escape it, the spikes on its tail detracted from the appeal. When it seemed to have taken full form, its eyes snapped open to reveal stones that burned with an even greater fervor than those which stuck out from its body.

It heaved itself into the narrow tunnel and balanced on the edges of the slashed open earth at their feet. It pushed against the ceiling with its back and caused it to crack. The three of them turned and ran. Simon extinguished his sword and put it back into a pocket on his waist; he felt that it might only serve to anger the creature. Despite the seeming impossibility that the ruby-encrusted golem could run in the tunnel, it charged them like a train through a narrow mountain pass. Its giant mouth opened to receive them like a cattle guard would deflect debris. The walls around it snapped and groaned from the pressure its massive body caused on them.

"What is that thing?" Simon asked.

"It's called a bularaz," Adger said. "They used to be quite placid until they were turned into these tools of destruction—"

"Save the history lesson," Filch interrupted, "Anytime now, Adger; we need to leave."

"It's not an exact science," he said in between breaths. "We might end up in a wall twenty feet up or in the *middle* of a wall, or, we could—"

"Just do it!"

Adger fumbled with a small wooden object he pulled from his jacket. A hole of light opened in the tunnel beyond them. The darkness was replaced with the arch of an opening that appeared from thin air as the one had for Filch in the alleyway. Blue skies and clouds could be seen. The fresh and cool autumn air that was coming in from the opening sent an unexpected wave of nostalgia flooding through Simon's mind.

He thought of lazy days on blankets and having picnics with his family. He saw his children, much younger than at his deathbed, still light enough to be held in the air above their daddy's head, while holding their arms out as if flying. He thought of smiling laughs, soft kisses on cheeks, and unarticulated words from mouths too young to speak clearly. The full force of the unbridled and indefinable love he felt for his family washed over him like a wave of frothing sea. The sadness he felt was nearly enough to collapse his legs beneath him. He somehow continued to stumble down the tunnel behind his companions. His eyes welled with hot tears as the longing for his family forced him into a stupor. His vulnerability affected his speed and the red, rock monster rapidly closed the distance between them.

The dark tunnel continually filled with daylight as the hole widened. Adger and Filch dove through the portal and disappeared from sight. Simon was steps away, but risked a glance behind him. The creature was so close; he could feel the heat of its breath envelop his body. Simon stumbled backwards through the hole and felt a rapid shift in gravity pull him back towards the tunnel mouth. He groped for a way to gain purchase and escape through the exit which Adger had provided. The bularaz prepared to strike. The daze Simon was in prevented him from reacting appropriately, but Filch and Adger grabbed him and pulled him the rest of the way through. They were standing on the wall outside the tunnel mouth.

Simon looked down at the hole in the wall to see the bularaz was nearly at the exit. Adger pushed a button on the wooden control in his palm and the tunnel snapped shut.

"Snap out of it, Simon," Adger said as he shook Simon by the shoulders.

Simon's senses started to return, and he noticed he was standing on the wall too, but it only added to his confusion. After another stupefied moment, he realized that they weren't standing on a wall but were standing in a street.

"I told you, Filch," Adger said as he supported Simon. "We should've come out through the side of a building, not up out of the street. The tunnel was upended; perpendicular to its proper orientation. You can't rush quantum manipulation even when being chased by a bularaz. This is the kind of crap that happens." His usual chipper attitude had turned sour but quickly changed when he addressed Simon again. "Are you all right? Don't worry, it happens to everyone. It's a smell, or a painting, maybe a flower or a taste; whatever it is, it's the flashbacks of your previous life. When you learn how to suppress those feelings, it becomes easier to bear. You should actually be grateful; most people don't remember a thing about their previous life. When did you start remembering?"

"It is weakness," Filch said, unsolicited. "We have bigger problems, anyway." Filch pointed down the street at a group of people fleeing in their direction. There were more of the bularaz running through the streets alongside the city guards. The three of them prepared to be attacked, but the group ran right past them. A second group, however, stopped in front of where they stood. The closest guard bent down and thrust his face within inches of Filch's.

"Redeem your crimes by defending your beloved city!" the guard shouted. The guard stood there with his face inches away from Filch's as he waited for a reply. When one was not forthcoming, several other guards circled around and pointed their weapons at them.

Filch stared down the guard defiantly. Adger was wise enough to know that appeasing these guards was their only path forward, but he failed to formulate an appropriate response.

Simon weakly said, "Our reparation will aid the defense of Canton."

Simon knew nothing of the city but hoped the guard was satisfied. He wondered if he had mixed himself up with the wrong people, but after seeing what they could do, he felt obligated to learn more. The moments of silence that followed were unnerving.

The guards eventually lowered their spears and regrouped with the squadron, but the singular guard lingered another moment, still staring down at Filch. He then strode to the others and they all moved on down the street.

Adger exhaled loudly as if he had been holding his breath. "Good job, Simon," he said. "Let's get going."

"I feel awful," Simon said, still disoriented from his stupor in the tunnel but able to walk.

"It's the curse of Dyurndale. Either you remember and cope with the sadness, or you don't and live your life wondering. People don't remember anymore—not many of us anyway. How long have you remembered your life before?"

"Since I got here," Simon said as he shook the disorientation from his head.

"No one remembers when they first get here," Adger said skeptically to Simon while glancing to Filch.

"We shouldn't stand in the open street," Filch interrupted.

With subtle glances over their shoulders and a turn of a corner, they dashed behind an outcropping of booths and crates.

"There must be an attack on the city," Filch said, "We were had; the guards never let people go unless there are far more pressing matters to attend."

"We need to get to my brother," Adger said.

"For once—and this is your only freebie—I agree with you, Short-round; we need his help." Filch whispered.

Adger opened his mouth to protest the insult, but she pressed her hand against his mouth to silence him. She pulled them both lower to the ground and deeper into the shadow of their shelter. Another garrison of towering guards ran past their hiding place.

"Couldn't you just do your black hole thing?" Simon asked.

Simon and Filch laughed quietly.

"No, I could not," Filch said wryly. "You wouldn't understand the complexity of what it takes to—"

The boxes next to them exploded in shards of wood.

"Deserters!" a guard shouted, pointing at them on the other side of where the crates once stood.

The three of them ran in the opposite direction and hoped to reach a bend in the road or another dark alley.

They escaped the angry shouts of the guards and sprinted towards what Simon could only assume was the home of Adger's brother. The friction of his clothes and the sweat on his brow made him feel lively and invigorated. He feared the wrath of Canton's army, but as the trio fled past empty stores, he caught fleeting reflections of himself in the store windows. With his coat fluttering behind him like a cape and his comfortable leather boots pounding the cobblestone streets, he started to feel like a real adventurer. He felt compelled to press on, and each time he escaped danger or narrowly missed a hazard, he started to think his destiny was something he could believe in.

The sound of guards on the chase was easily perceptible in the empty streets.

"We need to get back into the heart of the city and lose them in the crowds," Filch said.

"I *have* to find my brother," Adger said.

"We don't exactly have the luxury of asking them to stop chasing us."

The shouts of the guards were close behind them and more cries of conflict could be heard further away in the city.

"You're welcome to go if you'd like," Adger said to Simon, "but my concern lies elsewhere."

"I thought you needed me," Simon said.

"I do, but this attack on the city changes things," Adger said. "At the moment, I need to find my brother."

"...Lead on," Simon said. "I will help you find him."

They fled from the sound of battle and ran through the winding, declining, and inclining streets of Canton. They sprinted onto one of the stone bridges and Simon could see the breathtaking, outlying boroughs again. He noted that the waterfall was no longer visible and assumed they had exited the plateau from the opposite side. The further they went, the quieter the shouts of the guards became; it seemed the focus of the attack had been on the city center. When it was safe to assume that they had lost those chasing them, they slowed their pace. Simon was just as lost in the outer regions of the city, and whatever meager sense of direction he had before was obliterated. His fate rested entirely in the blind faith that he entrusted to his companions.

They came to a part of the city with narrower streets and buildings with slits for windows. The doors on the homes were just as slender and looked like they couldn't fit any piece of furniture without prior disassembly. They stopped in front of a darkened house with a door that was opened inwardly on its hinges. Adger rushed inside. Filch leaned her back against the house in contrast to the obvious angst that Adger had shown in his haste. He scurried around in the house as he called out, "Bromle! Bromle?!"

Simon stepped inside the doorway and noted the overturned living quarters within. There was a fireplace in the opposite corner that seemed too small to even hold a pot. Fading red embers in the hearth showed that the fire had gone out hours ago, and two chairs sat adjacent to a table barely big enough for two plates. Climbing above the fireplace were stairs sized for a child's width at best. It was surprising enough that the hovel had a second floor but even more so that Adger didn't bring it crashing down in his frantic search. He clearly shouted, "Una! Where are you?"

He came back down the narrow stairs and pushed his way past Simon to the narrow street. "Bromle's gone and so is Una!"

Filch seemed unaffected by the news.

"Did you hear me?!" Adger shouted at her.

"Try Ketay," she said calmly.

"Of course!" Adger said cheerily in contrast to his concern before. Adger fished inside his pockets and pulled out a mottled green stone. "Ketay," he whispered to the rock, "find Una."

The rock sprung to life but not in much form. It fell from Adger's hand and rolled into the house with Adger close behind. The stone rolled directly into the dying embers of the fireplace and sent a burst of sparks up the flue. The embers ignited the charred wood around it and although there seemed inefficient fuel to burn, flames rose to life. A glowing form rolled out of the fireplace and solidified into a red and green mottled creature similar to a raccoon.

"Unaketay!" Adger said, "Where is Bromle?"

Unaketay jumped around excitedly as a dog might greet its owner. Adger hurriedly pet it and asked it the question again. It stopped, as if it had to consider the question, and then darted past the trio into the narrow streets.

"We're coming to get you, Bromle!" Adger said excitedly.

Unaketay retraced their journey to Adger's home. Although Simon was disoriented, he recognized some of the squalid livings and people in the streets they had passed before. The people who took notice of them seemed startled by the stone raccoon and hurriedly went inside. The more they ran, the closer they got to the city center again.

They had just crossed over the bridge again and back onto the plateau when Unaketay stopped and looked to Adger. It sat back on its haunches and then, with its tiny slender hand, pointed up towards the tower in the center of the city. The creature purred and made several gestures with its hands like a secret code that Adger seemed to understand. It dropped back down to all fours and repeatedly nudged Adger's leg, but he stared at the tower in a daze.

"If he's there," Adger said to Filch with a pause, "then we could lose everything."

The stone raccoon nosed his leg again, actually knocking Adger off his balance.

"Okay, alright; here." He reached in his pocket and gave the creature some kind of reward after which it immediately shrunk into two small stones: a blood red, and a mottled green stone again. Adger reached down to pick them up and then put them in separate pockets.

As intrigued as Simon was, he assumed it was not the best time for more questions.

They all looked up towards the tower in the center of Canton. The distant cries of struggle still floated on the air.

As they stood there, Simon couldn't help but feel a bit awkward, and he wondered what they were going to do.

"He could still be fine," Adger said, trying to be encouraging; as if to himself. "He's probably—he's definitely in one of the lower sections."

Simon opened his mouth to speak again, but an explosion stopped him. A fireball decimated the upper parts of the spire; sending the pinnacle teetering down towards the city beneath. Several stories below, another explosion erupted and spewed debris, ash, and fire into the open air. The tower shuddered and then additional sections began to fall.

Adger was noticeably distraught by the explosions. Simon assumed that his change in disposition towards the tower meant that his brother must have been inside.

"This city's not under attack," Filch said as her eyes narrowed. She said quietly, "This is an invasion." She glanced back at Simon, giving him a divisive, sideways stare.

"I don't know anything about this," Simon said holding up his hands in innocence.

Undulating clouds of vapor raced through the sky from behind one of the buildings nearest the tower. They appeared to be clouds but it was as if they were directed or controlled. As chunks of the tower continued to fall towards the streets below, more clouds raced from other directions towards the crumbling tower. It seemed the tower was summoning the formations.

It took a moment to tell but Simon exclaimed, "Cool; there are people on those clouds!"

Filch shot him another unpleasant stare, but he was too focused on the new development to notice.

Two of the clouds raced towards the tower from behind them and flew just over the rooftops of the buildings; close enough to see partial details. On each one was a trio or pair of armor-plated creatures. The creatures piqued Simon's curiosity like so many other new experiences, but his interest was quickly suppressed when he noted the knurled weapons they carried. Even more terrifying was the dragon that flew in their midst. It continually vomited massive balls of vaporous wind into the city streets. The creatures converged in a cumulous mass that soared in wide arcs around the remnants of the crumbling tower as if establishing a watch. All the while the serpent lazily glided in the midst of the cloud riders. When the clouds ceased their amassing, the dragon stopped abruptly and turned towards where the three of them still stood. It started descending towards them with a gaze fixed in their direction.

"We've been spotted," Filch said.

The creature bellowed so loudly that the windows around them shattered. All the armor-plated creatures followed along behind the dragon towards where the three stood, too. The echo of footsteps could be heard in the streets around them too.

The invasion, it seemed, was coming just for them.

7 The Brother

The sounds of marching guards resonated behind them, in front of them, and beside them. The looming footsteps seemed to approach from every window and dark corner of the buildings.

Simon wondered if the aerial pursuers were Veadus' warriors coming for him. It seemed to make sense, and the inevitable guilt he felt was exacerbated by the confusion of his purpose. Kapell had been very helpful to him in guiding him on his quest. Trying to find his way to the next life seemed impossible without appropriate direction. Simon was in the middle of a monstrous city in a canyon with no direction and only a couple of cryptic companions who were leading him to a crumbling tower to save another mysterious person. He wondered if he should tell them who he was and if seeking their guidance might be in his best interest, but the new threat they faced together preoccupied his judgment. In that moment, it seemed better to confide in the safety of numbers.

"This seems like the opportune time to step through a wall," Simon said.

"We can't; they'll see us," Adger said.

"Doing anything is better than standing here staring at them," Simon said.

Without any further debate, Simon moved towards the dark corner of a nearby alley. It was short and ended in a wall, but it seemed a better option than being in the open streets.

"Where are you going?" Adger demanded.

Without reply, Simon quickly moved into the shadows of the corner; thankful for the darkness it provided. He promptly opened the pouches on his belt and searched for anything that might have been of use to him. His hilt did not seem like his best option because he still didn't fully understand it. He hoped to find a similar wooden object like the one that Adger had used to open the tunnel, but he wouldn't know how to use it.

There was a circular metal object that resembled a pocket watch. Simon thought it might be a compass, but when he opened it up, there was nothing inside. There were also several pieces of folded paper which Simon hoped were maps, but it didn't seem the most opportune moment to open them. Next to them in a small pouch were remnants of shells that might have been the center pieces or outer flakes of large conch shells. With them, there was a small metal frog and a golden loupe; neither of which Simon could imagine the practicality of. Inside the hardest of pouches to open were four incomparable rings; each one more entrancing than the last.

Despite the intrigue of all those things, Simon had hoped to find something more obviously useful. He searched the remainder of his pockets and then his coat. When he patted down the outside of his coat, the plain drab colors it had created before were shaken off like soot. The pressing need to be hidden gave him an idea. He furiously patted his coat, which produced even more sooty black dust. The cloud of darkness continued to grow, and Simon backed farther into the darkened corner.

"If you don't want them to see where we go, now's the chance," Simon said from within the cloud.

Filch and Adger appeared through the haze in front of him with bewildered expressions on their faces.

"There is more to you than I thought," Adger said with a smile.

"I would recommend getting that tunnel maker out, Adger; or, Filch, why don't you start punching some puddle-holes in the wall."

Adger quickly fumbled in his pockets, "Of course; I just—I've never seen—" he said while he looked at the cloud Simon's coat was creating.

"Here!" Adger said as he thrust out a wooden object. It was straight, rectangular, the length of a pen, and the thickness of a carrot. He squeezed it with both hands hard enough to make his knuckles turn white. The top sprung open into four parts which flattened and connected into a square. A straight, flat blade shot out of the handle. Adger quickly stepped to the back of the dead-end tunnel, stood in a wide stance, and raised the sword into the air.

"Stop!" said a voice from the narrow street that was only steps away from them. Adger froze with the sword raised, and Simon stopped beating his coat. The dark cloud still concealed them.

"What business do you have here?" said a guard outside the cloud.

"It is none of yours!" said a watery voice, descending through the air.

A fearsome roar shook the ground, followed by a quaking impact which was the flying creature's violent landing.

Cries of conflict ensued, which afforded Adger the time to finish his swing. He struck the wall at the end of the tunnel, creating a crack in the stone. Filch hurriedly ran over to the wall and leaped into the air. She extended her foot and kicked at the center of the crack. The impact of her strike caused the rift to widen and a gust of air escaped it, blowing away the shrouding protection of the haze. They looked back towards the narrow streets and saw the creatures from around the tower in combat with the city guards.

The creatures they defended against had an obvious advantage. They were shorter than the guardsmen but broad and stocky. They were more bestial than man; all with plated, azure armor covering their backs and shoulders. Their pauldrons were covered and lined with short razor spikes that made any physical grapple with them hopeless. Their weapons were various forms of swords, or spears, that flowed in sweeping curves.

Even amidst the fray, several of the Steward's soldiers noticed the miscreants that the cloud of smoke had been hiding. The trio immediately looked back towards the crack in the wall that had widened. It was still barely big enough to squeeze through. Other parts of the city could be seen beyond the wall, but the hope it conveyed was insufficient to outweigh the threat they faced. They all looked back towards the guards again, and each took a preparatory stance to fight.

The wall behind them erupted in a cloud of debris and dust, knocking the three of them to the ground. Chunks of the wall narrowly missed them and struck the guards moving in their direction. They looked back to see a figure as broad and tall as the sea creatures but quite obviously a man. His hands were as big as shovels and his shoulders: wider than a door frame. His bearded chin was like the hilt of a sword; its sharpness visible through the bushy beard. His red hair was one shade to the darker side of brown and fell from underneath a balmoral cap in a thick singular braid; the short hilt of a dagger could be seen sticking out from the braid near its top. He wore leather armor across his torso that connected to buckled straps and leather pieces on his shoulders. His arms were like the trunks of maturing redwoods; too big to even get two hands around. His legs were equally as muscular and were partially obscured under thick brown boots and a plaid kilt that hung down above them.

"Bromle! But I thought—" Adger said joyfully.

"Follow me little brother," he said in a deep voice with rolling r's that sounded like they might force a laugh at the end of each sentence. "We need to go back to the tower."

Without any further debate and welcoming the rescue, the three of them scrambled off the ground and rushed towards the hole in the wall. Bromle stuck his arm out to block Simon after Adger and Filch had passed.

"He's with us," Adger called back to him from the other side.

Bromle hesitated a moment longer and then dropped his arm to allow

Simon to pass. In the same moment he stepped through, more weapons clattered around the opening. The group rushed down the alley on the other side of the wall towards the open streets of the city. Bromle stopped after a few paces, turned, and slammed his open hands together. The air around his gloved fingers seemed to shimmer like ripples in a calm pond, which rushed towards the weakened remnants of stone. When the ripple reached it, the houses and bricks around it all crumbled on top of the guards that were pursuing them. For the moment, the chase had ended.

The other three stopped and watched the alleyway fill with rubble. They quickly fled the scene but slowed to a jog once they were back in the streets. People were still running in different directions with panicked looks on their faces, but it was noticeably less chaotic in that district.

"We have to go back to the tower," Bromle said.

"Why would we do that?" Adger said, "Why would we willingly risk going in that place? It's falling down!"

"It's the answer we've been looking for, brother! I think we might finally know how to go back home."

"What are you talking about? This is our home. There's no going back, there's no leaving the city, there's no getting out of here!"

"It's not the tower I want; it's what's underneath it!"

Filch turned away from their conversation to hide her involuntary reaction to his comment. She was uneasy because she knew what Bromle spoke of and had no desire to revisit it.

"We can't go that way!" Filch blurted out.

"See?" Adger said. "Even Filch agrees with me."

"Children that died in the life before used to be sent to the realm of Kylthame," Filch said as if she was forced into speaking for having blurted out her warning. "Kylthame protected them from the tyranny that now reigns here. It allowed them to grow in peace. It was the kindest and most peaceful place in all the realms of Dyurndale."

"I've never heard of it," Adger said. "Sounds like a nice place, but I don't understand the relevance right now. How do you know about it?"

"Rumors and stories from traders out west," Filch said.

"What does this have to do with anything?" Bromle interrupted.

"There are other realms within Dyurndale that Etnian is determined to rule. For him, total dominion here would open the possibility of entering the old world—the 'real world'. The more he has, the more powerful he becomes. He seeks to corrupt purity in every form and the purest of the realms would have been Kylthame."

"We all know how evil he is, but—" Bromle started again.

"Kylthame used to be on a river that flowed underneath all the realms of Dyurndale," Filch continued. "That's what you're after, Bromle; isn't it? It's too dangerous; even for you. Etnian is probably still searching for

Kylthame and any other place he can take over."

Filch's mind wandered. She had said more than she was accustomed to and more than she should have. If they pressed her any further, she may be found out.

It wasn't traders that Filch had heard about Kylthame from; she had lived there. Filch had died as a child. In the early days, it fell under the insurgent attacks of Etnian's scouts. His forces were destroyed and the river was dammed; not before captives were taken though. Filch was one of them.

She was dragged away to Etnian's realm and forced into servitude. She grew in her resentment of the world she found herself in. Having died at a young age, she had no recollection of her previous life; the only life she knew was the oppression of Etnian. She eventually gained his attention and was forced to be one his personal courtiers.

She resisted at first but then learned to play along and use her position to gain knowledge. When her horrid keepers were prey to inebriation—which was often—she would wander the empty halls of Etnian's castle: Gorfel. When her master would go on ventures to overtake other cities, she would follow in their ranks to plan her escape. She spent years planning it. She pieced together maps from archives and from the campaigns she secretively went on.

While searching the castle library one day, she found a book tucked in a corner. It mentioned the living water that surged beneath the ground of Dyurndale. She was surprised to have been directed to the book at all but one reading took her to another, and another that led her to it. Yet, despite this revelation that there was a network of other realms all connected by this stream, no campaign she had been on or read of ever made mention of it.

She knew what she had to do: she had to escape to one of these other places. She was ready. She was strong enough and learned enough of combat to defend herself. She was unsure of how to choose a destination, but she spent enough of her life in that place not to care. She planned to escape by following a very small scouting campaign that left late one night. She stumbled upon the group during one of her evening wanderings. The hushed conversations mentioned the book she had read and rivers of interconnected transportation. Whether it was wisdom or curiosity that guided her that night, she was never able to discern.

The small band of soldiers (being 300 in company) was set to attack a city that had a direct connection to the rivers below it. When she rode out on the horses, she soon discovered it would be farther than she had ever been before. When the first night turned into the second, and then fourth, she realized there would be no excusing her absence. She knew her presence would be missed by her deplorable master and felt no remorse in knowing that her absence would mean her keepers' deaths. Each time she considered turning back, the band of soldiers was either too densely encamped, or they were on patrol; leaving was implausible. By the time the eighth night turned into the tenth, she resigned to see the journey through. The only option that she had was to continue and despite the danger, she was happy to have escaped from Etnian. She steeled her nerves and focused on how to find a new home when the opportunity finally arose.

On the fourteenth night, the group of soldiers had arrived at their destination. A more permanent encampment was established, and the machines of war were assembled. A wide beaten road led to their target that was surrounded by bare trees stripped by the colder season. The castle belonged to a small fortress and a meager town. The guards within its walls were fearsome and fearless; unbeknownst to their attackers. Nevertheless, Etnian's forces were greater and more ruthless. The battle was Filch's opportunity to disappear in the bodies of the war and the shambles of the razed buildings; both of which there was an abundance of. She disguised herself in the garb of the enemy long enough to be overlooked and mistaken for dead. Etnian's soldiers moved from body to body, ensuring each combatant and citizen were assuredly demised.

She was hiding among the corpses and realized her subterfuge would be her destruction. With no other options, she leapt up and fled. The guards were in vehement pursuit, lobbing spears and any loose debris they could grasp as they chased her.

She ran into the destructed castle; pieces of the wall, freshly hewn from their proper place, were still crumbling down around her. One gigantic piece landed on the soldiers who sought to capture her and took out the stairs below them. The wall plummeted towards the ground far below and landed with a deafening crash that opened a visible fissure in the ground.

The impact caused the remnants of the tower to tremble and shake. The rest of the castle started to fall with her in it. She could see the fissure below grow as it swallowed the ground around it. It grew to a large enough space where she could see glowing streams flowing far beneath it. She realized that the castle sat directly above catacombs that led to the streams she had heard of.

She nimbly leapt from falling wall to plummeting stone and maneuvered herself to aim through the fissure. Projectiles and roars of frustration from the forces nearby rang out as she barely squeezed through the gap before the rest of the tower crashed onto the ground above her.

She kept her body tucked tightly as she fell through the crevice towards the cavern and water below. She neatly flipped and cut through the water, barely making a splash.

The water pulled her rapidly along and almost pushed her under before she was able to scramble on top of a door that found its way into the river with her. She floated along, and in and out of consciousness, for what felt like days; her body was exhausted. Eventually, her raft bobbed against a stony wall that the water ran underneath. She awoke and saw a narrow passage, leading out through the stone with daylight on the other side. She had spent so long in the dark that her eyes took time to adjust to the brightness.

She climbed out onto a small outcropping that looked out into the open sea, which she hoped separated her from the life she knew. Above her head was the top of the cliffs she emerged on, reachable by a short climb. Away and to the south, she saw a lonely stone pillar that could have served as a fortress if only there was a way to reach it.

She climbed to the top of the cliffs onto moorlands that rolled away into the horizon. Beyond that, even at the distance she was, she saw the tops of a city rising out of the ground. Over the few hours she walked closer, she realized it was a massive city set inside a tremendous network of canyons.

When she laid eyes on it, she knew what she had to do: she had to prepare a force to rise against Etnian and go back up the rivers to fight against him.

She learned that the rumors of his tyranny had spread and she joined those already set to resist it. She protected her past and claimed to be the sole survivor of the small town above the river. Her story was made more believable because when she arrived, she was still wearing the colors and garb of the town.

She joined with Adger and Bromle specifically because they didn't ask a lot of questions of her. They spent their time planning and scheming, and Canton became a haven for her. She grew more comfortable in the confines of the walls, and when her hopes grew that she could forget her upbringing, she ran into Simon. Despite the knowledge she had and how it might help them even then, she was reluctant to be more forthcoming.

"Filch!" Bromle said as he snapped his fingers in her face. "I said, what are you thinking about?"

"I was just thinking that the tower isn't our best choice," she said. "We could be walking right into his hands."

"Like I said, Brom." Adger said, "She agrees with me."

"I never said that I agreed with you, Short-round."

"Don't call me that! I hate when you call me that. Brom, our fight is here. We have to stay true to the Kalinaw and continue fighting until hope arrives."

"Those lies were made up by your crazy old friend in the woods," Brom said.

Simon watched the interaction quietly and nearly missed Adger's mention of the Kalinaw due to the distant sounds of the city wide invasion. Up until that point, he felt unwittingly dragged along without choice. The alternatives would have been less desirable in each situation. His time for control had arrived. He felt compelled to take a stand and demand more answers. He worked himself up to be brazen, confront these strangers, and be the leader instead of the follower. He had a mission to complete, and thanks to serendipity, he had been a part of the resistance over the past few hours. He worked up his confidence just enough to ask about the Kalinaw, but when he opened his mouth, his stomach took over.

"I'm hungry!" was all that Simon said. Yet, it was a surprising enough comment to make the others cease their bickering.

"Hear, hear!" Adger said, "Let's get some food."

"How can you possibly think of food at a time like this?" Filch said disapprovingly.

"I understand there's an invasion going on, but…I'm still hungry," Simon said. "Can we get some take out? Maybe a fruit stand, drive thru, shawarma…crackers?"

Adger excitedly nodded his head as Simon spoke, the two of them were kindred spirits led by their stomachs. Filch and Bromle looked at Simon with blank expressions. Simon's cavalier approach to seeking sustenance caused him to unwittingly make the mention of at least one element from his previous life that seemed incongruent to this one. Simon thought nothing of it, but Bromle had noticed.

"Come on, Simon! I'll lead the way," Adger said as he hurriedly led Simon down the street away from the tower. "No good adventure began on an empty stomach, I always say."

"You've never said that," Bromle called after them.

Bromle and Filch reluctantly followed them, lingering slightly behind them.

"He said 'drive-thru'," Bromle said to Filch.

"I am unaware of what that means," she said.

"It's something from his previous life. It's where a person would order food then drive around the outside of the building and pick it up from a window."

She stared at him with a blank expression on her face—as could only be perceived by her eyes due to the mask she still wore over most of her face.

"You get my point though, right? He *casually* remembers something from his previous life. Most of the Kalinaw have to be taught to remember."

"He says he remembers even from when he got here," Filch said.

"That's not possible. Where did you two find him?"

"In the market square; Adger had the usual affliction of not being able to close his mouth. I had to create a diversion, and since your pontificating brother also knows how to disappear quickly, I knocked Simon down. I stole his sword, and he chased me."

"Sounds like you're getting a little slow."

Ignoring his attempt at jocularity, she said, "He has a legendary weapon."

Bromle's expression of humor was replaced by one of surprise and alarm. "Does Adger know?"

"I don't think so. Simon had it alit when we were taking one of our usual shortcuts, but Adger didn't see the hilt. It has markings on it that I've never seen. That might not normally be cause for alarm, but I couldn't activate it; it's connected to him. Do you think Orvar is right?"

"Orvar is crazy and lives in a tree," Bromle said, matter-of-factly. "Any story from that old man is caused by mental instability from eating forest plants."

"We need a hero. I wonder if he could be…" Filch didn't finish her quiet thought and instead they both ran after Simon and Adger.

8 The Tower

Simon and Adger hadn't made it far from the other two. They were in a small shop on the street where some collection of meat rotated on a spit. Simon had no idea what the food was and was constantly aware of the pressing matters in the city, but he was unable to focus on account of his hunger.

"Adger, we don't have time for this," Bromle said as he came through the door.

"What's going on out there," the cook behind the counter asked when Bromle and Filch came inside.

"An invasion," Bromle said, "and these two can only think of filling their bellies."

"There's always time for food!" said the cook as he handed each of them a bag.

"See?" Adger said, "I even got it to go."

"Come on," Bromle said.

They left and turned back towards the crumbling tower.

"I thought we talked about this," Adger said in between mouthfuls of food, "There's nothing there but a guaranteed spear in the chest." A dribble of white sauce ran from the corner of his mouth.

"Or maybe a burial from the tower," Simon said with his own mouthful of food. He loved what he was eating; it tasted no different than a lamb filled gyro he had enjoyed many times. He was glad that his new friend had picked such a delicacy. He felt inclined to take Adger's side after the past few moments, and he desperately needed an ally in a world of aggressors. After learning that Adger had some form of allegiance to the Kalinaw—and not least, his stomach—Simon was more inclined to trust him.

71

"This town won't last much longer," Bromle said. "Our place isn't here anymore."

"It's not without its defenses, but that doesn't matter. We should stay here," Adger said. "Besides, aren't you glad to see that tower fall?"

"Of course I am, but we need to go home, and not to that squalid closet we were crammed into. You want to find a way to help the Kalinaw, right? You want to strike fear in the enemy? This is the way to do it; we strike the very heart of the enemy!"

"I don't think it will be as easy to fight him as you assume," Filch said.

"Of course not, but the river may take us back home where we can rally our kin. Or, it may help us find out where Etnian lives so that we can end his reign with a well-aimed blade." He thrust his hand out as if stabbing an enemy.

"And what would you do when you get there; when you're face to face with that monster?" Filch asked. "*If* you got there. I don't think you've thought this through. No one on this side of the sea has ever seen him or knows how to kill him."

"I've heard stories that he's a beast with wings of pure flame," Adger said. "He has the neck and head of a dragon, with a body as wide as twenty houses. All of it supported by legs like barbicans. Clintok told me that he's been there before and saw what he looked like."

Bromle rolled his eyes in exasperation. "Your friends are idiots," he said.

Despite the attack on the city, the sector they were in was seemingly unaffected. Distant cries and shouts could still be heard, but there was no evidence that the immediate area had been attacked yet. People rushed between buildings or occasionally a lone guard ran by with a weapon readied for attack, but there were no destructed buildings or groups of enemies. It felt unnaturally at peace. Simon imagined that at any moment, a surge of enemies would rush around a corner to attack them. It provided Bromle and Adger the opportunity to argue while Simon quietly enjoyed the rest of his food. He eyed a couple of watchful faces in upper windows of homes nearby, but they too seemed uninterested.

The brothers' continued their argument, and in seeming reaction to Simon's foretelling, the eatery behind them erupted in molten chunks and steam clouds. The fiery debris popped and clacked against the adjacent buildings, and they sparked up in flame. Multiple bularaz crawled out of the crater in the ground where the eatery used to be and spread out from the hole like an army of ants might rush to defend their fortress. Fortunately, the creatures had not spotted the four adventurers, and they needed no additional encouragement to disperse.

"Brom, how 'bout that tower, then?" Adger said while turning to run.

Simon shoved the last couple bites of food in his mouth, assuming that he might not eat again soon based on the events since his arrival. He chased after Brom and Adger with Filch close behind. He wondered about Bromle even though Adger seemed trustworthy; Filch was no more encouraging than when they first met. Bromle struck him as arrogant and not as forthcoming as he should have been about his time in the tower.

Almost involuntarily Simon asked, "Why were you at the tower, Bromle?"

Bromle stopped and turned to look at Simon. "I don't think that's any of your business."

Simon immediately felt uncomfortable at the sudden confrontation. Bromle's secrecy made him even less confident that the tower was the best choice, but his companions were his only link to the Kalinaw. Heeding Kapell's warning, he still hadn't revealed his origin and didn't feel compelled to do so since they had not yet done the same.

Even hurrying towards the burning tower, Simon felt grateful that they weren't being chased again, but Bromle's insistence on the tower made him slightly paranoid. It seemed that the whole world was chasing him and he didn't want to go find the trouble out at the moment. It was obvious that Bromle's haughtiness was linked to his size. He puffed up his chest and looked down at Simon which, given Bromle's height, was quite easy to do. Simon was reminded of past-life experiences with attitudes like Bromle's. He seemed like the kind of person who might belittle the ignorant and castigate the foolish. A certain amount of credit had to be afforded the brute for his dedication to his form, but his hauteur was nearly unbearable to Simon. Still, being on the wrong side of Bromle's aggression was not a place that Simon wanted to be, and it reminded him that he was still a stranger in their midst. He was grateful when Adger broke the tension.

"Yeah, Bromle, what *were* you doing at the tower?"

"I was down at Tuger's Place, minding my own business, and some guard thought I looked at him wrong, so they hauled me down there...but I broke out!" Bromle said proudly.

"That's ridiculous," Filch said, "No one has ever broken free from any capture that Canton enforced on them."

"I'd be the first then. It was a daring escape; tons of guards and fighting."

"I thought you promised to stay away from Tuger's." Adger scolded. "That place is a snake's den. I wish it'd fall into the ground along with all the thieves and criminals that go there," Adger said.

Bromle ignored his brother's chastisement as he responded, "They have good food. Come on, we're almost there."

Simon's suspicions were growing. In the present moment, he knew he hadn't the time to grapple with the unknowns; the tower warranted all his attention.

Warriors on vaporous clouds still flew around the crumbling minaret, but they were so high that the approach of the group was unnoticed. They came to the tower from the opposite side of the wide road where Simon first met Adger. The curvature of the tower was so wide that it stretched almost flatly in both directions. A narrow alley went in both directions along the tower wall. There were massive remnants of the upper tiers in the street around the base of the tower and some of the buildings around it had been crushed from sections that had fallen on them. The stone remnants were mostly made up of pale orange rock similar to the stone of the ground and canyon walls. Some of the other portions that had fallen from the more ornate sections of the tower were clearly made of marble. There were pieces of steel rods sticking out of some of the chunks of stone and it gave the impression that the structure did not fall with ease. There were even portions of the balconies that he had observed before.

"This might be a problem," Bromle said looking around at the street. "There was a hatch here somewhere."

"I highly doubt there was a hatch right out here in the open," Filch said. "It would be quite well hidden now."

"Well, it wasn't just wide out in the open on the street. It was underneath some stones like it had been paved over. Like a back door or something. It was…" Bromle trailed off in thought. He walked over to the low remnants of the wall of a house and put his back against it. He took a few steps from it, turned, and took a few more steps over the broken pieces of buildings. "Okay, stand back," he said.

He rubbed his massive hands together, and a bright blue smoke began to emanate from in between them. He extended his hands and arms out to his sides. The palms of his hands each held a small, smoking ball: one was bright blue and the other a blazing yellow. Bromle clapped one thunderous time, aimed his hands at the ground, and was launched several feet into the air. A green ring of fog shot out from around him.

Adger and Filch seemed unsurprised by it, but Simon's eyes and mouth involuntarily opened wide. No matter what unexpected thing he discovered in that world, his imagination was repeatedly surpassed. His reaction had gone unnoticed though, due to the cloud of debris Bromle caused. The explosion he created caused an alarming but expected amount of dust and sand to fly into the air. The haze that filled the small end of the road was a comfort due to the noise the explosion made. As the dust began to settle, Bromle stood over a giant crater he made in the broken debris on the street. Simon instinctively looked up at where the flying warriors circled the pinnacle of the broken tower.

They were no longer patrolling the remnants of the tower and had noticed the commotion below them. They descended quickly and started throwing weapons at the group beneath them.

"Here!" Bromle said as he reached down and pulled at the stones in the street.

After a few tense moments the sound of grinding stone was encouraging. Bromle lifted the hatch from the road and it creaked loudly on thick iron hinges. He held open the door for the others to climb inside.

Simon didn't like the thought of being confined in another tunnel, but whatever Bromle was after seemed safer than the clang of spears on the stones around them. He climbed over the debris in the street and entered the hatch directly after Filch. A cool gust of stale, moldy air hit him in the face as he reached the opening and descended the rusty ladder within. Bromle held the hatch open for Adger and then squeezed down past him. Simon noted a flint striker that Adger held in one hand as the light from the street above disappeared under the closed hatch. Adger stayed at the top of the ladder and could be heard fumbling with the trinkets of his coat pockets. Sparks lit up the darkness of the tunnel until a steady blue flame appeared at the end of a pistol that Adger held. The handheld torch could just be determined in the welding that Adger had started. He smelted the corners of the hatch, which immediately turned into viscous red liquid that slowly oozed a short way down the adit.

Once it cooled off and the red liquid darkened, they were plunged into pitch blackness.

"That should hold them," Adger said, "for at least a few minutes."

Despite Simon's reservations, there was no option but to go down and follow the ladder.

Bromle leaned his back against the wall of the narrow shaft and kept his feet pushed against the ladder. He then slapped his hands together until a soft blue light emanated from his palms. "We better get going," he said. "That won't hold them forever." He formed the blue light into a ball like a sculptor might shape a vase. He held the small ball of light between his hands and started to push his palms together until the sphere popped like a softened tomato. The blue light dimmed but steadily glowed from his palms. It was just enough to continue their descent with meager visibility.

"Where are we going, Bromle?" Simon asked, eager to learn more about their destination.

"I wasn't in their prison for long, because—let's face it—I'm me, and I can't be contained. I heard a guard mention that they found 'it' below the tower. The guy sounded scared but, being the weak little tower-guard that he was, I shrugged it off—."

"They're ten feet tall," Simon said.

"Well, compared to me they're little. Anyway, I managed to lure a guard close enough to my cell to knock him out and take his keys. I got my gloves back shortly after and fought my way out of there. Before I left, I wanted to find out what the guards were talking about. So, I headed deeper into the tower, and after I smashed a few heads together, one of them told me that they found a passage to a river under the tower. I thought he was just feeding me useless information but when I pressed him more, he told me that it wasn't *just* a river. He said it connected to…oh man, what was it called? Baynacrock or something—he said it was Etnian's lands. So, I went down there."

"You went down there—deeper into an enemy stronghold?" Adger asked skeptically.

"Of course I did! I wasn't scared. I got excited because I could hear a scuffle as I descended deeper into the darkness. I was getting bored just walking around—"

"How did *you* have any idea where you were going?" Filch asked with that same note of derision that seemed common in her tone. Even she sounded like she was done listening to him.

Simon eyed her as she took up the argument. These irregular lapses in her composure and silence showed that she knew more than she let on. Simon had no estimates how long this trio had been a group, but there was an element of experience in Filch which couldn't be ignored.

Bromle boasted on; "I heard some guys at Tuger's talking about the tower; one said he found out about something that would change the whole city. I had to *convince* him to talk about it. I had to loosen his tongue a bit, and that's when that guard had to stick his nose where it didn't belong. I managed to get just enough information out of him before I went with the guard."

"*You* went willingly?" Adger asked.

Simon got the impression that Bromle wasn't being entirely honest about the situation but from Bromle's previous reaction, Simon hesitated to probe for more information. For the moment, he was happy that Bromle's attention was diverted away from him.

"I overheard some of the guards saying that the river connected to other places," Bromle continued. "Right before I knocked them out, they said the river connects to whole other realms and cities. Maybe we could find allies, Adger."

"Since when was your faith renewed in the Kalinaw?" Adger asked him.

"It could even get us back home, little brother!" Bromle said.

"Where are you from?" Simon asked, knowing that whatever location the brothers said would be meaningless to him.

"A small town far out west called Yingu," Adger said. "It was over a desert, through a forest, and nestled on towers of stone covered in green. Our home may not even be there anymore. We were taken when we were young but old enough to remember. There was an incursion from a neighboring city—or maybe it was just a group of dwindling bandits looking to grow their numbers and purses—we were young and strong so, either way, we were ideal candidates to be indoctrinated. They killed any who resisted, and our town was too small to fight; just a bunch of farmers, really. We lost our family, friends—"

"We lost everything," Bromle interrupted.

"We were 'drafted' into the enemy's ranks," Adger continued. "We were bound and carried away for days. By the time our bonds were cut, the way home was lost. Which is why," Adger said to Bromle, "this is a waste of time!

"We managed to escape," he continued, "but by the time we did, any hopes of going home were gone. We joined a group of traders headed here and have lived a meager but happy life ever since."

"Speak for yourself," Bromle said.

Adger longed to return home, but he tried to accept the life they had been given. He missed his home, but his positivity made his experiences less severe. Bromle never settled in Canton. He was the older of the two and always longed to find a way home; no matter how unrealistic it might be. The disparity of their perspectives had frequently caused contention between the brothers. The Kalinaw was something that Bromle tolerated for Adger's sake but not something he took very seriously.

"Are you with the Kalinaw?" Simon asked, risking the exposure of his own agenda.

They all stopped moving down the ladder. The moments of silence that followed in the dark were palpable.

"We can trust him, Bromle." Adger said.

"That's not what worries me. Just the same, what does it matter to you?"

Growing tired of Bromle's skepticism and negativity Simon said, "If I was an enemy, do you really think I'd get myself locked in this hole with the three of you?"

Bromle laughed. "I don't think the enemy cares enough," he said, as if changing his mind about Simon's question. "The whispers of the Kalinaw would gain nothing more than a queer glance and an empty seat at the bar. The enemy doesn't care about us anymore. We're all that's left. What worries me is why you would even ask. "

They continued their descent down into the tower.

"We're not *all* that's left," Adger said. "Orvar's not dead yet, and he says there are others."

"Exactly; he's old and crazy. You can't really count him; he doesn't do much," Bromle said.

"But you *are* the Kalinaw, right?" Simon asked.

"For what we're worth, yeah."

"This might not be the best time to bring this up but…" Simon hesitated, but this small group was the only hope he had, "I was told to find you."

Bromle laughed even harder than before. "You," he said into between raucous laughter, "You were told to find *us*? Welcome aboard then, but there really is no Kalinaw anymore." Bromle continued laughing.

Simon thought this would have been more of a revelation to them, but they were unaffected.

"Well, I was told you could help me find my way to the other side."

"We're there," Filch said before he had a chance to explain further. The ladder stopped on a stone floor and Filch reached it first. "I'm assuming you know where the door is, Bromle?" she asked.

After Bromle's instruction, Filch kicked a latch on the floor and a mechanical lock released the door. She put her ear to the wall and after a moment, she leaned her shoulder against it. Light from the passage beyond flooded the closet sized shaft. She peered out of the opening and motioned the others to descend.

Bromle closed his hands and the blue light disappeared. Despite having descended the ladder for so long, the empty halls they passed through went steadily downward. The halls and empty rooms were lit by flickering torches that hung on the walls. The twisting passages puzzled Simon, and he worried that they were being betrayed.

The only sounds they heard during their descent were the occasional echo of some faraway thump, or the shudder of the crumbling tower above.

"I see how difficult it was for you to escape," Adger said sarcastically.

"I don't know where they all went," Bromle said, "but there were plenty of guards to share in a fight. They're probably all just up on the streets fighting, or something."

They came into a banquet hall that had a vaulted ceiling that reached far into dark upper levels of the tower.

"No one has been here in years, Bromle," Filch said. "Dust is covering everything."

A thick layer of dust did indeed cover almost every object in site. Dinnerware of every sort was scattered around the space and on the long banquet table in the center of the room. The food on the plates was rotten and consumed by time far beyond that of an evening. The hall looked as though it had been without an attendant for much longer than since the invasion began.

Despite the odd scene around them, Simon was captivated by the architecture of the building. He wondered how deep they were, since the dark ceiling above him was unbroken from the tower's destruction. He thought the high ceiling seemed to be a waste of space. He was looking upwards towards the dark ceiling and inadvertently kicked some bowls and plates scattered on the floor. The sound echoed into the unseen rafters and around the corners of the entrances to the hall. Each one of them froze in mid-step and slowly turned to glare at Simon.

He silently mouthed apologies and shrugged his shoulders.

"That thumping," Adger whispered, "it...it stopped."

"That was probably just the fighting on the streets," Bromle said somewhat casually given the tense few moments.

"Shush, Brom! Listen."

He tilted his head at his brother's direction and strained to hear anything in the stale, still air.

In the moment of silence, the smell of the hall was more noticeable. The moist air that permeated each object and every fiber of the deep parts of the tower was unmistakable. There was another smell though; something more putrid.

"Something smells like a dumpster," Adger said. "It must be this food."

"It's not the food," Filch said with a hint of knowledge in her voice. "We need to go."

"We can't leave," Bromle pleaded. "This river is important."

"I told you before; it's going to be swarming with Etnian's army."

"The Kalinaw need this victory."

"I thought you said the Kalinaw isn't much bigger than you three?" Simon said.

Filch shushed them both.

The stench grew stronger. It was a foul odor that made their lunch gurgle in their stomachs. Adger and Simon both felt sick from the smell, and they both felt as if they might vomit. The fetor brought to mind dead, burning animals; volcanic, putrid, popping hair and bone.

A quiet voice echoed through the hall: "Dust to dust."

The voice alone was enough to strike fear and motivate the bravest warrior to flee; indeed, Simon started moving back the way they had come, even though he still had no idea what enemy they might soon face. His knees felt weak and his heart pounded in woeful anticipation. He noted the beaded sweat forming on Bromle's brow but the temperature deep below the tower was cool. The stout man looked resilient, but his hand trembled almost imperceptibly.

One of the entrances to the hall filled with an ominous presence. Even though an elongated shadow twisted on the wall, it was obvious that it didn't belong to a human. Simon had seen enough. "We should go," he whispered.

They all turned to run, except for Bromle, who stood defiantly to meet what came towards them. The banquet hall began to fill with light from the doorway as if it were being spilled from a jug. A dark green, almost black, fog crept along the floor preceding a subtle orange light.

"You can't win this battle, Brom," Adger said.

Bromle hesitated a moment longer.

"Come on! We don't know the way, brother!" Adger pleaded.

Bromle turned to lead his companions.

"What was that thing?" Bromle asked his brother as they ran.

"I read about it in the Kalinaw library."

"You mean the one shelf of books?"

"There's more than a shelf!" Adger replied defensively. "Scrawled in corners of those old tomes were notes about a creature in the Enemy's employ. Foul breath, it said; breath that could turn a person to ash. Breathing the foul fog is enough to—well, you saw the dust on everything. Do you think that hall was full of people? "

"That's tidy," Bromle said. "Imagine if we could unleash that thing on Etnian."

"That's sick, Brom. I read somewhere that it's called Asah. Seems like too simple a name for something so awful. That smell though…ugh; made me so sick."

"Talk about morning breath," Simon said, mostly to himself.

"I can only assume that must have been it, and I don't want to wait to find out. We need to find this river of yours and get out of here."

"It'll be worth it," Bromle said, "I'm sure of it…I didn't exactly make it this far before."

They continued their hurried retreat, all the while faithfully following Bromle. The longer they fled, the more distance they seemed to create from the creature; its smell lessened.

As they went around one final declination in the curve of the tower, they heard sounds of metal against stone and rushing water. The echo of voices drifted down the passage. Despite all of their growing urges to put as much distance between them and the Asah, they were wise enough to slow to a hurried walk instead of a sprint. They came to a flight of stairs that led downward, and they descended the stairs quietly as the voices and clanging metal sounds continued to grow.

Darkness filled the bottom of the stairs and pushed back the torchlight from the stairwell.

Filch moved back up a few paces, flourishing her cloak and extinguishing each torch as she moved back down the stairs.

The group moved into a cave, which was lit only by the subtle glow of shimmering illumination from below the water; the source of which was not immediately apparent, but it gave the pool an eerie feeling of significance. The group knew full well that they were far underground, but the ceiling above them looked as if it was an entire night sky, brimming with constellations. Luminescent splatters covered the cavern walls as well, like stars falling to the ground. The glowing insects that wriggled and crawled along the rocks gave the whole underground pool an otherworldly appeal; even when compared to the stupefying creatures above. The edges of the underground aquifer were difficult to ascertain in the low light, but its far reaching shore could be seen stretching out into the darkness in the distance and its edges curved away in each direction. Simon guessed even his most adept throw of a stone would not skip to the outer most reaches of the lake.

Away to their right in a dark corner of the cave, on a small shore against the wall, was a group of figures with torches and machines that hammered away on the cave wall. The vibrant bugs and illuminated patches receded in the miners' presence, and their torches washed out the detail of their features. It was obvious though that these were not the guards from above; they were much shorter, even shorter than a normal sized man.

The adventurers stepped through the entryway and onto the shore. They moved the opposite direction of the miners and to the left. They squatted down behind a group of rocks and boulders on the small band of soft earth that encircled the underground lake and for the moment, they were well hidden.

"I don't see how this was supposed to help us, Brom," Adger whispered angrily. "We have garbage-breath behind us and a lake in front of us—with no way out! What was the point?"

"I didn't know *what* was down here, but this has to be good. We got that thing," he said pointing to the stairwell, "and these things," Bromle whispered, pointing to the creatures in the corner. "Anything with that much attention must be worth the time."

"I can't believe I followed you down here. I'm so tired of your wild ideas. When are you going to accept the fact that our home is gone? *This* is our home, Brom! I have worked so hard to pay for that place you call a closet, while you waste our money in a tavern!"

"I contribute!"

"Doing what?!" Adger whispered angrily.

The whispering argument they were having had reached its height which interrupted the rhythmic thumping of the creatures' drilling machine. The creatures were all looking towards where the companions were crouched behind the boulders. As the workers turned towards the array of glowing surfaces, their faces were more visible. Their heads were long and disfigured like a rodent's; they seemed more animal than human, but with the low amount of light, it wasn't clear whether it was due to masks or actual features.

"See what happened now, little brother?"

"Will you both shut your mouths?!" Filch said in a hushed whisper.

The miners on the other side of the lake started moving around the periphery of the water, stretching their legs and craning their necks to see what had piqued their suspicions. The machine stood silently, the lake was placid, and the only sound was the soft squish of wet earth under the miners' footsteps.

"We can take these guys," Bromle whispered, nearly inaudibly.

Bromle started rubbing his hands together and the familiar blue light began to emit from in between his hands. Filch put her hand over his to stay his attack and shook her head to keep him still.

The miners moved close to the group's position. The eight of them had their backs hunched over from their years of labor. They wore various leather masks covering their faces that had enormous goggles. They stood on the other side of the rocks and moved their heads around as if sniffing the air.

Simon noted a new sound. It was a low, steady grumble, like water forcing its way through a weak dam. The miners unanimously jerked their heads back towards the mining machine. From their work site, a geyser of water rocketed out of the loose stones and plummeted in to the glowing lake. The underground lake erupted, too, but in a much larger geyser. It rammed into the dark ceiling far above and interrupted a colony of bats' silent slumber. The air was filled with their screeching voices, and the companions were grateful for the distraction.

Between the cloud of bats and the two geysers of water, the miners had forgotten about the adventurers. The majority of workers ran to the smaller geyser of water and ducked under the stream; fumbling with wet machines and controls. The additional miners ran towards the stairs directly adjacent to the group and overlooked them. Wet footsteps could be heard fading over the rush of the water. The adventurers stayed put and watched the scene unfold.

The geyser in the lake settled as a small island rose out of the water. The pinnacle of the land was crowned with the hull of an old ship. The structure that crested the small mound was covered in various pieces of sea-growth, which signified its long duration under the water. There were no masts or equipment that might indicate the ship's design besides the bulwark that surrounded the island periphery.

A portion of the island broke away from the main body and slammed into where the miners furiously fought back the water. The spewing geyser was dammed with crumbling wall and their bodies. The water ceased along with any further hopes that the twisted creatures had of living out another moment of their enslaved existence. Another part of the island slammed into the entrance that led to back up into the tower. The stairwell collapsed from the impact and prevented an escape back up through the tower.

The island spun around to face the adventurers' small hiding place. It was difficult to tell what the creature was exactly, but its silhouette was smooth, unlike the craggy makeup of Kapell. Another peninsula jutted from the island with more articulation than the others. Its mouth moved as a creature was expected to do and shouted, "Explain your place, and tell me why you, too, should not suffer the same fate!"

9 The Cavern

"I am Tortuse Ripa, Lord of the River," the creature bellowed in the cave. "Your presence is an offense against mine and one worthy of elimination. None are allowed in these parts any longer! Explain yourselves!"

The creature shouted enough to make them all momentarily cower, despite their best elements of bravery; even Bromle.

"Speak, creatures!" he shouted again.

Simon surprised the others when he stood up gallantly and stepped out from behind the boulders to face the creature.

"I am Simon," he said. "We've come here by way of chance—"

"No such thing," Tortuse interrupted loudly. "You decided to be here unless you were taken!"

Tortuse rose out of the water to show his full form. He looked like a tortoise but, contradictorily, appeared to spend his time in the water. His shell was seated on his body like a tortoise but was interrupted halfway up and ended in the ship's railing. The light was still too pale to see its detail, but the bulwark was a prominent feature that seemed to defy the expectations of a testudine or any other natural creature.

"Do not lie," Tortuse said. "I can *feel* your truth." He moved his head to look down at Simon's feet, which were in the edge of the water.

"We have come here by way of choice then," Simon continued, appeasing the supposed expectations of the creature. "We do not, however, come here to infringe upon your home. We seek a weapon to help our resistance—"

"Shut it, Simon!" Bromle shouted.

"Your companions' presence is known to me," Tortuse said. "Your efforts are known as well, but there is no weapon here."

A soft thump came from behind the bolder. "I told you!" Adger said to Brom as he hit his brother. "There's nothing here."

"There is not nothing—but not the something you hoped to find," Tortuse continued, "I know the Kalinaw as well, but I know it as what it *used* to be. You are a sad representative of their former glory."

The insult meant little to Simon, but he assumed those behind him felt its sting.

"Then you know we are friends," Simon said.

"I know they may be, but you…" he said, "You escape the depth of my knowledge. From where do you come?"

Simon felt panicked, and inadvertently his heartbeat quickened. His lack of an answer was noticeable even to those who weren't graced with the intuitive sensitivity of vibrations in the water.

"Speak!" the creature bellowed again; this time, taking a step towards Simon. "What lies have you spun to those you crew with?"

Simon's eyes flicked towards the collapsed stairwell.

Tortuse continued; "That way is gone to you; although, I dammed its way for the sake of your safety more than your containment. You have but a moment to answer my query…"

With little other answer to provide, and feeling the need to fill the silence Tortuse's pause created, Simon said, "Your shell is magnificent and the bulwark that accompanies it becomes you."

"And flattery does not become you."

Simon was truly impressed with the creature, even though its full grandeur could not be appropriately appreciated in the minimal light. Simon's mind scrambled to continue the dialogue. He had not heard the names of any towns that he might use to feign his origin. He fumbled for an answer, but nothing came to him. His first impression was to consider simply saying his home had been Canton as long as he could remember, but he knew little of Dyurndale and whether or not his answer would satisfy Tortuse. A better fiction than that was beyond him. He thought about pledging his loyalty to the Kalinaw, but his desperation would have been obvious. He was unsure if this turtle meant him harm but was sure that if he did, he could have accomplished it without conversation.

Despite the surety that Lord Ripa could withstand Simon's best and uncoordinated attack, he reached into his pouch and wrapped his hand around the warm metal hilt of his sword. Although the air deep inside the cavern was cool, the hilt was warm as if it had been in his hand on a hot summer's day. He felt the symbols on its sides and thumbed the upper edge to ensure he had oriented it correctly. If needed, it wouldn't be his first time defending himself against a water birthed creature, and based on Veadus' vehemence, he doubted it would be his last. He tightened his muscles and gripped his hilt till his knuckles burned. He pulled his hand out and moved the hilt behind his back grasping it in both hands.

"Your heart beat quickens," Tortuse said. "You cannot hope to defend yourself appropriately." He took several slow steps closer to Simon.

Without a lie to protect his identity, Simon resigned to confess his origin. He stayed ready for any sudden movements from the island-creature. "I was sent this way by instruction of Kapell dun Shan."

Tortuse took a step back into the water obviously caught off guard by Simon's answer.

"He told me to find the Kalinaw, which I have," Simon continued. He gestured towards his companions who were still crouched behind the boulders. He waited for a response from the turtle, but his silence was filled with nothing more than the quiet movements of the water, occasionally interrupted by dripping teardrops from the speleothems.

"Kapell said that he was told to wait for me, but he didn't know what I was supposed to do; nor do I know, to be honest. Did you send him?"

The turtle remained still, and the lack of an answer made Simon unbearably uncomfortable. He slowly took a couple steps back and readied his stance in preparation for what he thought might come next. He glanced back at his companions. It wasn't obvious to Simon whether they were frozen by surprise, or too fearful to help. Their hesitation might be perceived as wisdom by some, whereas Simon's confrontation would seem foolish.

His only thought was encouraging this creature to help instead of harm them. He reflected on Kapell's suggestion to walk the path. He was unsure how he could provide hope for Dyurndale, but being stuck inside this luminescent cave would help no one. The silence wore on his patience.

"Tell me, are you friend or foe?" Simon said. "I have yet to receive the direction I need, and I must find the path to leave Dyurndale. I was told the Kalinaw could help and were many in number, but here, there are only three."

His companions could hold their tongues no longer. Bromle stood up first to object at Simon's depreciation, but when he opened his mouth, Tortuse spoke instead.

"Tell me," Tortuse asked, "did Kapell make mention of Kynn Veyor?"

"The only thing he told me was that he thought I should 'restore the purpose of the path'...something of grandeur like that. When I left him, he was in a pretty bad fight with Veadus," Simon said.

"That witch!" Tortuse said spitefully. "I had hoped she fell into the great depths of her watery home and been forgotten, but it seems your arrival was not a quiet one. Come, we must send you on your way."

Simon felt elated that his adventure was about to receive appropriate direction.

"Pardon me," Adger said as he stepped out from behind the boulder, "but I'm not quite sure I heard you correctly. Did you say 'Kynn' as in THE Kynn Veyor, that is?"

The other two also abandoned their hiding places, assuming that the dangerous tension had passed. In all their conversation, Filch remained still and silent. She too had heard of Kynn, but if the brothers learned where she came across the information, too much might be revealed. During her slavery, Filch experienced the vast resources of her master's library. Adger didn't have the same luxury, but the limited books he had found in the dark corners of the few Kalinaw bookshelves gave him enough to learn of Kynn Veyor.

Tortuse slowly nodded his head in response to Adger's question.

"Brom, this is him! This is the one I was talking about: he is the hope of Dyurndale! The book said he will find the way back to Haeophan."

"You can't seriously believe that garbage," Bromle said.

"He's here! He's right here!" Adger said as he rushed over to Simon and gestured at him emphatically.

"Why? Because a turtle said he is?"

"Of course not; it's in the library. It talks about the hero who will once again find the opening of Naru. How can you seriously be so skeptical of the person standing right in front of you? What more proof do you need?"

"He does have the sword," Filch said. "Legendary weapons aren't easy to come by, nor are they fixated to one person." She walked towards Simon and looked him over as if she had just seen him for the first time.

"That is the *first* sword," Tortuse said. "You came for a weapon, yet you have already found the greatest one to hope for."

Tortuse was unable to gesture except with his massive head. He nodded at Simon and the realization of what he meant came to them a moment later. Bromle pointed at Simon with an expression of perplexity.

"Simon *has* a weapon," Adger said.

"No, he *is* the weapon," Filch said.

Bromle said nothing in return. He may have seemed resilient, but his skepticism was well founded by his life's experiences and the betrayal of others.

"I want to believe you are Kynn," Tortuse said, "but I must see the sword and shield to validate your claims. Every great hero has a story, and Kynn Veyor is no exception:

The sword of guarding and the unbreakable shield,
Cannot be found but only provided.
The flame of the depths with the dark heat it shall wield.
The consumption by death the device keeps divided.

Their holder will be a man born on the sea,
From the lone tower and cave beset by the waves.
Protection he'll need from the water born creed,
So until that new day, the mountain will stay.

"The heroic poem promises more, but our presence here is known, and our time is running out," Tortuse said.

In time with Tortuse's warning, muffled voices came from the other side of the collapsed tunnel.

"If you have them both that will be enough proof for me, but you may have to fulfill more lines of the poem for others."

Bromle smiled. He remained skeptical and regarded his brother as an often too whimsical person. He looked at Adger and saw the excitement on his face. Adger was ecstatic that the suppositions he had might be true.

"Show me the sword and shield," Tortuse said.

Simon felt another fleeting moment of panic; the same kind he felt when he thought he heard the turtle mention it in the poem. Simon had the necessary surety of who he was but having to prove it made him falter. He had the sword in his hands, but Kapell had said nothing of a shield.

"I have the sword right here," Simon said and brought the sword out from behind his back.

He recalled how Filch had struggled to make the sword work which diminished his confidence even further. He grasped the hilt firmly in both hands and willed the blade to extend. Nothing happened. He pulled his hands back and thrust both his hands forward again with no success.

"Maybe there is a button," Adger offered. "On the side there where the…" he trailed off as he looked up at the turtle. He took a step away from Simon and, more intentionally, away from Tortuse.

Tortuse had no perceivable reaction to Simon's struggle.

Simon stepped back and took the hilt in one hand. He stepped forward and tried spinning his hand in a flourish, hoping that the movement would encourage the blade, but he dropped the hilt instead. He felt burning embarrassment heat his face.

"I don't understand. It worked before—twice even!" Simon said. "Ask Filch. It worked!" As Simon said the last word, he grabbed the hilt with both hands and swung it down hard. The sword burst to life with feathers of fire that rose from its end. The flame extended into the water, causing steam to exude in a steady stream from where the blade penetrated the lake. Simon's eyes opened wide and he grinned.

"Now the shield," Tortuse said, still unchanged by Simon's success.

Simon's pleasure quickly vanished as he remembered that the sword was only part of his proof. He again felt that honesty was the only choice he had.

"I don't have the shield. Kapell didn't say anything about one." He dropped his hands to his sides and the flame went out. "I am who you say I am, though: I came from the cave, Kapell helped me escape Veadus—I even fought her creature in the Vareex!"

More voices echoed down from the collapsed entrance leading back to the tower.

"You must show me the shield," Tortuse said, almost pleadingly.

Simon felt panic-stricken; a burning, writhing sickness swam through his veins. He wanted to satisfy the tale and be the hero. Despite the fearful situations he had been in so far, he wanted to fulfill every expectation of his arrival. He had purpose, but he was unsure of how to prove his worth to Tortuse.

He thought of the pouches on his waist, and he moved his hands to search them.

It must be in there, he thought. *Something I overlooked.*

He dug through each pouch looking at the same objects he had seen before, pulling them out one by one, turning them over in his hands, and looking for instructions or buttons. There was nothing that resembled a shield or seemed like it would be a component of one.

As he scrambled for answers, he hooked his thumbs on his ornate belt buckle. He looked down at the buckle; it was large, but insufficient to serve as a shield. When he moved his hands away from his belt, there was a minor resistance as if the hilt was drawn to the buckle. He moved the hilt back towards the buckle and felt the same invisible force pulling at it like a strong magnet. He loosened his grip, slid his fingers onto the side of the hilt, and it snapped into place on the buckle with a metallic twang.

Simon pulled on the handle, but he could not separate the two objects again. He tried several variations of efforts, but the two did not release their grip until he twisted his hand and the buckle along with it. The buckle popped from his belt with a satisfying sound but seemed locked into place on the protruding markings of the hilt. He fumbled with the conjoined objects until he managed to slide them apart. He held the disc in his other hand and it fit just inside of his palm. Judging from the way the sword seemed to manifest its blade, Simon was not too quick to assume the disc was without similar abilities. He flipped it over and ran his fingers along the subtle curvature, but nothing signified how to activate it. The only attribute he could discern was that the sword seemed to attach on the convex side. He balanced his hilt and moved the disc back towards the sword. The buckle snapped into place on the hilt again and the sound of the impact echoed off the water and chased the darkness to the highest reaches of the ceiling.

He reached for the disc again, but his hand passed through the material like lowering his hand into a cool puddle. The metal rippled and enveloped his fingers and hand. It retained its chrome finish despite the disruption. He had his hand about halfway covered when his fingers touched a hard object inside the buckle that felt like a handle. He wrapped his hand around it and pulled but instead of pulling an object out of the disc, it separated from the hilt.

The disc burst to life, and a bright crystal spike jutted from the center of the expanding metal. Its edges glowed with a bright, orange light as it seemed to fabricate new confines in an instant. It grew into a circular shield big enough to cover Simon in a crouched position.

Simon looked over at the turtle and thought he saw a smile on his face.

"You *are* Kynn Veyor," Tortuse said.

His entire demeanor had changed. He relaxed his heightened stance and sank a little lower. He took a step backwards and dropped his head to the water and bent both his front legs as if bowing to Simon.

"I, too, have been waiting for you for an age out of mind. I apologize for the challenge, but I had to know that you are who you claimed to be. The time has come, companions, to decide. Will you help him?" Tortuse stood back up.

The three of them remained quiet but their individual reasons were not obvious.

Simon touched the sword hilt to the shield, and it rapidly shrank back to its smaller form. He let go of the handle within the silver water, pulled his hand out, and returned the weapons back to their places.

"If you stay," Tortuse said, "I will be unable to aid you in overcoming the evil that passes through that debris."

"You would leave us here for that garbage-mouth demon?" Bromle said.

"I do not mean to be without compassion, but I must focus my efforts on helping him escape. If you come with me, you would do me the honor of escorting you away from this threat."

The sound of rubble being cleared from the collapsed tunnel seeped its way into the cavern.

"I must be allowed to return home and gather some things, but I will go," Adger said.

"You must leave with what you have and hope that what you have is what you need," Tortuse said. "You will not be without help, but this journey is long overdue, and it must start now."

Adger shuffled his feet a bit and looked down at the water. He didn't have much, but what he had at home he didn't wish to lose, no matter how trivial the belongings were. Nevertheless, he felt best prepared as he might be to get underway. He looked up at the turtle and nodded.

Filch said, "I will go," and she said no more. Her expression was hidden, and she was grateful for it. She knew where this path would lead.

"And you, Bromle?" Tortuse asked.

"Someone's gotta be the muscle of this outfit," he said. "I'm in. What do we need to do?"

"We cannot leave that way," Tortuse said nodding towards the tunnel. "We can leave through the water. The lake leads out past Canton and away from the battle above."

"You mean, we don't get to fight our way out?" Bromle said jokingly, but Simon got the impression he was serious.

"Come, climb on my back and we will depart," Tortuse said.

"I don't know about the rest of you, but I can't breathe underwater," Simon said.

"There will be no need; come."

Tortuse crouched down, and they moved towards his back. Bromle linked his fingers together to allow each one of his teammates a leg up. Adger clambered over the bulwark crowning Tortuse's shell. The deck of the turtle's back was wide and flat like the deck of a ship. The bow of the deck was broad and curved, and it tapered towards the stern as it ended in a sharper point. Various crates and piles of rope were at each end of the deck, but beyond that, it had no additional elements of a boat. Adger wondered if this was part of the creature, or an apparatus affixed upon him. His wondering was interrupted when Filch landed on the deck behind him.

"And we're going underwater how?" Filch asked.

"Have patience," Tortuse said.

The other two had barely stepped on the deck when the collapsed stairwell exploded into the cavern, and rocks flew into the lake. Hordes of creatures poured into the cavern, crowding the shore and fanning out around the periphery of the lake. There were Canton guards commingled amidst the cloud-riders; which contradicted their obvious disparity in the streets above. Creatures the same species as the miners scrambled at the feet of the larger enemies and were readying slings and daggers. A rapid thunderous vibration echoed through the cavern, and rubble started to rain down from the ceiling above. After a few more disturbing impacts, a fissure ruptured through the ceiling, and ten bularaz dropped into the shallow waters of the lake. The fall seemed far enough to have killed a man, but whatever stone these creatures were made of was tough enough to handle the descent. The mix of creatures prepared to attack: flourishing swords, notching arrows, and twirling slings.

"Why are they after us?" Adger wondered aloud.

"Word of your arrival has spread, Simon," Tortuse said calmly. "It appears that they found a common enemy in the knowledge of your arrival, young hero. Or, what worries me more, good minds have been corrupted."

The shuffling of anticipating enemies quieted and stilled; there was a moment of silent tension.

"So you shall be unmade," said the voice from before, but it was even more sinister this time. It was like the rumbling of a tremor and the distant rolling thunder of a storm.

Simon pulled his weapons back out and went through the same steps as before to create his shield. This time though, his fiery blade blazed alongside his shield. Bromle prepared for an attack, too; his hands glowed with smoking fireballs, ready to be combined into a shockwave of destruction. Adger pulled out his wooden sword and extended its blade. Filch was…

"Where's Filch?" Simon asked.

"Right next to you," said the empty air next to Simon. "Not all attacks are made effective through showmanship."

"No need for attack this time," Tortuse said. He lifted his leg and slammed it down into the water. Even as shallow as the water seemed, a tidal wave launched towards the ceiling and extended outward around them. It slammed into every enemy and knocked them to the ground or killed them on impact.

"Time to dive," he said.

Small hatches all over the deck simultaneously popped open. Little creatures, which looked like smaller turtles, rolled out of the holes and spread out across the deck. Each one of them stopped at the supports of the bulwark and kicked little hatches that opened to reveal small wheels. They all reared back on their hind legs and started rolling the small wheels with their front ones. A blue light started glowing from the top of the bulwark and a thin wall extended upward in a hexagonal pattern. The rising wall met at an apex and formed a barrier around them. Simon imagined that the shape of it might be what the inside of a translucent tortoise shell might look like. The translucence faded and eventually became so transparent that it disappeared completely. As quickly as the small creatures had appeared, they rolled back towards their holes and went below deck.

The remaining enemies got up and fired whatever projectiles they had towards the dome, none of which penetrated the protection. Tortuse moved towards the center of the lake and began his submergence. The water surged as he went underwater and quickly became placid as the visible remnants of the cave disappeared above the surface of the water.

Filch appeared a few steps from where her voice was a moment prior. She looked at Simon with a gleam in her eyes that showed her satisfaction in his surprise.

The four passengers continually looked up and watched as they were drawn deeper into the water. They descended a straight shaft leading to the complicated system of submarine tunnels. The darkness of the cave above was eradicated by the light around them from luminescent creatures shifting in the currents. The tunnels were also filled with pale, blue light that emanated from coral and seaweed on the walls. Instead of slick, or rocky stone walls, every crevice was teeming with life; small animals that had found a home in the subterranean labyrinth. From the light the creatures produced, the adventurers could see more of the deck they stood on and the detail of their rescuer.

Tortuse's pale head was covered in black and mottled brown diamond shapes that extended down the sides of his face and onto his neck. What they couldn't see were his wide legs that dangled helplessly as they descended. Four long and wide fins folded out from beneath his torso adjacent to each leg. This was more to Simon's limited expectations of a turtle that spent the majority of its time swimming. He had learned to embrace the beauty of the creatures he met in the new world but did not lose the amazement that came with it.

"Lord Ripa, if you don't mind me saying so, you are a magnificent creature!" Adger said with eyes wide in fascination. "In all my years in this world, never have I seen such beautiful life!"

"Thank you for your kind words, Adger," Tortuse said from the other side of the dome. His voice was as clear to them as if there were no barrier. This only made Adger's eyes somehow become even wider.

"And we stand on your very scales," Adger said looking down, having expected to see wooden planks but, instead, noted the massive hexagons of Tortuse's shell. "Canton has nothing so beautiful—in all my life…I will never return with the same opinion of the world; nor do I think I care to return to that hole in the earth."

"He already saved your life, little brother," Bromle said, slapping Adger on the back. "No need to butter him up."

"Well, I mean to say that I thought I needed my meager belongings, but now I see the only benefit to returning home would be to aimlessly reminisce over miniscule objects. I have my bag of gadgets and no longer feel the sadness for what I've left behind."

As they swam, more underwater creatures joined their continued descent and added to the mysticism. Creatures of brilliant colors and massive sizes travelled alongside their vessel, darting up and over the dome; some even coming to rest on Tortuse's head.

The mouth of the lake above was still a black hole against the light of the shaft. Pieces of the darkness broke away and moved with apparent intention. Filch was the first to see it.

"We've got pursuers," she said.

"You really are a bunch of anxious creatures," Tortuse said. "When you sit and wait for as long as I have, you learn not to fret." He waved one of his giant fins up towards the oncoming aggressors which sent a shimmer through the water. The black spots above them vanished and the dark hole that was the mouth of the lake closed.

"Get comfortable," he said, "we may be travelling for some time."

10 The Tortoise

Their descent eventually stopped, and they moved more laterally inside the vast array of underwater passageways. The tunnels had a pleasant, blue radiance that seemed to emanate from the life that covered its walls. Wherever they looked something was moving, swimming, or darting. Bromle and Filch were less affected by the beauty than Simon and Adger who were as ecstatic as children.

Bromle sat on a box and aimlessly produced glowing balls of various colors in his palms, repeatedly snuffing them out by closing his massive hands. Occasionally, he would release them to roll around the deck until they withered and disappeared.

"Now it's on to destroy the evil overlord, right?" Bromle asked.

Tortuse answered from beyond the dome, and his voice penetrated the water again as if wasn't a hindrance, "We must send you on your way, but I believe that you will need more help on your journey than I can offer. If we go to the kingdom of Maydanok now—where the Vile Monarch lives—I cannot hope for success. We need to rally an army."

"'Maydanok,'" Bromle chuckled to himself. "Nailed it."

"But the Kalinaw is not what it once was," Adger said sadly. "We used to be a resistant force in the name of the people trying to free the people from that wicked steward, but now—"

"We were a bunch of hopefuls that did little more than attract unwanted attention," Bromle said.

"I admit our goals were lofty." Adger turned and spoke mostly to Simon since the others knew the story well. "We hoped to one day grow to such a size to seriously consider traveling out to Maydanok—was it? Never did know the name—and rid the world of Etnian's evil for good. I think we were becoming enough of a threat to gain the unfortunate attention that caused our downfall. Some of us started disappearing, and those that remained couldn't figure out where they went."

"They got smart and quit."

"I've said this before, Brom; that's ridiculous. We were so close, and you were right there with me!" He turned back to Simon, "We were months away from making an attack, but it felt like days. Our biggest obstacle was the sea. The Kalinaw didn't have the ships to take us out over the waters where it was said that Etnian lives."

"You didn't know where he was?" Simon asked, trying to be gentle in the challenge, but his surprise couldn't be masked.

"We know he always came from the east—over the water—but, no, we didn't know exactly where. We sent out scout ships but never found a safe way across the ocean. Dozens of people went out in several ships but only two returned. One of them was so maddened with fright that the information he gave us was useless. The other man died shortly after his return, but not before he managed to tell us that they had found Etnian's borders. He too died before he could find it on a map of the known sea. Brom's hope about the river was the best news we've heard in years, honestly."

"*Does* the river lead to Maydanok?" Bromle asked Tortuse.

"It used to," Tortuse said, "but that way is gone now. I was given the charge to keep the enemy's forces at bay as best I could—at least by way of the river. Those creatures are frequent vermin in that cavern; ever trying to reconnect the path between his realm and ours. He's obviously found ways around the obstacle of the sea."

"What about you, Filch?" Simon asked her. "I've heard their story well enough, but what about yours? You haven't said much at all."

"Oh, we don't—you don't have to talk about it," Adger said sympathetically.

"No, it's okay; he should know. I came from far out west," she lied. She had told the story so often, sometimes she almost believed it.

Maydanok was far to the East beyond the sea, but the town she feigned her origin was indeed far out to the West.

"Etnian slaughtered everyone I had ever known. I hid underneath the corpses of my neighbors and by the graces, I was overlooked as the soldiers beheaded every survivor they found to ensure none were left alive."

"I see why you don't talk about it; that's terrible," Simon said.

"I have a vested interest to see him atone for it." She concluded with bone chilling sincerity.

They sat in silence, allowing the moment to be fully absorbed. Bromle was uncomfortable around those kinds of emotionally tense stories and was anxious to break the silence. He had been through enough difficulties in his life to mask whatever emotional upset he had with pride and arrogance. His habituation made others' emotions unsettling to him. Thankfully, for him, Filch narrowed her eyes and asked a question of her own.

"And what of you, hero, from where do you come?" Filch said derisively, as seemed to be her nature for those she considered beneath her. "To be chosen for such a destiny, you must've been a great hero."

Simon could not tell if she was being genuine or was attempting to debunk the beliefs he had for even himself.

"I...well, I was—I wasn't a hero, but I feel like I was a pretty good person."

"A good person?" Bromle asked, standing from the crate where he had been so quiet. "Intentions won't be good enough when you have a blade on your throat, or an arrow aimed at your head."

"I agree," Filch said. "You must have some predilection for swordplay then."

"I can't say that I've had very much experience with—ya know—swords and all."

"You can't use a sword?!" Bromle said, a bit more bothered. He took another step towards Simon and his aggression made Simon recoil ever so slightly. "You know how I got these things?" he said, spreading out his fingers to display his gloves.

"Well, no I have no—"

"I took 'em right off the cold dead hands of a Valquerian Ballistic; so damn scary, your nightmares would be paradise."

Simon looked helplessly over to Adger, who was smirking and shaking his head in disagreement.

"That's the kind of hero we need," Bromle continued. "We need—"

"What we need is often not what we expect," Tortuse interrupted the ranting Bromle and fuming Filch. "Your expectation is a hero with such valor that the Dark Mongrel himself would cower at the mention of his name. A craftsman can be a king without proving his worth of vociferous anticipation."

Tortuse's rebuke somehow forced them into silence.

"So, where are we going, Tortuse?" Bromle finally said.

"We cannot go back for certain," Tortuse answered. "That way is closed and only by considerable force, or my will, can it be reopened. I've kept Veadus' disgusting forces from entering that way for many years. By doing so, I've protected some of the deepest and closely guarded secrets that I doubt even Etnian has discovered. This used to be one path that people could travel on the way to Haeophan; the creatures here are so unique."

"But where are we *going*?" Bromle interrupted.

"Such hasty things, you are. From your display in the cavern and your recent discovery of the weapons you have, Simon, it is evident that you do not fully understand the tools you were given. I know of the sword and shield, but effectively using them is something beyond my capabilities. Before you raise an army—and certainly before you fight alongside it—you must learn how to use that sword. We are going to a place called Sophron. It is a temple filled with age and wisdom. The ascetics who live there have kept their practices and knowledge guarded for generations of the recipients to its halls. It seems that the most likeminded people congregate in similar places. Maybe it's the peace of the water that drew them there. Either way, they can help you, but that is where we must part ways. I must ensure this path is continually guarded and closed to the vile forces who wish to overrun it."

They were left to their own thoughts or quiet conversation for the remainder of the many forks in the path and even longer tunnels of undulating undersea life.

Simon found his way over to Adger, who he had found a certain level of comfort in confiding in. "Who were you before this? You and Bromle told me once that you hadn't forgotten like all the rest. Do you remember?"

"I do! Although it took some time to recall. Bromle and I...we weren't—aren't—actually brothers, but when we first arrived in this world, we assumed we were, because we had no recollection of the world before. Eventually, I learned that I was a clockmaker before I died, after nearly a century, and I enjoyed the work immensely. My propensities from then manifested in my tinkering here; making things like this," Adger said as he gestured towards his tool roll he kept tucked under his coat.

He pulled it out and rolled it on the deck made of Tortuse's scales. It was filled with assorted tools that stuck out at various angles; all of which were lost on Simon.

"What is all that?" Simon asked kindly; trying to show his genuine interest.

"You arrived with your tools for adventure, but I have had to improvise in my time here. They have many uses, but thankfully the weapons haven't been needed until now."

Before Simon could satiate his curiosity further, Tortuse informed them that they had arrived at their destination.

A dark void opened in the water beyond them and on the upper right portion of the tunnel. Tortuse slowly emerged out of the water and folded his fins underneath his body. They had entered another dark cave that seemed more like a tremendous cathedral than the wet cavern they started in. Shafts of light came in through openings in the ceiling and added an antiquated appeal to the space that was redolent of abandoned beauty waiting to be rediscovered. In front of them was a dark marble ramp that led down into the water. Tortuse easily made his way up it to a flatter space where even more dazzling architecture had been left in the dust of the darkness.

More than a dozen statues, as tall as buildings, encircled their landing. Each of them was a noticeably different metal or material. Some of the statues were gold, or silver, while others were made from stone that seemed to absorb the closest particles of light and make them even brighter. The figures were in various stances and looked formidable even in their stillness; their grandeur was intensified by the adornments that their weapons and armor had. Huge precious stones ornamented crowns on their heads and the hilts of those who carried swords. The amphitheater had many exits leading out of it into dark chambers and hallways, which Simon could only hope held such beauty as the monuments to whatever people had been worthy enough to pose for them. The massive openings in the ceiling illuminated such detail on the statues that Simon thought he might be charmed by appreciation alone. His spell was broken when he noticed the surrounding carvings that covered every space of the walls. He fervently wondered what secrets the inscriptions contained.

Tortuse climbed the marble landing, and the many holes in his scales opened as before. The small turtles hurried to the bulwark walls and the dome around them started to shimmer and retract. Before it had disappeared, one of the well-lit openings above was darkened.

"Stop," Tortuse said. "The air smells like…"

"Welcome, Lord Ripa," the dark shadow above growled, "Long has it been since you have emerged from below. After all that time, you grace my home with your presence. You may stay, but the manner in which you do so has certain…conditions."

"Cineris, is that you my old friend?" Tortuse said happily craning his neck upward.

"Indeed, it is," the shadow purred.

"My friend, how long has it been?" Tortuse said jovially, as he moved to get a better sight of his friend. "So many cycles have come and gone that I have nearly forgotten the time when we would travel together. What happened here? There used to be so many people in this temple; great warriors and scholars alike."

"Therein lies your answer, Tortuse; the population of Sophron became too great of a threat."

"A threat to whom, Cineris?" Tortuse said with a note of concern.

"Those scholars, as you call them, thought they could establish a peace even amidst the chaos; a vein hope to find existence when there was none to be had."

Tortuse started to back away from the center of the amphitheater and he placed his hind feet on the ramp to the open mouth of the tunnel where the surging luminescent river rushed along.

"Those sound like the words of influence, Cineris."

The creature spit a small flaming shot down on the ground below him, and in that brief moment, Simon caught the yellow madness of Cineris' eyes.

"Influence that has been much needed! These foolish monks blindly followed in the vain hope that some savior would come free them from their mindless servitude."

"You sound as if they became your enemy," Tortuse said with an increased note of anger in his voice. "We have spent time here in peace with these people. Since when did you so readily confuse peace for aggression? You were one of them, Cineris!"

"The world has changed, Lord Ripa, and your companionship is no longer as valuable as it once was."

The shadow above them lengthened and stretched as the creature moved from the opening in the ceiling. Simon held his hand to block the light but Cineris was indiscernible from the darkness around him. The creature stayed in the darkest corners of the ceiling, and anything more than his terrifying size could not be seen.

"Please tell me the Sinister Chief has not tainted the wisdom I so readily sought a lifetime ago," Tortuse said.

"My wisdom is as clear as it has ever been," Cineris said.

"What you call wisdom sounds like folly. What could evil offer you to surpass the satisfaction of peaceable existence?"

"His ascendancy is imminent, Tortuse. You would be wise to heed it!"

A great sadness filled Tortuse's voice, "I hope there is still good left in you when the time comes, brother."

Cineris roared, and the amphitheater turned red with flames that he spewed.

"Is there anyone who *doesn't* want to kill us?" Simon said as he dropped with the others below the remnants of the receded dome.

The protective dome raised back above their heads much faster than it had before. The flames broke on it like water on a beach. The passengers inside remained unscathed, but the same could not be said for Tortuse. He let out a cry so loud that his passengers clapped their hands over their ears. He fled back into the water and waved the tunnel closed with his great fin.

"Lord Ripa!" Adger said, rushing to the closest side of the dome.

Simon ran to the prow of the deck with Adger, but there was nothing they could do for their chauffeur. The skin on his head was no longer as beautiful as it had been; flakes of skin floated in the water and the raw red flesh made them all cringe. Even Bromle and Filch had been noticeably bothered by his injuries.

The tunnel shuttered from an impact on the other side, and a muffled roar made its way through the water.

"This world has changed since I last spent much time in it. I have stayed too long underneath that tower," Tortuse said feebly.

"Where can we go then?" Simon asked. "And what of you; you desperately need medical attention. Can any of you heal him?" Simon said anxiously to the others.

"Orvar will know what to do!" Adger said. "He knows this world better than anyone I've met—except for Tortuse in his day, maybe. If there's anyone that can help us, it's him. He lives on the western most edge of the Canton canyon. Can you make it, Lord Ripa?"

"I can find the way," Tortuse said.

"I still think that the old man is crazy, but he might be our best bet," Bromle said. "Our alternative is wandering around inside here hoping that this old beast will survive long enough to give us the open air again and preferably not in the den of some other foul beast."

"How can you be so callous?" Simon shouted at Bromle; his emotions, once again, getting the better of him. "If not for him, we'd have been killed; twice now."

"Don't get so excited, Hero, I didn't mean it like that."

Simon ignored Bromle, but he understood he had reacted harshly. He wanted to be angry at someone because he felt so helpless again, like he had been with Lazuli. "Tell me what to do, Tortuse. How can I help?"

Tortuse drifted towards the side of the underwater tunnel and ran into it so hard that his passengers were thrown. A piece of the dome flickered above their heads and fell to the deck and shattered like glass. Water rushed in through the opening.

"Please tell me we're not far away," Bromle said.

The small turtles still on the deck climbed up the transparent walls of the dome and centered on the steady stream of water. They formed a network inside that seemed to slow the leak but not eliminate it.

Whereas urgency was not his priority before, Tortuse swam speedily through the tunnels.

"We're almost there." Tortuse said.

His weak voice became harder to hear over the torrent of water. More of the dome started to flicker, fall, and shatter. Water poured in from multiple places. The little turtles rushed to the various leaks, but the dome was filling faster than they were able to manage.

The four adventurers stood helpless, watching the small turtles rush to stop the leaks. The myriad of sea creatures beyond the dome frantically surged to their aid. Sea turtles landed on the outside of the dome, providing an additional layer of mitigation, but their efforts were not enough.

"We're getting…" Tortuse's voice trembled, "we're getting close."

Despite his waning strength, the speed that Tortuse swam through the water was impressive. He slowed for a moment to wave his fin and an opening on the ceiling far up the tunnel appeared. Bright light splintered in to the currents around them.

The small holes in the dome became even bigger and the level of water increased rapidly. All the animals weren't enough.

"We have to do something," Simon shouted. "We can't just stand here! Bromle, what can you do with those gloves of yours? Can you make fire?"

"Gladly!" Bromle clapped his hands together and bright, red, smoking orbs appeared in each palm as he pulled them apart. He ran to the largest hole and put his open hands over it. The water around the outside of the dome bubbled furiously as the evaporating water he created tried to escape the burning fury of his gloves.

"Adger," Simon said, "can your tunnel maker do anything for us?"

"I've never tried it underwater, but I think I have something else that might work better," Adger replied. He fumbled in his pockets and pulled out a tube almost as long as his forearm and about half the width; it widened at one end like a trumpet's bell. He placed a crank handle in the back, put it at the end of the tube, and started turning. He ran towards one of the gushing holes and the gale he produced pushed the water away from it and several others adjacent to it.

"Filch?" Simon asked. "Can you—"

"My weapons would not help us here. I can help though." Filch ran to Adger and took over turning the crank when his arms grew tired.

Simon had his own idea. Getting inspiration from Bromle, Simon pulled out his sword and shield, igniting them both.

"Simon, not the sword," Tortuse said. "The fire is too great even for my shell.

"The shield though," Simon said.

"Even I don't fully understand its power; it is too dangerous here."

Simon put his things away and ran to Bromle, whose arms were noticeably growing tired from the force of the water spewing down on him. He supported Bromle's elbows as his hands started to fall.

"I don't need your help," Bromle said.

"Stow the arrogance, Brom," Adger said. "This is not the time for your bravado."

He glared at his brother but was silently grateful for the help.

The water continued to rise, but with the combined efforts it slowed, and not a moment too soon; it had reached Bromle's thighs which was nearly to the rest of their waists.

Tortuse had reached the opening in the tunnel ceiling and stopped abruptly to begin his ascent. The group lost their footing in the sudden change of momentum and fell to the floor of the deck. Torrents forced their way into the dome and knocked over the inhabitants when they attempted to fight their way back up.

They were all forced to the floor again as Tortuse began his rapid ascent.

A sickening sound rang out clearly above the rushing water as the dome cracked. The adventurers locked eyes and couldn't hide their inescapable fear of what was about to happen. The moment before the dome collapsed, time seemed to slow long enough to impress their helplessness down upon them. There were at the mercy of elements beyond their control.

The decimation of the dome allowed all the water to envelop the adventurers. Each one of them reached for something to keep them in place. To their advantage, the small holes that the barrier builders had exited were still open. Each one of them had the clarity to grasp the handhold closest to them despite the force of the water that threatened to wash them all away. Unlike their vehicle, they were unable to effectively maneuver or—more importantly—breathe underwater. The fear and hopelessness of their situation was weighing as heavily on them as the volumes of water. Each one of them found what small air pockets were left within the dome and filled their lungs with as much air as they possibly could.

The moments were agonizing even for the strongest of them; their lungs all burned with the fire of asphyxiation. Simon recalled his agonizing rebirth in the tunnel. Instead of a tomb of stone, his tomb was to be water.

Just when Simon thought he couldn't hold back the impulse to breathe any longer, Tortuse broke free from the watery depths of the underground river.

The speed he exited the tunnel caused him to fly through the air uncontrollably. He had launched his body up out of the ground amidst a forest densely made up of enormous trees. The tenants of the mighty woodland were each three times as circumferentially broad as Tortuse; some even more so. Tortuse's shell slammed into one of the trees, sending him spinning. His passengers were launched from the deck in different directions. They flew through the air and landed on the ground, rolling to a stop; bruised, but alive. Tortuse landed on the bare forest floor and slid a short distance. Despite Simon's graceless exit, he was grateful not to have ended his adventure prematurely.

They took a brief moment to enjoy the function of their lungs again before their senses fully recovered. The sunlight far above the lofty reaches of the forest canopy found its way to warm the saturated adventurers. Each one was glad to be freed from the cold cling of the water. Although their clothes were encumbered with the tunnel's river, their bodies felt invigorated by the fresh breaths they inhaled.

Simon took the least amount of time of respite but not out of stamina or ability. His concern was mainly for Tortuse. He ran to Tortuse's head and impulsively placed a hand on his crown as if the touch would heal him. The majestic creature's skin was more noticeably charred and blistered; a hideous sight that was imperceptible in the chaos of the tunnels below. He felt a great sadness within him, not out of shame, but true remorse for being the cause of another injury and loss of life. Simon took a step back and glanced into the deck of Tortuse's shell. The barrier builders were busily working in the deck but to what end Simon could not determine.

"This is not your fault, Kynn Veyor."

"But you were only there because of me," Simon said, a slight tremble in his voice.

"I made that choice, not you. You will learn that those who follow you will do so of their own volition, not yours. I will heal, and my small hatchlings will help, but I'm afraid I can no longer be of service to you," Tortuse said weakly in labored breaths. "I can help you no further."

"But there's so much I still don't know," Simon pleaded.

"You will find what you need; I believe it. You are Kynn Veyor, and you may find that most of the answers you seek will find you."

With the perplexity of Tortuse's last comment, he stood up with great difficulty. He slowly lumbered back towards the tunnel they arrived through. As he turned, Simon could see a wide crack in his shell and noted the massive tree that had caused it. Simon watched him sink into the hole in the ground and the water from the tunnel underneath rushed up onto the forest floor. The tunnel closed behind him and left dry ground with no traces of having been a tremendous passage. Simon stared at the ground, still reeling from the intense experiences he had just endured.

He inhaled a long, fresh breath and tilted his head back to admire the scene around him. The air was cool and crisp; carrying the scent of autumn and fallen leaves. The only sound that interrupted Simon's observations was the movement of the wind through the branches. He found a restorative power in the tranquility of the forest that almost made him forget what he had set out to do.

His companions had all satisfactorily refilled their lungs and stood, watching Simon lost in his respite.

"He's enjoying the world the way it should have been," Adger whispered to the other two. "Is Tortuse okay?" he said to Simon.

Simon broke from the forest's spell and turned to face them. "I don't know. He said he will be, but—who was the creature that attacked us, and how does Tortuse know him?"

"You know as much as me, friend. Wherever it is, it had access to the ground above. I'm not sure how far Tortuse took us, but I think we should get out of here." He looked at Simon as if asking for permission.

"Where's your friend?" Simon said.

"Let me just see where we are. It looks like the trees are thinner over there."

He pointed behind them where the forest seemed to stop abruptly.

The trees ended with a small amount of space that prefaced the sheer depths of the canyon that Canton was centered in. They had come to the western side of the city. The canyon below was full with a fog like a sea that made the canyon depths imperceptible. The fog was split by the sharp point of the plateau that was like the bow of a ship, sending the sea of fog down two massive rivers around it. The city ended at the edge of the cliff as if it might spill over into the sea of fog below with the slightest breeze.

"I know where we are," Adger said. "This is my favorite view of the city. It makes you forget the difficulties of its confines. Tortuse got us close to the old man's home. I know the way from here."

Smoke rose steadily from Canton. Simon wondered how much of it had been his fault. He feared that the battles being fought in Canton's streets were in pursuit of him, and that familiar guilt crept in again. He found solace as he recalled what Tortuse had told him. There would be many more battles fought in defense and support of Simon, and he was determined to properly defend those that would risk their lives for him. To mount any meager defense though, he first had to learn how to fight. He hoped the old hermit could help him do just that.

11 The Cabin

The walk through the woods was quiet. None of them spoke for fear of finding the creature that almost caused their death. Simon assumed a sufficient distance had been put between them and Cineris, but from the very little he knew of creatures of that size that could spit fire, they were excellent trackers. His knowledge was based on stories, but he kept his silence nevertheless. When they arrived at Sophron, Simon assumed it was the best place to learn the necessary skills to fight, and he was disappointed that he still didn't know how to properly battle with a sword. When he held the hilt, he felt sure of his capabilities, but logic dissuaded him from the naivety. His only hope now was that Adger's old friend could help him.

His usual tendency was to watch the ground beneath his feet as he walked, but the world around him was too indescribable to take his eyes from. Pictures he had seen throughout his previous old age could not compare to the vivid colors of reality. Being in that forest, he understood the intent of a place like Dyurndale: a place to appreciate nature's splendor. For some it might be the shores he awoke on, but for him, it was the trees and what lived around them.

"Where's the wildlife?" Simon asked, realizing that it was scarce.

"That's what worries me," Filch said behind him. "We've seen very little of it."

Simon was beginning to learn more about his companions in the still moments when they weren't being pursued. He saw Filch as keen and adept. He thought her mask was curious but deceptive; it was difficult to make appropriate assessments of her reactions. She spoke infrequently, except to make such observations. Simon wasn't surprised by the lack of wildlife when he considered four people noisily marching through the forest. He wasn't foolish enough to consider his gait nimble, and the heavy footsteps of Bromle would be enough to disturb the dead.

Bromle was difficult to read; Simon assumed he often let his cynicism overtake his restraint, but making an accurate assumption was difficult. His attitude seemed reasonable for a person of his size, but Simon thought it could cause complications if a contemplative decision was required in lieu of a more immediate one. He struck Simon as the type of person who might shroud his emotions for the sake of repute. Bromle's initiative to lead the small group, despite Adger's claim to know the way, exhibited his perceptions of his leadership capabilities. Simon was pleased to let him lead the march, though. Although Simon could appreciate Bromle's capabilities, they were not entirely ones he wished to characterize. Simon found the contrast between Bromle and his brother particularly entertaining.

Adger was a kindred spirit to Simon and he was glad to have befriended him. He saw a good natured person who cared about others before his own wellbeing. Adger's ingenuity would be of particular aid to the future of his adventure and had been a salvation three times so far. Simon assumed though that whatever legendary weapons this group possessed, Adger did not own one. The few gadgets that Simon had seen so far were certainly nothing to be underestimated, but their offensive capabilities were incomparable to those of his brother's. He had seen little of Filch's offensive capabilities either, but an ability to disappear completely was a skill that could not be underestimated. Simon's assertions were interrupted by their arrival to what looked like another indiscernible grouping of trees.

"There it is," Adger said from behind Simon. "At least, I think it is."

"Haven't you been out here dozens of times, little brother?"

"Yes, but Orvar always moves his house. You can tell which tree he puts it in if you look at it in just the right light."

Simon looked up towards the trees as they walked, expecting to see a suspended cabin.

"Not up there, Simon. Look there, at the base of that tree to the left."

Simon looked where Adger pointed, but most of the trees looked too similar to identify, and he certainly saw nothing resembling an abode.

Adger continued, "He usually opens up by the time I get this close. Let's—here, Brom—just here behind these bushes. Wait a moment. I think I have a key here somewhere." Adger patted down his pockets. He pulled out his leather tool roll and whipped it open to reveal a myriad of things Simon childishly wanted to toy with. As Adger looked over the tools within, running his finger over them, he reached into his pockets and pulled out the various things he had used so far and put them back in their appropriate places.

"Ah, here it is." Adger pulled out a black curved rod that was far too long for the pocket it came out of, yet Adger continued to pull it out until he had what appeared to be the limb of a bow without its string. It was a black so dark that it was more of a void of color than an applied lacquer; except for when the sunlight caught it just right, the darkest of greens shined from within. Adger pulled out a bowstring from the adjacent pocket, notched one end, stepped over the bow, bent the longbow back, and notched the other end.

"Cool," Simon said involuntarily.

"It gets better," Adger smiled to Simon.

Adger reached into the bush and twisted a branch from within it. It was covered in fresh green leaves and was frayed at one end where Adger was unable to snap the branch because of the life it still held. He positioned it in front of the bow and dragged it over towards the nock point of the bowstring. As he pulled the useless branch across the arrow rest, a black light enveloped the branch; straightening, shaving, and coloring the branch into a useable arrow. Once Adger had drawn the arrow far enough back to release it, he blew on the end closest to his face and black fletching sprouted from the shaft.

He let the arrow go, and it speedily found its target, while narrowly weaving its way through the forest. Simon was unable to clearly see what Adger had aimed for. The enormous tree the arrow stuck in shuddered from the arrow's impact. Adger put the bow and string back in its place and returned the tool roll to beneath his jacket.

The outer bark of the tree started to blur like a mirage coming into focus. The majority of the upper portion of the tree disappeared completely. In its place was the enormous stump of a formerly tremendous tree. In its center was a cabin made from planks as red and healthy as the wood around it. It was primarily shaped from the walls of the stump as if the entire tree had been carved down to create the house. There were much smaller trees and bushes that shaded the house like those that might be expected aside a normal residence. A second story of the home extended beyond the reach of the small trees. The roof of the next story was covered in a thick layer of moss and grass as if it had been grown instead of built. The curtains were open enough on a bay window to the left of the door to see that there was no movement inside. A short staircase in the front of the house led up to a worn, red door covered with assorted horse-brass plaques.

Adger's arrow had landed in the exact center of one of the plaques centered on the door.

"That's one way to knock," Simon said.

"It's a good way to do so without being seen," Adger said.

"But, you just exposed the whole house."

"It's only visible to the guests that know where to knock—or something like that; Orvar explains it better than I can. He showed me where to shoot and assured me he wouldn't be found."

A long moment passed with no movement in the house. Birds sung in branches far overhead and the stirring of underbrush made Simon nervous. He hoped it was the inhabitants of the forest and not another enemy. The team stayed crouched behind the bushes, waiting for an indication to move forward.

"He's not there, little brother."

"Where could he be? Do you think he's been…no. No, they wouldn't be able to find him." Adger moved from the cover without waiting for the others. He darted from tree to tree, looking around the woods each time he stopped. Conversely, Bromle leisurely walked behind him with little regard to whatever might be hiding around the corner.

"What are you doing?" Bromle asked Adger.

"I, I'm—Brom, get down!"

"There is *no one* here. You could have just walked up to his door and knocked."

Simon followed behind them and turned to beckon Filch along with him, but she was gone again. He turned to look back at the cabin and Filch was already at the top of the stairs with Adger. He hurried to catch up with them.

Adger quietly opened the door and slowly stepped through. The rest of them followed behind him into the entryway of the home. Stairs leading up across from the front door divided the house. To the right was a dark dining room with a long table that seemed too big to fit in the house when considering it from outside. To the left of the stairs was a comfortable den filled with books that any bibliophile could happily spend a lifetime in.

The smell inside the home was redolent of pipe tobacco and old books. It was filled with dark woods and weathered furniture. Bookshelves lined the walls, interrupted by a glowing hearth. There were a plethora of various sized books, enough to disprove Bromle's assertion that the contents of the Kalinaw library were nothing more than a shelf. Layers of overlapping carpets covered the floor, held in place with several deep armchairs and plush couches. Every side table had a lamp and assortments of objects worthy of closer examination. There was adequate light provided from the bay window, but some of the lamps were still lit as if someone left hurriedly in the night.

"Orvar, are you here?" Adger called out. "I'll check upstairs," he said to the others.

Simon wandered around, touching the books on the shelves and reading the various titles. There was no obvious consistency to the organization of the books; neither by title, size, or color. Piles of the books were stacked on the floor and the furniture. The sheer number of bookshelves was staggering; they covered the walls except in places where pieces had been cut away to accommodate maps or pictures on the wall.

Adger returned from the upper floor.

"He's not here, and the rooms upstairs are a mess. He either left in a hurry, or someone was here looking for something. I'm guessing the latter though, because I found this."

Adger held out an arrow much like that of the Canton guards at the tower.

"It's a mess down here too," Simon said.

"No, it always looks like this. This is actually pretty clean," Adger said with a chuckle. "I know where to find some of the books you'll need, Simon."

He walked along the walls, quickly reading the titles and pulling several books down as he went.

"How is reading going to teach him to fight?" Bromle asked.

"I always told you, Brom, there's more to these books than just words. We still need to find Orvar, but these should help. Here," he said, handing the books to Simon.

Adger looked around the room and grabbed a leather rucksack from underneath a table. He looked inside, dumped the contents onto the adjacent couch, and then handed the bag to Simon. Simon put the books in the bag and swung it onto his back.

Adger looked at the things he dumped on the couch and, finding nothing helpful, moved around the shelves as he looked for something else. He went from shelf to table, tipping out books, running his hand over frames, and picking up objects.

"What are you looking for now?" Bromle asked.

"Clues to where Orvar might be," Adger answered without slowing down.

"Maybe he just went for a walk."

"Why would he leave his house like that," Adger said as he pointed upstairs, pausing his search.

Bromle ignored the banter. "I still don't understand how this old man is supposed to help us."

"He's more capable then he lets on, and your insults cause the reservations he manifests when you're around."

"I'm just asking how he can help us."

"He's a mystic!"

"Well, I've never seen the proof. You honestly believe his ramblings— all that mess about blind faith?"

"Sometimes faith is all we have, and believing in him has never done me any harm. If anything, it's given me more hope than I would have had otherwise."

"Then hope away. I still think he's just a crazy old hermit, little brother."

"Yet another reason to believe him. He's older than anyone I've ever met. The way he talks about the world sounds like he remembers it before it was corrupted."

"But hasn't it been hundreds of years?" Simon asked.

"That's exactly my point. He's been around for ages."

"So, you think that Orvar is believable simply because he's a wrinkly old man?" Bromle said condescendingly.

"This house isn't proof enough? Can *you* make a house disappear?"

"It's a good trick, but Filch can disappear, and she's not a mystic."

"When I first met him in the market years ago, I could sense there was something different about him." Adger stared at the floor while recalling the memory. "He had an aura that was more lighthearted than the usual gloomy inhabitants of Canton. I couldn't fully explain it, so I struck up a conversation with him. I saw him several more times thereafter and we became good friends. Eventually, he told me who he was and I *wanted* to believe it. I wanted to think there was something more to the life I was in." He broke his trance and looked back at Bromle with a stern expression. "He taught me how to remember my life before Dyurndale, and that was proof enough for me to believe in him. He helped you too, brother."

"I would have remembered on my own, eventually."

"You're so obstinate!" Adger said as he grunted in frustration. "How can you be so relentlessly stubborn? Don't help me then, but we need his help. I've spent the majority of my life in Canton, and to think that I've spent so long ensnared by its grandeur is enough motivation for me to leave. I believed that city was all there was to life before I met Orvar."

"Are you saying that you thought Dyurndale was your first and only life?" Simon asked. "I remember everything from before."

"After the dark times, people stopped remembering their previous lives—or they forgot; I'm not sure which. It seemed like most people still have flashbacks, but the ones who don't understand it, and choose to dwell on it, go mad. Orvar helped me remember things completely instead of in pieces, which totally altered my perspective on Dyurndale. I had my doubts at first."

"I still have mine," Bromle scoffed.

Adger ignored him and continued.

"When Orvar told me about Naru and the Kalinaw, I knew that I had to do something to help. We've been fighting ever since. I think he can help us get you to Naru and maybe tell us how to stop Etnian on the way."

"What can I do to help?" Simon asked.

"I'm hoping there might be something here to help us find him."

Adger started looking through the room again, picking things up and turning them over. Simon also started moving from each table to the bookshelves, searching for anything that looked out of place, but the conglomeration made that discernment impossible. Bromle threw himself down on one of the many couches, sending a cloud of sunlight dust into the air. Filch indifferently watched the other two work and leaned against the door frame of the entryway.

Simon enjoyed examining the hermit's belongings while imagining why each object was important enough to be displayed. The consideration that the belongings were little more than clutter didn't occur to him. Adger appreciated the eclectic collection but thought there was a superfluous amount of belongings.

Simon felt drawn to a space in between the bookshelves that was made to accommodate an old map on the wall. The map showed the land around Canton extending beyond the edges of the map, except on the east where the sea pushed back the land. The map hung in a carved wooden frame that had a dragon on all fours sides of it. The dragons were painted in faded colors that showed the same age as the map they bordered. Simon recognized two of the serpents as one from the river and the other from the air around the crumbling tower. Simon reached up to touch the one that looked like the serpent that attacked him in the Vareex. He thought about Lazuli and hoped she had escaped the clutches of that foul beast. The dragon's eye on the frame seemed to catch the light coming from the windows, giving it a life that was both alluring and disconcerting. It was no bigger than a button and was clearly the same color of Lazuli's skin: ultramarine with mottled yellow and black.

Filch watched Simon with more interest than before as he extended his finger towards the blue stone. When the moment of interface arrived, the tip of his finger passed through the surface of the stone like with his shield. The definite sound of a latch releasing its lock captured the attention of those in the room.

"What did you break?" Bromle asked as he stood up from the couch.

Filch and Adger walked towards him as well.

"I looked here, but I didn't feel any buttons," Adger said defensively. "What did you do?"

"I just—I don't know. I just touched the eye here," Simon said.

Adger touched the stone but it was as inactive and solid as the rest of the frame. He looked back at Simon, who shrugged. Adger pulled the frame from the side which easily pivoted on a hinge behind it. Behind the map was a small shelf with a weathered envelope and a folded parchment. He pulled out the contents and delivered the folded paper into Simon's outstretched hand. Simon unfolded the paper to show a map just like the one in the frame. Adger opened the envelope which had his name on the front of it.

Adger read over the letter inside. From his mixed expressions, the others were able to tell the message was unexpected or misunderstood.

"It's from Orvar and he knows about Simon," Adger said. "The letter says he's gone ahead to prepare the army."

"How could he know about Simon?" Bromle asked. "We only just met him. And what army?"

"I told you he was enigmatic. He says the map will help us find...can you tell what that says?" He held out the letter to Simon.

"Looks like...'Rhin Geatu,'" Simon said with a shrug.

"He always did have bad handwriting. Rhin geatu...that does sound familiar. I think...Adger trailed off mumbling to himself as he went to a shelf nearby and pulled a book from it. He thumbed through it as he walked back to Simon. "Here it is: 'rhin geatu; or: secret gates.' They're doors or something; I didn't study this language very much."

"Save the schooling, little brother," Bromle said, picking his teeth absently and poking books on a nearby shelf.

"Anyway, the letter says to find the Kalinaw Council and that these gates will get us there. The map will help us navigate between them apparently."

"The Kalinaw Council?" Bromle asked. "There is no Kalinaw; we're it. This was a waste of time!" Bromle threw his hands up and retreated back to the couch.

Ignoring his brother, Adger asked Simon to show him the map. "It's the same one as in the frame."

Adger took it over to the window and held it up to the light.

"There's something here but it's too small to see."

"Oh," Simon exclaimed, "I have a loupe."

"Why do you have a loupe?" Adger asked.

"I honestly don't know," Simon said. "Unfortunately, I didn't get an instruction manual."

Simon reached inside one of his pouches and pulled out the loupe and the rings along with it.

The rings captured Filch's attention. She hadn't stolen something in far too long, and Simon's rings reinvigorated the desire. If Simon's shield and hilt were any testament to the power of his belongings, the rings would be no less impressive. She saw them for only a moment, but the way they reflected the light was enough to catch her eye.

He held the rings in one hand and walked over to Adger, extending the loupe in the other.

Adger only looked through it for a moment. "It's filthy; looks cracked too," Adger said and handed it back to Simon.

Simon stepped towards the table to take the loupe back. As soon as the loupe was in his hand, the glass grew and widened until it was a disk so wide he could barely hold it with one hand. The glass was prismatic and cast rainbows all around the room.

"I guess you weren't using it right," Simon teased Adger through his own surprise.

Simon leaned over to look through it, and the light it refracted revealed red markings on the map. There were paths drawn in between the cities and towns on the map; some of them led into open fields, or even across the sea. Each path ended at an arc with numbers next to it. Down in one corner, there were numbered notes corresponding to the arcs that read "Destroyed,""Dammed,""Immured," or "Open."

"Well, there you go," Simon said. "Where's the closest one?"

"The map says there's one near us, and…" Adger trailed off. "…and…yes, the note says—oh, the note says 'Home.' I believe we're right around this area, but I'm not sure how we find it. I would assume Orvar made this."

Simon leaned over the map and one of the rings jumped out of his hand. It hit the table and split into three pieces; all of which snapped into different places on the map. Simon put the other rings back in his pocket and reached to pick the pieces back up. Before his hand made it to the first piece, lines of light connected the pieces of the ring across the map and all the rhin geatu illuminated.

Simon chuckled, "I love this place."

Simon reached out and touched the rhin geatu closest to the cabin. The house shuddered and the muffled sound of wind whistling through a forest could be heard in the silence of the room. They looked around at the windows and the door but nothing had opened.

"It's here!" Adger said excitedly. "Quickly, search the house. There must be a hidden door, or hatch."

Simon reached for the ring pieces again and they snapped into place on his finger. Markings appeared on the ring and formed a red symbol of a single rhin geatu. He looked at it for a moment longer and was pleased he was given something so impressive. He grabbed the map and as he folded it up, the loupe shrunk back down to its normal size. He stuffed the things back in his pockets and quickly started his search in the rest of the house.

He was excited at the prospect of a secret passage and happy to have the opportunity to look through Orvar's other rooms. The den was so intriguing that he thought the rest of the house must be as captivating. He left the room and went into the dining room. There was a long table covered with books and scrolls, chests, and even several weapons. The desire to look through the contents was overwhelming, but Simon knew he had a hidden door to find. He looked under the table and around the cabinets on the far wall but saw nothing obvious. He saw a doorway at the back of the room that led to a kitchen.

The kitchen, like the dining room, was disproportionate to the cabin exterior. Long counters covered with various containers and food lined the right and far walls interrupted by a stove and deep sink. Pots and drying herbs hung from the low ceiling, and shelves and racks of plates lined the walls. Paintings of breads and vegetables were on the walls that looked real enough to reach into and eat. The kitchen was rich with aromas of fresh oregano and basil that made Simon hungry for another meal. He stopped his search to inhale the delicious smells that surrounded him.

A creak of the stairs above him broke the trance and he continued his search.

Filch darted up the stairs to begin her search. She arrived on the landing which led to several small but inviting rooms, filled with plush beds and covered with deep red carpets. Dark wood furniture complimented the amenities that distracted from the belongings haphazardly thrown onto the floor. The muffled whistling wind faded the further that Filch walked down the hallway. She turned and went back towards the stairs, assuming wherever they needed to go was further in the depths of the house.

Bromle left the den and walked through the doorway in the back left corner of the room. It led to nothing more than a bathroom. Bromle stepped back into the den and watched his brother frantically move from shelf to shelf.

"It has to be here somewhere," Adger mumbled to himself. "He wouldn't...he wouldn't have—what would be the point? Orvar, where are you?"

He leaned some of the books off the shelves, hoping to find an unimaginative secret switch; muttering out loud all the while. "It must be—maybe this one? Maybe it's here, or—oh, that book looks old! No, that's not it. Where is the—this one! No, not there either."

Filch had returned from upstairs and joined Bromle in the observation of their companion's hurried search. She shook her head at Bromle to indicate her disapproval of Adger's tenacity and her unsuccessful discovery upstairs.

"What if those red lines are just the markings of a crazy old man," Bromle said. "What if they're nothing more than what used to be the connections to each home of the Kalinaw?"

"No! That can't be all it is. There's more to it all than that. Plus, his letter said that it's a way to get around. Here, look."

Adger handed the letter to Bromle and didn't wait for him to read over it before continuing his search. He noticed one of the many carpets had been moved amidst his search and saw scratches on the floor underneath it. They weren't very long and indicated that the adjacent bookshelf might hinge out, but there wasn't enough room to make a passage. Under usual circumstances the scratches might have been overlooked, but the situation was abnormal. Adger grabbed one of the lower shelves and began to pull.

"Help me, Brom!" Adger pleaded.

He wanted to be right about Orvar. If he was wrong and the old man really was crazy, then Adger had wasted years devoted to learning all that Orvar offered him. Bromle shook his head but cared enough about his brother to do as he asked.

He rolled his eyes but walked over to the shelf that Adger tugged on and, with one hand, pulled on the shelf. The bookshelf started to pivot which caught Bromle's interest and he used his other hand to pull the shelf even harder. Adger stepped aside as Bromle pulled a little farther and a little harder. The bookshelf had many things on it that made it even heavier, but after a few more inches, the bookshelf sank into an unseen detent on the floor. The release of a lock was heard elsewhere in the house.

Adger's excitement should have swelled, but it somewhat diminished. He expected a passage, a sinking bookshelf, or a bright light—something more obvious. He looked at Bromle who just shrugged his shoulders. Adger had an inward moment of panic.

While the brothers had been pulling on the shelf, Simon was still in the kitchen enjoying the aromas. He was doing more than inhaling; possibly tasting the food in the pantry. He tried the usual places that a secret switch might be: candelabras, ladles on hooks, and panels on the floor, but the most he managed to accomplish was to satisfy his craving. He was just about to go back to the den when he heard a click and noticed a crack form in the furthest corner of the kitchen.

"Hey guys," he called out to his companions in the den after swallowing a hunk of bread. "I think I found it."

Heavy footsteps came from the den and then a crash as someone ran into the table and knocked some of the items onto the floor. Hurried steps preceded Adger at the entryway to the kitchen.

"I think it was me—I found it, it was the bookshelf. See?" he said over his shoulder. "See, Brom? Wait, did you touch anything?" he said to Simon quietly, who shook his head. "See, Brom!" he said with a wide grin on his face. "What did you find?" he said quietly to Simon again who pointed to the crack in the corner.

Adger rushed over to the wall and pushed with his shoulder. He motioned to Simon for help and the two of them pushed a panel inward and slid it into a recessed portion of the wall. Behind it was a set of narrow wooden stairs that led into the basement of the cabin. The sound of the rushing wind was even louder once they opened the door. "What did you do?" Simon asked.

"The bookshelf," he said with an expression meant to denote how obvious it should have been to him at first.

Bromle and Filch joined them in the kitchen. Bromle was smiling and Filch's expressive abilities were repetitively impossible to determine.

"I owe you my apologies, little brother," Bromle said as he followed Adger and Simon who led the way down the narrow stairs.

Despite his skeptical tendencies and usual arrogance, Bromle was not above some semblance of humility.

Adger flew down the stairs with a quiet chuckle and childish excitement. "Think nothing of it, brother!"

The stairwell was short and narrow. The basement was well lit by window wells filled with daylight. The basement didn't have the expected musty smell but was congruent with the floors above. There were stores of food and barrels of drinks that filled the basement; enough to feed one person for years, or host parties to fit the table above for months. The floors were clean and dry, and the stores of food had an organization that the rest of the house could not manage.

Beneath the stairs was an arch of stone not much taller than Adger. It was the source of all the howling winds. Inside the archway was a scene of the forest outside, the same trees that kept the cabin hidden.

"I don't understand," Bromle said. "Aren't those the trees outside? I thought the rhin geatu were supposed to help us get somewhere else."

"What about the map?" Adger asked

Simon pulled out the map again but it was no longer lit the same way it had been before. The once visible rhin geatu had disappeared. He smoothed it out completely on an open shelf and pulled off the rhin geatu ring. He put it on the map, but it did not break into pieces like before. He tapped it on the shelf and it was as solid as any ring might be expected to be. He put the ring back on and looked at it and then the map. He touched the rhin geatu symbol on the ring and the invisible red lines appeared again.

"There we go," Simon said aloud. "It's working again."

The brightest symbol on the map was the one nearest the cabin. Simon touched one of the other symbols and the scene inside the rhin geatu changed to rolling hills of stone leading to lowlands of water. Simon looked at the map and the brightest arc was the one he touched.

Filch watched what he was doing quite closely. She reached over the map and pointed to an arc far out to the west from where they were.

"I came from here," she said and touched the map.

The scene behind them vanished and the archway was empty with only the wall of the basement within it. Simon looked back at the map and noticed the note corresponding to it said, "Destroyed." He avoided commenting on it and beckoned Adger to look at the map too.

"We're from here!" Adger said excitedly as he too touched the map.

The scene behind them changed to a dark black room lit only by faint shafts of light coming from an unseen window elsewhere in the room.

"We can go home, brother!" Bromle said.

"I don't know about that," Simon said. "Look, it says 'immured.'"

"It means we can't go home, Brom. If we try, we'll be walking into a prison."

"Where's the Kalinaw Council?" Simon asked.

"The letter doesn't say. I...I don't know actually. Like Brom said, I thought we were all that was left. Orvar didn't tell me about there being a whole council of Kalinaw, let alone where they are. He didn't tell me about an army, or—any of this."

"I don't know the way either," Simon said. "I know just as much as you."

"So far, it seems that you've stumbled through this adventure," Filch said with so much venom that Simon looked away from her spiteful gaze.

"I'll admit that I've been fortunate, but I don't think it's chance. I refuse to believe that arbitrary circumstances have brought us here."

He looked at the rhin geatu ring. He willed it to work and rubbed the symbol, but nothing happened. He looked at the map, hoping for a change and touched the ring again, but the paper remained unaffected. He thought of the other trinkets in his pockets and remembered the folded papers. He quickly pulled them out and laid them next to the map on the shelf. They were blank with only the creases of folds on them. He touched the ring again, and it remained unchanged. He pulled off his ring and put it on the largest piece of blank paper, and it split like it had before on Orvar's map. The pieces slid into their assigned places on the parchment even though it wasn't obvious what those places might be. Red lines burned across the blank paper and darkened into black. Simon reached for the ring which jumped into place on his finger.

"It's a whole new map," Simon said. "It looks like it lines up here and...yes it overlaps this corner here."

"Unexplored reaches of Dyurndale," Adger said with wonder. "Orvar said the woodlands that separate here from there are so treacherous that traversing them is unheard of, but obviously someone did."

Beyond the forest that Adger spoke of, there were symbols of other cities and rhin geatu. The largest of the symbols seemed to retain some of the bright redness of the initial manifestation of markings. Simon was drawn to it and was learning to trust instinct over logic. Whether from foolishness, or an innate knowledge, he wasn't sure, but Simon pointed at the city and confidently said that the Council was there.

"How can you be so sure?" Filch said.

"It's the biggest city on the map," he said. "And it's one of the few that's marked as 'Open'."

He touched the symbol and the scene behind them changed. Within the arch it was dark, though minuscule bits of light could be seen.

"Lead on, map wielder," she said mockingly.

Simon folded the maps and slid them in a coat pocket. He stepped through the archway, not knowing where they might come out. He hoped that his first real effort at being a leader would be a good one.

12 The Gun

Simon stepped through the arch and expected to feel a noticeable transfer of matter, but it was no different than stepping through a doorway. The temperature of the new place was colder, and there were different smells, but other than that the transition was seamless. Despite the benefit of an uneventful arrival, his surety was still weakened. His doubts about his capabilities as a leader weighed on his mind heavily, and even more so now that those he brought with him trusted in his decision; it was a new experience for him. He never thought of himself as a leader, or a warrior, and not knowing how to fight made things worse. Nevertheless, he trusted his intuition.

He was determined to find this mystic, Orvar. If he really was as old as Adger thought, then maybe he could provide additional insight as to the validity of Simon's purpose. Maybe he could help Simon understand why he had been brought to Dyurndale; why *he* was the one to be chosen and if Orvar had anything to do with the choosing. Until then though, Simon had to trust the instinct that guided him.

The room around him had very little light but even in the darkness, it gave the distinct impression of somewhere more modern than what he had seen so far. As he stepped onto the floor he thought he noticed a glare of light reflect off a polished floor. Not a surface like dark wood; something more synthetic. He could smell the sour odor of old dirty water that might be in the dark basements of an old building. For a moment he was lost in thoughts about days of familiar smells in his former existence. There were aspects of his old life that he sorely missed, and they primarily consisted of the family he left behind. The smell was certainly not a memory he felt the desire to retain, but it was something familiar unlike the creatures he had met so far. This world was incredible enough to be the most amazing experience of either existence, but the longing for his previous life made his new one seem impassible.

What of my children; my wife, he wondered. *If I fail, what will happen to them?* He thought of the aurora Kapell mentioned that carried souls past Dyurndale. This might have given him some comfort if he didn't doubt the limitations of the stone giant's knowledge. *He couldn't remember why I was supposed to come here, after all.* He was sure that Orvar would know more.

His companions came in behind him and interrupted his thoughts. Filch pulled an orb from inside her cloak and slid back her mask to gently breathe on it. The rare opportunity to see what Filch actually looked like escaped him though, as she opened her mask away from him. The orb in her hand slowly illuminated a pale, purple light that lit several pipes that ran from the ceiling to the floor. The wall had caved in on one side, and underneath it, there were remnants of a doorway. Rubble had poured in from the door and removed any hope of leaving the room by normal means. The room was longer than it was wide, and several cinderblock pillars held up the ceiling. A few runs of smaller pipes and wires ran down the length of the room. One corner was fenced off, and inside were parts of machinery and pallets leaned against the wall. Stagnant puddles of water throughout the area reflected the purple orb's light, giving the dank room even more misery.

Simon pulled Adger to the side while the other two searched for another exit. He kept his voice low so the others couldn't hear him.

"Adger, I have to be honest with you, man: I'm just guessing here. I don't *know* what I think I'm supposed to know."

"That's okay, Simon" Adger said. "That's to be expected; we'll figure it out as we go. When I arrived in Dyurndale, I was so lost and confused; I didn't even know my name. Bromle was there though, and he watched over me. We must've been some of the last few to arrive in Dyurndale, I think. There was a large group of people, and most of them were captured right on the spot. There was so much confusion that Brom and I got away."

"Well, I'm glad you did. You've been a good friend in the short time I've known you."

"It's been a long time since I've had a friend," Adger beamed. "Relationships are fleeting here; at least in Canton. It wasn't a bad life, but sometimes I felt like we were just living to survive."

"You certainly have a friend now," Simon said and clapped him on the back. "I'm most worried about leading an army, though. I was merely a salesman in my old life, and certainly no commander of forces."

"I wouldn't fret much about that either."

"How can I not worry though? I'm afraid that I'm not the person that poem says I'm supposed to be."

"People of worth rarely recognize their best qualities, but I see your worth, and I believe in you. I don't think our meeting was by chance."

"Neither do I, friend."

Adger beamed again.

Filch walked up and her mask was unfastened at one corner. Simon noticed, and she quickly put it back into place.

"Why do you hide your face?" Simon braved to ask her.

"Why do you not know who you are, and who you are prophesied to be?" she retorted rather quickly as if she had been waiting for the opportunity to use the comment.

"Such venom," he said like he might scold a grandchild. He nearly forgot that, in her eyes, he was her age; if not, younger.

"Such ignorance," she said, equally as scolding.

Simon realized that any new information about her would have to be offered, and requesting it was fruitless.

"I see no way out," she said a bit louder so the others could hear her. "It appears that your intuition was misplaced, Hero."

"No." Adger said defensively. He felt invigorated after their brief conversation. "We're in the right place," Adger said and looked at Simon with a smile and a slight nod.

Simon thought for a moment and peered around the room in the darkness. "Filch, please put out your light."

She hesitated but granted the odd request.

"There," Simon said and pointed at the wall with the doorway filled with debris.

A small amount of light very near the ceiling forced its way through the disaster.

"Bromle, could you use your gloves to get us out of here?"

"I wouldn't choose to force anything out of here while we're inside of it." Bromle was sometimes overeager to disprove his brother's fantasies, but considering Simon's discoveries of the map and rhin geatu ring, Bromle was inclined to believe. "But...maybe I can *pull* something. Stand back and be ready with that shield of yours if things go sideways."

Bromle walked towards the doorway while the others moved to the opposite wall with the rhin geatu. Simon pulled out the map, touched his ring, and pointed back towards the mystic's cabin. They all looked at him.

"Just in case," he said as Orvar's basement became visible in the gate behind them again.

Bromle turned his back towards the archway and rubbed his hands together in a manner unlike the way he had before: he crouched low and stuck out his elbows as if preparing to thwart an incoming enemy's tackle. Black orbs with smoking white froth formed in his palms. He widened his stance and lowered his center. He thrust out his open hands towards the pile of debris and pulled them back as if pulling the stones from the pile. After repeating the movements several times, the dirt began to move. Small pieces of earth fell into the basement and were quickly followed by larger chunks of rock. The pile continued shifting from the structure around it without incident. The small bit of light at the top of the pile became a hole big enough to squeeze through and then big enough to crawl through. Eventually, the hole was big enough for even Bromle to pass through without concerted effort.

He closed his hands, extinguishing the orbs. Simon closed the map and the arch behind him became solid stone again. The four of them stood in silence waiting for the rubble to stop moving. For a long moment thereafter, they remained in their places listening for any movements or voices in the building beyond. Simon recognized the pieces of stone that fell into the basement; it was so unlike the structures of Canton that Simon felt he was back in his previous life in some derelict warehouse.

Simon broke the silence by pulling out his hilt and unlatching his shield from his belt. He left them sheathed in the confines of their metal bodies but kept them out in the event that their arrival had not gone unnoticed.

"Let's see where we are," Simon said and moved towards the opening. He climbed the pile of debris and looked back at his companions. "Staying here won't help us," he said. "We have an army to lead." He put his doubts aside, even if just for the moment.

He turned back towards the opening and the others followed him. They emerged in an enormous building with machinery of various kinds piled in the corners and strewn about the floor.

"What—why are there machines here?" Simon asked. They were not altogether odd to him, but in the context of what he had seen so far in Dyurndale, the rusted metal was sorely misplaced.

"Right you are, friend," Adger said. "Never have I seen such... sculptures. They must be art of some twisted kind; what other purpose would they serve?"

The rafters far above them held cooing birds that were undisturbed by the group's arrival. One upper corner of the building had collapsed, leaving a massive hole where the city beyond could be seen reaching into the sky. The skyscrapers made the world feel even more alien when compared to Canton. From the few buildings that could be seen through the hole, it was obvious that the city had architecture unlike any of them had seen. The buildings were tightly packed and of varying sizes; some reaching into the clouds while other clambered at their feet. They were more than straight squares that rose in singular angles; the buildings were sculpted in varying bulges and inclinations like tulips on thick stems. Windows speckled the buildings like porous bread and provided vantage points that would likely be sights enough to leave the viewer breathless. Even with beauty of the architecture, it was clear they had been neglected like the machines around them; the buildings looked derelict and forgotten.

The machinery on the floor was ancient and rusted; it looked like a gentle touch could crush them to dust. Crumpled papers and trash littered the spaces in between them. Both it and the buildings outside were the least of expectations for anyone in the small group and Filch was the least likely to voice her bewilderment but it escaped her composure nonetheless.

"What is this place?" Filch asked, unable to contain her amazement.

Simon was unimpressed by the contents of the building despite recognizing that it all seemed out of place when compared to the level of technology he had seen in Canton—and ignoring the miraculous weapons he carried.

"It looks like a factory," he said.

"I don't understand," Adger said. "Never have I seen anything like this."

"You and me both; I thought Dyurndale was more archaic."

"Than what?"

"The time I'm from has many places like this. Factories are a way of industry, but from the little I've seen of Dyurndale, I thought this kind of thing was beyond it. When were you all from—before you died, I mean—what do you remember?"

"Nothing like this," Bromle said. "Metal was limited to weapons, doors, and parts of buildings but not—nothing like this."

"And you, Filch?"

"Come, we don't have the luxury of remembrance," she said.

Filch and Bromle led the way and Simon confided in Adger again. "Does she strike you as a bit odd?" Simon said to Adger.

"Yeah," Adger snorted. "She's overwhelmingly secretive, and I can't say I've actually seen her face, but she fights alongside us and for that, I trust her."

"Hold on, you've never seen her face?"

"Nearly—but no; you learn to discern her moods from what you can see, though. I'm assuming her face is horribly scarred. Bromle used to tease her fiercely and eventually she said it was in mourning for the loss of her people. Whatever her reasons for staying around, I'm glad for her company. You haven't seen her true abilities."

"Becoming invisible is pretty impressive."

"Yes, but you haven't seen her fight. It is truly a wonder to behold. Let's see where your choice has taken us, friend."

Simon and Adger quickened their pace to catch up with the others. They all weaved through the machinery to the far wall of the warehouse. It took them more time than they expected because of how enormous the building was. The factory had an open floor the whole width of the building.

They reached a set of double doors that groaned with age when they pushed them open to the streets beyond. They stepped out into an alleyway filled with bags of forgotten trash and overflowing dumpsters. They walked down the alley to a wide six lane road with rusted cars and sprouting weeds. The foliage growing out of the streets showed that nature was reclaiming the city.

Cities were not new to Simon, but the others had never seen a building that reached to those heights. Some of the buildings had wide stairwells leading to connected landings that led even higher into the city. The architecture was more artistic than the stark skyscrapers Simon knew. Each building was unique from the ones adjacent to it. Skywalks connected many of the buildings and from his vantage point he saw none that escaped the ravages of time. The lower levels of the buildings were overtaken by trees and long grasses that had forced their way through the windows.

Simon didn't recognize the vehicles that littered the streets, but they seemed similar enough to ones from his previous life.

"What are those, Simon?" Adger asked.

"They're cars," he said. "They're like...carriages that don't require animals to pull them."

"How does that work?"

"I think the more important question is why this technology never reached Canton."

"What is that sound?" Filch said, hushing them.

A low hissing sound coupled with a mechanical clicking chirped in the silence.

"I recommend we find a place to hide," she said.

They turned to go back down the alley towards the warehouse but as they did, the approaching sound culminated in a machine that flew over the building at the other end. At a glance, it looked like a large bird and as it got closer, it was apparent that it was something they shouldn't wait to meet. It had a pair of long wings that helped it glide into view. Its body was sleek and portions of it reflected the daylight revealing a dark patina. The head of it was long, aerodynamic, and ended in a sharp point. Thin horns twisted from the back of its head towards its back. When it caught sight of them, it opened its narrow mouth, revealing rows of sharp teeth.

They ran into the street to find another place to hide, but two more of the metal creatures were approaching from opposite ends of the street, hissing and clicking all the while.

Simon, hilt still in hand, extended his fiery blade and shield in preparation for an attack. Bromle charged his palms and his brother created a black arrow from debris on the street. Filch was nowhere to be seen.

"We can take 'em," Bromle said with growing orbs in his hands.

The orbs were getting larger than the ones Simon had seen before, and they were billowing smoke that fell onto the street.

The metal creatures all converged from opposite directions; another two were now approaching from the wide, intersecting road behind them.

"Whatever Filch can do," Simon said, "she needs to do it swiftly. We are completely exposed. Each of us needs to take a bird."

"But there's five of them," Adger said.

"I've got these two," Bromle said and faced down the newest pair.

"Adger, take the one there and I'll do my best to draw the attention of the other two."

They all turned their backs to each other and gave enough space to defend themselves. The metal birds were getting closer and still showed no signs of obvious aggression besides flying directly towards them. As they got closer, the defenders realized the birds were much larger than they initially assessed.

"Don't attack yet; they've shown no signs of hostility."

"We've had very little hospitality so far; I don't have much hope that they will change that," Adger said.

The flying creature aiming for Adger exploded in a fireball that spewed out a spinning chakram. The weapon turned sharply back towards its origin. Filch materialized and was standing atop one of the rusted cars holding a second chakram in her other hand. She caught the first one as it came back to her.

She flipped off the car and ran towards the corner of the building and the alley they had emerged from. She sinuously made her way, darting around cars and jumping over objects in the road. Simon was impressed and was glad to see her abilities extended beyond disbelief of him. As she stopped moving at the corner and waited for the first flying creature to emerge from the alley, she began to fade into a shadow against the building. She took a couple more steps towards the alley corner and became slightly more visible. Simon was impressed but took note that strength sometimes couples weakness; he was no less amazed by her abilities though.

When Bromle heard the explosion, he only took a moment to realize what had happened and turned back to the two creatures he was preparing for. He followed Filch's lead and decided to attack. He thrust both hands towards the enemies, and two large flaming orbs rocketed towards them. A fuchsia orb hit its target which erupted in an orange blaze. His second missile, however, missed its mark and banked sharply before impact. The second orb, maroon in color, immediately turned into the air as it passed the bird and began a descent back towards it again. The creature was becoming uncomfortably close to Bromle. He clapped his hands together again, slowly pulled them apart, and two more brightly colored magenta orbs appeared in his hands. He slammed his open palms together and knocked the creature back. The metal bird was forced into the path of the incoming maroon orb and was destroyed like its companion.

123

Only two creatures remained: the one coming down the alley and the one facing Simon. Bromle turned to face the other two with his companions. The destruction of the other three had only taken a moment, but it seemed like there was still no time to prepare for the last two. They rapidly shortened their distance to the group. As they approached, each one extended four mechanical legs out of their bodies. They flipped and twisted into place like shafts stored under the pressure of springs. The one in the alley slowed as it exited and passed Filch. She raised her weapon to attack but stopped when she saw the transformation the creature had taken.

It landed directly on top of a car nearest to Filch. The other one landed in between two others, pushing them aside like they weighed nothing. Their wings did not have feathers or blades but were solid membranes; canvas tightly stretched between bright, brass rods like the wings of a bat. Their legs hissed and released puffs of steam as they put the full weight of their bodies onto them. The legs were mechanical with struts and tubes leading down to the feet that unfolded as the machines landed. Stabilizing toes unfolded from the base of the legs and pressed into the pavement with such force that small cracks crept out from the digits.

The brothers and Simon held the machines' attention while Filch moved to take advantage of the opportunity. As she stepped towards the machine closest to her, it quickly unfurled a wicked tail from between its wings with a ball on the end. Filch stopped and then darted behind an adjacent car to find a safer side to attack from. The creature's tail slammed into the car Filch was behind. Despite her imperceptibility, she had been seen. The car flipped into the air and exposed her. The way behind was blocked by more debris, and she had no other route to escape by. She ran towards the creature that had turned to face her and narrowly jumped over its bite, spitefully driving her heel into the top of its head. She ran down its back and flipped over the tail, catching her leg on one of the spikes. The pain was preferable to being caught in between the machine's jaws. She sprinted to the others for the safety of numbers.

"Filch, you and Adger take that one. Bromle, you and I will take this one," Simon said as he gestured towards the machine with its tail out.

Both creatures leapt into the air and started circling the group like carrion predators. From the side of one creature's head a small spark flared, quickly followed by the outward blast of gears and mechanical components on the other side. The heavy beast fell to the ground, leaving an indention in the pavement.

The other creature roared mechanically and a glowing fire could be seen building in its throat. Filch threw both her chakrams, but before they reached their target, another spark and explosion dropped the last creature to the ground. Filch caught her weapons as they returned to her.

The four of them turned to face each other, unable to make sense of what had just happened. Each one of them either shrugged their shoulders or shook their heads, not knowing who had destroyed the last two creatures.

They walked over to the closest machine with their weapons drawn in the event that there was still life within it. Its head leaked viscous brown oil and small mechanical components flowed out with the fluid. The air brought no new alarms, and it seemed they were no longer under attack. They could not explain how their enemies had fallen so easily. The group stayed ready for more battle, but the air was still and quiet. It made them feel even more uncomfortable than when the machines were on an intersecting course. The perplexed quartet walked over to the other creature to ensure it too seemed as inoperable as the other one.

The bronze color of the machines was mottled with age and neglect. The aggression of time in the city was no more merciful on them than the rusted cars around them.

Adger felt anxious, though Bromle and Filch were happy to have finally had an opportunity to destroy something. Simon felt pleased for directing the team and was glad they were all unscathed.

Adger knelt down on one knee to look at the machine. Its head was similar to but larger than any crocodile he had ever seen. Its body was as proportionately massive. He stood and walked around the thing several times, occasionally stopping to kneel and look at various aspects of it. He walked back towards the group, nodding his head as if he had learned something about it.

"Any idea what these things are," Simon asked him.

"Not a clue," he said and shook his head.

"Hello there. Don't shoot; I've already done all the shooting after all," said a female voice calling out to them with a thick, Highland accent. "I call them alaidak."

They all quickly raised their heads to see a slender and fully masked person in a spotted, hooded cloak making her way between the cars. She held a rifle raised in one hand that was short in length but taller than it was wide; it seemed impractical, but Simon was well aware of what it was although the others were not. The mask she wore had dark colors and one eye piece was larger than the other, giving it a mechanical appearance akin to the alaidak. The cloak around the mask was mottled with darker camouflage that, when the colors weren't shifting, seemed to blend in with the colors of the city. The four of them prepared to attack, assuming that this new threat was in league with the alaidak that had attacked them.

"A thank you would be nice," she said.

The four of them slightly relaxed.

"You did that?" Simon asked pointing to the alaidak closest to them.

"Aye. And I'd be happy to do it ag'in too. The name's Thaygin

Guneelda, but you can call me, Gin; not like the drink, mind ya'—though I do enjoy a drop or two on occasion," she said with an infectious laughter.

She took off her mask, which folded outward when she touched it and wrapped around the back of her hand. Red curls stuck out from the sides of the hood which bordered her fair skin and pleasant features.

"Well you have our thanks, Gin. I'm Simon, and this is—"

"Haven't you learned anything?" Bromle interrupted him. "We can't trust her; we don't know her. What if she has machines to spare, and she destroyed those two just to gain our trust?"

"Oh, I'm sorry," she said. "Orvar sent me and I'm with the Kalinaw. He told me to wait for ya while he went ahead. I've been here for days and was beginning to think I lost ya. I see who *you* are," she gestured to Simon's sword and shield. "For now, you'll just have to trust who I am. You can stay here if you like, but I'm sure they're more of those comin'."

A silent moment passed as they considered her offer. The rustling of paper carried by a new breeze in the streets was the only sound.

"I am Adger and this is my brother Bromle. The silent brooding companion there is Filch."

Bromle stood with his arms crossed, and Filch gave little more than a head nod.

"Pleased to meet you all," Gin said.

A hiss and click interrupted their exchange.

"We've run outta time," Gin warned. "Prepare yourselves or run, but whate'er you do, the choice is about to be made for ya."

High in the air and down the main street they were on, four alaidak careened around the corner of one of the buildings. They were flying faster than the ones before and with more intention. They descended low towards the road and kicked up debris and vehicles in their wake.

"Don't get in their way, but attack as they pass," Gin said. "And be wary of their wicked hands; they'll grab ya as they fly past if they can."

She hastily moved parts on her gun, pushing some pieces down and pulling others out, until its shape changed from something short and tall to an object that was narrow and long. She moved her hand towards her face and the mask that was on the back of her hand crawled around to the front and affixed to her face. She turned towards the group of four still watching her work.

"I guess you've chosen to stay then, but I would recommend ya don't just stand there."

They dispersed and took varying positions around the area to make their potential death or capture—whatever the alaidak's intentions were—more difficult.

Gin turned her back to them and raised the rifle to her mask. A scope on top of the gun unfolded after her manipulations. Gin hunched over on the gun and moved her face close to the scope which locked into place on her mask through gears that extended from the gun. She squeezed the trigger and fired several shots from the long barrel. There was no sound or flash like that which might occur with a regular gun; just subtle recoil that Gin absorbed well from practice. Two of the alaidak dropped dead from the air and slid along the street, knocking obstacles out of their way. A third was glanced by Gin's shots but was otherwise undeterred.

Gin pulled her gun from her mask and dropped to one knee on the ground as the remaining two alaidak speedily approached. She quickly worked on her rifle again, and when she was done, it had returned to the form from before. The long rifle and scope were gone and the weapon was more akin to the thickness of a book resting on its spine. She took aim, squeezed the trigger, and repeating blasts spewed from the short barrel of the gun. Unlike the previous shots, they were loud and were accompanied by wicked bursts of varying colors.

The two alaidak flew next to each other, low to the ground. One of them almost grabbed Gin as it flew past but only managed to tear a corner of her cloak. She kept the gun pointed at them as they flew overhead. Bursts of impact caused shards of metal to fall to the ground behind them.

Simon yearned to participate in the destruction of the alaidak. He quickly retracted his shield and stored it back on his belt. He grabbed the flaming sword in both hands, took a full breath of air, ran up the back of one vehicle, and leapt into the air. He roared ardently as his feet left the car and didn't consider whether it was fear or excitement. Simon's timing had been perfect; he would intersect at least one of the alaidak with his blade as they passed. When he swung his arms downward though, the fiery blaze of the blade became a volcano of fire extending past the first alaidak to also strike the second. They were both hewn in a sweltering swing and thereby eliminated as a threat. Simon nimbly landed on the ground a second before the remaining alaidak crashed into the street, leaving deep gouges in the ground. The city was still again, and no more hissing or clicking was heard.

Gin quickly ran between the remains of the alaidak closest to Simon and pulled out pieces of its inner components. She stuffed what she found in the bag on her back. The other four congregated in the open space the impact of the creatures had made.

"Thanks again, Gin," Simon said.

"And a thanks to you," she said. "Looks like you didn't need my help at all."

"I didn't even know I could do that," he said with a laugh. "We should probably get going; I'd rather not wait for more to return."

"Aye, of course," she said. "Some of these things are hard to come by, though."

She ran to the one of the halves of alaidak closest to them and crawled inside.

"I need just one more thing," her voice echoed from within.

She came back out with handfuls of components; spurting hoses and sparking wires. The black liquid that fueled the creatures smeared her cloak and dripped from her hands. She stuffed the parts into her bag. Simon held out his hand to help her up.

"A hero and a gentleman," she quipped. "Let's go."

She reached up to her mask, which wrapped around her hand in the same manner as before.

She led them along the sides of buildings and down the boulevard; stopping frequently to listen for any more machines.

"I don't understand this place," Adger said as they walked.

"You must be quiet," Gin said.

"I can't, this place is too amazing! Flying machines and these cars—where did all this come from? Why haven't we seen this before?"

"Ages ago—predating the Kalinaw—this city was the central place for all life in Dyurndale. For thousands of years, people lived here in peace without complaint or upset. When the Vile Tyrant arrived, this was the first place he came to. The Elders of Origin reached out to him in peace, but he mercilessly struck most of them down, and so, too, many inhabitants of this once great city. We weren't without resilience though, and a war began. We failed in victory, and he stole what weapons and technologies existed. The alaidak are ancient, sleeping remnants of that long and awful war. They were thought to be inactive—extinct—but they awoke a few days ago. And as for your second question, Adger, the city fell before my lifetime here, and I doubt Etnian would share anything, let alone an advantage. We have some left, though. You'll have opportunity to see it soon enough."

Adger had more questions but also enough to consider. He followed along behind the others silently and was lost in thought. He admired the city in the same ways that Simon had. He wondered what it might have been like full of inhabitants—peaceful inhabitants, at that. Canton was not a place of war, but it was not one of equality either. He thought of his small home and, like his brother, did not miss it except for the comfort of familiarity.

They walked through the city streets in silence. A shortcut through a deserted building seemed to take a more direct route towards their destination. They exited the other side of the building on a smaller street that wasn't nearly the arterial route of the previous one. There were no cars cluttering the streets, and the buildings that lined it were lower and less ornate but no less impressive or unique. They hesitated at the exit of the building, once again listening in the silence.

"I think we might be in the clear," Gin said. "The entrance is right up there, but stay here just in case."

Gin darted from the entrance way and ducked behind a small, one-sided structure, likely used as a bus stop. She picked up a metal rod with a hook on one end and a handle on the other. She quickly moved to the center of the narrow road and caught the edge of a manhole cover as she sprinted. She pulled the metal disc to reveal a tunnel leading down below the city. She gestured for the others, pointing at the hole in the road. They looked at each other, unsure of the rescue that was being provided. Gin nodded her head at them with a reassuring smile and mouthed, "Come on."

Simon was the first to move, and the others followed after him. He descended the ladder in the street hesitantly.

"We won't be underwater, will we?" Simon asked Gin.

"My, no," she laughed. "There're no gills on this girl."

They descended into the sewers, and Simon was pleased that neither the smell nor appearance met his expectations. They came out on a small landing in an intersection of wide, semi-circular tunnels that were bordered by broad sidewalks. In between them were riverbeds that may have carried waste and water in decades past but had long since dried up. Several smaller tunnels branched off of the main tunnel they were in. Some of them were arched tunnels while others were circular tubes rising and turning away from the main way; their dark shadows reaching towards the center like a creature's slender fingers.

"The alaidak shouldn't find us down here, but I wouldn't let your guard down," Gin said. "There's no telling what remnants of war may have been awoken in the dark corners of these tunnels. I only hope my time out there hasn't been too long and my rover hasn't been stolen or destroyed. Otherwise, it will be a very long walk; there are miles between us and my home."

They walked down the tunnels as quietly as they could, but their footsteps echoed off the walls despite their best efforts. The subtle sounds of their march became uncomfortable for fear of alarming anything hidden in the shadows. The jingling of trinkets in Simon's and Adger's pockets was amplified against the silence of the subterranean labyrinth. They didn't take many turns, but it was easy to lose their sense of direction.

They turned down one circular tunnel that seemed even darker than the ones before. Filch pulled out her orb and brought it to life, causing an eerie, purple hue to highlight the group's faces.

"Doesn't anyone have a flashlight or something?" Simon asked. "I mean, your purple bubble is great, Filch, but nothing beats a plain old flashlight."

Adger pulled out his tool roll and unfurled it in his hand. He ran his fingers over his tools and pulled out several pieces, assembling them into something about the width of a weapon hilt. He shook it a bit and pushed a button on its side. The dark tunnel was illuminated in white light with the palest of blue tints.

He looked at Filch. "Mine's better," he said and smiled.

"That would've been good in the warehouse," Simon said, teasing Adger.

"It's just up here," Gin said.

They turned a dark corner and Adger's light illuminated a metal contraption that filled the tunnel. It rested on six, wide tires that sat flat on the tunnel walls but at an angle to the vehicle they supported. It had no outer coverings but had symmetrical metal pieces rising in sinuous curves and smooth waves up from the front and over the cabin of the vehicle. A bronze metal housing sat at the back of the vehicle which held its engine.

"What is that?" Adger asked excitedly.

"Oh, good graces; it's still here," Gin said. "That is the fastest way to the Burgh. It would have otherwise been a long and defenseless walk. Come, let's get underway."

They all climbed into the vehicle that allowed them sufficient space to sit on the cushioned seats, of which there was an extra. Gin sat in a chair with no more controls than a few pedals and levers. She grabbed the shift next to her, and the vehicle hummed to life. A chirping buzz, disproportionate to the size of the vehicle, was barely audible over their conversation. Adger quickly took the seat next to Gin and immediately started asking questions about the vehicle. She happily told him all about it as she pushed forward on the controls. The rover lurched forward with no more sound than when at idle.

When the tunnel turned, the wheels would ride up the sides of it while keeping the vehicle level. It moved quickly through the dry tunnel and had no more difficulty when they transitioned to the wider semi-circle tunnels. The extensions that the wheels attached to leapt over the dry riverbeds and rode on opposite sides of the sidewalks as if they had an autonomous dexterity responding to Gin's orchestration.

They made one final turn and entered a wide open area that seemed to be a central convergence for all the various tunnels. There was water there unlike the sewers they had seen so far; it was a shallow, underground lake. Gin parked the vehicle on a dry central island amidst the water. A small dark, derelict, and crumbling hut was away to their left.

"We're here," Gin said.

The others looked at her questioningly.

"Oh, yes; I forget that you're unfamiliar with this place."

She pushed a button on her wrist and the shack disappeared revealing a hole behind it.

"Now we find out if the Council believes what I do about you, Simon. If not...well, let's just hope they do, for your sake."

13 The Arrest

Simon was excited to see that electronics had not disappeared from the world. He wondered how the hologram that hid the passage worked. The passage was dark and cold, but it was still exciting, since it had been hidden so well until commanded to do otherwise. After a long time, a glow and warmth slowly filled the tunnel that eventually turned into a humid breeze. They stepped out into a vaulted cavern that had several holes in the ceiling, allowing the warmth of the world above into the dark confines of the sewers. Massive mounds—that might as well have been mountains—rose up towards the openings of the ceiling far above. Even a well-aimed shot from Gin's gun may not have reached the highest peaks.

"This is one of the few protected places left in this part of the world," Gin said. "From above, it looks like nothing more than an empty field beyond the outer limits of the city. Our people have mastered subterfuge; looks truly are deceiving amongst us," she said and gestured to her coat.

"I thought so. I have one too," Simon said opening his coat.

Gin took the opportunity to examine his outer garment.

"Yes, I see it. I hadn't taken the moment to notice it before. It *is* one of ours. Where did ya get it?"

"Well, I…I came with it, so to speak."

"You are a strange one, friend. Come; let us see what the Council thinks of ya."

They walked out of the tunnel and towards the closest hill which was smaller than the rest. The cavern walls they passed through stretched away to their right and their left and were made unadorned and unfinished. The dark stone walls were black and craggy. They stretched away to the ceiling so as to swallow the underground city like the gaping jaws of an enormous

131

whale. The place made Tortuse's pool seem laughable in comparison. It was beyond Simon's wildest imagination; never had he seen—even in pictures—any cave that had mountains inside of it! The gap in the ceiling far above let the blue sky reach its encouraging fingers down in the darkness and spread some semblance of reality to the grotto. A ray of light landed at the adventurer's feet and beckoned them onward.

A smoothly paved path led from the tunnel entrance. It ended in between two of the largest hills in front of them. There was little else to be seen of the city that Gin spoke so fondly of. The dark walls curved towards the two hills and disappeared around their sides. Whatever confines the underground world had was hidden behind the two mounds in front of them.

"This is it, then?" Bromle said. "How many of you could there possibly be holed up in two tiny hills like blind moles? How can you have a weapon like that but have nothing more than this for a home."

"We're but on the outskirts," Gin said, stopping to turn on Bromle. "Your limited perception will do you no kindness here. Know that this city has been a refuge few outsiders have ever seen. You should consider this an honor."

"Calm down, Ginger." Bromle said, rolling his r's again.

The accents they each had sounded similar, and it amused Simon to think of them as related; especially the way they were playfully bantering. His humor faded quickly though, when he considered the oddity that that there were no soldiers guarding the tunnel that they had entered through. There was not even a gate through which they passed.

"This place is protected, Gin?" Simon asked her. "It seems like we got in pretty easily."

"Aye, it seems that way, but we'll be getting some company quite soon," she said with a smirk and a nod back towards the city.

Farther away towards the city, people could be seen walking casually from one hill to the next. Gin's attitude added to the relaxed atmosphere, as if the citizens they saw were fearless of discovery.

A small group of uniformed people carrying long weapons spotted them and started walking in their direction.

"Stop!" one of the soldiers boomed when he was close enough to be heard.

Four well armored people ran towards them. Their faces were covered, and their features were indiscernible beneath their armor of noticeable age. It was smooth at the wider places but turned in sharp angles, giving them the appearance of a machine-made-human. Their eyes and some of their faces could be seen behind the masks which put the group a bit more at ease than if they had full masks like Gin. They all carried long lances that ended in what appeared to be the stocks of rifles.

"You are covered by the sights of several. You cannot hope to resist," the larger one continued.

"May the light never reveal you and the shadows always hide you," Gin said. "And the peace of the sky be ever in your vision."

"Welcome home, sister," said the apparent leader and raised his hand in a closed fist. "May your sights remain polished, and your missiles always fly true."

That was the customary response to a blessing of those people.

"And a welcome to your companions," the large guard continued. "This is Burgh Sceadwia; the Burrow of the Shadow. You will find rest and wisdom in this place. If you need anything, all you need do is ask. We will give you guidance, or protection, as you require it."

Gin thanked them, and the group entered the closest of the large mounds. They passed underneath an archway with a wide and well lit avenue that ran straight through the bottom of the hill and out the other side. Several smaller hallways and staircases led out of it on the sides. Gin led them up several flights of stairs to a room that was plentiful in its comforts. The furniture was soft and plush, the tables had plates of food and pitchers of drinks, and the most breathtaking of elements was the view through the windows. They were on the opposite side of where they entered the hill. The subterranean world had been hidden by the mound they were in, but the large single pane windows allowed them an extraordinary view of the rest of the city below.

There were many more buildings and smaller hills that had portions carved out to accommodate the rising floors of other structures. Between the businesses and homes were streets that had plenty more people milling about and going about their day. The daylight from above beamed down on the city and gave it a pleasant appeal, even there beneath the ground, hidden in a cave.

"Make this place your home for the time being," Gin said. "These are the guest's quarters, and there's no telling how long we might be here. The Council is not known for brevity. I will go see them and tell them what I know."

"What about Orvar?" Adger asked eagerly. "Is he here?"

"I would assume he is, but at this point, I know as little as you do. I was in the city above far longer than is customary."

With that, Gin left, and it was just the four of them again. Simon was grateful for the change in pace. He immediately took the bag off his back and threw it with his coat on the floor. He went straight for the table of food, and Adger soon followed. The other two lingered but eventually dropped their burdens as well. Filch walked over to the window to gaze on the city.

"I don't like waiting like this," Bromle said strolling to the window too, grabbing a fat roll, and tossing it into the air. "This was too easy." He looked out the window at the city while he tore a hunk out of the bread. He watched for a while and noted Gin walking deeper into the city and out into the streets. The further she got from them, the harder it was to see where she went. He lost sight of her for a moment and looked to Filch. She pointed without looking at Bromle. Their suspicion was similar.

"That's only because everything else has been so hard," Simon said.

"Shouldn't we have had a hero's welcome? I thought you were the harbinger of victory and the fall of Etnian," Bromle said.

"It doesn't seem that my arrival came with a shout; more of a whisper."

"Everyone hopes for a hero," Adger said. "Once people realize who you are, word will spread."

After they had eaten, Simon took the opportunity to pull out the books that Adger had given them. One of them was a bestiary, another on swords, and the last on various, peculiar elements of Dyurndale. The relaxed pace was pleasant but somewhat unnatural. There hadn't been much peace in his journey.

Even Bromle and Filch took the time to pick at the buffet. Filch walked back to the window with a plate of food and continued staring out at the city which was becoming darker. Lights in the streets started to turn on, and the sky in the opening of the cavern far above gave way to the littering of stars. Simon and the brothers all found comfortable chairs to sit in and all three of them soon dozed off.

Hours passed and Filch stood watch while the others slept. Streetlights cast an orange glow on the streets below, and white lights illuminated the sides of many of the hills. The lights weren't able to eliminate the oddity of the underground city, but it did give it a metropolitan appeal.

"We have a problem," Filch said sharply enough to wake the others.

Bromle jerked awake and jumped up to join Filch at the window; the empty plate that was resting on his stomach clattered to the ground and roused the others. Simon quickly awoke and rubbed the sleep from his eyes. He stood up a little shakily and slapped Adger's feet to wake him. Filch was standing at the window and pointing down towards a company of guards that was running in formation towards them from the direction Gin had gone.

"I told you!" Bromle said. "I knew she'd betray us."

"What are you talking about?" Simon said while unable to stifle a yawn.

"Get your things, you two," Bromle said. "We need to leave."

"Hold on, what makes you think anyone's coming for us? We're expected."

"Look!" Filch said, still standing at the window.

Adger and Simon walked over to the window to see what she was pointing at. Far down in the streets below, the company of guards was getting closer to the hill they were in. One guard stayed ahead and to the left of the squadron to lead as he was running with them. The guard pointed up in their direction and the company stopped for a moment to look. They all started running again with a quickened pace; their arms swung more fervently, sacrificing a modicum of form for the sake of speed. Streetlights glinted off their armor.

"I don't understand," Adger said in the middle of a yawn. "Why would they be coming for us? They must be pointing at something else."

"No, not them; to the left there, beyond them," Filch said.

Two of the armored people were struggling with a much smaller figure; dragging her out of a doorway.

"Gin!" Bromle said.

Her hood was pulled back, and her red curls could easily be seen even at the distance the group was from the ground.

"See, Brom? She *didn't* betray us," Adger said.

"We need to get out of here," Simon said.

Adger and Simon quickly gathered their belongings without further argument. Despite still being a bit drowsy, Adger quickly walked over to the table and grabbed several pieces of food, stuffing them into his bag; Simon followed his lead. Judging from the urgency the guards rushed in their direction, they both assumed it might be best to get their provisions from what was available.

Filch ran to the door and quietly opened it. She stepped out into the hallway to see if it was clear. She turned and nodded at the rest of them. She opened the door, and Bromle charged through, taking the lead.

"Keep quiet," Simon said and ran after him. "Bromle! We can't win this fight. We need to understand what's happened here before we decide to take the whole city on."

Bromle stopped and turned in the hallway. "Okay then, what's the plan?"

The other two companions joined them in the hallway.

"We need to find out what happened with Gin. Going out the main entrance might not be the best idea. I suggest we get outside on the hill. The city is dark and we might go unnoticed if we stay off the main roads. We can only hope one of these windows opens."

"At the end of the hallway there," Filch said. "It looks like it may be an escape route."

The window at the end of the hall had signs around it to suggest it was an escape in the event of a building fire, or similar disaster. They rushed to the window and threw it open. They clambered out the frame and onto the grassy side of the mountainous building. It was inclined in a way to make it easy enough to ascend but only while walking, using hands as well as feet.

Filch was the last one out and closed the window behind her just as the guards rushed onto the floor where they were staying. They kicked in the door and rushed into the room that the group was in.

By the time the guards had an idea where they might have gone, they were halfway down the outside of the hill. Another mountain-building connected to the one they were on. They ran up the side of it once they descended the other one. They ran around the outside of it with minor difficulty, but the incline made the task more arduous. They circled on the side closest to the cavern entrance to avoid being seen in the lights of the city. The darker side of the hill gave them a minor sense of safety.

"What are we going to do?" Adger asked.

"Filch, did you happen to see where they took Gin?" Simon asked.

"Only that they were dragging her deeper into the city. I suggest we get to the top. At the very least, it would give us a better vantage point."

"Scout ahead and report back to us. We'll do our best to stay hidden for the time being. We don't have your advantage of invisibility."

She nodded her head and disappeared up the side of the hill into the darkness.

"What about us?" Adger said.

Bromle chimed in, "We need to chase those guys down and—"

"You'll get your chance, Bromle," Simon interrupted, "for now though, we need to understand what's going on without rushing in."

"What could have possibly happened?" Adger inquired. "I thought Orvar was going to be here already. What if those guards were there to escort us to the hero's banquet—to the hero's welcome—I mean, the food that we had was good but, I don't know. The reception was kinda lonely."

"The only escort we were going to get was to a cell," Bromle retorted.

"I think we have to face the possibility that creating an army will take some convincing," Simon said. "Bromle took some convincing; maybe they thought she was lying. You don't survive genocide without paranoia. Maybe she was taken for something else entirely, but the amount of people that were heading our way would suggest otherwise. And judging from their armaments, I don't think they were coming to escort us to a banquet."

"Then what do you suggest?" Adger asked.

"I suggest we move quietly and you lower your voices," Filch said from the shadows above them on the hill.

"What'd you find out?" Simon asked.

"There are a lot of guards down there. It looks like they're going from building to building. It is possible that they don't know what we look like. Either way, anyone they meet on the streets gets forced back inside. Whatever we choose to do, we need to stay unseen."

"We're not breaking up. Whatever we do, we need to stay together."

"I think we should just leave," Bromle said. "You have the books. Can't you learn what you need from them?"

"I just grabbed those because I thought they might help," Adger said. "Besides, where would we go?"

"Maybe the map will tell us."

"We're not leaving without Gin; we owe her our lives," Simon said. "And Orvar may be the only one that knows where Naru is. For now, we rescue Gin and, at least, find out why she was taken."

They all nodded their heads.

"Did you see where they took her, Filch?"

"Unfortunately, no. Without knowing the city, I am unsure where to look. The streets are swarming with those guards though. Exploration will be difficult. I did notice where the majority of them were headed. There is a larger mound about three hills away. It is also the most well-lit in the city, whereas the rest are darkened."

"So, you want to go where the most soldiers and lights are?" Bromle asked.

"I doubt they would keep her in the darkest and least guarded."

Bromle had no retort because he knew Filch was right.

"What if you're wrong?" Adger said. "What if this is all a big misunderstanding?"

"I admire your optimism," Simon said, "but I don't think we're that fortunate—based on the welcoming I've had so far. No matter what, staying here deliberating isn't helping us. We should head that direction and trust Filch's assessment. Could Unaketay be of any use to us?"

"Of course she could!" Adger said.

"You have Una?" Bromle said with a nearly indiscernible amount of weakness in his voice.

"And Ketay, but I thought you didn't care about anything back home."

Bromle's demeanor changed as he realized the momentary lapse in his composure.

"Adger, please," Simon interrupted. "Our allies are few, and time is not one of them."

Adger pulled out both stones and held them together for a moment before he dropped them to the ground, and they glowed to life as before. The light it produced was uncomfortable to them in the darkness, but the shape of Unaketay quickly emerged. The stone raccoon excitedly jumped at Bromle in the same way that it had with Adger. Bromle tried to hide his reciprocal joy at seeing the pet but was unable to mask the smile that found its way onto his face. He reached down and rubbed the creature's back.

"Now, who has something of Gin's for her to pick up the scent," Adger asked as he looked to the lot of them.

The group was silent as the only hope they had was rapidly fading. Simon looked down at his hands: empty but dirty from Gin's search of the alaidak.

"My hands!" Simon exclaimed a bit too loudly for the concealment they hoped to maintain.

They all looked at him with perplexed expressions.

"Well, not my hands but my arm; here. I couldn't get this alaidak gunk cleaned off."

"That may work," Adger said.

Simon held out his arm to Unaketay.

"Stay in the shadows, girl," Adger said to the creature.

Unaketay sniffed Simon's arm for only a moment and turned around and ran. The group chased it and Simon couldn't help but feel the excitement of pursuit. True to Adger's order, Unaketay stayed to the shadows. They all ran up and around several more of the mounds in the city. The windows were dark within and if ever they came to one that was open or lit, the raccoon hurriedly altered its course without command. The last hill they were on ended in the streets below and the safety of the shadows ended in a definite line of light.

Unaketay stopped just at the edge of the light. Without slowing their pace in the pursuit of the animal, Filch pulled something from her cloak and pointed it at the light above. The light flickered and went out. Unaketay immediately continued its lead and stopped each time to wait for Filch to extinguish the lights.

They ducked behind the buildings in the streets. After a few additional tense moments and bated pauses, the group arrived high up on the brightest and busiest of building-mounds. The four of them had waited farther down on the hill in an especially dark dip in the mound. Boulders provided additional cover for them along the way up the hill. The raccoon had gone ahead to search for Gin and was excitedly pointing at a dark and barred window further up. Adger beckoned the creature back, who split into pieces with the reward and praise of Adger. Bromle bent down and picked up Una, the red stone; Adger picked up Ketay, the green one.

"She's there," Adger said. "If Unaketay says she's there, then she most certainly is."

"They'll be watching her cell for sure," Simon said.

"I'll go see if she's there," Filch said and got up to move.

"No; let me this time. I know I don't have your abilities, but I'll go."

He looked to his cloak which turned a mixture of blacks and grays with subtle hints of dark greens. It was the perfect camouflage for ascending a dark hill. Simon slowly made his way up the hill; stopping occasionally to listen to the sounds of the city. The sound of crickets was reassuring to him; giving him a semblance of peace despite the threat he was in. He heard no shouts or alarms that might signal his discovery. He took his time avoiding the lights of several windows on the hillside. Unaketay's size and agility was a luxury that Simon did not have, but he was no less determined to make the short ascent quickly. He came just below the barred window and whispered Gin's name. He was worried that she wasn't in there, despite Adger's assurance. He wondered if there was a group of guards waiting to spring the trap he was sure he was walking into.

A long moment passed. Simon could barely hear his own voice let alone hope that anyone inside the cell would be able to.

"Simon?" Gin's voice whispered from within; also barely audible above the crickets echoing through the cavern.

"Yes! Yes, it's me!"

"You have to get out of here."

"Why were you taken? We saw you from the window of our room."

They both kept their voices low and barely audible.

"The Elders of Origin—the Council—they've...I'm afraid they've lost their way. I hadn't actually spoken to them before. I might'a forgotten to mention that they didn't actually send me. I thought I would've had more time to explain, ya see? Orvar found me in the ruins a few weeks ago—not sure how that old man did so either; I thought I was better at staying hidden. I almost shot him when I first saw him. He told me about ya and where to watch for ya."

"But why are you in prison?"

"They don't believe in you, Simon! They think that Orvar is crazy and that I'm trying to stage a coup."

"I thought my arrival was a good thing. Aren't I supposed to rid the world of evil and all that?" Simon thought aloud, mostly to himself.

"There are those who will take more convincing than others. It's been a long age of oppression and rumors of salvation do little more than remind people of that. Our entire civilization was decimated, and now we hide here in the ground. There's not much hope for someone like you, and your arrival is late. Some people are happy to hold on to hope while others, like the Council, see your coming as the end of their control. People have to have faith in what's given to them, and the Council, for all their faults, is the one who's been providing for our people for centuries."

The weight of the realization pressed heavily on Simon. He hadn't once considered that there would be resistance from those he was there to help.

"Has everybody here lost faith? Orvar said he came to raise an army so he must've believed there would be some who would listen."

"A lot have faith, yes, but more have doubts."

"Where is Orvar?"

"I didn't see him. I barely told my story to the Council before they dragged me away. Their chambers are not far from here but if they find you, they'll surely kill you. They've been in power too long to give it up. I hoped that my fears were wrong, but their actions proved me right. I'd wager you'll have to rally the support of the people before you can eliminate the majority faith in the Council. You need to forget about me and find Orvar. I've done my part to get you here, but I'm not sure I can be of further use to ya."

"Bromle could probably blast this wall out."

"No! If you do that, you'll be caught. We're lucky enough not to have been heard yet. If you can change the minds of the council, my freedom will come. This isn't the first time I've found myself in here. The council may be corrupt, but they're not without mercy, or hospitality."

"You give them too much credit," a muffled voice said.

"What did you say?" Gin said.

"I didn't say that," Simon said.

"I said it," said the voice. "And if I can hear you, the guards likely can. I would guess they've allowed your conversation more than overlooked it."

"Orvar?" Gin said.

"Yes, it's me. I'm in the cell next to you. You two were scheming so well, I didn't want to interrupt you. I had to give up my room with a view to get this one when I heard they caught you, Gin. There are some loyal Kalinaw left yet. Simon, is it?"

Simon walked over to the window adjacent to Gin's. Orvar's room was dark, and Simon couldn't see where he was. Orvar came into view from the side closest to Gin's room and startled Simon. He had a bare chin and a white mustache that fed into wide flared chops that framed his face like a saucer.

"Pleased to finally meet you," he said and thrust his hand through the bars.

Simon took his hand, which Orvar vigorously shook.

"Oh, yes, that's a good firm handshake. You'll do just fine. Why don't you get my good friends, the brothers, and have Bromle get us out of here. I could probably have talked my way out, but once I realized the Council had lost their faith, I figured you'd end up here too. So, I stay put."

Simon was a bit skeptical of his confidence, which brought to mind questions about how Orvar knew as much as Adger said he did.

"How could you have possibly known that I would find Adger?"

"I can't give up all my secrets, but if you must know, the Kalinaw is the only strength left in this world to fight Etnian. I knew that of all people who would believe in you and find a way to help you, it would be Adger. I left the letter for him because I knew your paths would cross."

"You didn't really answer my question."

"He has a way of doing that," Gin said in the cell next to them.

Orvar continued, "I've been a part of the Kalinaw since long before Kapell fell asleep in the sea."

Simon thought how old that would make him based on what Kapell had told him. His face revealed his confusion.

"Yes, I'm quite old. I'm glad Kapell at least pointed you to the Kalinaw. Although...it seems this branch of it has long since lost their understanding of what is right, and what is corruption. Come now, let's be on our way."

Simon checked on Gin before descending the mountain to where the others had waited for him. They were farther down than he remembered. Some of the boulders he passed looked familiar, like where he thought they had been waiting for him; his anxiety began to grow. He turned a dark corner of the hill to see of a swarm of oversized mechanized dragonflies buzzing in the air with the city's guards as riders. They all had spotlights mounted underneath them and were shining them where Simon's companions were crouched and vulnerable in the open.

Simon started to step out to challenge the guards and rescue his companions. He reached for his sword, but Filch caught his eye. She shook her head nearly imperceptibly. Simon stepped back into the shadow of the large stone he was behind. Guards swarmed over the hillside and rushed at them. Bromle hit a couple, but his resistance was more spiteful than productive. Extra guards ran to Bromle and it took a group of them to eventually subdue him. Adger, all the while, was shouting at his brother to settle and go peaceably; Simon couldn't rightly hear what he was saying, but it was obvious he was trying to placate him. Bromle sidestepped the first two guards that rushed him and caused them to nearly lose their footing down the side of the hill. Another two quickly rushed towards him and grabbed his arms, but he slammed them into each other as easily as closing a book. The remaining guards pointed their weapons at him as the others rushed to begrudgingly tighten his restraints.

The guards dragged the three of them away until the hillside was dark again. The crickets were unable to offer Simon any peace. He felt completely alone. He ran back up the hill to Orvar and Gin and told them what happened.

"I think I can get you out of here," Simon said and pulled out his sword.

"Wait," Orvar said. "You need to stay close to them. Follow them, and if they are taken to the Council, take care not to be seen.

"I...I need your help though."

"There will be a time when you must walk this path alone. For now, it is to our advantage that you haven't been found. If you raise an alarm by granting our freedom now, our element of stratagem may be forfeit. We will be fine here. Now go!"

Simon turned to go, unsure of which way to start.

"Wait!" Orvar called after him a bit loudly. "Find a guard. On their wrists, they wear a communication device of sorts. Don't be scared of it...it will help us speak at great distances."

"We called it a radio where I came from."

Orvar sounded surprised. "Really? ...I have many questions for you; another time though. Pull the dial up and turn it..." He looked down at a device he pulled from inside his coat. "...four—no, five clicks to the left. Push it back down and we can speak to each other."

Simon's confidence weakened. Not only was Simon chasing a group of flying guards with his companions in tow, he now had to subdue one of them. Instead of heading down, Simon climbed up the hill hoping to get a direction to continue his pursuit. As he climbed the hill, he also made his way around it in the direction his companions were taken. The closer he got to the city-side of the mountain, the more apprehensive he became.

Lights from the city below were directed up towards the hillside and were focused in spots on its face. Various features were highlighted that Simon easily could have descended to. That side of the hill had several entrances and balconies sticking out into the city, but the way they were illuminated made them the poorest of his choices for descent. Guards repeatedly walked out onto the balconies or out of the entrances far below. There were none above him, and it was slightly darker where he was crouched but not enough where he would be overlooked under the scrutiny of a keen eye. He planned his descent and where he should go next.

His companions were quickly being pulled out of an entrance at the base of the hill by a much smaller group of guards on foot. The urgency with which they were ushered along gave Simon a surge of encouragement. A guard walked out onto the balcony closest to him, and without giving it much thought, Simon jumped and landed on the guard's back. The fall wasn't without discomfort, but it was enough to render his victim unconscious.

Simon flipped him over briskly, and the guard stirred; his eyes fluttered open. Simon was grateful the guard's face wasn't covered like the others and he punched him hard. The guard stilled. Simon found the radio and quickly removed it from the guard's wrist. It was a circular metal disc on a leather strap, and for a moment, Simon wasn't sure if he picked up what might have been the guard's watch instead. He crouched down and looked again, but there was nothing else that matched Orvar's description. He looked at the face and there was a dial around the perforations of a speaker screen. He turned the dial as Orvar instructed, and when it clicked into the fifth detent, Orvar's voice came through.

"Simon, is that you?" he whispered. Simon jumped as Orvar's voice trumpeted into the quiet around him.

"How do I turn it down?"

"Ah, there you are! Turn it to the right. If you need to silence it, turn it all the way down and continue turning until it closes."

Simon turned the device down to a whisper.

"I see them down below," he said. Simon climbed over the balcony and back onto the face of the hill. He crawled underneath the outcropping in case another guard snuck up behind him.

"They're likely taking them to the Council, who seem to control the judicial balance that the Sceadwians—these people of the Burgh—were once known for."

"Well, how am I supposed to get close to them?"

"How large was the guard? Gin mentioned your coat is like the Sceadwians. If you wear some of his armaments, you may pass as one of them."

Simon climbed back onto the balcony and quickly took some of the guard's armor. Despite how heavy the pieces looked, they were as light as paper. It was easy for him to slip on the chest piece over his shirt, and the rest of the armor fit over his clothes without difficulty. He had to remove the pouches on his belt and consolidate some of his belongings in his bag. Underneath one of the pouches there was an empty place on his belt that he hadn't noticed before. It looked to be about the same length as his hilt and deep enough to serve as a receptacle for it. The pouch his hilt was in was indeed the largest of the pouches that Simon had, so he removed it and the hilt fit in his belt perfectly. It blended in so well that unless a person knew the weapon was there, it was easily overlooked. He was pleased with the concealment the belt provided for his weapon and the armor fit him better without the superfluous pouches.

He put his coat on over his armor and the bag he got from Orvar's home. He pulled a scarf from the guards remaining clothes and wrapped it around half of his face. The guard hadn't moved, despite being stripped of his armaments. Simon dragged him to one side of the door leading to the balcony and tore the man's shirt to use as improvised bindings.

He assumed running down the side of the hill towards the street would seem out of place, but he didn't want to get lost inside a structure he was unfamiliar with. He jumped over the balcony and let gravity do its work: rushing him down the incline until he reached the streets below. He tried his best to stay in the darker places of the hill during his falling sprint. Having not heard any shouts when he finished, he assumed he had gone unnoticed. He could see his companions still being escorted down the road and they were nearly out of sight. He looked around the streets that were mostly unoccupied; only a sparse soldier or briskly paced citizen was noted. He sprinted towards his friends, hoping to keep up with them.

He followed them through the streets, taking turns and passing through wide roads underneath several mountains. All the while he closed the distance between them. The guards led their prisoners to a stone mountain that wasn't covered with grass like the other ones he had seen so far. The mound was carved with intricate images and scenes, impossible to ignore; Simon was unable to look away. He had seen similar things before, but only in museums, or pictures of ancient civilizations recording their history on the walls of their tombs. It seemed slightly out of place, considering the technology the city seemed to possess, but it only made the building exude more grandeur. Simon's feet kept him moving towards his companions who slowed as they approached the mountain.

"Guard! You! Why are you falling behind? Come help us with these heretics."

It took Simon a moment to realize they were talking to him. He tucked his chin a little lower and hoped the guards didn't all know each other well enough to betray his disguise. He walked over to the group and grabbed Filch by the arm as she was closest to him. He saw the recognition in her eyes as they flared ever so slightly. The group started moving again towards the large carved mountain.

"We need to take these ruffians directly to the Council to see what they think of them," the guard said. "And we'll all be standing there proudly to receive the commendations we deserve for making the arrest."

Simon's stomach tightened. Instead of rescuing them, he was escorting them to the one place he was meant to avoid.

14 The Council

Simon followed along with the group of guards and their captives, knowing that it would be better to be close to them than hope to find them later on his own.

"You lot will fetch us a nice heap of money," the lead guard bragged to Bromle, Adger, and Filch. He wore a golden band around his right arm with a crest of a phoenix on it. It was the only thing that set him apart from the others, and he was the only one who spoke in the group. "That's roight," he kept on in a cockney accent. He shouted and laughed boisterously as the other guards shoved their captives along.

Simon stayed to the back of the group out of the direct sight of the guards and kept his head low.

"That Thaygin girl thinks you lot are supposed to be some bit of heroes," the lead guard said again.

"What did you do with her?" Adger demanded.

One of the other guards spun and backhanded him. A cut emerged on his face.

"That's what questions'll get ya. She brought outsiders here—twice—and as such, she got herself in a bit of trouble. They might go more easy on you if you tell us where your other friend is."

Adger glanced back at Simon when he thought the other guards wouldn't notice. Simon shrugged his shoulders to express his confusion of what to do. Adger started slowing moving a hand to the protruding handle of some weapon Simon could just see sticking from beneath his jacket. Simon held up an open hand to Adger and mouthed *Wait*.

The group approached the gates of the mountain fortress at a more casual pace than when they were walking through the city streets. Simon assumed that the sight of the mountain put the guards more at ease. As they got closer to the massive, building-sized doors, a smaller one opened to the side of them. The guards shoved the prisoners through, and Simon followed along behind them while a guard closed the door. Simon kept his head low and was relieved that the small entrance they were in was dark. It connected to a hallway that turned sharply towards the interior of the fortress. After a moment in the stifling hallway, they stepped out into a cavern within the mountain. He shook his head in amazement despite the situation they were in.

"What you shakin' your head about," said the guard closest to him in a thick accent.

Simon was grateful that his fear was masked. He lowered his voice and tried to sound a little tougher than his natural tone might sound.

"Just looking forward to getting rewarded," Simon said.

The guard stared at him for a second and Simon felt the blood rush to his forehead as if he was about to start perspiring.

"Not more than me!" the guard laughed and slapped him on the back.

There were more guards in the fortress sparsely spread out at various doorways of the buildings that were carved out of the stone and were as ornate as the outside of the mountain. Scenes of battles were depicted on every blank wall, which gave the place even more brilliance. The guards all wore the same kind of armor as what Simon had stolen; blending in would not be a problem for him. Still, he wondered how well the guards knew each other and worried he was obviously an outsider.

He walked with the group of guards, escorting his companions down the narrow paths of the fortress. He was walking close enough for any other guard to see he was out of place, but he went unnoticed. Their march went on until they came to the largest building that was a round tower that curved backwards to intersect the outer wall. Buildings were conjoined beside it but were smaller and plain, demanding less attention; even with their inscriptions. This massive structure dwarfed the others and reached to the upper limits of the mountain and pierced through its uppermost domain.

The guards led them inside where two of the guards left the group. Simon felt less comfortable with reduced numbers but continued to follow his companions. They descended several flights of stairs to a short row of rooms with small barred cells. They put each one of the prisoners in a separate cell.

"We'll see what the Council decides to do with you in the morning," one of the guards said.

Simon pushed Filch into a cell and whispered to her, "I'll get you out of here."

"What'd you say?" one of the guards said to him.

"I said, let's get out of here," Simon quickly replied.

He followed the guards up and out of the building back onto the street. They walked towards the front gates, patting each other on their backs, proud of their capture. Simon used their excitement to his advantage and turned down a dark corner as the guards walked away from him. Once they left the mountain, Simon turned back towards the cells. His inclination was to sneak in the shadows, but his subterfuge had been successful up to that point. He tried to walk casually, but his efforts seemed to gain lasting looks from the guards. He quickened his pace until he entered the building with the prison cells.

He made his way back down to the cells and checked on each one of his companions.

"Bromle, can you break out and get the others?" Simon asked.

"They took my gloves."

"And my tools," Adger said.

"Maybe I can get us out of here," Simon said and pulled out his hilt.

"Wait!" said Orvar over the wrist radio. "If you break them out inside that fortress, you might as well lock yourself in one of those cells. There must be another way."

"Maybe I can get some keys from one of the guards."

"That would work," Bromle said. "Just take that sword of yours and run 'em through!"

"I doubt that's your best choice," Filch said.

"They don't know what I look like though," Simon said.

"So, you're going to just go up to one of the guards and ask for his keys?"

"Trying to get any of us out of our cells isn't an option right now," Orvar interrupted. "For now, you must be patient, Simon. Stay close to your friends, but I would not stay too close. There's nothing you can do for any of us right now. For now, you must wait and listen. There may be something more we can learn in this situation. If we're lucky, the guards won't realize what they've taken from your friends."

"I would start by finding us a way out of the Burgh," Filch said.

"I'll see what I can find out," Simon said and left his friends in the cells to go explore the fortress.

Simon was tired but could neither find a place to rest nor could he possibly be at ease. He left the guard tower behind to venture in streets that were even emptier than before. The entrances to buildings were no longer guarded, and only a couple sentries walked in the space between the buildings. The reduced presence of guards made Simon feel more exposed. He walked along the streets to gaze at the carvings on the walls and also to create a mental map in the event that he would need a hasty retreat. From what he could tell, the only exit amongst the buildings seemed to be the gates.

"Orvar," Simon said into his wrist.

"I'm here," Orvar whispered.

"What do you know about this place?"

"Burgh Sceadwia was once a haven for the local cities. It's not a perfect place by far, but it's managed to stay hidden from the enemy for centuries. The Elders of Origin were some of the oldest and self-proclaimed wisest of the survivors. They easily filled the vacuum of power that the war created, and now they lead by exclusive consensus with no outside influence."

"Did you say, 'Centuries'? How is that possible?"

"Time moves differently here; that's one of the worst exacerbations of Etnian's evil reign. People have been under his thumb for a very long time, and a good portion of them have been around to experience all of it."

"Wouldn't old age claim them eventually?"

"If the Council died here, they'd likely be put right back into power. My thoughts lean towards collaboration."

"Once again, you didn't exactly answer me," Simon said with a nervous grin.

"Even before the end of Dyurndale's beauty, there was still the possibility of accidental death on the Path. If something like that happened in the past, the unfortunate person would be given another opportunity to experience the wonderful walk of Dyurndale. The fissures, that would allow people to reemerge in the world, were quickly discovered by the Foul Tormentor. He built prisons around every crack he could find and—to the best of my research—he's nearly found them all. He happily kills people over and over again, or deceives them with promises of power. Most people choose servitude over endless death."

"I can see why. Do you know where the Council members are?"

"I have no knowledge of where they are individually, but their seats of power are in Fort Burgh."

Simon looked back towards the tallest of the buildings where the cells were. He craned his neck up towards the ceiling where it seemed to protrude from the crest of the cavern. He wondered if there was a way out through the roof, and he went back inside the building to find out.

"I think they took us to the fort," Simon said.

"If I've learned anything about the Council, they'd have a back door close by," Orvar said. "Finding a different way out of here is likely your most advantageous task."

Simon listened for any sounds when he entered the building again, but the hallways were quiet. He heard the distant scuffle of someone moving in the building and sped along to find a quiet corner to sit in until the clarity of direction came to him. He wasn't sure how elaborate the hallways were, or how he would lead his companions through them again if he managed to rescue them.

How am I supposed to help them, he thought to himself. *How am I supposed to save this world?*

He continued his exploration with only the quiet company and whispers of Orvar.

"Orvar, I…I really don't know how to be a hero. I feel like I've been luckier than I have been heroic, and if I'm to actually defeat Etnian, I need help."

"You have the sword and you have the shield, don't you? Gin told me how you handled those alaidak in the streets. Only a hero could have made that kind of an attack."

"I've used the sword before, but I haven't exactly been able to use it consistently. I've tried a few times, and I can only seem to make my weapons work by accident."

"It's likely fear or excitement that's helped you in the past. You need to have more faith in the strength you have inside you. The strength to wield those weapons has always been a part of you; that's why you were chosen to be our hero. It wasn't an accident that brought you here; you were *chosen*."

"I was nothing special before this though. I made just enough money to provide for my family—we weren't poor by any means, but—well, it was enough for us. I was nobody in my life before."

"But you weren't nobody to everybody," Orvar said.

"I had a family, yes: a wife and three beautiful children."

The recollection made his voice quiver and he almost lost his composure especially there on his own. Simon's mind drifted to them and that swooning sickness returned; the same kind he had felt the last time his family was the focus of his thoughts. His knees weakened and he braced himself against the nearby wall.

"Be cautious!" Orvar's voice gave him clarity. "Thoughts like those can consume you. Knowing there was a life before is important but knowing how to suppress it is even more so. And whatever you do, guard that knowledge. If the enemy knows you remember, it can be used against you. Death would be a welcome escape. But, that's not what is meant for you, so think nothing of it! I can help you learn how to use your weapons efficiently, but the *ability* to do so is already within you."

Simon stopped to listen for any sounds in the hallways. Silence on the other side of the radio told him that Orvar was doing the same.

"Did Adger have the foresight to grab some of my books?" Orvar asked, a glint of pride in his words.

"Yeah, but I haven't really had the time to read them."

"You should read them in depth but, for now, we might be able to get you some preliminary knowledge of the sword. Can you suspend your search for a moment and find a place to sit down?"

Simon spent a few minutes searching some of the rooms closest to him. There was a dining hall, several locked rooms, empty bunk rooms, and even a small library. He chose a quiet corner behind some shelves in the library.

"Okay, now what?" Simon asked.

Did Adger manage to bring the book called, *The Guide of Nyawa Geni?*

"Yup, it's right here," he said, pulling the book out of the bag. He turned over the worn red leather tome in his hands and admired its strong binding. "Who is Nyawa Geni?"

"Nyawa Geni is not a person; it is a mindset. It is the fire of the soul and the key to understanding how to fight from within you, before you fight from without."

Simon was confused, as was often his reaction to the old man.

"What does it smell like?" Orvar asked him.

"What?" Simon asked as he scrunched his face, sure that he had misheard.

Orvar patiently repeated himself. "What does the book smell like?"

Simon hesitated but obliged and sniffed the edges of the book. "Old; like an old bookstore with—it smells like your house actually."

"No, not what's on the outside. Get your nose in the binding. A good book is like a breath of fresh air."

"I'll admit, I've enjoyed the good sniff of a book here or there, but this is getting weird."

Nevertheless, Simon opened the book and breathed in deeply. The smell from inside the book was stronger than that of the old pages and pipe tobacco on the outside. It was a fresher smell; sweet flowers in full bloom. It was enticing. Simon breathed deeply and felt peacefully drowsy. His face fell into the book and he drifted into hypnagogia. Images flashed in his mind of swords and fighting stances. He didn't just observe the things he saw, but he was able to retain them. His face was pulled deeper into the binding of the book and the images he saw became even more frequent and vivid. The library disappeared from around him and Orvar's fading words that chased after him fell away.

Reality slowly returned to him and he awoke to a bright, sunlit new scene. He was standing on the foliated edge of a small lake, nestled in the crater of a dormant volcano. The water's placidity was interrupted by the pinnacle of a short mound that sharply rose from the center of the lake. He turned around to see that the crater was surrounded by a fog, like it was floating in the clouds. There was no other living thing there except him.

A rumble in the ground made him wonder if the volcano was as lifeless as this new reality. The ground rumbled again and concentric ripples started to emanate from the small apex that pierced the lake. The vibration continued and Simon was reminded how Kapell had awoken to greet him so long ago. His first instinct was to wait and happily receive Kapell with a friendly salutation.

As Simon stood there, watching the ripples disturb the scenic water, the peak in the center of the lake exploded. The shockwave from the eruption knocked Simon down. Ashen clouds filled the sky in plumes dark enough to blot out the sun. The clouds stopped pouring from the pinnacle and were interrupted by the spewing magma that had percolated underneath the lake. Red light cast a fiery reflection off of the water, and steam quickly filled the crater as the lava started to splash into it.

Simon looked back towards the source of the eruption and thought he saw the outline of a man. He regarded it as another delusion in the already chaotic scene until the outline of the Man remained and even stepped out from the volcanic emission. The creature was made of the same molten rock that was shooting into the sky and he left flaming footprints behind him as he descended towards the steaming lake. The brightness of his fire diminished and darkened until his skin became more akin to cooling magma that had just started to solidify. His face was only composed of smoking blue eyes with bright flames that rose towards his forehead like wild eyebrows.

He bent low as he walked and dragged a hand in the streams of viscous rock beside him. He pulled his hand away and slowly extracted a string of hardening lava as he continued his interception with Simon. The rock continued to blacken and grow until a blade reflected the red of the streams pouring into the water below. The sword was three hands wide and twice as long as Simon was tall, and it became apparent that this was no emissary of Kapell.

Simon got to his feet and quickly went through the motions of extending his sword and shield; each time he did, it became more natural for him. The volcanic creature had reached the water, and when his toes first touched the steaming moisture, he started to run across the top of the water, raising his sword upward and backward. Simon readied for the attack and resolutely prepared to defend himself even though he was terrified. His enemy flipped over his head, flying through the air and struck at Simon.

Simon dropped to one knee and when the Man hit the shield, prismatic colors splashed onto the ground around them.

"Who are you?" Simon asked as he backed away and readied for the next attack.

The Man just looked at him with flaming blue eyes and Simon realized the thing had no ears to hear the question or mouth to reply with. Instead, the Man rushed Simon again and forced him into action. Simon thought of the flashes he saw while entering this strange delusion and felt an innate tightening of his muscles. He parried the incoming attack and deflected the additional swings that followed it. Simon swung with his shield that burned as brightly as the erupting volcano. He thrust his sword and missed but successfully avoided being severed by his enemy's weapon.

The two of them fought along the edge of the lake and the longer they did so, the more steam filled the crater. The moisture swirled around them and fled with each attack they hurled at each other. Simon's muscles burned with fatigue, but he felt empowered. He thought of what Orvar said; about believing he had the strength inside him to overcome the Man. A power grew from within him, like his lungs and stomach were filling with a mighty roar. He reflected on his actions in the streets of the abandoned city and remembered how it felt to use the power of the sword to overcome the challenge. He felt the strength flow from his gut and into his arms; a chill electrified his spine. The Man charged him one last time as the lower half of his face ruptured with a gaping tear for a mouth and vomited a burst of blue lava. Simon deflected it with his shield, crouched low, and thrust his sword upward through the Man's head.

The scene disappeared and Simon's eyes snapped opened to reveal the library again. He was unsure of how much time had passed.

"What happened?" Simon asked Orvar. "I was…somewhere else…there was—I *know*—I know how to fight!"

"There's more than one way to read a book," Orvar said. "Knowledge is one thing, but technique and experience is something else entirely. I would recommend you thumb through the other books Adger gave you, but focus the very little time you have going over the book on swordplay. You may have to use that knowledge sooner than you think. There are many footsteps here for this time of night; even more than necessary for the disturbance that you and your companions have caused. I think the owner of your armor may have been found."

"How can I read at a time like this?"

"I will contact you if anything changes, but there is little else you can do until we find out what the Council wants with us all."

The radio went silent. Simon spent a few minutes thumbing through the books, especially the one on swordplay, but his ability to focus was infinitesimal. He put the books away and shook his head. He wondered how Orvar could seriously consider this as an appropriate time to study. He was grateful for the supernatural impartation the book was capable of; he couldn't imagine spending any time reading for the same effect. Despite his lack of practical application, Simon could not, in good conscience, leave his friends imprisoned while he studied; he had to find a way out. He was determined to find an alternative to them facing the Council.

He left the small library and continued wandering the halls looking for a way higher in the building. All the while, he kept his hand on his hilt in its new place. He heard no noises or voices in the building which made him less comfortable than if he heard voices he could avoid. There were several times he had to backtrack, but he was otherwise successful in his exploration. The greatest of his accomplishments was finding a small armory that had the group's belongings casually lying on a table.

"This is too easy," Simon said out loud.

"I admire your optimism; has your journey been met with ease so far?" Orvar's voice came over the radio.

"No, not that; I found their things just laying here."

"It's doubtful that they would fear an enemy inside their walls; especially inside the armory."

Simon took all their belongings and stuffed them in his bag which somehow held more than it seemed capable of.

The higher he climbed in the building, the more often the natural stone of the mountain pushed through into the passages.

I must be getting close, he thought.

With one final turn in the hallway, he entered a rather homely room with a few empty cots, carpets, and trunks. There was a ladder leading up to the roof and Simon excitedly rushed towards it. He climbed it and eased the hatch open that was at the top. A gust of fresh air almost pushed him back down the ladder, but he kept his footing. The hatch was in the lower part of a field with hills surrounding the basin. The ground around the hatch provided such camouflage that if he stepped out of the hatch, he feared he'd never find it again. The rays of morning's first light were burning the sky behind the hills. The air was warm and refreshing, compared to the cool, dark city below.

Simon was broken out of the spell though, and realized his time for rescue was almost gone. He quickly closed the hatch and descended the ladder. He retraced his steps as his memory could best manage. Voices echoed through the hallways as Simon quickly moved back towards his friends.

The buildings were filling with awakening life. He rushed past open doorways, hoping that he would continually be overlooked. He ignored the caution that had kept him occupied for so long.

He still hadn't formulated a plan, but knowing where an exit to the city was, he started developing one as he ran. He was unable to adhere to Orvar's advice; waiting for his friends to receive judgment felt unrealistic. Simon would break them out and then make his way to Orvar and Gin, fighting every guard on the way if he must. He skipped stairs and jumped to landings. He almost tripped several times, but having no knowledge of what the routines of this place were, he knew urgency was the only thing he could guarantee. He made it to the final turn in the stairs and heard familiar but slurred voices. He slowed his sprint to a crawl and stayed at the corner of the hallway to the cells. He peaked around the edge and saw a few guards standing before his allies' cells. They were a stone's throw away but too far to overcome them before they had time to react once Simon announced himself as their enemy.

"We're gonna be rich," one of the inebriates said.

"Let's get one thing straight—*hic*," said another voice. "I found these guys first."

A third voice, "Whatdya mean 'first'? There was ten of us."

"Okay, fine. We'll take credit and leave the rest of them—of those losers—on the…on the…the pub floor where they belong."

The second voice laughed and the others joined him.

Simon was able to rightly infer that these were the guards he had helped earlier in the night. They had been prematurely celebrating their capture of Simon's companions. Simon was determined to prove them wrong and foresaw no difficulties in subduing three intoxicated guards, no matter their size.

"Let's get them out of here and—*hic*—then we can get some sleep—"

"After the money!" said one of the other guards fumbling with the keys in one of the cell doors.

Simon stepped out from his hiding place, trying to look as strong and defiant as possible.

"Who are you, then?" said the one who had bragged the most earlier that evening. His head wobbled on his neck like a yard decoration on a spring.

"You're not going to get all the credit," Simon said. "I had a part in this too."

"Where've you been all night? I didn't see you with us at the…" the guard prattled on.

"I was here, watching them to make sure they didn't escape."

"I guess that's worth some credit. No trouble from their friend? No one's seen him—*hic*."

"Not a worry," Simon said. "It's been quiet all night."

"Hey you," said the lead guard stumbling a bit again, "Where's your mask there, guy?" The guard wobbled and widened his eyes to fight his fatigue and inebriation. Then he squinted, trying to focus on Simon again; he closed one eye as if looking down the sights of a gun. Both his eyes opened wide when he realized Simon was not at all an ally. "You're that— he's the other one!" He backhanded his closest comrade in the arm to rouse him and gain his attention and then inaccurately pointed in Simon's general direction. "He's the—*hic*—the last heretic!"

Simon thought he'd have more time to plan his attack, but realizing his ruse was discovered, he made his move. He reached to his belt, pulled out his hilt, and extended his sword to such intensity that the flames blackened the ceiling above.

"Well that's a fancy torch—*hic*—" one of the guards said, unimpressed by Simon's weapon.

Simon eyed the dangling keys in one of the cell doors. As if Bromle had heard his thoughts, one of the cell doors burst open, nearly breaking off its hinges. Bromle charged from it like a raging bull, even though his hands were still bound behind his back. He slammed two of the guards against the wall and they slid to the floor unconscious. The last guard spun to attack him but tripped on his own feet. Bromle laughed as he caught the falling guard in the chin with one knee. When it was apparent there was no threat from the guards, Simon extinguished his blade.

"Where have you been?" Bromle said. "I thought you'd break us out of here right away. Were you off drinking with your new friends?"

"Of course not," Simon said defensively. "I found the way out of here, but we need to get Orvar and Gin out first."

Simon rushed to the open cell door and grabbed the dangling keys. He released the others and removed all their bonds.

"So good to see you Simon!" Adger said excitedly, once Simon came into view of his cell.

Filch's face was still covered, but Simon thought he saw the effect of a smile around her eyes. "Thank you for coming back," she said with genuine appreciation.

"Well, I wasn't going to just leave you guys; I just had to develop an exit strategy. Orvar, are you two ready over there?" Simon said the last part into his wrist.

"They don't exactly have anywhere they can go," Bromle said as he was crouched over one of the guards and pulled a coin purse from his belt. "Hey, we should be compensated for our time here," he said defensively to his brother's scrutinizing glare.

There was no answer from the radio. Simon looked at the others.

"Orvar, you there?" There was still no answer.

"That's not good," Adger said. "We need to get our things back and get the others."

"I actually found your things." Simon handed them his bag.

"That's convenient," Bromle said. "Let's get to the hatch."

"What about Orvar and Gin?" Adger asked. "I can't believe you would actually leave them there, Brom!"

"It's not like they're being tortured. I'm sure they're comfortable. Besides, we don't even know Gin, although...she does have that fancy weapon."

"If Orvar vouches for her, then I trust her," Adger said with a rising inflection. "She helped us in the city and has done nothing to make us doubt her. She's a trustworthy person."

"Orvar is crazy. You can't actually believe—"

"Stop it!" Simon said. "Both of you. We're going back to get them.

Bromle, we'll need your help, but if you're adamant about staying, fine, but keep this place from being overrun. Filch, I need you to take the lead and scout ahead; you can move quickly without being seen. Take one of the guard's radios and we can follow behind."

"You'll need my help," Bromle said. "You can't actually hope to take on the whole city without me."

Adger rolled his eyes and Simon had a similar sentiment but was glad Bromle was arrogant enough to help. They all put their belongings back in the appropriate places and were ready to face the city.

"The sun is coming up so we won't have the benefit of darkness this time," Simon said.

The rattle of an armored person sounded from down the hallway. A guard stepped into the doorway with three more behind him.

"Finally," Bromle said and pounded a fist into his other hand.

"I got this," Simon said and stepped in front of him.

"You don't even know how to turn that thing on, do you?"

Simon pointed at the charred mark on the ceiling.

"Okay, yeah, but do you know how to *use* it?" Bromle said.

Simon didn't answer him but turned around, widened his stance, and extended the blade from the hilt again. The flames roared to life and again licked the ceiling above. Simon's companions took several steps back from the heat. Eyeing the burning fury of the sword, the guards took a slight step backward too. Simon closed his eyes and drew in a long breath. Flashes of his fight with the Man returned to him and he recalled the power that welled up from within him as he fought the muted creature. He could feel that familiar excitement at the confidence of being able to use the weapon he had been carrying for so long. His hands were warm with the heat of the handle, and it felt as if the weapon became an extension of his own arm.

The guards had widened eyes but stayed in place from their sense of duty. Their weapons were too long to be of much use to them in the limited confines of the hallway. They leaned their lance-guns against the wall and stepped towards Simon, drawing their own swords. They were short, and wide, and glowed around the edges from an internal illumination. The guards all charged Simon at the same time.

The flash of Simon's blade against the first guard's made the other two aggressors guard their eyes. Simon parried and pushed him back towards the other two. The guard stabbed at Simon and he deflected the move, stepped to the side, twisted his blade, and removed the guard's hand from his arm. His mouth opened to scream, but Bromle silenced him quickly by forcing his face into the wall like the two guards before.

Simon looked up at the other two guards and they charged him at the same time. Holding his sword in both hands, he deflected their slices and strikes both in front of him and at his back. Even in the confines of the small passage, Simon stepped nimbly to the side of each guard as they wildly swung at him. Their efforts were worthless when compared to how easily Simon wasted their strength.

The guards were quickly fatigued, but Simon's control and his fluidity allowed for a steady expenditure of energy. He stepped towards them and beat them back towards the doorway. They retreated under his attack but held their ground as best they could against the blazing sword. In one blinding motion, he gracefully swung his sword and cleaved the others'. The remnants of their weapons clattered against the floor. The guards looked at their swords, then at Simon, and both turned to run.

Filch threw her chakrams out the doorway after them, narrowly missing Simon's head. The weapons bounced off the walls and chased after the guards. The sound of metal sinking into flesh was followed by the sound of bodies falling to the floor. Filch went to retrieve her weapons and returned to wipe them off on one of the guard's cloaks.

Simon retracted his blade and turned to see the surprised expressions of the brothers.

"I'm a fast reader," Simon said with a wink. "Thanks for the books, Adger."

"The books helped then? Great!"

"We might make a hero out you yet," Bromle said and smiled.

"We need to get going," Filch said, trying to spur them to action.

The reunited companions made their way out of the building without resistance and rushed into the narrow streets of the mountain fortress. They froze in place on the stairs exiting the tall tower as they were opposed by an army that filled every available space in the streets. Simon and the others backed away towards the doorway they foolishly sprinted from, but when they started to move again, the groan of stretching bowstrings stayed their retreat.

From the center of the armored mass, in the main street that led back towards the giant gates, a group of guards parted like a choreographed formation to allow ten elderly people to step from amongst them. Their age was only apparent by their wrinkled faces and silver-haired heads; otherwise, the group seemed fully able-bodied. The elders were dressed differently than their guardians and had been well hidden by the mass until they had chosen to do otherwise. Their clothes were made of brighter color and grandeur than had been seen in the cavern so far. Long robes covered each of them that just barely touched the ground. They were of varying heights and builds, but their clothes were each tailored to fit them and it was apparent that they were not an adornment of ceremony

"Welcome to the city of Burgh Sceadwia!" said the central most person of the group of elders. He had silver hair combed back underneath a short mitre with the crest of a phoenix on the front. It was the only thing that set him apart from the others. He gestured to those around him, "We are the Elders of Origin; the Highest of Councils in the Kalinaw. We were told that you seek our help."

Simon was confused by their greeting. How could they welcome him before they imprison him? He stepped forward and tried to speak more confidently than he had done yet.

"I am Kynn Veyor, the hero of Dyurndale." Simon got chills from saying the words. It was a confirmation for himself as much as a declaration to the Elders. "I've been sent here to seek your aid in the downfall of the malicious beast: Etnian de Aithna. Yet, you've treated us as bandits."

"That is wonderful news!" said the Council member ignoring Simon's demand for an explanation. "I am Deocran Twinzinlee."

"And self-proclaimed leader of this senile group," Bromle said quietly so that only the four could hear him.

"Tell me," Deocran continued, "what proof have you that you are who you say you are?"

"I have the sword and shield of the hero."

"Who are you for us to take you at your word? Many have come before you with similar assertions. Plenty believe, but proof is something else entirely. *Show* us the weapons so that we might determine your truth."

Simon hesitated. It seemed that it would not be in his best interest to reveal where his weapons were hidden. Although his belt was ornate, he naively hoped that it was somehow just simple enough to be possibly overlooked. He hoped the Council didn't know more about him than he knew about himself. The song that Tortuse had told them was only a part of a longer ballad, and Simon had no idea if it told of his wondrous belt too. Either way, he wasn't about to give away the singular advantage he might have.

"I will show you who I am only if you extend a gesture of good faith by letting Orvar and Gin go. What crime have they committed?"

"Those dissenters are sowing seeds of corruption and are not worthy of freedom. Would you cast your lot in with them?"

Simon noticed a sudden change in the Council's demeanor. Orvar was right. The Council had lost its way, but the question was how far they had gone into the darkness.

"The only harm they cause is to the diminishment of your power. You fear losing your grip on this city. Instead of fighting the enemy, it seems like you've become one. How can you represent the Kalinaw and imprison those who would stop Etnian?"

"You sound like one of those hermits in the canyons out east. Your kind is ruled just as much as these people. You only serve to diminish your reputability. Our populace needs leadership; they want to be ruled. They are not wise enough to make decisions for themselves; we do it for them so that they can live their lives in peace."

"Age and wisdom don't always coincide. Fresh perspective can derive sound council."

The oldest council member laughed.

"That antiquated way of thinking is what got us here in the first place! Now we hide underground waiting for a hero that does not exist. You want us to believe you were sent here to provide salvation? We the Council are the voice and strength of this people. Only by submitting to the powers in this world are we able to remain at peace."

The four of them fully realized what he meant.

"You're in league with him too?" Adger shouted angrily. "Being a bunch of tyrants is one thing, but how can you actually submit to a creature who desires for more power, more death, and only destruction?" Adger's face turned red with anger. "I have friends who have died under the blade of his soldiers!" he continued. "You have that blood on your hands!"

Deocran was unaffected by Adger's accusation.

"He allows our order its strength and his permission allows us to flourish," Deocran said. "How could we continue developing who we are as a people? Do you honestly think a city of this size has escaped his sight? Do you truly believe that the Kalinaw would be such a mighty force yet expect my master to remain idle? If you are who you say you are, we will bring you to him and let *him* determine your worth. Your chances of liberating anyone, especially yourself, are disappearing as fast as your legend is. Your truth is of little consequence to me, but this does provide us with the opportunity to solidify our power."

"Orvar was right," Adger said. "He means to kill us all."

"We'll have to come back for Orvar and Gin later," Simon said as the four prepared to turn and run.

"Do you remember where to go?" Bromle asked.

"I hope so."

A group of guards exited the doorway behind them and leveled their lances at their backs.

Bromle cursed.

They had no other choice but to concede.

"Bromle, start something," Simon whispered to him.

"I may be me after all, but there's a thousand of these guys!" Bromle said.

Without trying to convince him further, Simon shoved Bromle into the group of guards. Others rushed to their aid and the stairs that led back down to the streets were quickly filled with more guards. Simon shoved Bromle again as the brute effortlessly regained his footing.

"What is your problem?" Bromle shouted as he shoved Simon back and sent him flying off his feet and crashing into some guards.

It hurt, but it was the distraction Simon needed. He wasn't foolish enough to believe he could fight this whole garrison but he was wise enough to know his belt would likely be among the things confiscated during their capture. As the guards he impacted scrambled to their feet so as to restrain him, he quickly extracted his sword hilt and shield from the belt. He elbowed a couple guards to add to the brief chaos and managed to shove his armaments into his boots before they regained control.

The guards handled him and Bromle rather roughly as they shoved the four towards the council and threw them at their feet.

"How would killing us benefit you?" Simon asked breathlessly from his knees on the ground.

"If you truly are Kynn Veyor, your survival would herald a new era for this world. And in that world there is no place for the likes of us."

"No matter what you do, we'll overcome it."

Deocran laughed. "Your hope is decimated, Hero. If you try anything at all or lash out again, these fine men and women will skewer you so excessively that your blood will drain from your body faster than water is poured from a bucket. And know this; you *will* die, but the question is the manner in which you do so. We will show the people how foolish it is to believe in a single man for victory. Your death will be the final push for them to wholly put their faith in *our* rule."

15 The Stadium

Hundreds of guards surrounded Simon and his friends. They took their bags and weapons and were less than gentle about it. To Simon's disappointment, they did not overlook his belt. He was grateful that his weapons were stuffed into his boots and didn't even mind the discomfort they caused; it was a pleasant reminder that he was still armed. The other three looked at him with hope in their eyes but the reality of being outnumbered was a discouragement.

The council members led the horde out of the fortress but instead of squeezing through the small door to the side of the gates, the massive doors slowly swung outward. The morning light filled the entombed city through the large openings in the cavern ceiling. Simon wondered if there was indeed some form of camouflage that hid the holes from the outside, or if it was another lie that the Council fed people to make them feel at ease.

"Do you think everyone knows they're in league with the enemy?" Adger whispered to the others.

"No way," Simon said. "They can't all have given in. They were forced into hiding, and their city was taken from them. People wouldn't forget that no matter how much time has passed. Some must remember what the Kalinaw used to stand for."

"Quiet!" one of the guards barked.

In the faintest of whispers a voice of one guard said, "I remember."

"Me too," came another voice.

There was still hope left to encourage.

The city was awakening in the morning light, and people were moving about the city streets to start their daily tasks.

161

The guard who had silenced them called out to people as they walked. "Come see the fall of the hero, Kynn Veyor!" he shouted, "Come see the lies made truth as the Vanquisher falls by the sword!"

People looked up from what they were doing and many began to follow; it had been a long time since anything extraordinarily interesting had happened in that city. Many more joined them as they went, and word quickly spread about the capture of the adventurers. There was a buzz of excitement in the streets. Every few years, someone claimed to be Kynn Veyor, but never had there been so much focus as Simon and his companions were receiving. The worst punishment a person received for claiming to be Kynn Veyor was being tied up in a public place as a means of humiliation. Even in those instances, it only took a pair of guards; certainly not an entire battalion.

The unanimous march of the soldiers echoed off the city buildings, interrupted by the beckoning of the heralding guard.

They led Simon and his companions to a stadium so great that it could have easily been mistaken for one of the mountains inside the cavern. The Council led the crowd into the main gates, but Simon's group was led down stairs and narrow hallways with no idea where they were going. Unbeknownst to them, the stadium was filling to capacity above them. All the townspeople were slowly pouring in to see what the excitement was about.

The group of prisoners was shoved towards dark cells in the lower levels.

"You sure do have a lot of cells in this place," Bromle said.

A couple of the Council members were close at hand watching their imprisonment.

"We will gracefully allow you to keep the armor you've stolen; you will need it." One of the Council members said, "It won't help you, but it may give you more peace about the death you are about to experience."

Whatever the guards hadn't taken before, they stripped them of now. All their cloaks and outer garments were taken from them; even Filch's. All three of her companions pushed against the guards as they were forced farther down the dark passages. They had never managed to see Filch's features, and this was a mystery they were anxious to solve no matter the threat they faced. Long, straight, black hair fell from within her outer garment as it was torn from her. Her skin was fair and her features, alluring. She had striking green eyes that were more vivid without the obscuring cloak.

The three men stared at her. Even the guards stopped shoving them to admire Filch's beauty. Her loveliness was ensnaring, and for a moment, none of them moved. She looked towards the ground, and her saddened expression was no less detracting.

"I thought maybe you were just ugly," Bromle said, breaking the silence.

"Or maybe had a really bad scar," Adger said.

"Or buck teeth," Simon said.

"One could only wish for such things," she said mournfully.

The other three felt confused but glad to have finally seen her face.

"That's enough, all of you," one of the guards said and shoved them down the hallway.

"We are kind enough to have granted you this chance to die honorably," one of the council members said. "Will you die cowering in fear, or will your death be worthy of remembrance?"

The four of them were forced into a dark room so black that they couldn't see each other. The door closed behind them with a loud metallic lock. The only sound was the breaths of those imprisoned.

"Filch, I don't understand," Adger said.

"And you still won't, Short-round," she said. "Beauty is not always a thing to be desired."

"Adger? Filch?" a voice said in the dark.

"Orvar?" Adger said. "Simon can you—"

Simon flared up his sword before he could finish. The light revealed Orvar and Gin in the dark room with them. Adger walked over to Orvar and firmly grasped his hand and embraced him to pat his back. The room they were in was wide, and even the bright flame of Simon's sword didn't reach its darkest corners.

"It's fortunate that they brought you here," Adger said and released his friend.

"I don't think fortune is the appropriate word in this situation," Orvar said. "I doubt that our reunion is something to be celebrated. Nevertheless, I am glad to see you, Adger, and that you are unharmed; you as well, Brom and Claire."

"Who?" Simon asked. Bromle and Adger looked equally confused. Orvar gestured to Filch.

"I prefer the nickname," she said.

"Simon, I see you've managed to keep your weapon hidden," Orvar continued.

"The sword fit in the belt quite nicely; I had hoped they would have overlooked it, but I stuffed it in my boot just in case."

"Well, it is good you did. Otherwise, all hope might have been lost."

"Quiet," Filch said.

"...Aye, I hear it too," Gin said.

The faint sound of applause and cheering seeped through the walls.

"Does anyone else have any weapons?" Gin said.

Filch pulled three daggers from beneath her clothing; handing one to Bromle, who pulled another one from within his braid. Adger reached inside his pockets and ripped some of the seams inside. He pulled out parts and pieced them together to make a dagger with curved blades on both sides of a single handle.

Gin pulled up one leg of her pants to reveal a metal case around her skin. She knocked on it and an empty space could be heard within. "I lost the real thing to an alaidak. Lucky for me, the condition of every citizen's appendages isn't public knowledge." She pushed and slid three pieces on her leg to reveal small compartments. She pulled out pieces of metal and fit them together to make a pistol.

"Where can I get one of those?" Bromle said.

"It's not much when compared to my rifle; that took a lot of time and questing to obtain. This one fires metal, whereas the other is imbued with an enchantment—the only kind like it in the world. I hope they don't dismantle it."

"I wouldn't mind having my gloves back, but this'll do just fine for the time being," he said nodding to Filch.

"Let's see how hot this sword can get," Simon said and stepped towards the door.

He raised the weapon but the loud sound of locks releasing interrupted him. The ground they were on started to rise and, for a moment, they believed they might be crushed into the ceiling but it began to open up. Simon quickly extinguished his blade and slid it back inside his boot. The others hid their weapons as best they could.

The ceiling opened to reveal a gargantuan stadium, larger and taller than Simon had ever seen in any days of attending sports events while he was alive. There was no roof on the structure, which allowed it to open up to empty sky beyond. It was situated under one of the holes in the roof of the cavern. The group of adventurers was directly in the center of the stadium floor. When the morning light of the sun illuminated their platform, they noticed two lifeless guards lying on the floor. They had been overlooked in the darkness. They had been stripped of most of their armor and had no weapons of their own. If it wasn't for their armored boots and the embroidered crests on their black shirts, it might not have been obvious who they were.

Gin stepped towards them and knelt down to see if there was any life left in them. She roused them both and they dazedly stood up, blinking in the light.

"I guess this is what we get for showing support," one of them said. "I remember what the Kalinaw once was; even at the cost of doing so."

The crowd greeted them all with raucous applause. The sight of the group caused the audience to become even louder, although none of the group understood why; all but the guards. They knew where they were and what was about to happen.

They all stood in a field of grass with several boulders and pillars positioned throughout. The walls around them were high enough to make escaping into the crowd impossible. Thick, barred gates interrupted the smooth wall in various places. The field provided little advantages, if any at all.

In one prominent position in the center of the seating on one side of the stadium was a lofty, roofed platform above the crowds. In it sat the Council, several prestigious looking citizens, and a few sentries. In the center sat Deocran, on a small throne. He raised his hands and the crowd's cheering slowly diminished.

"Sceadwians of the Burgh," he spoke, his voice filling the stadium, "we have gathered you all here to witness the downfall of the most heinous heretic our city has had the fortune to contain. His group of dissidents has tried to corrupt our graceful city and have gone so far as to kill our own!"

The crowd erupted in hateful jeering.

"Not only are they murderers, thieves, and corrupters, they are from Canton!"

Somehow, the crowd became even more aggressive and louder; some of them even threw things into the field in a futile effort to hit them.

"I guess they don't like our home, little brother," Bromle said.

"He casts us as criminals!" Orvar said to the group. "He is truly a wicked man."

"The most egregious of their leader's crimes is that he claims to be the Hero we long for: Kynn Veyor."

The crowd's demeanor changed again. It seemed that most of them weren't sure how to react.

"The old promise is sacred, and we, the Council, are here to show you that we are the ones to provide for the people until such time as that hero arrives. We represent the people and are ruled by the people, but this insurgent is trying to undermine what we stand for! What say all of you to this criminal?"

The groups that seemed unsure before had their doubt apparently eradicated as the masses shouted and applauded together.

"The people have spoken, my illicit captives," Deocran continued.

Deocran disappeared, and a few moments later, he exited a small gate at the field level of the stadium. Guards fanned out behind him as he approached the captives. He proudly walked up to Simon and leaned towards his face.

"If you are who you say you are, then you should have no trouble saving yourself and your companions," Deocran said so that only they could hear him. His voice no longer echoed through the arena. "Know this: when you die, you will awake in the clutches of my master, and he will not be so merciful. I have already sent messengers to inform him of your arrival, but the manner in which you arrive to him is up to you. No doubt you will die here and then suffer your death for an eternity to come, but I'm mercifully allowing you this secondary option."

"You rule the people with a lie," Simon said.

"*You* are a lie!" he shouted, losing his composure. "The promise of a hero is dead! There is no hope left in this world and we are the only thing left to provide it. I serve the people, and by killing you, I am doing what is best for them."

He calmly turned and left the group of prisoners standing in the center of the stadium. The guards followed behind them and the gladiators were left on their own again.

Simon turned to the captive guards, "What is this?"

"You are to be sport for some of the Council's pets," one of them said.

"You're their sport too there, little man," Bromle said.

"You can't win, no matter what weapons you have. They are armed with natural weapons and are equipped with armor that no weapon can pierce."

"We'll see what this can do," Simon said as he bent down and pulled out his sword and shield; each small, inactive object in one hand. He slid the longer end of his hilt up one sleeve so as to better conceal it.

The larger gates around the field started to open.

Out of the largest of the gates came an elephant, unlike any kind that any of them had seen. It was taller than five men and had long curved tusks covered in plates of spiked armor. Its hide looked tough enough on its own, but it too was armored in sharp barbs.

Out of another gate came an enormous feline, fifteen feet long with long sharp front teeth that scraped the ground. It was covered in a studded leather hide that protected it all the way down to the tip of its tail which ended in a spiked hook. It was a creature from an age before man.

From two other gates came two more prehistoric monsters: a Gorgonopsid and a Daeodon. The Gorgonopsid was a reptile with a long rectangular head on the muscular body of a dinosaur. Its back was ridged and plated with curved spikes protruding up and backward. Like a dog, it cantered on four muscular legs, circling around some of the protuberances in the field and its group of prey. It repeatedly opened its mouth to show rows of teeth only made for the purpose of tearing flesh from bone. It wore no armor but didn't seem like it would be slow enough to need it.

The Daeodon was similar to a boar but larger with longer teeth. Its head was covered in fur that diminished to a ridge down its back. It stopped walking shortly after leaving the gate and started pawing the ground. It was draped with a coat of mail and wore a helm with a long horn like that of a rhino. It was unclear if this was an adornment or part of the creature, but it was frightening either way.

"I don't think daggers will be enough," Gin said.

"I doubt your gun will be either," Filch said.

"I can manage to kill at least one of these, but any coordination of attacks and even this sword would be ineffective," Simon said.

They all stepped off the platform and into the field. The platform lowered back into the ground and the hatch closed above it, leaving them no means of escape.

"We can do this; we just have to work as a team," Simon said.

"Better weapons would help," Adger said.

There was no other preparation to be had and no better way for them to prevent the oncoming attack. The ground shook as the animals began to charge. They had no projectiles to fire—except Gin's small pistol—and no efficient way to dissuade their predators from their task. The crowd cheered as the battle began.

"Look, there," Orvar shouted, pointing at three guards. Through a small gate, they trampled into the theatre and sprinted in the adventurers' direction.

They were carrying bags in their arms. Filch spied the glint of one of her weapons.

"They have our things," she said excitedly.

Simon looked back towards the Council who was shouting and shoving several of the guards nearest them, pointing in the direction of the guards carrying the supplies. At the Councils direction, a barrage of arrows halted the betrayers who barely made it out of the small gate. They all dropped dead, with the weapons clattering out of their grasp and towards the prisoners.

The imprisoned eight ran for the weapons, but the Council's archers fired more arrows to deter them. The crowd booed the archers, but it was not enough to sway their steady arms. The reverberations from the charging beasts waned and they slowed their assault to a trot. Simon ran towards the weapons and ignited his shield; it was just big enough to block the arrows and retrieve the bags. The archers stopped firing but kept their arrows fixed on Simon as he slowly moved to rejoin the others.

"We are not without allies in this city," Filch said as she quickly equipped herself with her belongings.

The others did the same and donned themselves for the battle. They gave up their meager weapons for their preferred ones, except for Orvar, who took two of the daggers as he seemed to have no other weapons. Filch had her chakrams, Bromle wore his gloves, Gin pieced together her rifle, and Adger notched an arrow on his black bow, while holding several more in his other hand. Simon ignited his sword to match his shield. He even managed to drag along two lance-rifles from the fallen guards which the two that remained picked up and brandished with ease.

The animals renewed their charge at the behest of a sounding trumpet.

167

The guards dropped to one knee on either side of Gin, and all three of them started firing at the Gorgonopsid which was closest to them. Most of the shots hit their target but the creature seemed undeterred.

"Keep firing," Gin shouted.

It slowed, but not before it wrapped its jaws around one of the guards and whipped its head to knock Gin and the other guard away. Gin landed next to one of the boulders and narrowly missed being bashed against it. The second guard was not so fortunate and fell lifeless to the ground after being slammed into the boulder. The reptile fell to the ground with half of the first guard's body in its mouth; both of them were motionless.

The crowd erupted with applause. Gin stood up, dazed but otherwise unharmed. She looked up towards the Council; several of them were standing up from their chairs and bending over the rail around their loft, cursing and pointing. Gin regained her balance and enough wit to look up at the council and flick her chin at them. The crowd cheered even louder than before.

The Daeodon ran towards them, and Filch ran to meet it. She threw the chakrams, but they bounced off its armor and came back to her. She still ran towards it and flipped through the air onto its back as it otherwise would have run her over. She threw her chakrams towards the ground, and they turned sharply before they hit the field and severed the creature's front, unprotected legs. It squealed and slid along the ground. Filch jumped off of its back and put it out of its misery with a quick slice of its throat. The crowd became even louder in response to Filch's triumph.

"I'll take the saber-tooth. Can you guys handle that elephant?" Simon asked the brothers.

They both nodded their heads and moved towards the incoming elephant. It moved slowly, but its size gave it an advantage. Adger fired his arrows at the elephant and it started to pick up additional speed. Bromle created orbs of smoking fire and repeatedly threw them at the elephant, which only angered it more. The brothers reloaded and fired again. Adger's arrows hit their mark that time, and he gave the elephant one arrow for each eye. It reared back on two legs and landed on the ground with such force that it left two small craters. Whatever speed it lacked, it found after being blinded. It rushed towards them. Bromle clapped both his hands together and pulled them apart creating an orb bigger than he had done before.

"Keep firing little brother; I only need a second more," Bromle shouted.

The crowd was on their feet then, deafening in their roar. This was just good entertainment to them. There were plenty in its midst that were cheering for each side, but mostly their enthusiasm was in support of the action, whichever way it went.

Adger fired several more arrows into one leg of the elephant. It started leaning to that side in response to the pain and due to its loss of vision ran into one of the stone pillars in the field. It stumbled but was unfortunately redirected by the pillar and was now barreling down on the brothers' position.

Bromle raised the orb with a swirling myriad of fiery colors above his head. He shouted as he threw it towards the charging beast. The orb seemed to grow even greater in size just before it hit the creature's face. The orb stopped it dead as if it had hit the side of a mountain. A loud crack echoed through the field and the elephant slumped to the ground without another breath.

The only opposition left for them to defeat was the oversized tiger. It had been circling them on the outer most part of the field as it watched the other creatures fall.

The rest of Simon's companions grouped around behind him.

"This shouldn't be a problem," Bromle said and clapped his hands together readying another orb.

"No," Simon said. "Let me take this one."

"There's no reason to be the hero. We can do this together."

"I would normally agree, but the crowd is cheering and they're cheering *for* us; they need me to be the hero. Let me show them who I am and what I can do. You've all already done so much. Stay ready in case it goes badly, but let me at least try."

"You can do this, Kynn," Orvar said, nodding his head.

The others did the same, and Simon felt an electrifying chill crawl up his spine. His companions' faith in him was empowering.

Simon still held his weapons ready and burned his shield even brighter. The tiger responded to the luminous defense by charging at Simon. It was still at the other end of the field, but it closed the distance quickly. The ground in the center of the field started to open as it had before, and the platform below started to rise.

"Simon, let me kill this thing and we can get out of here," Bromle said pointing at the rising platform.

The group turned to jump down into the hole in the ground, but the platform was not empty. A pair of soldiers stood in its middle. They were warriors forged from the very fires of the earth, as evident in the way that a burning light shone through their flesh. Their skin was stony gray and black with visible veins filled with fire. They had bright red pieces of armor that covered their legs and arms and their chests were carved of stone. They carried shimmering red swords; one of them a claymore as tall as the creature that held it by the handle aloft with the point in the ground by his foot. The other warrior wielded a shield and a khopesh sword that was straight near the hilt but then curved outward like a scythe. Each of them had helms with flared wings on both sides that reached to a point above their heads and jutted forward like a horn. They were Etnian's soldiers; remnants of the war that forced the Sceadwians underground. The crowd grew silent at the realization of what these creatures' presence meant.

The roar of the feline was the only sound in the stadium and was enough to halt Simon's footsteps. He was paralyzed, and his terror was not enough to break the spell. The tiger leapt towards Simon and landed on his shield. It knocked him over and pressed him into the ground, but the charm had broken. His sword was knocked out of his hand, and he had to use both of his hands to hold the shield up. The weight of the tiger was suffocating Simon. It took all his strength to keep from being crushed. Simon roared in exertion and the tiger roared back, leaving Simon's ears ringing.

The crystal spike of the shield was inches away from the tiger's chest; Simon could just see the tip of it pressing into the animal's fur. Simon willed his muscles to push harder, but he knew the creature was toying with him. He glanced towards Bromle, who was starting to move in his direction; Gin had taken a knee and was aiming for the opportune moment to fire.

"No," Simon grunted. "Let...me—" He felt like he was running out of air. "Let me do this."

He looked towards his sword hilt, but it was far out of his reach. If there was anything to be done, he had to find the power within himself. He concentrated on his shield and pondered the way it extended at his will. He thought about the bright colors at its edges and the geode that adorned its convex face. In his rapidly fleeting strength, his confidence faltered and he cursed his adamancy at being left to succeed on his own.

The flame of the depths.

Simon recalled Tortuse's words about the ballad of Kynn Veyor. The thought of fulfilling the story made his chest burn. So, too, the orange edges of the shield started to glow more brightly than they ever had before. The clear crystal on its front burned brightly from within with a violet hue that looked bright enough to light the darkest walls of the Burgh. Both the edge of the shield and the crystal spike started to shimmer at their confines like they threatened to explode. Simon roared at the tiger again and the protuberance extended even farther than before. With a guttural shout, Simon felt the full control of the shield's properties, like his vision had been drawn down into the microscopic composition. The spike shot up and through the tiger, which howled in pain and fear. Simon's shield continued to burn until it spewed fire of varying colors in every direction. The multi-hued flames incinerated the legs and the majority of the creature. Its full, charred weight collapsed down on Simon.

"Help!" he squeakily cried from underneath it. "I'm ready for help now," he said with a smile.

His teammates rushed over to push what was left of the burdensome creature off of him.

The pair of hellfire, smoldering soldiers stood motionless as the platform had finally reached its height.

Simon ran to his extinguished hilt lying on the ground and ignited it when it was back in his hand. He was exhausted but resilient and ready for what came next.

The crowd was still and silent and most of them stood speechless.

"Fear not, my people!" Deocran called from the platform. "These creatures of war are subdued and controlled. They are no longer tools of the enemy but have served us loyally for many years."

Still the crowd was quiet. It was uncomfortable for them to see an enemy from the ancient war, despite the assertion of loyalty. Even the surety of the Council's supporters was weakened. The Council had enlisted their master's aid unbeknownst to the Sceadwians. These creatures had been sent to the city shortly after Simon's dramatic arrival. Their purpose was either to escort or kill Simon and any who supported him.

They stepped towards Simon and he grabbed his hilt firmly in his free hand. He leapt into the air, and swung it at the new combatants as he had done in the streets above. And, as it had done before, the sword became a geyser of magma, spewing towards the soldiers. Simon swept his weapon at them, but they nimbly jumped over it and landed in the same place they leapt from.

Simon retracted the fire and reduced the blade to an undulating length equal to the blade of before. There were many whispers and gasps at Simon's attack. It would not be enough to defeat them though; they would require a more direct approach.

"You still want to do this on your own?" Bromle asked.

The gates opened around the field and legions of guards marched inside. The guards fanned out and filled the outer rim of the field; several of them stepped forward and grabbed the defenders, all except Simon.

"I guess that answers the question," Bromle said.

The crowd was still silently staring, surprised at the pair of new enemies below.

"This will be a fair fight," Deocran said from above. "Your friends will not be allowed to help."

"How is it fair to have two versus one?" Adger said from the confines of a pair of guards.

The twins attacked simultaneously. Simon took the same stance he had before and deflected each of their swings with a grace that was new, yet natural for him. The knowledge the book bestowed allowed him the ability to repeatedly deflect attacks and dance around the enemies' assault. The soldier with the claymore was larger and stronger; the sword seemed easy enough for him to have wielded with one hand. The other soldier was smaller and faster, and his shield made Simon's offensive strikes few and ineffective.

The more they fought, the more the crowd seemed to respond. Their silence was slowly replaced by grunts or quiet cheers as the three warriors fought. The whispered voices became utterances when Simon gained some ground and gasps escaped when he was pushed back. The crowd, it seemed, was rooting for Simon. Their encouragement grew until people starting cheering and shouting again in support of Simon. His friends were the most adamant behind him and even a few guards started joining in.

The soldiers were tireless in their attack and at one point the smaller of the two slashed Simon's armor, leaving a deep gouge. He was grateful for having the chest plate but knew it wouldn't have saved him had the soldier been a step closer.

Simon needed something greater than the weapon he had. He needed an advantage that he couldn't otherwise create for himself.

"You are Kynn Veyor!" Orvar said.

"You are Kynn Veyor!" Adger said.

"You are Kynn Veyor!" the rest of his friends said together.

More people from the crowd started joining in on the chant. The Council above shifted as if they were covered in fleas.

"Show them, Simon!" Orvar shouted over the rising chant. "*We* believe in you, now solidify *their* faith. You must channel your friends. You need fire and you need earth!"

"How?" Simon said dodging the blows of the pair of soldiers, parrying and retreating as best he could.

His sword blazed and his shield shone; the crowd cheered, and his friends chanted on.

"You must use the strength of Kapell dun Shan! You have done it with your shield. You must find a way!"

He thought of Kapell's fiery kilt and his blazing eye. He remembered how it felt to see the giant stand up out of the water as he watched the sea fall from his back. He felt the grumbling and melodic echoes of Kapell's voice in his own chest as if Kapell was trying to speak through him.

The soldiers stopped their attacks and took several steps back. Whatever their intent, Simon used the opportunity to focus even more deeply, and he closed his eyes. He recalled how it felt to experience that first wild ride down the giant's leg and into the water. He felt the ground beneath his feet begin to tremor and shake like the steps of Kapell during Simon's waking moments of his new existence. He dropped his hands to his sides. His shield and sword retracted and Simon stood stone still.

He opened his palms to the ground and felt them swelter from an unseen heat source. All the while, he kept his eyes closed and hoped a sword wasn't about to penetrate him. He imagined he was pulling the ground from the earth, and the sand on the ground beneath his feet started to rise. The earth continued to shake and, unbeknownst to Simon, the twins hesitated. Simon imagined pulling at the ground harder and stronger. The distinct crack of stone echoed through the arena, and the crowd grew deathly silent again.

Simon snapped open his eyes and whipped his arms into the air. As if the ground beneath him was attached on cords, chunks of earth followed the motion of his arms. The pieces of earth hung in the air like they were suspended on strings; they slowly spun in place.

The Council realized they had misjudged this character pretending to be who he said he was. Many of them exchanged nervous glances and relaxed their heightened postures at the balcony wall; all except for their leader who stood as resolutely as he had in the fortress. He gripped the handrail around the loft so tightly that his knuckles turned white while his burning red face grimaced at his prisoners' success. The rest of the Council realized their obstinacy far too late; there was no time left to recant.

"Kill him!" Deocran shouted.

The two fire soldiers rushed towards Simon, and he thrust his hands towards them. The pieces of earth were sent forth like a meteor shower, picking up the soldiers as they flew. They were rocketed towards the farthest wall of the stadium. Most of the guards had seen what was happening and managed to dodge the disaster. The ones who didn't were knocked down but alive. The two soldiers of the enemy, however, were obliterated.

"Kill him now!" Deocran shouted hysterically, jumping in the air and nearly flipping over the edge of the platform.

The soldiers around him hesitated but some of the guards still in the stadium seating strung their arrows and drew their bows. Simon raised more chunks of earth from the ground and—like he had studied the graceful moves of an artist his whole life—directed the earth towards the archers obeying Deocran's command. The rubble rolled over them easily.

Once the guards were down, he pulled up pieces of the earth a third time, raised them above his head, and threw them towards the Council. The pieces of ground stopped only inches from their faces.

"Your reign is at an end! I *am* Kynn Veyor and the oppression of your master is no more!"

The stadium erupted more ferociously than in all the moments of the battle before. The guards dropped their weapons. It was clear that the Elders of Origin had lost any remnants of their former glory and power.

16 The Plan

A few days later, Simon and his companions were enjoying some much deserved recuperation. The days prior were filled with celebration, once the Council had all been imprisoned. Many "heretics" were released from their cells. They were people who resisted the Council when they enforced their antiquated reign, despite the public voice of disapproval. There were numerous guards who resisted the Council's downfall and ended up joining them in their new home. Otherwise, the city was largely unified by Simon's victory in the stadium. His demonstration showed people what he was capable of, and the city was buzzing with excitement. Kynn Veyor had finally arrived.

The group of six sat in the large den of a suite that was once reserved for the Council. They were individually recounting their adventures up to that point; Simon's were of particular interest, but the others had plenty of stories to share.

"I want to join you wherever this journey takes you," Gin said during a lull in their conversation.

"I think we all consider you a part of our team already," Simon said.

Everyone nodded their head in agreement.

"And where *is* our journey taking us?" Bromle asked. "I don't mind the break in pace, but we must be on some kind of deadline; aren't we?"

"I can provide you with knowledge," Orvar said. "I can further teach Simon how to fight, I can help us navigate the known rhin geatu, and I might even know the general direction of Etnian's home, but what I don't know is what we need to know: how to kill the enemy and exactly where Naru is."

"Who says he has to be killed," Simon asked. "I thought I just needed to find my way to—what was it, Adger?"

"Haeophan: the life hereafter the life thereafter."

"That's it: Haeophan. I thought I was just supposed to find my way there."

"Tortuse did not recite the whole song, did he?" Orvar asked. "It is a long tale and not one I can wholly remember, but I do know where to find the answers. There is a repository of knowledge far out west; farther than any map has ever recorded."

"How do you know about it, then?" Bromle challenged. He seemed eager to debunk people's assertion but it wasn't intentional; he was genuinely curious.

Orvar continued, "A seer was in the favor of the force that contains and owns the endless seas of the desert that separate us from what we need. He shared his knowledge with me before he disappeared."

"Why you?" Bromle asked.

"There were few of us in the beginning. We were explorers."

"Hold on, did you say there was a desert?" Adger said. "I'm not a fan of all that hot, gritty landscape."

"Well, the seasons are in your favor; it is cold this time of year and growing colder. The colder nights are what you need to fear there; the sun will be a welcome escape from the frost."

"So, you want us to cross a freezing desert to find an answer to something you can't recall?" Bromle asked.

"Long ago, I had visions—"

"I'm sorry to interrupt but I don't understand," Simon said. "How is long ago such a common term?"

"Time moves slowly here, but understanding it hasn't been my focus. My ability to remain free has been contingent upon understanding the mysticism this world offers. There are powers here that are impossible to understand; even if you have lifetimes to do so. There are bestowments too, given and not gained."

"I don't understand."

"And neither do I, in its entirety. I have done my best to record what I've learned but there are *volumes* yet to be read and assimilated. Despite my experiences, I don't fully understand this world. I might know the secrets of subterfuge and elemental manipulation, but understanding what drives those connections, or what might change the very path of this entire existence, is beyond me. I was fortunate enough to learn of the visions of the library far beyond rolling hills of endless wasteland. The path between was guarded by a terrible monster of endless torrential sands, but that is the most I know.

"And how're we supposed to surpass this 'terrible beast?'" Simon asked.

"Unfortunately, that's beyond me too. I know where to go but not how

175

to appease the storm. That, my friend, may be something left for you to discover."

"I still don't understand why Etnian needs to die though—I mean despite being...you know, evil incarnate."

"Etnian's death will completely change Dyurndale. It may not eradicate all evil, but it will diminish the influence that it has. He limits the potentiality—eliminates it really—that any will come here after you."

"Then we go to the desert, but I won't force any of you to come with me. I don't know what's ahead, and so much of each of you has been asked already. I won't make the decision for you."

Bromle stood up first. "I don't understand all this, but I will go with you. Someone has to do the heavy lifting, after all."

"I believe who you are and what role you have yet to play," Adger said as he stood up.

Filch stood up too but gave little more affirmation than a head nod.

"I've already pledged my desires," Gin said cheerily.

"And I will help you with what wisdom I have," Orvar said.

"Then it's settled," Simon said. "Except, what direction we need to go." Simon pulled out his second map with the markings of Burgh Sceadwia.

"Where did you get that map?" Orvar asked excitedly.

"I had it when I arrived, remember? I thought I mentioned that."

"I must've been miles away. The ring made the markings—ah yes, of course."

Simon smoothed out the maps on a low table that had cushions around it. Adger, Orvar, and Gin kneeled around the table with Simon. He touched the ring, and the map came alive with glowing rhin geatu in various locations across it.

"There," Orvar said. He pointed to the small markings of a city with a rhin geatu symbol over it. It was on the edge of a desert that bordered the majority of the west side of the map.

"How do *you* travel by the gates?" Simon asked Orvar.

"There are many special things that make the supernatural occur, but a ring is not one I have seen; especially one that acts in the manner which yours does. There's no time for more questions though. We must be off and ensure that Burgh Sceadwia prepares for the inevitable war that will ensnare us all. Let us see what contingencies this city has initiated in the vacuum of the Council. I'm also curious if the city will follow you, Simon."

"They were chanting his name," Adger said.

"They may believe who he is, but giving their lives for him is something else entirely. I know they are able...but I fear their reasons to fight may be lacking."

"Why does everyone require proof?"

"Not all people are so easily convinced. Shall we go?"

The group left the room and made way for the buildings that once housed the Council and their court. They soon arrived and the building was bustling with people of every kind from the city.

"It appears there are many candidates for the seats of power," Orvar said.

"Orvar!" said a plump man walking towards them in ornate regalia. His thick, bushy mustache covered his lips as if it was his facial hair speaking, the way it bounced when he spoke. The ends of it were waxed to a blunt, upturned end. His eyebrows grew uncontrollably up from his eyes and threatened to douse him in comedy, but he had a distinct impression of authority in his voice that eliminated the humor. "I heard you were in town; it is so wonderful to see you once again." The two of them shook hands in a hug. "And this must be Kynn Veyor; or Simon, is it? I am Senator Driscol." He vigorously shook Simon's hand. "What brings you all here?"

"We need to know if the Sceadwians will support our efforts to overthrow Etnian—" Simon started to say.

"Quiet your whispers of war," said the senator with his free hand aloft. "There will be time for that, but for now we must see what power will replace the Council."

"Are you in the running?" Orvar asked.

"Indeed. What else can I do for you at the moment?"

"We must leave for the time being. There are things we must make known."

"Orvar, you really must work on your ability to provide direct answers. You would make a splendid candidate for our new Council Head."

"I have no desires for politicking and negotiations."

"So, where are you off to, then?"

"That," Simon interjected, "must remain withheld for the time being."

"I see you've taught him well, Orvar," Driscol said gesturing to Simon. The senator lowered his voice and took a step closer to the group who leaned in to hear what he had to say. "I heard something that might interest you. We now know well that the Council was ensnared by their former master, and I heard a rumor that there was something worth being guarded in the dark corners outside the Burgh. The high-guards the Council enlisted were more secretive and isolated than even the Council members were. In the last couple of days, there have been quite a few efforts to wring all the old Council's supporters of information. We managed to find out that whatever they were hiding is in the darkest northern corner of the cavern."

"Driscol, you really must work on your ability to avoid being involved in every conspiracy," Orvar said. "I'm not quite sure how that helps us though, friend."

"One of them said something about—oh what was it called? A ring goat—no, that can't be it a..."

"A rhin geatu?" Adger asked.

"Yes! Be cautious with those words," he said looking around. "I believe the city is largely in support of going to war—it is long overdue, and our people have grown tired of hiding in holes—but this rhin geatu is something that took a considerable amount of…'convincing' to discover. I would not recommend sharing this knowledge. I am unsure what it is, but considering the lengths the Council went to keep it secret, it may help you."

"Thank you, Driscol," Orvar said and shook his hand again. "We must be on our way. I fear if we linger, we may lose focus."

"Here," Driscol handed Orvar a small purse. "This should help you with provisions. Whatever you lack, tell the merchants that I will pay it."

"We are indebted to you, sir. Thank you," Simon said.

"No debt needed, Kynn. I am honored to have this privilege. May the peace of the sky be ever in your vision."

"And may the light return to the city again," Orvar said.

With that, they departed and walked towards the market to prepare for their trip towards the desert.

"A rhin geatu, here?" Simon thought aloud.

"It seems that map of yours is incomplete," Filch said from the back of the group.

"Driscol is paranoid and usually has an ulterior motive, but he is not a liar," Orvar said. "His intent is never malicious either, but his position has been made through strategic alliances and relationships. For whatever reason, this gate is not on Simon's map, but if Driscol says there's one there, I believe him. If he's elected as the new head of the council, this city is in good hands."

"Good enough for me," Simon said. "Let's get what we need and get going."

The team split up into pairs of two: the brothers, Orvar and Simon, and Gin and Filch. They spent the better part of the morning haggling prices, gathering supplies, and stuffing their bags as full as possible. Some of them even bought new clothing, considering how cold Orvar said the desert might be. They gathered later that afternoon in the city center and determined where they should start their search for the city's rhin geatu.

"Is everyone ready?" Simon asked.

"What about the vehicles the guards had? Can we 'borrow' a couple of them to cross the desert?" Bromle asked.

"The sand would make it impossible to use them," Gin said.

The brothers looked at each other and Adger shrugged his shoulders, "See Brom, I told you it wouldn't work."

The group headed north to the outer edge of the city and talked casually as they walked. They were repeatedly stopped as people recognized Simon and rushed to greet him. The city was friendly towards all of them and the group was happy to receive the greetings. They reached the edge of the city and beyond it, the landscape was filled with darkness. The large openings in the cavern ceiling poured sunlight into the city, but it recoiled where the roads stopped.

"Not bad for a hole in the ground, eh?" Adger said to Simon.

He stood staring back at the city but didn't have the same affectionate grin that Adger had.

"What is it?" Adger asked him.

"Just...a feeling," he said quietly.

As he looked on, the light in the city quickly darkened as if a cloud had passed in front of the sun. Simon closed his eyes to take the mental image of the scene and focus his thoughts. His eyelids fluttered open and he heard a song develop in his head; a familiar trance that he should have recognized right away. His mind told him what it was, but he felt forced to ignore the warning as he stood there in the silence. A panicked, distant voice drifted to him in the quiet, and try as he might to understand it, he couldn't. The holes above the city continued to darken and then started to fill in with dark blue water.

"That looks cool," Simon heard himself say like someone was speaking for him. "It looks like a trampoline." He chuckled childishly.

"—Simon!" Bromle said shaking his shoulders and finally breaking the spell he was under.

"She's here!" Simon said the second he was free of the enchantment. "The Witch has returned!"

Each membrane that covered the expansive holes in the ceiling started elongating in swirling funnels towards the city below. Each water spout was as dark as the depths of a sea ravine.

"What now?" Bromle sighed.

Cries rang out from the city. The radios that Orvar and Simon still wore started crackling, and hurried, panicked voices came through saying, "Raise the alarm," "What are they?" and, "To the fortress!"

Orvar twisted the dial on his wrist, "Driscol! What's going on?"

A quiet moment went by.

"Orvar, they're...I don't know. They have the bodies of snakes."

"Veadus," Simon said.

"Who?" Adger asked. "Oh yeah, that's the watery giant that attacked you when you first arrived; right?"

"Yes, and she's loyal to Etnian," Simon said. "If she knew where to find this place, then it's likely that her master knows too."

"What're we going to do?" Adger asked.

"We have to help, we can't stand idly by."

"If you die here, we'll fail," Orvar warned.

"If this city dies, we'll fail just as well."

The group ran back towards the city center. As they approached the funnel that was touching the ground, they could better see the enemies descending it. Simon noticed that the invaders were the same kinds of enemies that he had fought at the shore. The speed at which they moved made them indiscernible besides the serpentine bodies of some. The cries of inhabitants amplified the closer they got.

"No one is running away; it looks like they're running *towards* the funnel," Simon said.

"We don't flee in the face of a fight," Gin said. "My people are fierce warriors who would battle to their last breath."

Enemies emerged from side streets and the group was forced into action. They all pulled out their weapons; even Orvar had one this time. Gin spent little energy as she shot those closest to her. Bromle, Filch, and Adger took on watery invaders by blasting, slicing, and striking their enemies. Simon drew his fiery sword and shield and vaporized any who attacked him. He thought his attackers would be seared, but when his blade struck an enemy, they turned to mist like boiled water. Orvar drew a sword from beneath his coat. It appeared to be a rapier except the blade was wider to one side at the serrated base of the blade and tapered up to the end. When he drew the blade, it extended from the handle; its length didn't seem to logically fit unseen on his hip. The thin knuckle guard and sweepings grew and wrapped around his hand like vines. The hand guard glowed green and solidified but retained a subtle sheen of the emerald hue.

"Where was that before, old man?" Bromle said, gesturing to Orvar's weapon as he blasted another incoming enemy.

"Your equipment was returned to you in the arena; mine was returned later."

With several more swings, shots, and claps, the group's enemies were defeated and they prepared for more attacks.

"What do you mean?" Bromle said.

"Filch noticed, but you, it seems, did not stop to consider from where your belongings were given."

Bromle opened his mouth to argue again.

"Come on," Simon interrupted.

The group rushed deeper into the city to aid in pushing back the incursion.

"It seems the towns you visit are often invaded," Gin said.

"At least I'm not running away this time." Simon vaporized another enemy as they ran.

The funnel of water darkened and the enemies that came through it increased. The water that poured down was confined to the whirlwind and didn't flood the city streets and buildings amidst the hills.

"We need to stop their assault somehow," Simon said.

"It's literally a tornado of water-born enemies," Bromle said. "What about the stuff you did in the stadium?"

"I've been trying, and—I don't know. I'm not getting the same feelings that I did there."

"Orvar," Driscol's voice came over the radio again. "Are you still fighting?"

"Where are you," Orvar asked. "We can get to you."

"No! They're looking for Simon and any of your group. You must leave; our people can handle these enemies."

"Aye," Gin said. "My people are not too weak to handle a few hundred fish."

"I would rather stay and help, but he may be right," Orvar said as he looked to Simon.

Simon glanced at Gin.

"They can handle it," she said confidently.

"Okay, then we head for the gate, then on to the library," Simon said.

They stopped and turned back to leave. They took one last look at the funnel pouring into the ground before they left. It changed shape and shuddered and the ground shook with successive tremors. The water tornado was annihilated as the gargantuan shape of a stone giant came swinging through the hole in the cavern ceiling while hanging onto the edge. It nimbly twisted and landed on one of the bare hills of the city.

"It's Kapell!" Simon said.

He turned and saw Simon even at the distance he was from him.

"Simon," he shouted. "I'm glad to see you're still alive!" From his perch Kapell carefully stepped into the streets below and started swinging at the ground.

"That is Kapell?" Adger asked excitedly. "Please tell me you will introduce me!"

Simon laughed. "Of course I will! He's pretty cool, isn't he?" he said proudly as if bragging of a personal accomplishment.

The funnel of water was gone and in its place, the light of day started shining back through. A smooth black orb rolled towards them and when it reached Simon's feet, a small shape emerged.

"What is that small creature, then?" Gin said, bewildered.

"His name is Sid!" Simon said kneeling down to greet the creature. "He helped me escape my previous encounter with Veadus."

"Hello again, Simon," the pangolin said. "Kapell has asked me to come with you." Without waiting, he jumped up onto Simon's bag.

"Kapell is okay then? Did he defeat Veadus? And what of—"

"I am okay, Simon!" Kapell shouted from far away. He stood up from where he had reached down from his perch to swat at enemies. He waved and smiled in Simon's direction with a handful of warriors in his tightened fist.

"He said you might need help with Sammos: Kapell's brother who lives in the desert. He's not as kind or patient as he once was. Now let's go; Kapell is capable enough to help the city!"

"I can't leave him again," Simon pleaded.

"But you must."

"I will be fine, child," Kapell shouted towards Simon again. He swung at the ground and the bodies of several enemies went sailing far into the air to meet the ceiling above.

"We will meet again, Simon; you are protected with Sid," Sid said. "Sorry, yes, I can speak for Kapell over short distances but he often prefers his own voice. In any case, you must not linger any longer."

"Simon, trust him. Their kind are reliable," Adger said, patting his pocket where the stone of Ketay was still hidden.

Simon stood looking back at Kapell again. "All right then; we press on."

They ran through the city streets and around the mountains in the cavern as they had come before. They met very little resistance all the while. What they didn't see was Kapell changing direction to continue assisting the Sceadwians; Veadus' forces had shifted their focus and were now converging on Simon's location.

"I hear the rushing of water," Filch said. "I recommend we hurry."

They all started running even faster but not before their feet started splashing in slowly rising water.

"The witch's forces are upon us!" Sid said.

Filch stopped and turned back towards the city. "Go!" she said. "I'll hold them back as best I can."

"No," Simon said as he stopped and turned. "We can't lose you to them."

"Aye," Gin said. "I'll stay and help." She ran back and stood defiantly next to Filch as they prepared for the incoming attack.

"You'll need me too, then," Bromle said.

"What is going on?" Simon said a little frantically.

"They will need you more, Bromle," Filch ordered.

"Hear, hear, Brom!" Adger agreed a bit selfishly. "No need for you to go...I mean to say—indeed, we'll need your help, brother."

"Listen to your brother, Bromle. Now, all of you go!"

"We need you both," Simon insisted.

"You don't have a voice this time, Simon. You must discover how to end this. Go!"

They turned and fled again. The discomfort they felt leaving Gin and Filch to die was more enveloping than the rising water. The women turned to face the enemy but before the others turned one last corner, they couldn't help but stop one more time to gain a last image of their comrades.

"We can't just..." Adger said, quickly wiping an eye and hoping the others had not seen it.

"We must, little brother," Bromle said placing a hand on Adger's shoulder and squeezing ever so slightly.

"Kapell will help them," Sid said. "Focus now on what you must do."

They ran past the edge of the city and the light from the holes rapidly abandoned them. Occasional glances over their shoulder told them that whatever efforts Gin and Filch had made was enough to halt the enemy's pursuit. The ground beyond the city was uneven and slowed them down. There were hills and mountains out there similar to those in the city, but glancing up towards their heights made most of the group uncomfortable. Not knowing what might be watching them was unbearable. The quieting sounds of battle put them more at ease, and they slowed down to conserve their energy.

"I'm assuming you know which way is north," Simon said to Orvar.

"I have a general idea, but finding the gate will be difficult."

A chime rang out from Simon's pocket. He reached in and pulled out the small pocket watch. It was softly emitting a quiet melody. A light was glowing from within. He opened the watch and the chiming grew slightly louder. It wasn't a watch but looked more like a compass after all. It had eight points on the periphery with a spinning golden arrow in the center. The end of the golden arrow had the same symbol as Simon's rhin geatu ring.

"What is that?" Orvar asked.

"You mean you don't know something?" Bromle teased.

"Not all the mysterious things in this world are known to me."

"It looks like a compass," Simon said. "And judging from the markings, it looks as though it has something to do with the rhin geatu. Let's see where it leads."

Simon used his sword to illuminate the way. The others kept their weapons drawn as well, not knowing what they might find in the darkest places of the cavern. Adger pulled out his light to help push back the darkness.

"It's getting louder," Simon said.

"Look there!" Bromle said proudly.

What they could see of the city between the hills behind them looked miles away. There was a large opening in the wall in front of them and the chiming song of the compass became even louder. The diminished group entered a small cave that had smooth walls and a tiled floor. Torches on the walls flamed to life when the group stepped foot in the small entryway. A hallway led out of the entrance and from it came two guards much larger and better armed than those they had seen in the city. When they saw that the visitors were not members of the Council, they immediately attacked.

Orvar skewered the closest guard and Bromle knocked the other one into the farthest wall with one of his orbs. Leaving a large crater in the wall, the guard fell to the floor. Simon still held his sword in one hand and the compass in the other. He extinguished and stored his blade as he pulled out his map of the rhin geatu. Simon touched the gate symbol on his ring, and a rush of wind sounded from around a corner down a short hallway nearby. He then touched a symbol at the edge of the desert on the map, and a new symbol appeared just outside the edge of the desolated city above the Burgh. Burgh Sceadwia and a new rhin geatu symbol were drawn onto the map.

An additional wash of light illuminated the hallway and a cloud of sand blew onto the floor.

"The gate!" Adger said excitedly.

They walked around the corner to see a gate with the image of a dark sea of sand. They stepped through and one by one entered the heat of the sun and desert.

17 The Sands

"Karawost is what they call this place," Orvar said as he recollected. "I think it means, 'the black sand.'"

"That's comforting," Simon said.

"It is a lot warmer than I thought it'd be," Orvar said as he took off his outer garment. "It was supposed to be colder this time of year."

The others did the same and shed a few layers to minimize the heat of the sun. They adjusted their packs and assessed their surroundings. The rhin geatu was facing the desert, but behind it was a small desolate town. Mountains rose up behind the cliffs surrounding the town which gave the four of them a sense of isolation from the rest of the world.

"We should block this gate up," Bromle said. "We don't know how far behind us Veadus' army was."

"But, what if Gin and Filch were right behind us?" Adger said.

"Bromle's right, Adger," Simon said. "I'd like to think they're about to step through the gate, but I'm more worried that something else might come through first."

The group found broken stones in a collapsed building nearby and were grateful for the rhin geatu being low and narrow gates. After a short time, they had placed enough stones in front of it to make it seem buried to anyone else on the other side.

"This won't hold them back though," Adger said.

"You're right," Orvar said, "but we also don't know how the Council opened their gates; nor do they know where we've gone. Whatever tools the Council used to travel through the gates may not be intuitive enough to help their allies discover our course. Karawost seems to have been forgotten, and hopefully our destination cannot be rightly ascertained. I think, for now, we are not in retreat, but that also means we are entirely on our own."

They spent the afternoon exploring the city, looking for an aid across the desert. As the shadows lengthened, they halted their search until the morning returned. The night was cold, as Orvar had warned, but they were all prepared to withstand it. In the morning, they found little more than the day before.

"How're we going to cross the desert?" Adger asked. "There's nothing here but the skeletons of what might have helped us."

Bromle walked up from around a corner. "I think I found us a ride," he said, beaming.

He led them to a building that was larger than those around it but only by a portion. It was still intact enough to keep out the relentless aggression of the arid environment. Inside was a skiff with large bulbous wheels. A sail was laying in it and there was space enough to fit them all. It was dusty but otherwise seemed unaffected by age.

"Good job, Bromle," Simon said. "This might just work. Does anyone know how to sail?" Simon asked, looking into the boat.

"I know a bit; maybe enough to get us underway," Orvar said.

After a few minutes, they pushed the vehicle out the wide doors of the garage and into the streets. They maneuvered it towards the edge of town and assembled the sail.

"Which way are we going?" Adger asked.

"I've been wondering that myself," Simon said as he pulled out his compass. "After we came through the rhin geatu, my compass changed. The symbol on it is now a fox. I think we should follow it again."

"And everything's just that easy for you?" Bromle asked.

"Your skepticism must be exhausting," Adger said.

"I'm not skeptical; it just seems that everything is way too easy. You have the compass, and the map, *and* the ring to make the map work? Not to mention your sword and shield. Every hero has to quest for their weapon, and yours was just handed to you. Legendary weapons are deep in the confines of fortresses or dungeons, yet you just woke up with yours."

"Nothing I've done so far has been easy. I look at it as divine intervention," Simon said. "I believe there is a higher plan to all of this that none of us might immediately understand."

"So you actually believe that there's some almighty purpose to this," Bromle said, gesturing to the town around them. "And to that cave, or Canton with the constant oppression and daily struggles? How could there be any righteousness to any of the evil in this world?"

"That's deep Brom," Adger said.

"I may not be as smart as you, or have read as many books, but any idiot can see that there's no god in this world; doubtful there's any in the next."

"I can only believe in purpose," Simon said. "Nothing is this random. I have to believe there is a good ending in all of this."

"Not every story ends in joy. For centuries Etnian has tried to take over all these realms. I remember my life before this, and had I known this was the afterlife…I would've sold my soul to avoid it!"

"Those are dangerous assumptions, Bromle," Orvar said.

"I agree with you that this world is terrible as it is now, but this isn't the way it was supposed to be," Simon said. "This was supposed to be a paradise and an interim journey to the next life. That's what I was sent here to do: restore the realms to their former glory."

"That's a tall order for someone who only just learned who they are," Bromle said.

Simon took a moment and looked at the ground. "I'm prepared to try and fulfill it. I need your help to do it, too."

"I just don't understand how we're supposed to continue only relying on hope. Are we supposed to navigate into the desert blindly, and pray that compass of yours and an unplanned breeze will get us there?"

"We aren't just victims of circumstance," Adger said. "Some of us have prepared. Look." He pulled out an extra bag from amongst his larger one and from it unfolded two pair of metallic wings. They were similar to those on the dragonflies they were captured by. They had a copper color and reflected the light like they had been polished. There were four of them and each wing was only as wide as Adger's two splayed hands; they narrowed at the ends and turned at a sharp angle to have their connecting joints hidden within the bag. The pack was dissimilar to the new wings: its fabric was worn and browned like it was made to look so to hide the treasure within. "I got them for a great price, too!"

"I thought Filch said they wouldn't work out here."

"You were just complaining how everything's by chance and that we're just lucky. Well, I'm telling you, that we're not just lucky; we're prepared. Plus, it won't hurt to try; maybe they'll give us an extra push."

After a few minutes affixing the wings to the back of the skiff, they looked like they were a natural part of the rig. They all climbed in, and Orvar manned the wheel at the back.

"Do you know how those things work?" Bromle asked.

Adger spent a few minutes adjusting the wings and pushed a button or two. A spark flew from the pack, and one of them turned at an incongruous angle to the others. Sheepishly, Adger looked at the others and spent a few more minutes adjusting something within the pack. The wings fluttered to life, flapping and humming; driven by a motor unseen.

"This is impossible," Simon said in admiration of the contraption.

"And your weapons are no less impressive?" Adger said with a smile.

The wings gave the vehicle a sudden rush of speed and the group was thrust into the dark wilderness of the desert. Orvar steered the vessel while the others occasionally adjusted the ropes and sails. Simon had forfeited his compass to Orvar who was using it to constantly adjust their course. They sailed over dunes and down into valleys of sand. The bleak landscape was only occasionally broken by the outcropping of stone cliff faces and vegetation. There were no natural landmarks in the desert that gave them a sense of direction besides the sun. They took shifts in steering the vessel the direction that the compass recommended. They traveled on like this for three days, only stopping to build a fire when their provisions required it.

"Why would this appeal to anyone?" Sid asked from Simon's pack on the afternoon of the third day.

"I forgot you were back there," Simon said. "Some people would find its immensity peaceful."

"I would rather be in the mountains, or on the coast where there's more water; although, the water seems to have taken a life of its own lately— maybe just the mountains, then."

"Speaking of water," Simon said, pointing towards the horizon at an oasis that was surrounded by trees on the crest of an encompassing hill except for the one side facing them. The bright sun could be seen reflecting off the water like a mirror.

"That must be a mirage," Orvar said.

"Well, is everyone seeing it?"

The brother's nodded their heads.

"I don't think it's a mirage," Simon said.

The closer they got, the bigger the oasis became, and it was apparent that it was indeed a reality. The small oasis was in the basin of surrounding rocky hills. There was a multitude of trees and even a lush carpet of soft grass around the pond. The boughs of the trees hung over the water and provided plenty of shade for them to escape the harsh heat. The four of them were glad to take a long break from the skiff and refresh their skin in the water of the small pond.

"What's your compass say now, Simon," Bromle asked. "I'd rather just stay right here than continue any further."

Simon pulled out the compass and was surprised to see that the arrow of the compass had melted. The golden blob bounced around inside the compass. He showed it to the others who had no grounded theories to provide.

"Did this thing seriously melt?" Simon said angrily.

Simon got dressed and walked up on the ridge of one of the sand dunes. The blob of gold in the compass stretched and pointed back down towards the oasis. He walked around the ridge of the dunes and the compass constantly stayed fixed towards the pool below.

"It's just pointing back to here," Simon said as he walked back down to the others.

"See? Just like I said, we should just stay here," Bromle said.

Spurts of sand burst from the dunes around them and several people materialized from the sand that spewed forth. They were all wrapped in tan clothing that nearly blended in with the colors around them, if not for the bright golden scimitars they carried and golden cuffs they wore. Their mummified appearances were also protected in pale leather tabards that had golden symbols pressed into them along the edges like scrolls of forgotten languages. The warriors were as tall as Bromle, almost uniformly, like they were all pressed in the same mold. Their faces were covered in the same wraps as their limbs and tightly packed around circular black lenses.

Simon was the most capable to defend against them, but only because he was the most dressed. All of their equipment, and most importantly, their weapons, were in the skiff on the other side of the water. Simon stood as ready as he could, but he had nothing to defend himself with, and he doubted the people were friendly. Simon's companions jumped out of the water and ran towards the skiff, but another of the sand creatures materialized in their path.

Simon was inches away from one of the creatures. It stood motionless in front of him, towering several feet taller than him. All of them were robed, and their faces were obscured by wrappings. They each carried scimitars that widened at the ends where they curved backwards. Some of them were straighter than curved and the flare of others was more pronounced. They encircled the pond and the adventurers; who all stood ready to defend against an attack despite not having any weapons. Several of the creatures were still materializing, and more were forming at the ridge of the dunes.

Sid rolled out from Simon's bag and into the water; unseen by the sand warriors, or by Simon. Like Lazuli had changed before, Sid too began to grow from his small size into something much larger. He jumped out of the water with a wide and long sword that seemed too big for any one person to wield. He swung it high and then low as he landed with the sword and sliced the warrior closest to Simon. The creature's hewn body turned to sand and was indistinguishable from the ground around it.

"Who are you?" Simon said, moving away from the new entity; not terribly threatened but still not comfortable either.

"It's me, Sid."

He had changed into the brawny form of a man, similar to Bromle in size but with greater agility. His back was a coat of long, drooping spikes that gave him some semblance of his previous form. The armor he wore was dark brown and covered in small studs interrupted by various spikes.

The warriors around them didn't move even when Sid attacked. He rushed off towards the next closest guard but was quickly swallowed by the sand as he turned to run. As quickly as he had jumped out of the water, he was enveloped by the ground. A second later, a black orb shot from where he was swallowed. Simon caught it in the air and realized Sid had returned—either by choice or force—to his solid obsidian form.

The warriors had finished materializing during Sid's attack and still stood motionless and quiet.

"What do we do, Simon?" Bromle said.

"What do you want?" Simon yelled at all of them.

The pool cracked behind them and a whirlpool formed in its center. The water rushed into the hole that was created. The sand of the dunes around them started to shift and portions of structure started to rise out of them. A large onion dome rose out of the water accompanied by several others, prefacing the rise of a palace that barely fit within the confines of the water. Its outside was laboriously intricate with flowers and designs that gave it a more natural appearance as if it was covered in foliage. It and the wall that surrounded it in the dunes had reached its pinnacle and stopped its ascent.

The four companions were ushered towards the front of the palace. A man and several of the warriors walked out from its entrance. He was dressed like a desert king. He wore a short robe that was girdled with a band of gold, encrusted with stones of teal and emerald. He wore a blue khepresh crown shaped like two upturned turtle shells sandwiched together. In the front and center of it was a malachite stone that was dark green with bright circles of paler hues. His bare shins were wrapped in bright leather sandals that wove up to his knees. In one hand he carried a short staff that had a narrow axe head on one side of the end and a golden orb behind it; a dangerous looking weapon for cutting or bludgeoning. His other hand rested on the hilt of an ornate opal dagger's handle that contained a scattered rainbow within the stone. If it weren't for the situation, Simon would have nearly begged him to look at the objects.

"Travelers, what business do you have in Karawost?" the man asked.

"We meant no offense in our intrusion and are only seeking knowledge," Simon said trying to remember his manners.

"This is a desert and not the best of places to seek it. And it appears that you seek more than that; you attacked my warriors. Who are you?"

"My apologies for any insult we caused. We have not received many warm welcomes in our travels. I am Simon, and these are my friends: Adger, Bromle, and Orvar."

"I am Sammos dene Sabuli, king of the desert. You have left out one companion, though: the Methatien—that shape-shifting stone creature."

"Sid? Do you mean the armadillo thing?" Simon said. "He's here." Simon opened his hand and Sid's pangolin form emerged.

"You?" Sammos exclaimed. "Then that means my brother has sent you, and any friend of his is an enemy of mine. Kill them!"

18 The Palace

The warriors pointed their swords at the group's necks and they did not move for fear of being cut.

"You need to get past your problems with Kapell," Sid said.

"He left when we needed him the most, and you defend him?"

"He left to defend Kynn's arrival," Sid said gesturing towards Simon.

"This person is Kynn Veyor?" Sammos laughed. "The time that my brother spent underwater has corrupted his mind. Kynn's arrival was said to come loudly, not for few to know."

"He has the sword and shield—" Bromle said.

"I've heard about the weapons you carry and word of your adventures has reached me already. Those antiquated weapons are nothing more than legendary relics you're fortunate enough to posses! The real hero the stories speak of has far more. Kapell may have taught you a few tricks, but that only proves where your loyalties are. Your allegiance to that towering mountain, I have the unfortunate burden of calling my brother, is enough to call into question any motivation or reason you may have in coming here. Kill them all, and bring me the Methatien."

The warriors raised their weapons to kill them, and Sammos turned his back as he walked towards his palace. Simon felt the same rumbling within him that he had before, but this time it felt smoother like the shifting of sands instead of the cacophony of falling rocks. He defensively raised his hands as the guards swung their weapons downward, and they all turned to harmless sand.

Sammos quickly turned with surprise. He moved in lithely gestures that the sand seemed to respond to. Where the warriors fell in small piles of sand, their forms began to grow again. They formed around the group and more were on the ridge of the dunes around the oasis. They all rushed towards Simon who still was unsure of how he managed to disintegrate the ones before.

Simon tried to envision and pull whatever sand he could. He raised his hands and the ground beneath the four of them rose, too. They were elevated into the air on a geyser of sand. Simon willed the sand to smash and disintegrate the warriors and lower portions of it did. He could feel each time that Sammos tried to materialize more warriors and prevented him from creating any reinforcements. Simon imagined the sand carrying them towards their belongings and it responded. Simon continually prevented Sammos from any additional attacks while they all quickly gathered their weapons and clothing. After a brief moment, they were better prepared to fight anything else that Sammos created.

"Yes, Simon," Orvar said excitedly. "I knew you had the capability within you to move the sands!"

"This would be a great time to teach him instead of letting him learn on his own," Bromle said.

"A lion cannot be taught to roar; it must discover its voice on its own to be truly effective," Orvar said.

They rushed over to the palace entrance where Sammos was still gesturing and trying to conjure more warriors. He changed his movements when he saw Simon coming. The area around them grew dark as a shadow blocked out the sun high above them. The four of them turned to see a giant as large as Kapell but made of sand and stony, jutting, red rocks similar to the cliff faces near the small desert town.

"I admit," Sammos shouted over at him, "I am impressed with your manipulation and tricks of the sand, but Rykos is beyond even you, whoever you may be!"

The sand giant, Rykos, stepped towards them and bellowed with a cavernous mouth that revealed an array of sharp, stony teeth. Its eyes were dark and silvery like pools of swirling mercury. It swung at them with a slow but powerful clawed hand that smashed into the ground. Its hand turned into a pile of sand and then instantly reformed. It stood even taller and extended two tremendous wings that swirled the sands around them into a funnel. The four of them stood at the bottom of the storm's eye and were unable to flee.

Although he was unsure about what to do, Simon picked the four of them up on another geyser of sand as he had done before. He had no plan of how to overcome Sammos or Rykos, but waiting to be killed was the least of his options. His only thought was to attack. He trailed his companions behind him as he rose up and over the top of the tunnel of sand the creature had created. Each time he raised them above the edge, the funnel grew with them.

"Bromle, prepare your gloves and the hotter you can create your orbs, the better," Simon said. "Adger—"

"I got this," Adger said and pulled out what looked like a rock sling.

"And Orvar—"

"My sword is of no use here," Orvar said, "but I have this." He pulled out a staff from one of his sleeves that didn't seem to sensibly fit there. Despite the obvious rigidity that the staff had, he wrapped it around his wrist like a rope and it extended a cubit past his hand. He spun his hand and thrust it towards Rykos, firing bursts of colors towards the giant. The blazing bursts punched holes through the funnel walls. The other two followed Orvar's lead and started attacking Rykos as they ascended, throwing whatever projectiles they could conjure.

"I'm assuming you have a plan," Adger said as he whipped his rock sling into the sand closest to them, scooping up more material to alter into a projectile. He swung it above his head, released one end of the sling, and then threw what he gathered towards the creature above. The projectile solidified and grew before it slammed into Rykos.

Simon reminded himself that he had no surety his plan would work, but idly waiting to be buried in a dune was enough motivation to try any poorly conceived plan. He pulled out his hilt and ignited the blade. It was brighter than he had ever seen it, and he could feel the heat from the flame, yet the hilt remained cooler in his hand. The flame grew and Simon imagined Sid's blade; the sword took on that shape.

"Hey, that's my sword," Sid said from Simon's pack.

Simon elevated the group up out of the tunnel and sharply turned down towards Rykos before the funnel could surround them again. He dragged his blade across the giant's face and the cut he made reflected the light after he had passed. He kept his sword dragging on the creature's skin as he flew around and down it. The trail of glass he created started to crack and slow Rykos as he struggled to fight against it. Simon weaved his way down to its legs and around them several times, causing them to become wrapped in glass trails. The giant stopped, his legs unable to continue. The glass stripes broke and the sand creature fell towards the ground on top of where Simon and his companions had landed.

Simon raised his sword and held it with both hands. He channeled the rapid beating of his heart towards the sword's intensity and willed it to burn even hotter. The giant fell and exploded into a cloud of sand and dust. When all the sand settled, a glass dome was around the adventurers. Bromle clapped his hands and the dome shattered outward. Simon picked them back up on another wave of sand and quickly surfed towards Sammos. They landed around him and leveled their weapons at him. Sid changed his form to the large brawny size he did before and joined the others in threatening Sammos.

Sammos raised his hands and the sand he still controlled fell to the ground. The sand-warriors around the palace raced towards them. Simon turned and blazed his sword in one hand, while with the other, he directed a stream of sand through the fire. It turned to missiles of glass that shredded the incoming enemies until they all fell towards the ground in heaps.

The oasis was as peaceful as when they first arrived except for the palace that had replaced it. Simon turned back towards Sammos with his sword and hand still poised to pierce him with glass projectiles.

"I concede," he said and raised his hands even higher. "It's apparent that Kapell taught you more than I thought was possible."

"Kapell taught me nothing of what you've seen here," Simon said.

"But how is this possible?"

"Because he's Kynn!" Adger said. "Why is that so hard to believe?"

"That is not a sufficient answer. The powers you've displayed are beyond even my own conjuration."

"Why would we tell you anything?" Bromle said and took a step closer to him. "You tried to kill us!"

"My brother's allies are no better than him. If you align yourself with him than you, too, are betrayers."

"Without Kapell, I would be dead," Simon said. "I wouldn't have even set foot in Dyurndale had I tried to do so on my own. He fought Veadus to keep me safe."

"Did he defeat her?" Sammos asked with a note of concern in his voice.

"I don't know, but it sure looked like he did. He slammed her face into the water and she disappeared. Her forces invaded Burgh Sceadwia though. So, I don't know if she's dead or not."

"If you come from there then you are surely enemies!"

"Calm yourself and listen!" Orvar yelled and pointed his staff's end towards Sammos' face.

"We overthrew the Council," Simon said. "When they found out who we were, they tried to kill us. Instead, we killed the beasts they released on us and even a couple of fiery soldiers—"

"They were Etnian's soldiers," Orvar added.

"My subjects have told me of the Council's betrayal," Sammos said. He let the wind fill the silence, and even with weapons pointed at his neck, he still commanded an air of respect; his chest was stuck out and his chin held high. He glared at each of them, examining them up and down now that he had the silent moment to do so.

"After seeing what you're capable of... I am inclined to believe your story. Etnian must have been more influential than I first believed. I foolishly hoped the Council's rule was just a lust for power and nothing more. I still disapprove of your companionship with this Methatien," he said and gestured to Sid.

"Your brother harbors no ill will for your disgust," Sid said. "The divide between you has been fabricated by you alone."

"He left us, Sid! When we needed him most, he fell asleep in the ocean."

"I already told you: without him, I would be dead by now!" Simon said. "He saved my life, *and* he helped us escape Burgh Sceadwia."

"You claim to have defeated the Council."

"We did, but when Veadus' forces invaded we were overwhelmed...we lost friends."

"We don't know they're lost," Adger said quickly.

"Look, Sammos," Simon continued, "we need your help. We need to find a library. Is it here?"

"Ta Khronika Metis," Sammos said. "It's known by many names, but most people know it as simply *Khronika*. That's where you're going?"

Orvar nodded. "I had forgotten the name; it has been centuries since I have heard it."

"To help you means to help my brother."

"He is worth helping," Simon said.

A long silence passed and the whistling of the wind in the empty reaches of the desert was the only sound to disturb the silence. Sammos looked at the ground lost in thought. He lowered his hands and extended his open hand to Simon.

"You can lower your weapons," he said. "I will help you, but first, you must tell me your tales. Come; let us find a respite even greater than that of the oasis. I will have the rest of your things brought into the palace."

They put away their weapons and followed Sammos into his palace.

"If you need me again, I'll be ready," Sid said as he returned to his smaller form and jumped back into Simon's pack.

The inside of the palace was full of deep, bright blues and gold. He led them to a wide pool that was entirely tiled with the same bright blues as the rest of the palace.

"These waters will refresh your wounds and strains. Take your time, and then join me for food when you are ready. My subjects will guide you there."

Three beige Fennec foxes with oversized ears walked around a corner and sat down at the edge of the pool. From another corner came three black Tesem adorned with wide ornate collars. The animals sat motionless at the pool where the adventurers stood. Adger, who couldn't help but be in awe of their regal beauty, reached down to pet one of the soft looking foxes.

"Please don't pet me, sir," it said.

Adger pulled his hand back quickly.

"They won't harm you," Sammos said, "but I wouldn't recommend treating them as a pet you own. I will leave you now."

The four of them lounged in the pool, letting the sand and soreness fall from their bodies. After soaking a while they got out and dried with towels nearby. In the time they were swimming, their clothes had been taken and cleaned, which they wouldn't have noticed if not for being folded and fragranced with a pleasant sandalwood. They got dressed and followed the animals.

They were led to a great dining hall with walls too high for candlelight to reach. The walls were filled with books and paintings so large that twenty people could not have lifted the frame. It was enough to retain any person's attention if not for the table in the center of the room, covered in food. Tall golden candelabras illuminated the table with green flames that shimmered like dancing emeralds. At their feet were silver bowls and trays with piles of breads, cheeses, and roasted meats with charred edges begging to be picked. A cornucopia poured fruits onto the table and the produce filled the blank spaces like the pointillism of an artist's brush. The tablecloth was a brilliant blue, hemmed with gold, and embroidered with hieroglyphs of stories begging to be told. The chairs looked more like they belonged in a lounge than at a dining table, and they begged to be sat in. Sammos sat at the head of the table in a tall wing-backed throne and they joined him at its end.

"Are you feeling refreshed?" he asked.

"Very much so," Simon said. "Thank you."

"This is far too much food for just us, your highness," Orvar said bowing low.

The other three awkwardly tried to follow his lead but were far less graceful.

"Care not for the food you cannot eat," Sammos said. "There are others in my kingdom who will be afforded the surplus; you are only allowed the first-fruits."

The brothers and Simon exchanged confused glances.

"If my palace has shown you any one thing, let it be that sight does not invalidate reality; what you cannot see may exist just the same. Now, please, come and tell me of your adventures while we eat."

Over the course of several hours, the group recounted their adventures and tales. Particular interest was given to Simon's recollection as the others were pulled into his story as it happened to him. When their stomachs could hold no more food and sleep threatened to subdue them, they finished their stories not long after.

"It seems you have had quite an ordeal," Sammos said. "I'm amazed that your sensibility is still intact. And you still don't rightly understand your manipulation of earth and sand?"

"Not fully; no," Simon said. "I didn't have the time to ask your brother in the Burgh, so I just went with what I felt. It seemed natural and when it happened, it only encouraged the feeling."

"You have convinced me well enough. I apologize for my hostility. It has been far too long since I have had the company of friends."

"So, you no longer consider us enemies from our allegiance with your brother?" Orvar asked.

"No, I see that it may be time to mend our broken bonds. Tonight, you will sleep here, and tomorrow I will send you on your way with provisions and transport. You may leave your skiff here, and it will be well tended to."

"You can keep it honestly; we just borrowed that from the town at the edge of the desert," Simon said.

"Ah, yes. What a fond people they are! I assume they helped you greatly."

The group looked at each other, and Simon spoke after nervously exchanged glances. "No, your highness, they've—they're all gone. The town was deserted."

Sammos' countenance dropped noticeably. "This saddens me greatly but only further strengthens my resolve to help you. Sid, will you continue on with them or can you carry a message to my brother for me?"

Sid's shape emerged from a stone on the table. He ran to the head of the table and stood in front of Sammos. "I will tell your brother whatever you wish so long as it is good for him to hear," Sid said.

"Ask him to meet me at the western mouth of the Pass of Stoikheion. I may be willing to help you, but there is a long discussion he and I must have before I consider our brotherhood mended."

"I will do as you ask."

"I will speed you on your way." Sammos summoned one of the Tesem and whispered something in his ear. He and Sid left the room quickly, and that was the last time the group would see Sid in such a pleasant setting.

Speaking to the others, Sammos said, "The library will give you the answers you seek. Like my brother, I cannot give you all of the answers as much as I would wish to have them. Your best hope is within the library, but locating the information will be difficult. You need to first find Countess Sophia Bodehaite; she is the librarian and without her, you will lose your way in the limitless shelves of knowledge. I warn you though, she is wisdom; the very embodiment of it. To gain her assistance, you will have to impress her. Think not on these things tonight, though. Please rest and allow me the honor to serve you all in the morning."

With that, Sammos stood and they all did the same. He bowed, and they responded in kind. They each left to separate rooms and found their beds to be soft and their dreams to be pleasant.

In the morning, they were fed well again, but their host did not join them. The table was not nearly as covered by food as the night before but was set for the four of them. They were pleased with the breakfast but slightly concerned that their host was not there. They were startled as the dining hall doors swung open. A sphinx was on the other side. It was a creature with the body of a lion, an almost beautiful female face, and wings so expansive and multicolored that they threatened to crack the doorframe as it passed through. Despite the disparity between the width of the door and the creature's muscular body, it folded its feathered wings and stepped through the door. They were all speechless at the enormity and surprise of seeing such a creature; it gave them more alarm than even the creatures they faced in the stadium. This magnificent being was a legend written about on the dark corridors of ancient worlds, not a living reality—or so they thought. It spoke quickly when it noticed their anxiety.

"Peace unto you," it said in a deep, calm voice that seemed overlaid with the reverberations of a darker power. "My master apologizes that he could not be here. His journey to the Pass of Stoikheion is long, even when hastened. He told me to ensure you continued your journey and instructed me to guide you to Ta Khronika. I will await you outside."

They finished their food and gathered their belongings that were piled in the corner of the hall. They made their way outside being led, again, by the Tesem and the foxes. When they stepped into the heat of the day, they squinted in the light. A blimp affixed to three masts of a great ship glinted in the sunlight. The ship reflected the light with gold trimmings and jewel encrusted planks. On its prow was a fleet of creatures similar to the foxes in the palace but drastically larger. Each had a pair of wings that shimmered in the morning light. A ramp led up to the deck and fourteen sand warriors were lined up along the path that led to it.

"And here I thought we were just going to get a few camels and a cart," Bromle said with a smile.

They climbed the ramp, and no sooner had they set foot on the deck then the warriors below turned and marched on the ship with them. They lined each side of the ship at the ramparts and stood facing outward. Otherwise, they did not move.

"You all ready then?" said a throaty voice from the helm of the ship. They turned to see a short man that had green wings like a scarab's. The wings fluttered and folded underneath a shiny shell that was dark green with concentric black circles that formed spots all over his back. "The name's Malachi, and I'll be your captain today."

"Are you a Methatien?" Simon asked.

"Indeed I am!" Malachi said in a chipper tone. "That be a problem for ya?"

"No, not at all; I find your species so fascinating."

"And I found yours to be bizarre. To the library then! Find a place below and stay there. We wouldn't want the great Kynn Veyor falling to his death, now would we?"

Not long thereafter, they were airborne. There were windows below deck that allowed them to see their ascent. It was a more breathtaking site than any journey Simon had had so far. The inside of the cabin was cool, especially when compared to the heat of the desert. There were no sharp banks or turns, and there was food, and small plates of breads and cheeses for them below. It was not an altogether unpleasant journey.

"Look, beer!" Bromle said, rushing to a keg with a mug he snatched up nearby. He quickly filled it with frothing liquid and tipped it to his lips, letting the froth run down his beard. He let out a long belch that went on for ages and even looked to the others with wide eyes and a nod. They all erupted in laughter and joined in the pleasantry.

Simon was comfortable below deck—having a good time even—but he couldn't resist the urge to see the journey from above. A short while after the journey began, he found his feet leading him to the deck above. His companions joined him soon thereafter.

The sun was setting over the distant horizon; the sky was an assortment of purples, reds, and oranges as if an artist's oil palette had been spilled in the sky. All around them was a sea of swirling sands, both dark, and golden. The shadows of the evening reached their spindly fingers towards each other between the dunes and hills.

"It's too beautiful to resist," Malachi said from the helm. "Just watch your step for me then, eh? I'll be liable for any harm that comes to ya'."

The darkness came and swallowed the sun as the sky bloomed with more stars than grains of sand in the desert below. The blimp above them shimmered and became transparent. The light of the stars shone through it like it wasn't even there. Simon couldn't help but feel weakness in the awe of the creation's beauty.

"Aye, there be your library," Malachi said, pointing towards the horizon. A beam of light shone into the sky far in the distance.

"I would get your things," Malachi continued. "We'll be there soon and I'd rather not linger on the balconies of the Countess."

Their flight took them away from the edge of the desert and above forest floors and rising cliffs of a mountain range. The steep rising and falling of the ground made the library seem inaccessible by any other means than flying. The dark greens and cooler temperatures in that part of the world were a welcome change to the harsh temperatures of the desert.

"How're we supposed to get out of here if you leave," Simon asked. "Are you coming back to pick us up?"

"My, no," Malachi said. "You're on your own from here. I was instructed to take you there, but this is not a place I wish to stay."

"Why? Is Sophia an unfriendly person?"

"For starters, I wouldn't call her anything less than Countess—if you see her at all. And her friendliness is something I have never been close enough to experience. From what I last heard about her, she may have been lost in the library."

"How could she be lost in her own library?"

"Khronika is not just a building; it's as big as a country, mate. It stretches out into all the mountains you see below you. It contains every thought and written word of all mankind from this life and the one before, all collected in one place; it is many shelves. The attendants that collect and catalog the information are—from what I heard—corrupted. They are fearful to be challenged by and faster than I think even Sammos could compete with."

"And Etnian's grasp hasn't reached this far?" Orvar said.

"Sammos protects it with his ownership of the sand. He has swallowed many attempts of passage from below and above."

Structures climbed the side of the tallest mountain in the range as if the mountain had grown around the buildings. They spread outward and their scarcity increased the farther they were placed from the congregate. The stone of the structure was pale and smooth like each stone was carved out of the very mountain face. Windows littered the mountains as often as the trees. Massive openings made thousands of shelves visible below. Pillars supported entire sections of mountaintops that roofed open areas filled with even more shelves. All of the shelves they saw were but a portion of what else there was.

"Are we welcome here?" Simon asked.

"You are not unwelcome, but neither are you invited. I have never been inside let alone landed on its premises. Any more advice I offer you is an assumption."

They approached a balcony that was large enough for the massive ship to land on with room enough for several more. The ship landed, and the four adventurers disembarked.

"Good luck, friends," Malachi said as he took off again. "May the sun set at your backs and the sand be still underneath your steps!"

"And may your foxes' wings grow large enough to carry his majesty's palace!" Simon said, unsure of the customary response but thought it might be appropriate.

The four of them stood watching the ship sail away, slightly concerned that they had no plan of escape. They turned to face the mountainous library and the entrance before them. An archway and the open-air hallway beyond stood illuminated by torches; sending flickering shadows along the floor. The sky above had no moon and only the light of the stars. No matter the length of their delay, an answer was not forthcoming. Simon took one last glance of the shrinking airship and wished he could have just stayed on it, enjoying the moment a while longer. He turned back towards the library and steeled his nerves for the next challenge.

"Well, gents," he said, "let's go find a book."

19 The Library

"I don't need a welcoming committee, but not being approached by a single guard or warrior is a little unsettling," Adger said.

"It is a welcome change from our last few encounters," Orvar said.

"Stay alert nevertheless," Simon said.

"Allow me to take the lead," Bromle said.

"We don't know where we're going, though," Adger said.

"What about the compass?"

Simon pulled out the silver object and opened it to reveal a dark, swirling fog filling the glass. "Well, that's disappointing."

"Maybe Unaketay can help," Adger suggested.

Bromle and Adger pulled out Una and Ketay, but when the stones merged, the small pet was no more help besides excitedly jumping around them.

"What other objects were you given?" Orvar asked Simon.

He pulled out the things he hadn't had the opportunity to use or look at: three rings, the small metal frog, his maps, some blank parchment, and pieces of a shell. "I'm not sure, really," Simon said. "I can't imagine what these shells might be useful for; they seem like trinkets." He shook one of the rings next to his ear like there might be secrets held within it.

"I'm sure you thought the same thing of the rhin geatu ring before you discovered its purpose. We may be able to find some answers here but locating the right book is another matter entirely."

"Well, what do you think they're for?" Simon asked Orvar, extending the objects to him.

"I have learned more than once, the unfortunate way, not to touch powerful items intended for another." He held up his hand to refuse the

201

objects.

Simon put the objects back in their pouches and unfolded the parchments that he hadn't looked at before. He had the two maps that still had the rhin geatu marks, but the other papers were blank. "Well that's useless," Simon said and handed the papers to Adger's outstretched hands.

"No, wait; look," Adger said, his eyes wide with excitement. The paper he held came to life with lines twisting and extending outward from the center which formed walls, hallways, stairwells, and bookshelves. "It's the library!"

The other three crowded behind Adger.

"What'd you do, little brother?" Bromle asked.

"I don't know. I...I just thought about the library and how overwhelming it is. How are we supposed to realistically find anything on our own?"

At the bottom and center of the map, the large balcony could be seen. The library filled the entire paper which was larger than any map any of them had seen before. It unfolded and couldn't be held on each end by one person.

"Each area of the library seems to have different subjects," Adger continued. "There's history, weapons, art—the list goes on—oh, there; cartography! Where should we start looking?"

"Probably weapons," Bromle said with a nod.

"I would think we start with cartography," Orvar said. "Finding Naru should be our priority."

"We just need to ask the map, right? Map, show me—what was it—Naru."

The map remained unchanged.

"I don't think it will be so easy," Simon said.

A crack of thunder sounded right above them, and the once clear sky poured rain down on them. They all rushed inside with Unaketay close behind. The creature rushed underneath Adger's legs.

"Unaketay, come here," Bromle said. He gave the creature something and it split into two stones as it had before.

"Let's head into the library and see what we find, but keep quiet and stay to the shadows when possible," Simon said. "Like Malachi said, we weren't exactly invited."

"Sneaking around is not the best idea for people who don't want to seem like a threat," Adger said.

"I'd rather choose to be seen than unknowingly watched. I think we should divide into teams to cover more ground."

"What about the Countess?" Bromle asked. "Or the map; we only have one of them."

"Maybe I can copy it."

"But that would take ages."

"There must be something in my collection to help with it. Maybe there's something that can take a picture of it."

Simon pulled out the other three rings and turned them over in his hands. One of them had what looked like a small observatory on its side with a compass rose on the other. It was a wide band with a large, black stone at its top. When Simon turned it in his hand it seemed to shimmer with a rainbow in its darkness.

"Hold out the map, Adger. No, hold it towards me so I can see it."

Adger turned the map around towards Simon. Simon put the ring on and pointed it towards the map. Smokey rainbow tendrils floated towards the map and moved all around it as if they were snakes smelling the air. When the ring seemed satisfied with whatever its task was and the tendrils retracted, Simon pointed the ring towards the wall behind Adger and a projection of the map shone as clearly as it was drawn on the paper.

"How could you have possibly known that ring would do that?" Bromle asked.

"I figured these rings must be for *something* and just let my imagination take over. If I had a special ring, that's what I'd want it to do in this situation, except…" Simon twisted the ring on his finger inward towards his palm and the image of the map was cast upon the ceiling. The image started to shrink and drop from the rafters, floating in midair. The two dimensional layer of the map expanded and grew until they were looking at a small scale model of the library that Simon seemed to hold just above his hand. "There we go," Simon said. "*That's* what I'd want a ring to do."

"You have a lot more on your map than I do here," Adger said.

"Just stay on this level. Why don't you and Orvar start in the map room; Bromle and I will head to weapons. Orvar, do you still have your radio?"

Orvar raised his wrist to expose the communicator.

"Good. Stay in contact, and stop if you're not sure of anything. Let us know if you find anyone, too. Maybe they can help us find what we're looking for. I think both our paths are this way."

"I don't see why we need Countess Sophia," Adger said. "Seems like we have the right rooms, we can probably find the information—"

Adger trailed off as they exited the entryway and entered what was marked as the lobby on their maps. The ceiling was so tall that it was lost beyond the reaches of the highest torches mounted on the walls. Bookshelves reached up into the tall ceiling and lined the walls in between the torches. There were so many books and the walls were so far from where they stood that the distinguishable features of the books melded together like a speckled painting.

"And this is just the lobby," Adger said. "We need to find that countess."

A shadowy figure drifted towards them from a door far on the opposite wall. It wore a white robe hemmed with golden designs.

"Stay ready, but don't show any obvious signs of aggression," Simon said.

The figure seemed to weave back and forth as it moved towards them, making it seem more like an apparition. It flew around them several times before stopping in front of Simon. It had no face until it spoke. Features formed from the darkness inside its hood. Its face was that of a woman's but was so pale with such sharp features, that she looked less human and more avian. It was disconcerting but did not appear to be aggressive.

"Welcome to Ta Khronika Metis. You are the first visitors this hall has seen in over a thousand years. You may read whatever you wish, but do not attempt to take anything outside the library walls."

"Thank you for your welcome," Orvar said as formally as he could. "Could you assist us with finding some information?"

The apparition floated away towards another door as if it hadn't heard Orvar.

"Excuse me," Simon called after it, "can you help us please?"

The apparition turned and floated towards them as it had before. It circled them again, stopped in front of Simon, and said the same thing through the same face that it had before. Once it was finished, it flew away again.

"I don't understand," Orvar said. "This used to be a lovely and welcoming place to visit. It seems that time has changed it too much. Something is not well here. We need to find Countess Sophia."

"Let's see if we can find what we're looking for first," Simon said.

The group split up and went in separate directions. They walked through varied rooms like the lobby, each of them equally as filled with books and all of them different in color and architecture. Openings to the outside allowed flashes of lightning to remind them of the storm, yet somehow, no wind blew the rain inside. The rain and an occasional distant rumble of thunder were the only sounds they heard. The rooms were each unique from the ones before them as if the place was a collection of books *and* wholly different libraries. They passed by globes, statues, and other relics amidst the shelves that made it feel like a museum in addition to a library.

"How're you guys doing over there?" Simon said into his radio.

There was a crackle and a moment of silence.

"Who're they," Adger's voice came over the radio. It was picking up his voice but not because he was speaking directly into it.

"I don't know," Orvar said.

A loud voice boomed through the communicator, "You should not—"

The communicator was silent.

"Orvar," Simon said into it. "Adger?"

"We need to get back there," Bromle said with urgency in his voice.

Simon nodded his head and they retraced their steps, but at the turn of a hallway connecting two of the rooms, a stone wall had replaced the doorway. Without hesitating, Bromle developed two orbs in his hands and launched a force of air towards the wall. He tried a couple other colors, but the brick was barely charred.

Simon tried the radio again but still there was no response. "We need to keep going," Simon said.

"This was an open hallway before."

"Either this place can move walls, or someone is moving them. Either way, it doesn't look like we have much of a choice but to keep going forward. It looks like there's another way back to them. Look." Simon projected the map so that Bromle could see it. He pointed to a passage that entered the opposite side of where the others would have entered.

Bromle and Simon quickly jogged that way while trying to keep their things from making too much noise. They didn't take the time they had before to notice all the minutiae of the shelves and artifacts. Instead, they focused on trying to discover what happened to the others as quickly as possible. They took several turns and followed Simon's map until they came to where the others should have been.

Bromle pulled out his red stone, "Find Ketay, Una."

The rock rolled under a shelf and a faint light emitted from underneath it. A second later, Unaketay appeared.

"Can you find, Adger?"

The creature sniffed around the room, weaving in between bookshelves. After a few moments, Unaketay had circled back to the door where they had entered.

"Up, up," Bromle said to it, and it hopped up onto his shoulders. "There's nothing here. If they left anything else, she would've found it."

"This certainly changes things. What are you thinking?"

"You're the leader here." Bromle paused to think. "But, I'd bet—no, I don't know."

"No, go ahead. What do you think? I have an idea, but I want to hear yours, too."

"Well, if they got swiped, I'd bet that Sophia lady isn't as lost as Malachi thought. This place looks well kept. It's got light, and it's pretty clean, even though we haven't seen anybody wandering around besides that owl-faced ghost. Whoever else is still living here probably had the same thoughts as you and chose not to be seen; including the Countess. I bet she already knows we're here."

"You're probably right. Now we need to figure out where to go next."

"Libraries always have a head office."

"Now you're thinking what I'm thinking." Simon pulled up the map again and they both scoured it for any notes or indications of a room smaller, or different from the rest, that might set it apart as an office.

"I'm not seeing anything that says, 'Office,' or, 'Here's the Countess,'" Bromle said.

"This place is massive," Simon said. "If I was running the show, I'd keep my office somewhere central. I bet she's in the highest place with the best view. There..." Simon said, pointing to the outline of a small room at the pinnacle of one of the structures.

"And you think she'd take them there?"

"I think that she'd want to know who's in her house. If Orvar and your brother were taken, yes, I think the Countess would want to meet them. We haven't been taken yet, so I'm wondering if we also haven't been seen. Don't worry, Bromle; they're still alive. I can feel it."

They ran for the central most room in the library, stopping occasionally to see if they were still heading in the right direction. All the rooms within were well lit—as best as can be with torches and candles. Even though the light found its way to the floor and around the shelves, there were occasional shadows that seemed to keep the light back of its own will. The darkness forced paranoia into Simon's mind and made him imagine creatures in the pitch.

They bounded up several stairwells that opened on the sides to views of the different rooms. The shadows below seemed to have grown even more from the dark corners they were hiding in before. The pair eventually came to the top of the stairs and the top of the Library at its center. They were at the end of a very long hallway with several books in glass cases on pedestals. Several rooms opened from the hallway into much smaller collections of books.

"These rooms are unmarked on the map," Simon said.

"I wonder if what we need is in here somewhere."

They stepped into one of the rooms and glanced at some of the titles. They were a varied collection that didn't seem to be limited to a particular genre. They walked through a couple more shelves and then stopped to admire the view when they both turned the corner of the last shelf. There was an archway that opened onto a balcony that looked far out into the mountains. The storm had stopped, and the darkness of the night was interrupted with innumerable stars again. A cool evening breeze blew in from the open archway.

They were so refreshed and captured by the scene, for a moment they overlooked their cohabitants in the room. Several robed figures like the one in the lobby were moving books on the shelves, except their garments were black with white bordered hems. In the darkness of the cloth, there were shimmering inscriptions that just barely caught the candlelight, making the foreign scripts seem to dance about. They had a corporeal form instead of ethereal; they walked around on lanky bodies. As they moved books, they easily reached high onto the shelves then shrunk to touch the lower ones. One of them noticed Simon and Bromle and they all turned to vapors underneath their robes. They unanimously flew towards them in a flutter of robes and stopped inches away from their faces before either Simon or Bromle had a chance to react.

"You should not be here," they boomed together in one voice.

Without another action, they fluttered back to their various places in the room, resumed their corporeal form, and continued adjusting books as if nothing had happened.

Simon and Bromle slowly backed out of the room into the hallway.

"Those must be the same things that took Adger and Orvar," Bromle said.

"Probably, but I'm not sure how to fight a ghost."

"They looked real enough to me," he said as he pounded a fist into his other empty hand.

"We don't know what happened yet," Simon said and put a hand over Bromle's to calm him. "For all we know, the others could have gotten away. We don't know that they were taken."

They backed out of the room and continued down the hallway, passing several more rooms that they hurried past. The hallway ended in a set of double doors. Each door had an elaborate scene of stained glass that was too beautiful to appropriately describe. The colors of the scenes were so deep and the glass so thick that seeing through them was impossible. On one door there was a scene of two figures in a furious sword fight, and there were flashes of light and sparks flying from the blades. The person who was facing outward seemed to be winning the battle against the one whose back was turned. He was pushing the defender back with one sword and held another high in the air. The defender had a shield and sword in hand; both bright with the life of fire.

The other door had a figure standing on a cliff above hundreds of soldiers fighting on an open battlefield. Amidst them, there were creatures that Simon recognized from Canton and Burgh Sceadwia. There were even several giants locked in an embrace like Kapell and Veadus had been at the start of his journey; indeed, two of them appeared to be his defender and aggressor from that time. Beyond the battlefield, there was a tall cliff with an illuminated crack. The light poured out and fell on the ground like a waterfall.

"These are me," Simon said as he pointed to the doors. "I think this is my future."

"Let us hope so," said a peaceful female's voice that drifted into Simon's mind as clearly as someone speaking next to him, but it felt foreign.

"What did you say?" Bromle said to Simon.

"That wasn't me; I thought that was you."

"That wasn't me…"

They both spun around with weapons raised but turned to see an open hand in front of each of them. They were unable to move. The woman before them kept her hands outstretched and her face calm. She was a few inches taller than Simon and as lithe as a lady might be expected to be, but the way her outstretched arms were tensed, the shade of muscles could just be perceived. It was easy to see the age behind her eyes, although her face did not clearly show it, except for the smallest of creases at the corners of her pale, golden eyes. Long blonde curls stuck out from a golden hemmed robe, similar in design to the other creatures of the library. It was otherwise of much more intricate design; closer to a gown than a simple robe. Its pleats overlapped so seamlessly, and the glimpses of colors in between glowed so brightly, that her garments appeared to sparkle. She wore a dress underneath that just grazed the floor. It was woven with a vast array of colors; each thread an artisan's effort and sewn so as to make the garment a wash of colors. She bore no weapon, but from the way she had captivated them, it was obvious she did not need one.

"I will not hurt you, but you mustn't attack me in return," she said.

Bromle tried to speak but found his mouth could not move either. The only words that he muttered were trapped in his throat.

"Your brother and your teacher are unharmed," she continued. "I am Countess Sophia Bodehaite; you may call me Sophia. Please, come and sit down."

She lowered her hands and the two of them were released from their invisible bonds. Unaketay jumped from Bromle's shoulder and ran to leap on Adger. They both introduced themselves and bowed slightly, as seemed the best thing to do when in the presence of a countess. The doors behind them opened to reveal Adger and Orvar, who sat in large armchairs with their backs turned. They pivoted as the doors opened and through mouthfuls of food shouted in excitement at Simon and Bromle's arrival.

"Forgive my subtlety," Sophia said. "I had to be certain that you would allow me to explain. Your companions were regaling me of your recent tales. Please sit down and refresh yourselves."

The office they were in was full of dark woods and deep green, leathered furniture. There were bookshelves filling one side of the room and, on the other side, an assortment of tables covered in various works of unfinished art. A balcony opened onto a wide terrace with a view looking out onto great forests and rivers in the vast mountain ranges. The sun was peaking over the distant mountain and the sky was glowing with the rising light. Adger and Orvar were sitting around a low table that was covered in breakfast refreshments. Bromle walked over and sat down in a larger armchair to accommodate his size. He immediately started picking up food and eating. Simon sat in a couch long enough to accommodate two people and followed his companions by participating in the food.

"Tell me, Simon," she said as she sat down beside him and turned to face him, "what knowledge do you seek?"

He was slightly uncomfortable around her; he could sense her lifetimes of knowledge and felt youthful in his own. "Well...I," Simon pointed at the doors they had come through. "I think that's me, and—well, I—I need the weapon and the way to Haeophan."

"You seem uneasy."

Simon did feel uneasy. He had been ever moving towards this moment of revelation through the threat of death and destruction. To be faced with what he was sure he already knew was an anxious experience. "I've—we've all been through a lot and to—well, I still wonder if I'm the right person to do what's expected of me."

Sophia stood up and walked to the other side of the room. She picked a book from the shelf. "I know these words well," she said as she walked back towards him, "but I want you to read them for yourself. You have been chosen and you are the one to give the faith to hope."

She handed him a dark green leather book with branded red markings that formed the outline of a mountain. On the front was a person holding a flaming sword and on the back was the shape of Simon's shield. Within the book's pages was a wide violet silk ribbon with lines of characters and symbols. He opened to the passage and at the top it read, *The Tale of Kynn Veyor.* Simon read the passage aloud involuntarily, as if thinking it wasn't enough.

The 'Dale has been scarred but all hope be not lost,
A hero will come and bring new life to this land.
With sword and with shield o'er the river he's crossed,
To come and destroy the Dark One's command.

The sword of guarding and the unbreakable shield,
Cannot be found but only provided.
The flame of the depths with the dark heat it shall wield,
The consumption by death the device keeps divided.

The wielder will be a man born on the sea,
From the lone tower and cave beset by the waves.
Protection he'll need from the water born creed,
So until that new day, the mountain will stay.

The hero's arrival will change Dyurndale's path,
And Naru will be freed from the enemy's wrath.
Not all of the walk can be heralded here,
But listen and think and seek out the seer.

The forces to fight will be of many and size,
An army he'll need with strength and resolve.
Unite them if lost to brighten the skies,
Find the way home, and the darkness dissolve.

But dead is the path that has been burned.
The people are lost and without new direction;
Hope will be given once his arrival's been learned.
He'll give light to the way and incite insurrection.

Guidance is needed for the tale to be heeded.
The mending of brothers will unite even others,
More ranks will increase from the anger's release,
And power perfected will be resurrected.

Dark towers shall fall and its weapons will rust,
So resign your doubts and strengthen your trust.
The blazing of Bere'dn: the Dark One's cessation,
Its fire the kind that will cause his cremation.

An age you may wait at new life's stone gate,
But the hero will be, you must wait to see.
So give faith to hope that you've not been lost,
'Cause the hero Kynn Veyor the river has crossed.

"That is your story, Simon," Sophia said when he was done reading. "And from what little your companions have told me, it sounds as if you have fulfilled much of it already. You may not believe you are the right person, but you have already proven that you are."

"I'm not sure I fully understand it all. Poetry wasn't really my thing before," Simon said.

"It was one of the first books to come to me, but its pages were blank when I found it. I kept it here because it was so odd for me to come across a blank book. Years went by—millennia actually—and then one day it fell to the floor while I sat right where you are now. It fell open on its spine and the words began to glow on the pages like they were being written as I watched. I spent lifetimes trying to understand it all, and it only became clear when the Maleficent King arrived. Do you indeed have the sword and shield?"

"I do," he said as he started to pull them out.

Sophia held up her hand. "I do not need to see them. I have spent many years reading of weapons and never have I enjoyed the study. I have my own tests for you. Please, empty your pockets here on the table."

Simon did as she asked and placed the few objects he didn't fully understand onto an empty space amidst the food: remnants of shell, the two remaining rings, the small frog, and the papers he had left.

"I see that you have discovered the use of the other rings?"

Simon nodded his head, "By accident, honestly."

"Sometimes the best discoveries are the ones found unintentionally. Before we continue, you must answer several questions."

Simon shifted in his seat. He had learned a lot since his journey's beginning but realized his knowledge paled in comparison to the vast resources of the library.

"Where do wisdom and knowledge begin?" she asked him.

Simon thought for a long while, and the longer he was silent, the hotter his face burned. He grew increasingly more uncomfortable and thought of the easiest of answers like *my brain*, or *ignorance*, but none of the things he imagined seemed appropriate. He was afraid that he could fail in who he was supposed to be in that very moment. And that's when the answer came to him: in his fear. "Fear is the beginning of knowledge," he said.

Sophia nodded her head. Simon let out the breath he was holding in suspense.

"And what is your greatest feat?"

Simon was quiet and felt less anxious to answer but was nearly overwhelmed with sadness as he thought about the family he left behind. He thought about the childish drawings his youngest children made for him: illegible lines and shapes that had meaning only when interpreted. They were priceless to him. He loved the smallest things his children made for him, or the stories they told him. He used to keep a journal of the simplest things they would say so that he could always treasure them and read them anytime he needed the remembrance. He felt a warmth well up inside of him as he thought of the love that gave him strength. A smile crept onto his face as he absently stared at the table in front of him.

"Love," Simon said mostly to himself. "The greatest thing I ever did was love my family."

Sophia nodded again.

"How much faith must you have to do what is asked of you?"

Her question interrupted Simon's nostalgia, and he was pulled back into the challenge.

As much as is needed, Simon thought. He had never quantified something like that, but it occurred to him that whatever small amount of faith he had must be enough.

"A grain of sand," he said.

"That's not very much," Bromle interrupted.

"With the smallest of faith, a mountain could be moved," the Countess said.

"That's ridiculous," Bromle said as he laughed and looked at the others. Their faces were stoic, and Bromle quickly went silent.

Sophia nodded her head and picked up the things Simon had placed on the table.

"Each object you were given serves a purpose. Whether you choose to use the gifts you were given is up to you, but you may find that neglecting them makes your journey harder. These shells are pieces of the whole to call upon those you need when the time is right."

More riddles, Simon thought. *I need answers, not riddles.*

"The figure of the frog is a marker; one to defend you in your battle."

Simon remorsefully thought of Lazuli and wondered why he was given a sore reminder of her sacrifice.

"The papers," she continued, "as you no doubt realized, are to help you when you become lost, but be cautious. They can reveal things to any with will enough to see them."

Simon was glad to have some semblance of explanation but frustrated that it wasn't enough of one to fully understand how to actually use the items. He was hoping for more than promissory grandeur but considered that when his need was greatest, the items revealed their use.

"What about the rings?" Simon asked. "This one, we discovered, activates the rhin geatu. And this other one seems to copy maps and even improve upon them." Simon turned over his hand to project the library.

Sophia picked up the other two rings and dropped one of them right away.

"My apologies. That ring is the life giver and the life stealer; a dangerous combination to hold. It's called the ring of Olim."

It rolled under the couch she and Simon were sitting on. Simon retrieved the ring and looked at it with newfound appreciation. It was half pure white and half black; as black as the dark void of space.

"It is volatile and has a mind of its own. I have only seen brief mention of it, but the words that describe it are hastily written and fearful. Despite the wealth of knowledge here, this is one oddity that has little written of it. The other ring you carry is the key to Naru. Only the wearer can pass through the crevice," she said as she pointed towards the stained glass scene on the door.

"But I thought that discovering Naru would open the way for all people to pass through," Simon said.

"You are hope and will give the people a sign that the way has been found, but when you pass through those gates, it will close until evil is vanquished once more. The way is narrow, but it will widen in time."

"Strangest key I've ever seen," Adger said.

"It is harder to lose something you wear than something you carry," she answered. "If you lose the ring, hope will be lost with it. The only sure way to change this world is to kill Etnian—I despise to say his name. He has done such horrible things that I simply cannot stand to say his name. You *must* kill him; it is the only way to be sure," she said with a subtle loss of her composure.

"Everything that I was sent here to do…" Simon paused for a long time to think about the weight his words would carry. "Everything the poem says, I will do my best to fulfill. But, I don't know where to find Naru, or even how to kill Etnian."

Sophia shuddered when he said his name. "The strongest of swords have been forged for ages, only to break on his steel. The mightiest of conjurations have been either turned to his pets, or made into trophies. The best of warriors have faced him and been sent to his deakylos, the 'death loops' as I've heard them also called."

"How am I supposed to kill him, then? Is this Bere'dn?" he said as he gestured to his sword.

"Unfortunately, I was close to discovering that answer when *he* came."

"Sammos said that Etnian never made it out here," Adger said.

"Sammos has spent too long in the desert. He forgets the darker days when the world was lost. The will of people was controlled and so, too, were my own archivists eventually consumed. They now wander the shelves aimlessly, and so my only option was to search for the answers alone. I believe the sword you carry is the weapon to alter the course of this world, but I must find the information vital to resolve my assumptions. I have spent lifetimes trying to find the information. There is simply too much for me to sift through; I need their help. I feel as if a book is somehow missing; the place where I thought the answer would be is not here."

"Orvar," Simon said, "You haven't said a word. You've been as quiet as Filch."

"There is much in that tale that I have heard. The weapon I have no doubt of; you surely carry Bere'dn, Simon. I fear that each deviation decreases our chances are of success. I would argue that Etnian's fall would restore the capabilities of your librarians and remove whatever control he has over Veadus. I wonder if the information you seek is even here."

"The information is here; this place contains all written information to have ever existed. I am unable to direct you to Naru without my archivists' help," Sophia said.

"Malachi said the library contained every thought, too," Bromle said.

"Malachi is even more delusional than Sammos!" Sophia said.

"Then maybe the information has yet to be written," Orvar said.

"The maps!" Adger said excitedly and grabbed the papers still on the table. "Show me Naru!" The blank paper burst into flames and vaporized in a small cloud of smoke. Adger remained still and looked around at the others without moving. "Sorry 'bout that."

Simon reached out and picked up the first map he took from Orvar's cabin and the second map he had made with the ring. "It must be here somewhere," Simon said.

"The whole world is unable to fit in such small confines," Sophia said.

"What about this," Simon asked and opened the green leather book again. "There are still blank pages in it." Simon flipped the book open, but when he got to the blank pages words began to form. Another story was being written as he watched.

"This is not a story that was written by a person," Orvar said. "The story is being written as *he* lives it. These pages were to remain blank until Kynn Veyor created the story."

Simon read through the passage and saw a narrative of some of his previous exploits interrupted by drawings of beasts and lines of maps as if it was a notebook he had filled himself as he journeyed. When he reached the point in the journal that seemed to be the bestiary, he recognized some of the creatures he had seen so far and four he recognized most particularly.

"I think these dragons were on your map frame," Simon said to Orvar. "And two of them, I've seen; one in Canton and the other just outside it."

"You have seen two of these creatures?" Sophia said in surprise.

"What about that thing in temple?" Adger said. "Was he one of them?"

"Are you talking about Cineris; Tortuse's old friend? I'm not sure. It was pretty dark, but if he looked like this I hope we don't see him again."

"They are myths even in our world," Orvar said. "If the dragons have resurfaced then our time to act and fulfill the tale is short. We need to find Naru. What else does the book say?"

"That's hard to say really; I mean, there's a lot in here. What about this seer?" Simon said as he flipped back to the poem. "Can't he tell us where to go?"

Sophia and Orvar exchanged nervous glances.

Simon started flipping through the pages again instead of waiting for an answer. He stopped on two pages that had been revealed when the book started writing more. They were written and drawn with a dark red ink whereas the rest of the pages were written with black or brown. There was a picture on one of the pages of a great, evil looking man with two swords, similar to the figure in the stained glass on the door. He held his weapons high in the air, slightly bowed over his shoulders. The figure had wicked looking armor and a dark helm that covered his face. He looked poised to cast a final strike on any defender against him. On the adjacent page was a picture and short description of Bere'dn.

"Oh, it's right here!" Simon said. "It's my sword. It says that the fire it carries is from, 'an age and darkness more volatile and destructive than the deepest furies that boil Etnian's blood. When its flames permeate the wickedness within him, his flame will be extinguished.'"

"That sounds great!" Bromle said. "So let's figure out where Naru is and we can get going."

"I think your journey will be more difficult than simply finding Naru," Sophia said.

"The information must be in here somewhere," Simon said as he quickly started thumbing through the pages again. He went from map to drawing to sketch, looking for anything that mentioned the gate or what might be on the other side of it. After scouring the pages while the others waited, he finally came across a page with a picture of the ring-key. The text spoke about how the wearer had to enter the gate while wearing the ring.

"It has a portion of a map, but it doesn't look like it's on these that I have here," Simon said. "Wait, it looks like...there; I think the gate is here," Simon said, pointing to a place on the map. "It also says, 'the gate is only permissible if the warring nations are brought to peace, and the devastating armies are united in opposition.' So, we need to intentionally bring the people trying to stop us to the gate with us?"

"That corresponds with what the seer told me and with the door, if that has any prophetic value," Orvar said.

"So, that's it then," Simon said. "Now we just need to find a way over the ocean, avoid Veadus (who will surely attack us in the water), find Etnian, kill him, somehow avoid being killed by his army, and then come all the way back *here*," he said pointing to the map, "and make it through the gate."

"Sure, no problem; we can do this," Adger said. "Let me just eat another roll."

20 The Gathering

Adger ate a few more rolls and the others joined him. They finished their food and got up to thank Sophia for her help and hospitality.

"This is a nice change for us," Adger said. "There hasn't been an attempt on our life for at least half a day."

"It has been a welcome change," Simon said, "but I fear that what lies ahead of us will be anything but peaceful."

"Allow me to take you to the library's rhin geatu," Sophia said. "I will send you to the eastern shores. From there, you will be able to find help across the sea."

"You have a gate?" Simon said. "I didn't see it on my map."

"The benefit of being granted my charge is that there are secrets I can choose to reveal; the geatu is one of them."

"Why not back to Burgh Sceadwia, though?" Simon asked. "We can't do this on our own; we'll need to have the support of any who oppose his reign. The journal says there's supposed to be armies involved, not four people with a few legendary weapons. Orvar, how far do these radios work?"

"I am unsure. Never have I tried from such a distance." He understood what Simon was thinking. He adjusted the communicator on his wrist and spoke into it. "Driscol, can you hear me? Senator Driscol, please respond."

A long moment went by and Orvar tried several more times. He even made additional adjustments and tried hailing additional people whose names Simon did not recognize. After a few more moments of silence, the communicator finally buzzed to life, and a woman's voice was on the other side.

"Orvar is that you?" the woman said.

"Gin?" Adger said excitedly.

"Aye!" Gin said. "We were all wondering if you made it to the desert."

"We did indeed and even farther," Orvar said. "We must set out for Etnian's kingdom, but before we leave, we need to know if an army is to join us. Tell me, is Driscol still alive?"

"He is, but he was badly injured in the battle. He will live but received a leg much like mine for the loss of his. Are the others with you and Adger?"

"They are. Were you successful in pushing back Veadus' forces?"

"We did what we could, but without Kapell, we would have all been lost. Many friends died and some were taken in the battle, but we were victorious." She paused for a long moment. "Filch was captured, but she fought valiantly."

"Oh no," Adger exclaimed. "Filch was taken? By who? Where was she taken?"

"A lot of us were taken," Gin said. "Right after you left the city, Veadus' forces swept down on us like a storm, but Kapell was there like a dam in a torrent and destroyed the last remnants of opposition. The ones that were captured were dragged away during the battle. Our scouts found the rhin geatu a few days later, but we had nothing to make it work. We thought you had been lost weeks ago."

"What do you mean, 'weeks'?" Simon said. "We've been gone for a few days, sure, but weeks?"

"My apologies," Sophia said. "The concept of time in Dyurndale is complicated but even more so here."

"That is unfortunate," Orvar said. "Has an army been raised in our absence?"

"Indeed, one has!" Gin said. "Driscol was nominated as our new leader, primarily because of his wisdom but also because of his heroics in the battle. He saved many lives and nearly lost his doing so. Many allies have rallied here; even refugees from Canton have managed to arrive with Kapell's help."

"Exactly how long have we been gone?" Simon said with grave concern.

"Nearly three months have passed since I last saw you. In three days time, we were set to travel towards the sea and hope to find you on the way. There is an outlet near the city that would allow us to sail to open waters. There have been so many people arriving here that we were forced to abandon our home below and return to the city. It's been an exciting time for our people despite the loss of friends."

"Where are you set to arrive on the coast?" Orvar asked.

"North of the Pass of Stoikheion," she said. "We should arrive within a week, from what I was told. Your revival will hasten us even more; I will tell Chancellor Driscol immediately. Where will you be?"

Orvar looked to Sophia, who pointed to the map that Simon pulled out for her to reference.

"If we hurry, we may be able to pass through the rhin geatu before your allies get to the coast," Sophia said.

"It appears that we will be slightly south of Stoikheion in a town called...Bakeez," Orvar said.

"Aye! We will see you soon then," Gin said.

With that, the communicator went silent, and the group was even more anxious to get going.

"Before we go," Simon said, "I have one last question—well, I have lots of questions but at least one most relevant to us right now. I'm curious who made these doors?"

"You might as well cease the ruse, Orvar," Sophia said.

"*You* did?" Simon said. "So, you're the seer too?"

"No, well I am *one of* the seers but, yes, I did make these doors. In my defense, I did try to tell you in Burgh Sceadwia, but I was not able to finish."

"What else do you know that you're not telling us?" Bromle said more critically than he intended. "Do I die? Does Simon make it? Does *he* die?"

"It does not work like that. I am not a fortune teller. In my time, I have been granted certain things to help shape change for the world, but the intent of those revelations is not to change the shape of the individuals. I know no more of Simon's success or failure than you do."

"So the seer that told you of this place—"

"Was me. I was unsure of our company at the time, so I hesitated to reveal everything about myself."

A moment of silence passed as everything settled in that they discussed.

"I'm good," Simon said and shrugged his shoulders.

"Me too," said Adger.

"Have you ever doubted Orvar, little brother?" Bromle said jeeringly.

"Not really," he laughed, "but I didn't know he was a seer until just now. That still doesn't change my trust in him though—I mean, I wish you would have told me, Orvar—it's pretty amazing!"

"I meant no harm keeping you in the dark, Adger. Knowledge is not always a power one should seek idly; sometimes it can be a burden."

"It very well can be," Sophia chimed in. "We have delayed long enough and too much time has passed. Simon, you may keep the green journal for now, but you must promise to return it to me when your story is finished and its pages are full," Sophia said.

Simon nodded his head and with that, the group of them proceeded down the long hallway. Sophia led the way past the smaller collections where the ghostly librarians archived and organized books in an endless cycle. As they came to the larger chambers, the sunlight from the morning illuminated even the darkest corners of the library as if unseen mirrors helped to reflect the light. The beauty of Khronika was even more impressive in the daylight than what the torchlight revealed. The shelves that housed the books were each exquisite; as much care had gone into their crafting as the books they held.

They had idle conversation about the library as they walked and eventually came to a bookshelf on one of the lower floors. It seemed like they had been walking for several hours, and they had even stopped at one point to eat a small lunch from a nearby table filled with food. Sophia pulled several books off of the shelves and rearranged them in an order that only made sense to her. The snap of a latch signaled a lock's release, and she pulled the shelf outward to reveal a hallway. They entered it to see that it was lined with artifacts.

"Why aren't these things displayed like some of those in the libraries?" Adger asked. "They're beautiful!"

"Some things are better left hidden until their theft can be convincingly denied," Sophia said. "Simon's success means more than just the obvious abdication of the Tainted Seraph; it will also bring a peace that will return the purpose of Dyurndale."

They passed through several rooms of relics, a couple locked gates, and a sturdy thick door until they arrived at a rhin geatu. It differed from the others they had seen in that its frame was wooden instead of stone.

"Even your ring cannot open this gate," Sophia said.

She touched a pendant around her neck and the gate came to life to show the ocean and a sandy shore. The geatu on the other side was in a cove; confirmed by the rocky coast in the scene that stretched out and back towards the geatu.

"This is goodbye," Sophia said. "I hope to see you all again, but a return to this place would be far out of your journey's path."

"I will return the book to you when this is all over," Simon said.

"About four days will have passed when you step through the geatu; you should have sufficient time to reach your allies. May wisdom be your guide and the excellence of knowledge preserve your life until your journey's end."

They were all unable to formulate a response, especially Orvar. He wanted to stay in the library and planned to return should the journey not claim him.

"If we are successful, I will deliver the book back to you myself," Orvar said. He embraced Sophia and she kissed him sweetly.

Bromle couldn't control his surprise and elbowed Simon as he pointed at them.

They thanked Sophia repeatedly for her help, and Adger was especially emphatic about the food. They stepped through the geatu onto the soft sand and turned to say goodbye one last time to Sophia.

The image of her in the library disappeared to reveal the boards of a wooden shack the geatu was on.

The cove they were in was heavily foliaged with just enough sand between it and the crystal clear water to sit and enjoy the warmth of the sun. Behind them were several levels of beach huts and shacks stacked on top of and behind each other, as if they only had a limited amount of space to build. The cove was wide enough to allow more homes, but it seemed that whoever had built them wanted to preserve as much of nature as they could.

"How long do we need to wait here?" Simon asked Orvar.

Adger pulled out the maps again. He had picked them all up from the table before they left Sophia's office. He enjoyed looking at them and his fascination with them allowed him to quickly determine where they were.

"We're right here," Adger said as he pointed at the map. "And it looks like the Sceadwians should come into the ocean right there. If we leave soon, we may be able to get there in a few days, but I'm not sure we will get to them before they exit the rivers.

"We're being watched," Bromle said as he pointed up at the shacks.

People were watching them from the windows in the buildings, but they looked fearful of their arrival; peeking out from the corners of the frames or from behind curtains.

"W—welcome to Bakeez," said a young man as he stepped out from behind a tree.

"We're friends," Simon said. "Do you get many visitors here?"

"Not many, and when we do it usually means one of our people has been taken by the Witch's soldiers."

"Veadus?" Orvar said.

"Don't say her name! It will conjure her minions."

"We're not here to take anyone," Simon said. "We're on our way across the ocean to free you from those threats."

"But how will you cross the ocean?" the young man said. "Our people have tried in hopes of returning those taken from us, but no one has ever returned."

The water beyond the cove swelled as if a sudden wave was building. Something moved underneath the water and caused a meager wake to churn behind it. It moved towards the shore, unbeknownst to the adventurers, until the man they were speaking to pointed behind them with a fearful expression. They all spun around with weapons drawn and started backing away from the water in preparation for a defense. A dark silhouette formed under the water as it approached them and came into the shallow part of the cove. Even as clear as the water was, it was difficult to tell what was coming their way other than that it was large enough to be a threat. The water sprayed upwards as a massive turtle broke the surface of the water.

"It's Tortuse!" Simon said excitedly.

Tortuse Ripa walked onto the beach and folded his flippers underneath his body.

"Man, is it good to see you," Simon said.

"It pleases me to see that you are well," he said.

"Have you healed?"

"Indeed, I have. I have been roaming the coast waiting for you."

"What made you think we would come here?"

"Etnian's forces broke through the dams underneath Canton, and I used the opportunity to enjoy the freedom of open waters after I killed them and dammed the holed behind me. As much as I would love to spend more time in the rivers underneath the world, it has been too long since I have swum these waters. I was not far from here when I heard your voices through the sea."

"Do you think we could get a lift? We need to join up with the army set to destroy Etnian, but it would be a long walk otherwise."

"Of course," Tortuse said and bowed so that they could climb onto his back.

Simon turned to the young man, "We'll find your people and do everything we can to bring them back to you."

As they departed to go north to join the others, Simon was thinking about what the boy said of Veadus, and it was not the first time he wondered how they were going to safely cross the sea. Finding safe passage across the open ocean was something that worried him greatly. Tortuse was a mighty creature, but being exposed in the ocean left him unguarded and without an opposing force like Kapell, they would be vulnerable.

"Why did you tell that boy we would find his family?" Bromle asked, interrupting Simon's silent thoughts.

"What do you mean? We're going to go find them," Simon replied.

"How can you know that? You've given him a hope that you can't guarantee."

"Hope can be more powerful than brute strength," Orvar said. "If we find them, we will return them, and if we don't, we will at least have tried."

"I think it would be better just to tell him the truth, or even recruit him, but leaving him waiting like that seems a waste to me."

"Well, what about Filch?" Adger said. "She's out there too; probably right along with that kid's people. I, for one—or two—hope we find them all still out there."

"And hopefully not driven half-mad by the deakylos," Orvar said compassionately.

"We're just a cheery bunch of sunlight then, aren't we?" Bromle said chuckling.

It took them two days to travel north towards the Pass of Stoikheion.

They talked often of what armies and navies they might enlist to their cause, but Orvar was often the bearer of bad news in that most civilizations had either been too weakened or subdued to help. Orvar looked at charts he had brought from the Library and no matter which course he plotted, the matter of making the journey safely could not be resolved.

"What about *underneath* the water," Orvar recommended.

"No thanks!" Adger said and shuddered. "I like swimming but not under threat of drowning! No offense, Lord Tortuse; I know that wasn't exactly your fault. I just...I just don't really like being submerged very much."

"I understand, Adger; no need to apologize," the turtle said in his calm, regal manner.

"Does anyone know where we'll actually land if we manage to get across the sea?" Simon asked. "Has anyone actually scouted his kingdom?"

"I know the land well," Tortuse said. "I am not very good at making maps, however."

"And I could not find anything in the Library," Orvar said.

"There are shores on the north-western coast of his lands that are not watched. It is an island, although it is large enough to be considered a continent. If we were to try and go all the way around his borders to the eastern most side, not only would we certainly be seen, it would take months to do so. Our best hope is to approach from an unoccupied stretch of land. It did not appear to be inhabited the last time I was there."

"How long ago was that?" Simon asked.

"About five hundred years ago."

"And you think it'll still be uninhabited?" Bromle laughed.

"It is still uninhabited. Veadus does not control every creature in the sea. I sent friends to confirm what I surmised so many ages ago. I was told many buildings have been developed on that coast but have since been abandoned. It is our best option."

"And what of the creatures she does control?" Bromle continued. "Sounds like a good place for scouts to see you coming."

"Or the Witch herself," Orvar asked.

"I worry less of scouts than Veadus and the sea she controls. The challenge of the sea is something that I hope we will find a solution for soon."

After another night, and a half day of traveling, the sun was falling back towards the ground over the coastline of the cliffs to their left. The ground had steadily been rising and seemed to reach an apex around a mountain by the sea. High up on the cliff faces (much higher than those that Simon had seen in the beginning) there were buildings and statues visible even at their distance. There were enormous sculptures of the same four dragons that

Simon had noticed on Orvar's frame in his cabin. Two of them were on each side of the canyon that severed the otherwise unbroken face of the cliff.

"The Pass of Stoikheion," Tortuse said. "Long ago this was a bustling epicenter of humanity but has long since been abandoned. Stoikheion is a wondrous place where the confines of the elements are weak and easily altered. You are not the first one to move the ground, Simon, but you are the first in an eon. The beasts you see there were, at one time, friends to all, but as Etnian reached, their kindness recoiled. I am not sure where their allegiances align any longer."

"So far, three of them have tried to kill us," Simon said.

"Yes, I am surprised we were attacked at Sophron," Tortuse said. "Cineris was once a travelling companion of mine; we would roam the world in pursuit of nothing more than scenery. When you humans first arrived, we would happily take you on journeys far across the sea to distant lands where scenery was so great, you had to close your eyes to catch your breath again. He was a good friend," he said sadly. "I fear that time and evil have corrupted his mind."

They all stared at the giant statues that were carved out of the sides of the canyon. The leviathan that Simon encountered in the Vareex had great fins sticking out from the side of its head and its mouth was open in a wide, silent roar. Simon could recall the foul stench of its breath.

"Saipere, the King leviathan," Tortuse said.

The statue of the creature they had seen flying around the tower in Canton had four wings that gave it the illusion of flight, even while petrified. Long whiskers started at its face and flowed towards its tail, giving it a life even in its stillness.

"Hekaze, the Queen of the clouds," he continued.

"Ol' Queenie has a beard," Bromle laughed.

The statue reminded Simon of a Chinese dragon with a mane and a ridge of flames down its back.

The figure of Cineris was wide and strong with two great wings and four tremendous legs. Its tail was curved forward with long spikes sticking out from its end. A cranial plate on his forehead flared outward and upward and was adorned with short horns around the edge. It had two tusks protruding from its mouth, and a wide horn stuck up from its snout.

"Cineris, you know, and the last one there is Jortho, the Count of the mountains."

The final effigy was almost overlooked due to the trees that grew from its back; it appeared to be part of the rock. It was wider and larger than the other three. The way that it was carved; it looked as if it was crawling out from the cliff and wriggling free. It looked more closely related to a pogona lizard than it did the others.

"Each of them, on their own, is extremely powerful, but together they represent a balance that helped form this world. They have existed since the beginning," Tortuse said.

"It's a shame they aren't on our side," Bromle said. "Their strength would be a formidable weapon."

"Indeed, it would be."

Not long after passing Stoikheion, the high mountains on the sea began to drop and the beaches were not as inaccessible as before. Remnants of eroded land stuck out from the water in lonely towers and mounds. The land dropped and gave way to the sea in slopping embraces that let the water wash up on the grassy plains. Occasionally, the shore was broken by outlets of water and coves that led to whole rivers leading inland.

"How do we know where they're coming out from?" Simon asked.

"I am uncertain of the exact location," Orvar said.

"They are close," Tortuse said. "I can hear them and there is hope in their voices."

"After my first encounter with Veadus, I can't say that I share the same feeling," Simon said.

Orvar put a hand on his shoulder, "Sometimes being a leader means holding onto hope, especially in the face of impossibility. Remember that you have to believe in the power you were given if you are to use it. Even if you lack faith in yourself, others have not lost faith in you. It will do them good to see you have not lost it either."

Simon nodded his head.

As they came around a stony outcropping, a fleet of ships was exiting an estuary wide enough to accommodate them. The stream of boats that flowed into the sea seemed endless and continued for the better part of an hour before they began to diminish in number and size. The group on Tortuse's back sat and watched in amazement at the various boats that poured from the river. Some of the boat designs were obviously that of the Sceadwians with sleek bodies and no sails; propelled by a force either underneath the water or by enormous sets of wings like those that Adger had attached to their desert skiff. There were other boats too that looked less advanced but no less impressive.

Some of the boats were great battleships with innumerable sails. Others were smaller and longer; weaving around and through the bigger ships. It was obvious that many allies had decided to join the fight. Seeing the various flags and banners hung high on the masts was not only encouraging but also invigorating. Simon couldn't help but feel chills climb up his back at seeing all the people rallied to the fight. Coupled with Orvar's encouragement, it was enough to alter the negativity he felt before.

He was still unsure how to peacefully pass over the sea and avoid Veadus and whatever evil she sent towards them. Despite the worry, seeing all those people gathered in a singular cause was enough to help bolster his courage.

"Orvar? Are you out there?" Gin's voice came in over the communicator.

"Yes, Gin, we're here with Tortuse," Orvar said.

"I can't wait to meet him," she said. "I'm in the forward most ship, here to your right."

They looked to see Gin waving on the bow of the largest vessel near them.

"We won't be able to sail out right away," Gin continued. "Our plan was to dock in the Pass of Stoikheion, but the way into it from the west was blocked. Most of our ships are here, but we cannot set sail quite yet. There are forces far in the north and some from the south that we must wait for. The fervor of the north is legendary, and without it, our success may take longer. The cunning intelligence of the south may provide the tactical advantage we need to coordinate this many ships into a singular attack."

"There is a sizable port inside the east entrance of Stoikheion," Tortuse said. "The larger vessels cannot hope to enter it, but many of the smaller ones can find refuge there until we are ready to depart."

Orvar relayed the message, and after a few silent moments, the entire fleet shifted south, back towards the Pass. Tortuse led the way and after a moment, the ship Gin was on came alongside them. She leaned over the side and waved vigorously down at them.

"Lord Tortuse Ripa," she said, "you are a magnificent creature!"

He looked back at her as they swam and smiled as much as a turtle can. Several other ships came alongside them and more people ran to the sides of the ships to look down at them on Tortuse's back. They whispered and pointed down at the adventurers. Simon wondered if they were intrigued by him or by Tortuse. They were indeed pleased to see Simon and his companions and found Tortuse equally exciting. The stories of their adventures had traveled far in the three months they had been absent. Simon's story was encouraging enough to bring many from the farthest reaches of Dyurndale to join the battle.

"Simon, Orvar, are you out there?" said another familiar voice on the communicator.

"Is that you Senator—*Chancellor* Driscol?" Orvar said, correcting himself to accommodate Driscol's new position.

"It is, old friend. There was worry you had abandoned us, but I wouldn't hear it! I knew you were just late."

"We were delayed, although not as much time had passed for us. I'm sorry to hear you were so gravely injured."

"That knee bothered me anyway," Driscol laughed. "Where are we going, friend?"

"There is more than adequate lodging in this old place," Tortuse said. "There may not be hot food or soft beds, but there is ample space for all of us."

Orvar relayed the message again, and in a short time, their feet were on solid ground.

The walls of Stoikheion went far into the air and narrowed at the top, high above them. An entire city was carved out of the interior sides of the canyon. It was completely overlooked from the water, but inside the canyon, it was apparent the place was far more than simply a pass through the landscape. Time was devoted to making Stoikheion a city to outmatch even the size of Canton. Buildings were stacked on top of each other in some places while wide open areas allowed the sky above to shine through.

The sky had become orange with the setting sun and darkness seemed to reach over the edges of upper crust of the ground. People were busily disembarking and carrying provisions, weapons, or torches, which they started illuminating the city with. Streams of oil that retained their flammability were positioned all around the city. As they were lit, they caused other fires to light, providing the city with a peaceful orange glow to match the sky above.

Gin ran up on the docks and happily greeted them again. She hugged Adger slightly longer than the others. Driscol showed up a few moments later while they were retelling their tales since their separation. They soon found an abode in which to leave their belongings; it was an improvement to the small space the brothers called a home in Canton.

"Join me later, over there," Driscol said, pointing to a large courtyard across the river. "There will be food and celebration. And then tomorrow, we will begin our plans."

That night there was a lot to celebrate for all the people that had gathered there. After sampling an abundance of foods, Simon became the center of attention. People begged him to regale his adventures. Simon may not have been the best of storytellers, but the crowd didn't seem to mind. When he was finished, people greeted him and shook his and his companions' hands late into the night.

"Don't lose your focus," Orvar said to him later, after the festivities had diminished. "Remember that you are an element of change and the excitement of others can induce pomposity."

"Understood; I certainly feel more sure of myself than before though," Simon said.

"And we will work to increase that surety over the coming days and weeks. There is a delicate balance between confidence and foolishness. I've been speaking with some of the other leaders and it seems that we have much planning to do. Even in our absence, the plans of war have not been completed. We may be here for a few weeks, but it will allow us to give you some of the training you will no doubt need."

Simon stayed with Bromle and Adger as they had become not only companions but his friends too. Despite the warm reception that he received from the thousands of others, he learned to be wary of strangers. Fortunately, the next few weeks were rather uneventful for them all; they were wearied from their adventures so far. Simon spent his time training with Orvar, Bromle, Gin, and Adger, who showed him the best way to fire a bow. There were more than enough people who were eager to help teach him, or spar with him. Whether they wanted to see his sword and shield, or simply use the opportunity to fight the legend he was said to be, he did not mind. The challenges helped him to apply the little that Orvar's book had taught him.

One afternoon, late into their third week in Stoikheion, Adger and Simon climbed to the highest point of the statues. They were perched on one of the heads of the great statues staring out into the sea. The sun warmed their backs, and the breeze kept them cool.

"I wonder if she's okay," Adger said speaking of Filch. "I didn't know her as well as I should have; especially for being one of our own."

"Well, you know more than me," Simon said. "I'm sure she's fine; she seems plenty capable. How are you holding up in all this? We've barely had a day's rest over the last few weeks—well I guess months, when considering the time we lost in the library."

"I'm great, but I can't help but miss my home in Canton. Bromle and I lived there most of our lives. Despite how little money we had, it was still a home and better than most. I certainly wouldn't want to be living underground in Sceadwia."

"Speaking of the Burgh, you and Gin seem to have gotten close."

Adger grinned and blushed, and Simon said no more. He just smiled and nodded his head. He closed his eyes and let the fresh, salty air fill his lungs. "You still think we can do this?" Simon said after a few moments of silence.

"Of course we can! No matter what happens, you've helped do something I never thought was possible: you unified people from all over the world."

"I didn't really have anything to do with it, though. Driscol probably did most of the work."

"Give yourself more credit than that. Granted, it's not just you they're following; it's the idea of what you represent, but they need that! This world needs to change, and without your arrival people would have remained stagnant. Not to mention, you're the one who threw out the Council."

"Well, I didn't do it alone, friend," Simon said, clapping him on the back.

"I did have some help from these legendary weapons, though," Adger said, patting his jacket where the tool roll was tucked away.

"What are they; the legendary weapons?"

"Your sword might be considered one, but it's something else altogether. I don't rightly understand them all, but from what I know, legendary weapons are made from some of the rarest stones, or forged in fires deep below the ground. Sorry, I know that's not really an answer; more of an Orvar-answer." He laughed. "The most I know of them is that the materials they're made up of come from either killing something much larger and more powerful than you, or finding one already made in the darker places of the world. We all found ours on various adventures to some of the more dangerous places outside the city. Our journeys would have been a lot shorter had Orvar mentioned the rhin geatu earlier. I always wondered why he repeated himself so often on our long treks. 'The exercise keeps the mind sharp and the muscles taut,' he would say—something like that. I made my bow from a broken staff we found when Bromle found his gloves. He was hoping to find a hammer or an axe, but the gloves were so large, they didn't fit the rest of us."

"And these weapons were just lying around?"

"You have to understand that the places they were hiding in were dark and awful, filled with creatures that even nightmares wouldn't do justice depicting. Nothing I saw in my life before, for certain. Speaking of which, what about you; who were you before? Who were you really?"

"Nothing compared to the life I've experienced here. I was a boring salesman, but despite its lack of giants, dragons, flying ships, and legendary weapons, it was a great life and I had a loving family."

"That look in your eye is the weakness that Filch was talking about—I don't think it's weakness, mind you—but it is dangerous."

"I can see why people go crazy without understanding their memories; that emptiness they must feel from a life now gone."

"Hello Simon; Adger," Orvar said as he climbed up the dragon's head behind them. "I've been looking for you. Some of the leaders want to talk with you again. Most of the nations we've been waiting on have arrived, but they hoped Simon could help rally the final heroes we need to secure a victory."

"Me? What can I do?" Simon said.

"Your journal has authored more notes. I have been studying it constantly."

"Yeah, I meant to ask you if I can have it back, actually; I'd hate to lose it and face Sophia without it," Simon said with a chuckle.

"Of course you can, but there is one passage I want you to look at first." Orvar opened the book to a pair of pages that had an image of an ornate conch shell on one page and a passage on the other. Simon read over it, silently nodding his head as he read.

"It says 'the hero will sound the horn of champions past and reunite the lost through the union of sound' but I'm not—I mean, I have no idea what that might mean, Orvar."

"Those pieces of shell you have might do it," he said excitedly. "Look at the picture. It is not the horn of an animal, but a *shell* made into a horn."

"But I have only pieces," Simon said as he pulled out the shell fragments. "Even if I glued them together, they wouldn't look anything like that."

Orvar was quiet enough to let him work it out on his own. Simon held the pieces in his hands, turning them over looking for an answer in their curves and twists.

"A horn, huh?" Simon said.

He imagined a military bugler heralding the coming of war, or preceding the march of a line formation intercepting the enemy. He picked up one piece of the shells that was about as long as his finger. It looked like the central most twirl of a larger shell. He expected nothing more than a whistle from it but still held the piece up to his lips and blew as hard as he could. Nothing happened at first but as he took another breath to blow again, and changed the shape of his lips on it, the other pieces snapped into place. The gaps in between the fragments stretched like growing vines of steely mercury to craft what was the shape of a conch shell. It was mostly covered in metal and encrusted with stones of dark blue and pale greens. It grew around his hand and inside his grip while his fingers held the smooth innards. He took another breath and blew into the horn with everything inside his lungs.

A long, deep note reverberated off the canyon walls and shook the water far below them. The entire canyon was still, and most of the people in it even covered their ears from the sound. The long call filled the Pass of Stoikheion, reached up and outward, and was carried to lands far away. Unknown to those closest to it, the horn was heard by those that needed to hear it.

People emerged from the rooms below to see what the sound was. Bromle joined them a few moments later on top of the statue. Simon stopped blowing his horn for a moment to look down at the many surprised faces that looked up at him. The horizon far out into the west seemed to darken with a storm cloud which might have made Simon nervous if it looked like the typhoon he had first experienced. Instead, this cloud looked like a tsunami of sand.

"Keep blowing, Simon," Adger said breathlessly from excitement.

Simon continued and tried to blow with even more fervor than before, despite the burning in his lungs. The cloud of sand fired bolts of lightning in response to Simon's renewed blast. The sand rushed closer to them in a burst of speed as if being urged by the cracking whip of a driving master. As the sandstorm sped in their direction, the ground shook with a successive tremor. It felt and sounded like the heavy footsteps of a giant. He feared the giants of the water, but here, on the land, it meant that help was coming. He stopped blowing the horn and waited for the hastening vibrations to reveal themselves.

"Have the Witch's forces come to take us?" a voice said from below.

"This is no enemy that comes to us," Orvar shouted down from their perch. "We are not without stronger allies, yet to join us."

More people had climbed the steps and ladders to the tops of the statues to look out on the planes where the sandstorm was continually growing and moving onwards.

"This can be nothing good," a voice said.

The sand began to glow as if someone carried a giant torch from within it.

"It is not Veadus who comes for us, but the very fires of Etnian!" another voice cried out.

"Stop your rumoring!" Orvar snapped. "This is not something for us to fear."

Just as Orvar finished his breath, Kapell broke through the cloud of sand in a sprint towards them, still leagues away. Even at the distance, his fiery kilt was a bright beacon of hope and the source of the glowing light from within the sands.

"It is Kapell!" Adger said excitedly.

Some of the others around them were not as enthusiastic. Indeed, a few shouted and scrambled down the statues shouting warnings.

"No, he is not our enemy; he was with you in the Burgh," Simon cried after them.

Some of them stopped, but those who let their fear overtake them, or had not seen Kapell until that moment, fled to lower levels of safety. Simon waved them off; their warnings would be interrupted and then the whole congregation would see this fantastic creature.

Kapell had a grin on his stony face which turned into a laugh as he saw them standing on the statues' heads. He had thick chains about his neck and hundreds of ropes lashed about his body. From the chains and ropes, hung vessels of the sea. And in his arms, he cradled many more boats. He ran straight towards them and as he became close, his sprinting footfall was so great, the earth cracked in several places. It seemed he meant to bowl them over, and even Simon took a step towards the stairs in doubt.

As Kapell neared them though, to the point where he would have to stop or crush them, he leapt over their heads towards the water. The people craned their necks to watch Kapell fly through the air. He splashed down into the water causing a tidal wave of water to launch towards the open sea. He placed all the many boats down in the water and stepped carefully to where Simon was standing.

"We heard you Simon!" he said with a stony grin. Birds flew from his mouth as he laughed. "My brother has come with me!" he said, pointing to the dark storm clouds that preceded him.

A few moments later the sandy storm cloud began to coalesce. The dark shadow the sand cast from blocking out the light of the sun began to diminish and the rays of light found their way to warm them again. The sand gathered as if being summoned in one place; swirling spouts of sand poured into a growing, gargantuan shape the size of Kapell. The legs formed first like the earth was magnetized to the stalks that grew. The form continued walking towards them even in its partial form. The body and thick arms began to form and this was more than enough to send more people fleeing down from the planes.

"Why are they so afraid?" Adger said aloud; his voice full of wonder and wide eyes fixed on the forming creature.

"The Sceadwians have remained hidden for many decades. Their subterfuge is their way of life," Orvar said.

"They stayed hidden because they were in bed with the enemy," Bromle said.

"But that affair was known but by a few; to the rest of them, hiding should precede a fight."

The sands finished their convergence to reveal Sammos riding on the hand of his sandy giant, Rykos, who had fully recovered from its bout with Simon. Even at the height that Sammos stood above their heads, his bright blue khepresh crown was brilliant enough to be seen. Rykos stopped at the cliff top and lowered Sammos down next to Simon.

"It is good to see you again, Simon," Sammos said. "I apologize that I was unable to see you depart."

"Malachi was very helpful," Simon said. "Thanks again for your hospitality."

They shook hands and there were a great many cheering voices coming from behind him. Legions of troops were formed up behind Sammos on the moorlands above Stoikheion.

"These are the most we could find to gather," Sammos said, gesturing to the troops. "Kapell and I have spent the last couple of weeks trying to gather them all and feared you might have perished on the way through Ta Khronika. We were amassing in an old city many leagues to the north; farther than can be reasonably explained through our hasty arrival. When we heard your shout, it was apparent you had succeeded—but this," he said gesturing towards the waters below with the whole of the Sceadwian navy, "I did not expect so many heads of allegiance."

"Neither did I, honestly, but they carried on while we were 'missing' and were set to head out across the sea," Simon said.

"Kynn Veyor has inspired a mass he cannot fathom," Orvar said.

"Orvar! Is that you, young child?" Kapell said moving to peer down at Orvar. He gripped the edge of the sea cliff and moved his face even closer to look at Orvar. A few more people backed away as he got closer.

"Not as young as I once was, my old friend," Orvar said waving up at him. "Who have you brought to us?"

"Yes, of course; they are allies! Simon, your call was heard so clearly. We gathered some of the mightiest heroes we could find and were going to escort them across the waters, hoping you all had made your way there. When I heard your call, I could wait no longer. I gripped the boats tightly and was prepared to run here as quickly as I could. Yet, your song carried us here before I took my first step; me and all these allies," Kapell said gesturing to the legions on top of the cliffs.

"I am quite glad to see you again," Simon said to him.

"Sammos, will you join us below in the war room?" Orvar said to him. "We are in the final stages of our preparation and would benefit from your input."

Sammos bowed to him and descended the stairs down to the operations room.

Simon glanced over towards Adger where he was still standing on the cliff's edge staring at Kapell who had moved his giant head down to look back at him. Simon could not hear what Adger was asking him but saw Adger pull out his stones to have Unaketay emerge soon thereafter. Kapell laughed and held out a hand for the Methatien to jump on, which it did fearlessly as if returning to an old master. Adger followed the small creature onto Kapell's hand and the giant sat down in the water.

"He is far braver than he gives himself credit for," Bromle said to Simon.

"Well, that's a nice thing for you to say," Simon said.

Bromle's demeanor changed, and he cleared his throat as if he realized he had made a mistake. "Well, you know what I mean."

Simon laughed and the two of them followed the others down the ravine.

People busily ran around the war room with maps and papers. The armies' leaders and generals were regrouping around the largest of the tables that was covered with maps, pieced together from stories and scouts.

The group of them walked up to the table, and after a few moments of excitement at the prospect of having two giants on their side, they turned their full attention to the papers covering the table. Sid rolled into the room a few minutes later and grew into the fearful warrior he did in the desert.

"I will be the ears and voice for Kapell dun Shan," he said.

"Good," said Chancellor Driscol who was just walking up to the table. "Let us begin. Tomorrow we end Etnian de Aithna's reign of terror."

232

21 The Departure

Their final battle plans went late into the night. Etnian's domain had many names it seemed; many of which could not be agreed upon. Most of them called it Maydanok; others had more profane descriptions. The incongruities made the maps misaligned, and no one had a clear idea of how their journey across the open sea should be plotted. Simon was not once consulted to be the battle leader for which he was grateful and was mostly left out of the plan for the main attack. It seemed his mission would be to stay alive as best he could and ensure he was ready to fight Etnian when the moment arrived. Still, no matter what they discussed, they did not address his largest concern.

"What about crossing the ocean," Simon interrupted at one point.

"We have our boats," one man said.

"Of course, but what I am asking is how will you avoid Veadus Naufrage?"

"Our boats barely disturb the waters. She won't even know we're there," one woman warrior said.

"Yes, but not everyone has your boats. Those that don't may be easily detected. There must be another way."

"I think we can help with that," Sid said gesturing towards Sammos. "Make no mistake that crossing the water will be difficult and we are likely to meet the torrent of the sea, but there's no other choice. Veadus may have rule of the ocean, but even her resources are limited."

"What about the rivers underneath the sea," Simon asked. "I was told that they would get us there faster as well as more covertly."

Most of them gave him confused looks, and it was obvious that not everyone there had the knowledge he did. The leaders continued their plans assuming that Simon had nothing left to contribute.

Simon turned to Orvar and lowered his voice. "I'm supposed to be the hero in this tale; why am I being ignored?"

Orvar turned from the group to Simon and spoke quietly, "Do not let your newfound abilities thwart your morality. There is more to leading than strength and ability; the general is not always the one with the most power. And as to your suggestion, if we use the rivers between the realms, it would surely get us there faster, but remember that Etnian is trying to come here on them. We would likely meet his forces somewhere in the middle and be severely outmatched without the use of our battleships. Take heart; your opinions are valued, but urgency often encourages disrespect."

Simon nodded his head. "What if we sent a small group of people, though?"

"Kynn," one larger general with a great big mustache interrupted. "Where is this Naru gate of yours?"

He couldn't help but feel a small bit of excitement at getting to contribute in the planning. He laid out the first map he had from Orvar's cabin and butted the second next to it. He opened his journal to the section of the book that he thought revealed the location of Naru and showed the others on the map where the image in his book directed him. Some of them disagreed and Simon's surety in his first assessment was shaken. The image in the book looked very similar to the image on the map.

"I've been there," Sid said. "I'm sorry to tell you that the gate is not there."

Simon's felt his heart drop.

"It's here," Bromle said gravely. His thick finger was rested on a rudimentary map of Maydanok, the realm of Etnian de Aithna.

"But the book showed it here; look it says that it's right there," Simon said hoping to avoid what Bromle had discovered.

"We have to go to Maydanok either way," Orvar said.

"Yeah, but now the way out is on *his* land. You think he doesn't know about it by now?"

"That changes nothing," Driscol said, trying to change the mood. "We knew this would be difficult. Our best course of action is to rest well tonight and sail at dawn. Generals, leaders, please ensure your warriors and soldiers are ready for departure."

The city was busy that night and Simon found it difficult to sleep. It did not totally evade him, but it was difficult to maintain. Before the sun rose, he gathered his things and climbed to the highest point on the statues as he had done the afternoon before. He sat with his bag on his back and thumbed through the books he still carried to include the journal. There was useful enough information in the books but nothing that would divert the tide they were about to face.

His mind wandered back to his family again. His journey occupied the majority of his attention but he was enjoying a rare opportunity of peace and solitude that allowed him to think of other things. He thought of his wife and children, and their children, and he smiled. He wondered if they would come to a place like this but hoped for their sake that they did not. He looked up at the aurora that sailed in the darkness, wondering if time moved slowly enough here that perhaps his wife was passing overhead.

The horizon was burning red, and in the farthest reaches of the distance, he thought he could see a speck of blackness that might be Maydanok.

"You couldn't sleep either?" Adger said as he climbed up behind Simon and sat down.

"No, there's too much to think about," Simon said. "Is that it; out there?"

"I think so, but I've never spent this much time this close to the sea, so your guess is as good as mine."

"You know, you didn't have to come this far with me. You don't even have to go now if you don't want to." Simon said gently.

"What do you mean? I have no home to go back to. Who knows what the state of Canton is now. The tower fell and those bularaz have probably overrun the city by now."

"Does Bromle share your sentiment?"

"Oh, Brom is happy just to have left Canton; he didn't care where it was we were heading. You were a good enough reason to leave. No, my place is here, and I'll do whatever I can to see this through to the end."

Simon clapped a hand on his back. "You're a good friend and companion," Simon said. "Is your brother still sleeping?"

"Oh my, yes; he has no apprehensions before heading into a fray. You'd think he was hoping for battle." Adger laughed.

"If—I mean, when—we come to the other side of this, what then?"

"I would love to return home one day—our real home in Yingu. It is such a beautiful place. It's like the mountains grew fingers that constantly reach upward. In between them are complicated canyons carving their way through the land. Our people lived on top of the spires and elevated planes of cliff towers much like the one you showed up on; you could see for miles from their heights. You have to understand: most of them are wide; wider than Stoikheion even. Great bridges of stone and wood connect them all. Around the edge of the canyons, there are trees thousands of feet tall. They gave us peace from the sun on hot summer days and protection from the sight of the outside world...almost. In autumn, the smell of the falling leaves is enough to reduce one into a stupor; entranced by the majestic life of the place. The animals that fly there and the animals that roam the canyon floor are enough to make it feel like a moment trapped in a time long gone. I could go on for hours."

"I'm tempted to let you; it sounds like a wonderful place."

"But if what they say is true, and Naru is reopened, I think I would go with you. This world is beautiful, but I would like to know the rest of the story, so to speak."

They both sat silently listening to the seagulls' call.

"Well, we should probably go rouse my brother," Adger said. "The sun has nearly risen, and he can take considerable effort to wake."

They went back down to their lodging, but Bromle and his belongings were gone.

"I don't understand," Adger said. "He was just here—we weren't up there for that long, were we? Usually it takes cold water or physical abuse to get him up this early in the day." Adger laughed.

They went to the war room, but he was not there either; it was mostly vacant. Papers were on the table and floor like people had left in a hurry and only a couple were left behind to gather maps or stacks of documents.

"Did we get left behind?" Simon said a bit concerned.

"No, all the ships were still in the water when we came down. Everyone's probably on the docks already."

They went down to the docks where hundreds of people were busily loading up ships and sailing out into the open waters, or loading small dinghies set to carry supplies to the larger ships. Hoping to find anyone in the mass of people seemed impossible.

"We are never going to find Bromle in this mess," Simon said.

"Oh, I'm sure he's on a boat already," Adger said, still searching and stepping up onto a crate to see above people's heads.

"You sure are looking pretty hard for not being too concerned about him."

"Oh, I'm not looking for Brom; we'll catch up to him. I was hoping to see Gin before we left…" Adger trailed off as if he hadn't meant to state his intentions.

Sensing his embarrassment, Simon said, "Look, there's Driscol."

Driscol was standing towards the end of one of the docks; directing people and trying to hurry them onto their ships as they departed. He stood like an orchestra conductor, pointing in one direction or another, barking orders. One leg of his pants was higher than the other and his new mechanical leg glittered in the sunlight. It was as intricate and beautiful as the Sceadwians' ships and weapons: polished and new, unlike Gin's prosthetic that was slightly more abraded and aged.

"There you two are," he said as he saw them walk up. "I was worried you had fallen from the heights of the Pass."

"Have you seen my brother?" Adger asked.

"Yes, I have, but he has been dispatched on a scouting mission."

"What do you mean?" he asked with a bit more urgency.

"I've sent him on ahead with Orvar, Thaygin, and a battalion made up of various armies. I assure you, they will be well protected."

"Where did you send them?" Simon asked. "And how did you manage to organize something like that so quickly?"

"Orvar developed the mission," Driscol said. "He said he knew something about a river deep beneath the sea."

"Yeah, that was me; I mentioned that last night, but he said it wasn't a good idea," Simon said with annoyance.

"I can't believe this! I want to talk to him," Adger said.

Simon handed him his communicator. "Use my radio," he said. "I'd like to hear from Orvar, too."

"Driscol, please," Adger said and handed the communicator out to him impatiently.

Driscol adjusted it to the right channel for him and handed it back.

"Bromle, what are you doing?" Adger said angrily into it.

After a moment, his brother's voice came through.

"Oh, hi, little brother," Bromle said cheerily dragging out the syllables. "I was—"

"You are so reckless! I cannot believe you would go on without the—I can't—whose idea was it?"

Simon held his hands up defensively. "You need to ask Orvar, not me; I thought that idea was off the table."

Orvar's voice came in a second later. "Simon, I am sorry that I was unable to tell you before we left. We did look for you but wanted to get underway immediately. Despite the support we have, this will still be dangerous and I would rather you be protected with the tens of thousands that will accompany you across the water."

"What do you even hope to accomplish?" Adger said angrily. "You'll all be killed!"

"We will surely meet resistance in the river," Orvar said calmly, "but based on what Lord Ripa told us, the side of Maydanok we arrive on is uninhabited. We need to ensure *your* arrival will go unnoticed."

"But why did *you* go, Brom? Or you Orvar? And where is Gin?" Adger asked.

"The time for restraint is gone," Orvar said. "Boldness if our best defense now. Your brother is more of a tactician than you give him credit for."

"But we would have gone with you!" Adger said slightly more choked up than he intended to show. He had no doubts in his brother's capabilities, but he worried about the danger he was in; even more was he worried for Gin.

"I know you would have, little brother," Bromle said. "I'll be fine as always; don't worry! Someone's got to look out for Simon anyway, and you're the best guy for the job."

"You better not die out there because the next time I see you, I'm going to punch you square in the mouth," Adger said.

"If you can find a ladder, I'll let you," Bromle laughed.

Simon thought he noticed a smile crack on Adger's mouth.

"Adger," Bromle said quietly through the radio. Adger quickly turned the communicator down to make it even harder for anyone else to hear. He stepped away from the other two and held the radio close to his face. "I'll keep her safe. You have my word," Bromle said.

"I want to talk to her," Adger said quietly.

"She's on a different boat little brother but...I promise I will tell her."

The communicator became silent and Adger handed it back to Simon.

"I'm sure he knows what he's doing," Simon said, trying to fill the silence between the three of them.

"You there," Driscol shouted at a dockhand carrying a crate, "that goes—yes, there, over there! If Orvar is with him, there is wisdom enough to be shared," Driscol said placing a hand on Adger's shoulder. "Come let us be on our way. It will take more than the day to arrive on Etnian's shores, and there is still much to be done."

The water near the dock was interrupted by the clear dome of Tortuse's shell slowly rising out of the water. He continued to rise until his shell was level with the deck.

"Lord Ripa!" Driscol said.

"I was just preparing your men for the journey we are about to take," Tortuse said.

His dome lowered to reveal five large guards similar to those in Burgh Sceadwia but their armor was black with bright golden accents. Their faces were covered and their individual features indiscernible. Their only difference was the weapons they carried. Great axes were on the backs of two of them, hook swords on that of another, a tremendous hammer on the fourth, and two smaller axes on the back of the last. They all stepped off of Tortuse's back and onto the deck in front of them. Their shoulders were just above Simon's head, and he felt small again in the face of such large people.

"These are my personal guards, the Thuaran; in the old language of Thaygin's people, it translates to *Night Shades*. They will escort you across the water," Driscol said.

"I'm glad they're on our side," Simon laughed. "I'm Simon," he said holding out his hand to be shaken.

"And I am Adger," he said extending his hand as well.

The guards stood motionless waiting for Adger and Simon to board.

"They're not the cheeriest of people, but they are the fiercest," Driscol said. "Do you have everything you need to leave?"

"We haven't eaten, but I think we're as prepared as we can be," Simon said. He looked to Adger who didn't look to be his jovial self.

"I'm ready," Adger said flatly. "The sooner we get there the better; my brother will need our help."

Driscol spoke something into his radio and after a brief moment, a man dressed in a greasy apron showed up with a couple of small boxes. "Some food for you, sirs," the young man said, handing the boxes to Simon and Adger. They were wrapped in red cloths, tied in a knot at the tops.

Adger and Simon took the food, and Simon thought he spied Adger's demeanor change ever so slightly at the prospect of sustenance. They shook hands with Driscol, thanked him, and boarded Tortuse. Being slightly closer to the guards now, they were even more intimidated. The guards' black armor was unblemished and darker than Simon had ever seen, like a void in space instead of a color of metal. The only thing that made their armor seem real was the golden accents on the edges.

"If all goes well, I will see you on the other side of the sea," Driscol said to them from the docks.

"We'll see you soon, Chancellor," Simon said.

"It's Admiral now," Driscol said proudly.

Always working an angle, Simon thought of Driscol. He was grateful for his help but skeptical of the way he maneuvered himself into his recent positions of power. Nevertheless, he was grateful for the powerful allies he had amassed so recently.

"We should depart within the hour," Driscol continued. "Some will stay here and guard our retreat and your brother's if needed—which I hope will not be required."

"But why can't we go after my brother?" Adger pleaded.

"I have closed the way," Tortuse said over his shoulder to Adger.

"Well, can't you just as easily open a way here, below the water, and let us help him? Or what of the place you sent them from?"

"I wish it were so easy, Adger, but there are only particular places that I can create such fissures without causing subsequent catastrophes. And I dare not make such an entrance in the Witch's waters; she is cunning and would likely overtake your brother faster than I could close the fissure again. No, my young Adger, we are forced to make our way with the fleet now. Going back would mean risking exposure of our plans to the enemy again; we nearly had…an incident the last time."

"What do you mean?" Adger demanded.

"I am bound to say no more; know that they were sent without harm and safely made their way."

"I am sorry, gentlemen, I can linger no more. There are many matters I must attend to in the short time we have left," Driscol said and walked briskly away without waiting for further adieus.

Tortuse made his way from the docks out into the fleet, Simon and Adger ate their breakfast and marveled at the vessels that had come from so many different places in the world. Adger recognized many of them and was glad to label them for Simon. Simon noticed his sullen attitude lessened with food and conversation. He wanted to ask more of his affection for Gin but thought any pondering of her might sadden Adger again.

They swam lazily amongst the boats; many of the decks towered over them as Tortuse was much lower to the water. As they entered less populated water towards the front of the fleet, they caught a glimpse of Kapell standing out in the open water. He was in the water beyond the ships and had a storm cloud of sand hovering above him, connected at his shoulders.

"Kapell!" Simon shouted up at him unsure if he would hear him at such a distance. The mountain of a creature turned and bent low to him, and Tortuse swam over to meet him. Kapell smiled his stony toothed grin at Simon.

"Is that your brother above you there, or is that Rykos?" Simon asked.

"It is both and all of them," Kapell laughed. "He prefers the storm of his sands before a battle. I find him quite itchy but am glad you have been so instrumental in our reunion."

A small part of the sandstorm separated from the cloud above and rushed down to the back of Kapell's arm where his hand sat on his giant knee. Sammos' shape appeared with a beaming grin.

"Simon, I am quite glad to see you once again; I too owe you my thanks. My brother and I have been silent for far too long. Although, he has been submerged for many ages."

"Why aren't you riding in your amazing airship?" Simon asked. "That would have actually made this journey a lot easier; Veadus wouldn't even be an issue."

"My wonderful companions would be able to cover this distance in the shortest of time," Sammos said proudly. "Alas, they have refused to leave the desert besides their recent escort to Ta Khronika. I implored Highkar, the eldest and wisest of them, but he said as long as Etnian was in power, he would not risk his labor or life for threat of such evil."

"That's unfortunate, I would love to see Malachi again; I didn't tell him about Unaketay," Adger said.

"The Methatien keepers have unnatural bonds to their pets."

"Unaketay is no more my pet than the sphinx is yours."

"I apologize, Adger, I meant no offense."

"None taken! If we come on the other side of this—when we do, I would like to visit your companions again."

"You will be an honored guest, youngest brother!"

Kapell began to stand up, but Simon called up to him again. "Wait Kapell, before you go, we haven't spoken much the two times I've seen you," Simon said to him.

"You have been rather busy," he said, still smiling as he bent back down.

"I've been meaning to tell you about Lazuli. I fear that Saipere may have…well, I'm not sure she made it out of the battle."

"Oh, Simon; do not worry of her well-being. She is of tougher moxie than any creature and warrior I have yet to meet."

Simon thought he sensed a meager amount of doubt in Kapell's voice and wondered if Kapell believed his own words.

"Well, I hope to see her again," Simon said. "I need to thank her for saving me back there."

"You will have your chance; I believe many of us will survive this war. I will be close, and you will be well protected. If all else fails, you may hide in the forests of my back."

"Why don't we do that now?" Adger asked excitedly. "With Sammos above you and the Kalinaw navies below, we would be quite safe—and the view would be splendiferous!"

"He may well be a larger force to protect you, but if Veadus arrives without warning, I can speed you away. If you are far above on Master dun Shan, I have no hopes of rescuing you," Tortuse said.

"And the last time I was hiding on Kapell, I hindered his defense," Simon chimed in. "No offense, Kapell."

"None taken, young one!" the giant boomed. "She is a wily—and vile—sorceress."

Simon shuddered when remembering the last time he ran through Kapell's forest.

"Are we not under threat of Veadus out here in the water, even now?" Adger said.

"I have been listening to the sea and have heard no threat from her," Kapell said. "I think, for now, we have not gained her attention.

"I think it might be best if we stayed with Tortuse for now," Simon said. "If we go underwater on Kapell, we're done for."

Adger nodded his head, although he wished he could have climbed on Kapell above even if for the moment before they left.

The time had come for departure, and Tortuse left his dome down as he sailed amidst the fleet of ships. The wind was refreshing and a pleasant distraction from the battles they were sailing towards.

It wasn't long before the entire fleet was under the force of the wind and aiming straight for the speck in the distance; straight towards inevitable conflict and hopefully the salvation of Dyurndale.

22 The Sea

"I told you that we'd be fine," Adger said. "I could've been riding up there on Kapell's shoulder, but we've been sailing for hours with not even a raindrop of a threat."

"But we're on Lord Ripa!" Simon said. "This is still pretty amazing."

"Oh, of course it is—and it has been, but did you know he has animals up there?" he said, pointing up towards Kapell. "There were birds in the trees, fish in some of the ponds—I think I even saw a deer!"

"I'm fine with just enjoying this breeze for the moment," Simon said, closing his eyes and inhaling deeply.

The sea was beautiful and the weather was calm. The breeze that carried the cool water's temperature combated the heat of the sun in the clear blue sky. Simon stood at the bow of Tortuse's back while Adger redirected his attention and tried to make conversation with Driscol's guards. Simon watched as the short man walked from one to the other. They stood there quiet and unresponsive. He walked back over to Simon and shook his head.

"I can't even get their names," Adger said. "I just get grunts."

Simon shrugged his shoulders and said, "You probably don't get to be an elite guard through friendly prowess."

"How many people do you think are with us?" Adger asked.

"I have no idea. I've never seen so many people in one place in all my life; let alone so many boats. Do you really think we'll be able to make it over there without being seen? I mean, look at this," he said, gesturing towards all the boats around them.

"They are the Sceadwians; they had a whole city hidden underground." Adger said with a smile.

"True, but Etnian found us there, too."

"That was from a betrayal and not from a lack of their ability. Our other advantage is that this would be the first time anyone has attacked Maydanok. When the war began, any efforts like this were stopped before they even started. He has no idea we're coming; trust me. There's just no way."

"We've already been betrayed so many times. I can't help but be wary with so many strangers alongside us. I wish we had some kind of advantage instead of just being dragged along until our time of usefulness arrives."

"Well, I'm glad you feel that way; you think a map of Maydanok would help?" Adger held up the same map that Bromle had identified the location of Naru on.

"He took the map?" Simon laughed.

"Bromle may infuriate me at times, but if he's anything, he's smart enough not to ask for permission. Plus, we need it more than they do. He swiped it in the war room, and I was studying it last night." Adger walked over to a nearby crate and smoothed the map out for Simon to see. "It looks like we'll land here. Then Etnian's castle is there, obviously; it looks like the only city for miles besides the one on the coast. There will probably be hordes of enemies between us and Naru," he said, losing some of the joviality in his voice at the thought.

"Wait a minute; I thought no one had been out here. How'd they get his map anyway?"

"I asked the same question. It came from one of those rough looking groups—you know, the ones that are all either missing an eye or a limb. Orvar said they sail out in tiny boats, mapping the land in hopes to find places to hide their treasures."

"Well, that's great for us. And what about his army; are they slaves too, or are they loyal soldiers?"

"I'm guessing they're people who have spent so long in the deakylos they've pledged allegiance just to stop dying, like Orvar said. I asked him once about how he was able to stay around for so long without losing his mind. After months of asking him, he finally told me that each time he died, he emerged from the rivers with a fresh new body; and always in a different place. He wouldn't tell me how he managed to avoid capture though."

"Look at that," Simon interrupted with an awestruck gasp.

Four blue baleen whales broke the surface of the water and were close enough for Simon and Adger to see the pupils of the creatures' eyes. The whales were bigger than Simon could have ever imagined the greatest of sea creatures to be. They rocketed into the air like torpedoes the size of buildings being shot from the surface of the sea. They slowed as they reached the apex of their breaches and started to fall back towards the water. When their tremendous bodies hit the sea, huge plumes of water exploded into the air; the outermost reaches fell on Tortuse like a heavy rainfall.

Simon and Adger laughed hysterically.

"That was amazing!" Simon hooted while trying to ring out his clothes from the water.

Additional shouts of praise rang out from nearby ships. The breach was a display that many were pleased to have witnessed.

"I've heard about whales before, but never have I seen them," Adger said.

"Me neither. Sorry, you were saying?" Simon said smiling and shaking the water from his hands.

"I can't even remember," Adger said, still laughing. "Oh, look at these guys," he said, pointing to the Thuaran. "How can you lot not have moved a muscle?!"

They both laughed heartily again and then turned their attention back to the map which had also been soaked.

"I'm glad this wasn't drawn on that flammable parchment you incinerated in the Library," Simon said.

"Hey, you guys aren't going to tell Old Driscol about this map, are you?" Adger said to the resolute guards. "Good." He turned back to the map. "Well, it looks like there's a wide open stretch of land north east of his castle... 'Gorfel,' it says. If we haven't subdued his forces sufficiently, we will be completely exposed on our approach."

"And if this map is too old to show that Gorfel has grown, then we're going to have a bigger problem. Do you think you're ready for that?"

"I'm ready for anything; I wouldn't still be here if I wasn't ready to die for this. How could anyone go back to living a normal life knowing they could have been a part of shaping the world?"

"This world is a place worth saving," Tortuse said over his shoulder to them. "Did you both enjoy the display my friends made?"

"Did we ever!" Adger said excitedly.

"There is more where that came from."

The small hatches popped open all over the deck to allow the small hatchlings to scramble across the shell to the bulwarks and send the translucent dome rising quickly. Simon spied a childish grin on Adger's face as his eyes lit up with the blue light of the developing hexagons. Conversely, the reflections were absorbed by the darkness of the Thuaran armor; Simon feared them even more for their ominous visage. He broke his stare when Tortuse submerged beneath the surface of the sea.

The bright sun above illuminated the world beneath the water; the whales were still visible as they opened their massive jaws to scoop up the clouds of krill below. They vocalized long, deep whale-songs that passed through the now transparent dome as easily as Tortuse's voice. In the moments of silence between their calls, the clicking of dolphins distracted from the whales' spell.

A super pod of porpoises swam around Tortuse like a raging rapid, all the while clicking and chirping.

"Away with you, children; your playfulness is a distraction," Tortuse snapped at them like an elder to his youngest of grandchildren.

When they passed, there was still more to be seen of the underwater world. Although the darkness of the sea loomed below them like a gaping chasm, the life in the water was so teeming that it seemed a compensatory comfort for the pitch below. Schools of reflective fish darted towards the surface and back down to let the light on to other scales. Wriggling serpents, as wide as the trees outside Canton, moved through the water without fin or dorsal protrusion, yet their speed would have been enough to hasten Simon's journey. The most paling of fearful creatures were the ten megalodon sharks that peaceably swam amongst the other fish.

"Are those—those aren't—are those sharks?!" Adger stuttered.

"They are, indeed, Adger," Tortuse said. "But you have no fear of them while under my ward. They care not for something of such little meat, but for a plump person of your size, they might be willing to make an exception," Tortuse laughed. It was a strange mix of aquatic sounds not altogether dissimilar from a chortled song of a whale; familiar and inviting.

They could see the pressing of the boats above them through the water too, but it was little in the way of impression for the sights around them. Despite the desire to stay and gaze at the aquatic life that distracted them from their impending duties, they found their way between the ships again and returned to the terrestrial world.

The rest of the day continued without incident but was not without Adger's repeated pleas to see the life below the water. The sun began to set and the ships slowed but did not stop.

"Tortuse, do you need to rest?" Adger asked.

"I do not require as much as you might," he said. "As for the rest of you, I would recommend you get what sleep you can find. There are bedrolls in a crate near the prow to soften the hardness of my shell, and I believe there might be a bit of food nearby there."

Simon was sure sleep would evade him again, but he fell asleep shortly after he lay down. Adger and Simon slept deeply and Simon was grateful for the lack of disturbing dreams like his first night in Canton. He assumed they would find him again, there on the precipice of war, but he slept without vision or thought. His sleep was restorative but seemed so brief that it was over as quickly as it had begun.

When they woke in the morning, the five guards were still standing nearby and it wasn't apparent if they had slept at all.

Adger woke up with a chunk of bread in his hand and immediately put it to his mouth almost as soon as his eyes opened. "Can't beat this bread," he said, sleepily tearing off a bite.

In the pale morning light, the speck of land they had seen the day before was now a land mass away to their starboard side.

"There it is," Simon said with a yawn as he stood up and started to put his things together.

"No turning back now, eh?" Adger said yawning.

"Not unless we can convince Tortuse," Simon joked.

"Your journey is nearing its culmination, Kynn Veyor," Tortuse said. "To forfeit a race with but one step left is as if you had never begun at all."

Simon's communicator whistled to life with a boatswain call.

"This is Admiral Driscol speaking to all vessels. All personnel, be ready. We are fortunate to not have met the enemy yet, and if fortune continues to favor us, we will land unnoticed. All vessels commence at full speed and prepare all artillery for combat. Confirm and disseminate."

Another boatswain call sounded on the communicator and then it was silent. Colored flags raised on the masts of most of the ships and flares fired into the air from a few of the other vessels. Sails opened across the fleet in response and the ships lurched forward under the influence of the wind.

"We would do well to prepare as best we can," Tortuse said.

The blue dome raised around the crew on Tortuse's back.

"Wouldn't it be better to stay above the water in case Veadus shows up?" Adger said.

"Just having a look around," Tortuse said.

He dove under the water and foaming water surged around them.

"I do hope we get to see those whales again," Adger said.

"As long as it's not that dark chasm of the deep sea," Simon said with a shudder. "The dark of the deep makes me—well, I'd rather not stare at it anytime soon."

"Looks like you won't have to," Adger said with a gasp.

The sea floor was much closer to them than it had been the day before. The water was clearer and the life that swam through it was so abundant that it threatened to slow them down.

"Even more impressive than the rivers," Tortuse said. "It has been far too long since I have seen such sites."

Schools of brightly colored fish darted around the shallow sea floor through twisting masses of coral and outcroppings of textured rock. Every surface of every stone had wavy formations of life, or spindly bushels of underwater bushes that moved of their own accord. Eels darted from their hidden coves and ambush predators fled from their camouflage beneath the sand as Tortuse passed. Three giant manta ray glided over Tortuse's head and Simon couldn't help but laugh.

"I think they might be bigger than you are, Tortuse," Simon said.

A cloud of ink proceeded the flitting of an octopus that quickly changed directions to avoid the snapping jaws of a nearby reef shark.

"Look at how bright those stones are, even here underwater," Adger wondered. "The ocean floor has as much life on it as there is just above it. Look at those bushy things there; how they keep going in and out and back in again. Tortuse, what of that bit there; that darker stone with the fluttering tassels like seaweed? It seems...well, it seems out of place with all the other life."

"That, young Adger, is nothing more than a bit of stone yet to be conquered by this tropical kingdom," Tortuse said.

"But even the fish seem to avoid it; look at the way they come close and then turn around it."

"Your scrutiny is commendable, but it is doubtful this many persons would have not seen a threat so close and it still avoid detection."

"Lord Ripa, would you mind if we swam over there and just had a look?" Simon tried to say respectfully. "Just to give Adger some peace of mind." He smiled and nodded at Adger to show his support.

"Very well; we are to be scouting about at any rate."

Tortuse drifted over towards the dark mass of rock and tilted one direction to allow a glance of the space below. The passengers steadied themselves against the bulwark as gravity pulled them downwards. The Thuaran even took the opportunity to lend their gaze at the suspect anomaly.

Simon peered through the clear water and didn't see anything in the dark space below; exactly the thing that made him look even harder. "Something is wrong, Tortuse, there's no life there."

Tortuse opened his mouth and released a bellow that was a strange mix of a whale's song and the growl of a crocodile, overlaid with the clicks of a porpoise. The water rippled from his mouth and shot towards the darkened space of seafloor. When it impacted it, a plume of sand vomited into the air. Before the dust even began to fall back towards the floor, figures shot from the cloud and Simon's heart leapt at the recognition of the shapes.

"It is Veadus!" Tortuse called back.

Before he finished speaking, Simon yelled into his communicator, "Admiral, the enemy is below us!"

"All vessels," Driscol's voice immediately called, "the Witch is upon us. Submersibles: fire when ready!"

The water around Simon and Adger flared to life with bubbling clouds of fiery ejections from allied vessels that sprung up around them from amidst the coral and rocky sea-life. The missiles impacted their target and sent bodies and small enemy ships spinning into the water. More enemy mounds sprung up nearby to the Kalinaw, firing their own projectiles. Simon still struggled to identify the Kalinaw through the bubbling clouds preceding swarms of missiles; the sea had become chaotic.

Amidst the resultant fiery explosions and bubbling streams of armaments, huge masses of seabed rose from the bottom of the ocean like great hills that had loosened the gravitational restraints of the globe. Simon squinted in the bedlam at the mounds and saw what looked like overturned three-mast vessels rising to breach the surface of the water above. When the keels of the ships touched the surface of the water, the decks could be seen as they quickly pivoted to turn back upright. Each deck was filled to the edges with underwater enemies, brandishing weapons and shouting unheard battle-cries. They were exactly the kind that Simon had fled from in the first moments of his afterlife existence: some half serpent and the others with shimmering skin like the schools of fish in the more colorful parts of the sea.

"We are no good down here," Simon shouted; unsure if Tortuse could hear him.

Tortuse swiftly rose from the underwater fray and broke the surface of the water to see upside-down vessels rotating into the battle like the keels were fixed on a spit. As the ships slowed their rotation, enemies were poised on the uppermost parts of the masts, ready to be launched towards the allied ships. When the ships were fully righted, groups of enemies were thrown towards the Kalinaw from the sudden stop.

As violent as the maelstrom below the water was, the conflict above was equally as hazy with the explosions of opposing ships. Enemy naval forces had swooped in on a swift wind and commenced their barrage on the Kalinaw. Explosions and smoke rose from both sides of the battle. It was hard to tell which side was winning despite the enemy being outnumbered.

Dragonfly riders, like those in Burgh Sceadwia, darted in between the ships. Alongside them, small clouds of sand were carried on the wind. Simon wondered if it was the conjurations of Sammos, but he had no real way to know. Cries rang out in the fray and in the blink of an eye, the threat of conflict had come to fruition. Opposing forces battled on the ships, in between them, and struggled in the waters around and beneath them.

Salvos from the warring ships made Simon jump and Adger dive for cover.

"This is madness!" Adger shouted.

"Tortuse, we must join this fight," Simon said. "Get us close to that ship there."

"My job is to keep you safe," he said.

"Hear, hear!" Adger shouted. "We don't have cannons! We don't have—we don't have an underwater warship!"

"'The time for restraint is gone,'" Simon said quoting Orvar. "Please Tortuse, I beg you; I cannot stand by when I know I can do *something*—anything is better than watching as our allies die!"

Tortuse reluctantly swam towards one of the larger Kalinaw vessels and partially opened the dome.

"Go, but use discretion and restraint in your actions!"

"Well, if you're set on going then I'm coming too! Tortuse, we can't make it to the bulwark though," Adger said, standing up quickly and moving towards one of the chests on Tortuse's back. "Do you have a bit of rope or something?"

Without waiting for Tortuse to answer or Adger to find what he sought, Simon leapt unnaturally high and cleared the bulwark of the ship above.

"Since when could he leap like a grasshopper?" Adger shouted hysterically. "You lot, stop just standing there and let's go help him!" he shouted at the Thuaran.

Simon landed directly in the heat of the battle on the vessel deck. The ship was nearly as wide as it was long and had no sails or masts; propelled by some force underneath the water. Everywhere Simon looked, there were enemies tangled in an embrace with one of Simon's allies. He whipped out his sword and shield and flared them with such fervor that the flames singed the planks of the deck. The closest enemies immediately recognized him; the legend of his weapons had spread swiftly. His opponents rushed towards him with battle cries and weapons held high.

By the time the five guards and Adger had joined him on the deck, he was through his first aggressors and already on his way, slicing and destroying other enemies in his path. Simon's ferocity had not consumed him but was spawned from the desire to protect himself and those that fought alongside him; the ones offering their lives to protect him. He disliked being a tool of destruction but with the opposing forces threatening those who so willingly were spurred by nothing more than the rumors of Kynn Veyor, he put every ounce of vigor into his efforts.

He leapt and twirled from box to crate; enemy to aggressor; all the while making his destruction of the foe seem easier than possible. The five guards and Adger stopped when they saw how swiftly he cleared most of the ship's surface, despite it being as wide as a field. The remaining opposition either surrendered to the Kalinaw, or jumped from the ship.

Simon noted that his influence had been effective but yearned to do even more. He spied conflicts on other ships nearby. He couldn't rightly surmise how he was able to make such a leap onto the deck but trusted whatever gifts he had been granted. He couldn't stop there, not while the cries of pain crawled across the deathly air.

Simon's heart panged with the death of those nearby. With little more thought, he ran towards the nearest bulwark and dove off the edge of the boat. The Thuaran ran to the edge to see Simon rise from his fall and sail towards an adjacent ship alongside Sammos on a cloud of sand.

"Good to fight alongside you this time, Master Veyor," Sammos shouted. "Allow me to give you a lift; although I doubt you need my help."

Sammos continued on to aid others as Simon jumped from the cloud and onto the next ship. Adger watched as Simon cleared it of enemies as he had done with the first one.

"Look at him go!" Adger cheered.

Before there was an opportunity to catch up to him again, Simon rushed towards the edge of that ship and leapt again, hoping that he could find the power of the desert and the rock. He felt the call of the earth as he had in the arena; the rumbling voice of Kapell grumbled in his heart. The open air was all that caught him for a moment and in that absence, he feared his powers had waned. He quickly focused on Orvar's advice about having faith in his abilities and dug deep for the belief that his gifts were not without purpose. The water far below him burped in spurts of froth, preceding the salvation that Simon hoped for. Instead of sand carrying him along, rock columns shot from beneath the water and met each step as he ran, like rocky stilts. He landed on another enemy ship and charged into battle again. Plumes of smoke blocked the sight his allies had and they finally lost sight of him in the fray.

"I did it," Simon yelled as he jumped onto the third ship. "I actually summoned stone again. I don't know if that was you, Kapell," he said aloud even though the stone giant was nowhere in sight, "but I certainly got the idea from you."

Simon landed on the enemy vessel with confidence and excitement. The feeling was invigorating, but his conscience begged for caution. He kept the enemy boat's crew in front of him. The muscles tensed in his arm and a burning fury flowed from his chest into the shield he carried. It extended farther than it had before and he slammed it into the deck. It ceaselessly widened and burned the ship until the creaking severances of wood signified the vessel being cleaved. Simon had cut it in half with nothing more than his shield. The enemies stopped their attack and clung to whatever was closest to them as the vessel started to sink.

A great stone spike exploded through the half of the ship he was still on. It destroyed the remaining masts in the process. The sun was darkened by a rising mass from the water and the sinking half he was on steadied. Simon looked up at the darkness in front of the sun.

"I owe you my life again, Kapell!" Simon shouted.

The giant had returned and quickly moved to the remaining enemy vessels, sending them sinking to the ocean floor below. Kapell stomped away, sending huge vessels beneath the waves faster than a leaf in a puddle under a child's footstep. Simon quickly dispatched the remaining enemies on the broken half of the ship with fire and fury; grateful that Death might find victims other than him. The battle across the fleet shifted as more of Etnian's warships sunk back down to the sea in ruin and ash. The enemy ships were quickly destroyed, but their attack had a significant impact.

Severed masts hung from their cracked stumps on decks and many ships had broken, splintered beams jutting in various directions from their sides. The fleet had suffered greatly. As the cries of conflict quieted, they were quickly replaced with the moans and screams of injury. It sickened Simon as he had yet to experience aftermath on such a scale. Allied lives and remnants of defeated vessels were lost; floating in the waters around him.

"Simon, are you out there, lad?" Driscol spoke over the radio. "Has anyone seen Kynn Veyor? And what of his stone protector who we have not seen since the dead of night?"

Simon's communicator had been decimated in his conflict; it stayed on his wrist but was broken and charred.

Sammos' sandy cloud landed on a vessel adjacent to the remnants of the boat Simon was left on.

"They are both here Admiral," Sammos said into a Sceadwian's outstretched communicator as he had none of his own. "They are on the south side of the fleet. Kapell was likely trudging through the deepest trenches in the sea, seeing as no boat you can construct is capable of bearing his weight. Are you well, Simon?" he shouted over to where Simon stood breathless.

He nodded his head and waved a hand at Sammos. The crew had seen Simon's final heroic actions and cheered for his wellbeing.

Another boatswain whistle sounded on the communicator.

"This is Admiral Driscol speaking. All vessels report in and prepare for another attack."

The whistle sounded again and the communicator went silent.

"I saw what you did back there," Kapell said as he walked back towards Simon. He stooped to lift injured soldiers and move sunken vessels that blocked the path of others.

"I thought maybe the stone stilts were you," Simon said. He sat down on a nearby crate and waited for his turn to be rescued from the marooned remnant of the ship.

"You have grown quickly," Kapell laughed. "So is the nature of you humans. Here," he said lowering an open hand, "let me take you and these others back to the right place."

Kapell took those he found back to various vessels, depositing the deceased and the injured to the places best suited to attend to them. Tortuse found the giant wading through the fleet and called out to him to retrieve Simon.

"Master Kapell, I believe you have a passenger of mine," the turtle shouted up to him.

Simon looked down to see the Thuaran and Adger standing on his back. Adger was waving up at him emphatically and shouting something too quietly to be heard from how high up Simon was.

251

Simon soon rejoined Tortuse and Adger although his friend was not altogether pleased with his bravado.

"You didn't have to run off on your own like that," Adger said slapping Simon on the arm. "What happened to discretion and restraint?"

"Would you have done any less?" Simon smiled at him.

"Indeed, I wouldn't have but—well, still—you went jumping off ships and swinging about!"

"I'm sure there will be plenty more opportunity for you to accompany me into battle," he said with a laugh.

They were summoned to Driscol shortly thereafter. Tortuse made his way amidst the fleet to the center of it where Driscol's mighty ship towered above them with three tiers of cannons stacked on top of each other, sticking out from the portholes. The bulwark was far above, so high that Simon had to shield his eyes to see the uppermost parts. When the wonder of how they would surmount such a warship wavered on the edge of his lips, ropes were tossed over the edge. The Admiral was lowered down on a platform and was soon greeting them with applause and beaming grins.

"Word of what you have done has spread quickly amongst the crews, Simon. Your efforts are no less commendable, Adger. My Thuaran passed the message on how you so valiantly pursued your companion. You both are impassibly appreciated!"

"How did they, being here, tell you, being up there?" Adger said with confusion and a glance towards the guards. He thought he spied the playful wink of one of them but thought better of the break in composure.

"Simon, I am grateful for your capabilities—very grateful—but...I need you to be more cautious," Driscol said as he stepped onto Tortuse. "My guards are incapable of such feats, and we still do not know what lies ahead."

"That was amazing though!" Adger said. "I think he can handle it."

"I must agree with Admiral Driscol," Tortuse said back to them. "Your capabilities surpass what I have witnessed in ages, but your true power should be used there," he said gesturing with his head towards Maydanok.

"I respectfully disagree; my abilities should be used on the frontlines," Simon said.

"We need you to stay safe and allow Kapell, his brother, and this fleet to fight what comes. We all know what we came out here to do, and we accept those risks. Your arrival has been an inspiration enough. Your heroics must be reserved for the final battle," he said, putting a hand on his shoulder as consolation.

Simon opened his mouth to argue again, but realized it was a dispute he could not win. Driscol returned to his ship and the fleet was soon moving again. Simon wanted to do more in whatever might come next but ashamedly realized how brazen he had been. He was glad to have come out the other side of the battle with his life but realized he was lucky. He promised himself a more stringent adherence to caution in whatever came next.

He caught glimpses of Maydanok in between the fleet ships around them. "Let's have a better look, Tortuse," he said.

The giant turtle maneuvered to the outer parts of the fleet and their destination loomed away to the east ominously. It had tall rocky shores that were black, even under the beating of the setting sun.

Night fell again, but sleep was harder to find than before. The moon was gone and clouds blocked the light of the stars, making the darkness they were in even more suffocating.

A crack of thunder in the east made Simon sit straight up from where he was laying. Tortuse's dome had been lowered and the breeze from the water was cool and sent a shiver down his back. Tortuse was still on the outside of the fleet with the dark shadow of Etnian's land in view. Their direction had shifted east as they circled the cliffs, which were still far enough away to feel a meager amount of safety from.

"It's her," Simon said of the storm, remembering the way it formed when he and Kapell spoke so long ago. He quickly roused Adger for fear of the way she sped upon him in his first days.

"What—why did you wake me?" Adger said amidst a great yawn. "That is too far away to concern us," he said as he lay back down.

Simon wasn't even sure if he had fully woken when he responded. "Come on man, wake up." He shook one of Adger's shoulders, and he popped back up from the deck again.

"What—why did you wake me?" Adger said with another yawn. His eyes snapped open when he saw the lightning.

Adger noted the way that the Thuaran had lost their stoic bearing and were leaning against the bulwark to look towards the brewing storm. The clouds were firing bolts of lightning into the water so repeatedly that they looked like a jungle network of vines. The rolling thunder echoed across the water towards them, uninhibited, and shook them to their cores. A light spray of rain pattered down on them like a gentle shower. The storm was still far across the water but the edges of the storm had reached them with the gentle caressing drizzle that preceded the violent strike of a deluge.

Flares from the ships behind them shot into the sky as before, and the fleet was quickly full of light and life again. Torches sparked across the fleet and sails were stowed to prepare for the coming typhoon. They slowed and eventually stopped to rock in the water. The sea was slowly becoming more turbulent as the winds from the storm disturbed the placidity.

Adger read the signs and quickly readied himself, putting his things back into his bag and tightening it to his back. Tortuse's many small turtles emerged and hurriedly raised the blue dome. It quickly became clear before Tortuse dove underneath the water.

"Not underwater again," Adger groaned. "Last time we went down there, we just found trouble!"

The sea beneath was even darker than the world above it. If there were enemies around them, they were even better hidden than the preceding day. They peered in the darkness, but nothing could be gained from continued submersion. Simon looked back towards the surface and, even though the waves distorted the world above, he could see the lightning flashes.

"The storm looks like it's right above us!" he said. "This is like her first assault all over again; except in the dark with more rain."

Tortuse resurfaced to rising swells that made navigation difficult, even for Tortuse. The light spray had become a heavy rain that blurred the world just outside the dome. Sheets of water flooded down the hemisphere.

"I can't see anything through the rain," Simon said. "Tortuse, maybe we should lower the shield for the sake of vision."

"No way!" Adger said. "If that is Veadus' storm, do you really want to be subjected to it?"

"Maybe you're right. We'll be safe enough in here at least," Simon said to him to try and ease him.

"There is no good place to be in this. We've thought we were safe in here before but almost drowned once," Adger said. "No offense, Tortuse," he said, quickly realizing his comment may not have been polite.

"Being in the open air is a much greater threat to you," Tortuse said. "Even if there are enemies below, my protection has been strengthened since Cineris' betrayal."

Waves began to rock the fleet more violently and the brunt of the storm was fully upon them. Dark clouds blocked out the moon, and flashes fired within them like fireworks. Lightning bolts broke through the blackened billows and hit the boat nearest Tortuse. A clap sounded so loudly above them that it felt like the entire globe was being torn apart. Pieces of the ship's hull went flying into the air and flames sparked within the gaping hole of the vessel. Several more bolts landed on the other ships around them with such specificity that it was clear a nefarious power was at work. Still, neither Veadus nor her enemies were visible. The allied ships struggled enough in the storm without the added difficulty of being under attack.

Tortuse stayed level while swimming against the tumultuous current despite the greatest of waves; they would pass over him while he kept an even keel.

In the flashes of light, Simon thought he saw Veadus in the distance but he was unsure if his fear was overtaking reality. Another flash of lightning lasted a fraction of a second longer than the rest and he saw her gigantic, lithely form again.

Simon started to call for Driscol but a boatswain whistled over the radio before he could. "Veadus Naufrage is coming," Driscol's voice called out loudly. It was difficult to hear him over the howling winds that overlapped his voice. "Gain as much distance from each other as you can."

"I don't mean to sound cowardly, but if protecting Simon is our priority, I would recommend we distance ourselves from her," Adger said pointing towards Veadus.

Tortuse turned his back towards the coming storm and gracefully weaved in between the ships that were struggling in the waves. He made for the western side of the fleet. Simon looked back towards the enemy as more flashes of lightning illuminated her rushing form; arms backward as she leaned forward. The shapes of ships around her could be seen, too. Their particulars were lost in the quick bursts of light, but there were many that filled the horizon around her.

Veadus' terrifying scream reached them even amidst the growing sounds of the storm. "You will all fail," she bellowed.

A surging tidal wave burst forth from her and a concentration of lightning strikes hit the waves the Kalinaw struggled to stay afloat on. The storm became a typhoon and despite the distance each ship had put between itself and those around it, some of them violently smashed into each other. Tortuse struggled to avoid collisions and dove under the water several times to avoid being crushed.

"Why don't we just stay down here," Adger said.

"There may come a time when our assistance is needed here," Tortuse said as they resurfaced again.

"What can we do, though?"

A wave crested near them and on it, a ship was subject to the water's will; it rose above them and started to capsize. Tortuse swam up the bottom of the wave with ease and crashed into the side of the boat to force it back upright. He beat the water with his fins long enough for the wave to break and release its merciless grip on the craft. Some of the crew dangling on the edge of the boat cheered at Tortuse before rushing back to their stations to try and maintain continued control.

An orange light pierced the darkness as thousands of cannons on enemy vessels gave light to the scene. Missiles tore through the rising waves and impacted the allied ships struggling on the water. The Kalinaw fired their own salvos, but the uncoordinated efforts were not at their best of capabilities; hindered by the wind and the waves. Cannonballs passed through Veadus without any deterrence as she pressed on towards the allies. The bombardments did hit some of her minions and the successful impacts caused a significant amount of reparation for the Kalinaw. No matter how many projectiles they fired though, it was incapable of slowing the Witch. The chaotic scene was a desperate defense; even Simon couldn't hope to be the saving grace this time. The constant explosions of thunder were unpredictably inconsistent and made his heart race.

The cannon fire was so constant and steady that it created a hazy orange glow in the dark of the night like the rising sun. It was enough to see that, even at the distance Tortuse had put between them, Veadus was nearly at the eastern edge of the fleet. In but a moment, she would reach the vessels that were already struggling on the losing side of the conflict.

"Kapell, where are you," Simon prayed quietly.

A mountainous shape rocketed out of the water between Veadus and the Kalinaw fleet; the rocky formation was shaped like a fist and an arm. It slammed into Veadus' jaw as she passed over it. Kapell erupted from the water as Veadus bounced along the sea from his attack as if she were sliding on a smooth floor. Kapell put a hand on his knee and stood to his full height from where he had been hiding in the more shallow water. He used the moment of Veadus' fall to turn and smash the enemy ships closest to him. He took out entire rows of vessels with each swift kick. He made movements, like Simon had in the arena in Burgh Sceadwia, and buttes launched entire ships into the air. He was faster and more aggressive than he had been in the previous conflict; the desperate opponent disparity certainly called for it. As he continued his attempts to tip the odds in the Kalinaw favor, Veadus stood back up and jumped on his back. For the moment, she halted her assault on the Kalinaw and sought to avenge herself of Kapell's attack.

Kapell grabbed her and slammed her into the torrential waves. She exploded like a crashing wave and instantly reformed, kneeled, and poised to jump towards him again. She would not be taken by such surprise again and called on all her abilities to overtake him. Fortunately for Kapell, he wasn't carrying Simon or anyone else, so the two of them were more equally matched than their last encounter. She rushed him and despite her more slender form, pushed him back. They continued pushing and leaning against each other. In one moment of her weakness, Kapell raised a hand and a mesa land formation sprung from the earth beneath the water behind her. The elevated land had a flat top and steep cliffs too high for even a giant to step over. Veadus had no time to react and tripped over it as Kapell ran and kicked her in the chest. She was sent flying backwards on the mesa and slid over the other side. Kapell used that momentary advantage and slammed his hands together repeatedly to send gale blasts towards Veadus' fleet, pushing those closest to him underwater or toppling over. His efforts were enough to disrupt the enemy fleet but not enough to stop the rest from firing upon the allies or engaging them in close combat if they were in range enough to do so.

The storm isolated the mountainous combatant and although he had no fear, his companions were desperate to help; all they could do was watch and hope to survive the challenges they, too, were facing. The constant downpour prevented Sammos from helping his brother or the companions he sailed with. He watched the chaos around him with a panged heart, but the most he could do was to assist in keeping the vessel sailing that he was on. Simon's magnificent heroics from the previous battle were also stymied. Tortuse was unwilling to let him fight in the battle and he wasn't entirely sure he would be able to brave the storm on his own.

"There must be more we can do," Simon yelled to Tortuse over the noise.

"The risk of losing you amidst the storm is too great. Even I would struggle to find you if you fell into the water," Tortuse said.

One tremendous wave washed over them inside the safety of Tortuse's dome. Simon saw that the battle had become equally as ferocious underneath the water. Enemy submarines had returned, and the opposing vessels were filling the water with torpedoes that only added to the churning chaos of the battle.

Simon paced back and forth with fret. It seemed his only capability was to be a solemn witness to the destruction of life on both sides. He prayed for a swift resolution to develop as it had in the last conflict, but each side exchanged and expended their mortality equally without securing the victory.

The battle went on for what seemed like hours until the water was filled with shards of vessels too broken to determine which side they belonged to. Tortuse helped right falling vessels and tried to ram those enemies that he could reach. Simon and Adger served as lookouts and prevented Tortuse from being hurt in the pandemonium; even the Thuaran discarded their bearing for the sake of keeping watch. The storm lessened as Veadus was weakened but the advantage that calmer water offered had long since passed. The night was waning, and both sides suffered from the effects of the battle. The light of the rising sun gave the battle a subtle glow that signified the dawn, but the light did little more than reveal widespread destruction.

"This is the time," Simon said. "We should help finish this fight now while they're weak!"

"Fear not, Simon; I think this battle is nearly won," Tortuse said.

Kapell and Veadus were slowing their attacks. The moments in between their blows became longer each time they pushed each other back. In a momentary lapse of aggression, Kapell kneeled in the water and was immersed up to his neck. He stayed there for a moment that seemed too long for the heat of battle. Veadus saw her opportunity and seemed invigorated enough to strike him down with one final effort. She closed the distance between them rapidly and raised her hands to attack.

Simon saw Kapell's immobility and shouted to him despite the impossibility that he would hear him. Kapell looked to him and smiled in a devious way that told Simon he was not without a plan. A quaking rumble sounded up through the depths of the water like a mountain was trying to birth its way into the world. Simon saw a strain in Kapell's face and couldn't imagine what was about to happen.

Veadus was only steps away from Kapell, and still he struggled in the waters with something below the surface. Whatever he wrestled finally broke free and he began to stand. The water in front of him immediately spewed a geyser of boiling steam as his hands rose from the surface. Simon saw they held the hilt of a blade and the more of it that emerged, the more focused the geyser became. The sword continued to evaporate the water until it broke the surface of the sea. It was a stony blade edged with a red heat like that of Kapell's molten kilt and was as wide as one of his enormous legs. It was made from a material as dark as the depths of the ocean and from it, rocky protuberances added to its size.

Kapell swung the blade upward from the water just as Veadus reached him. It cut her in two, straight up her middle. As the blade tore her flesh, instead of blood or some other foul fluid, shards of hardened turquoise burst from the wound like shattered glass. She emitted a horrific scream that echoed across the sea as she aimlessly grabbed at the sword to stop her demise. The sword silenced her as it cleaved her head in a fiery flash. Kapell stood with the sword raised in the air; the edge burning so brightly it was nearly white. The two halves of Veadus' body fell to the water and sunk below the surface.

As her grimace was swallowed into the depths, the raging storm calmed almost immediately. The dark storm clouds above the fray dispersed and allowed the rising sun to spread its light. As the torrential waves fell and the water calmed, the Kalinaw were able to fire ceaseless missiles towards their enemies. Many of Veadus' ships were destroyed so quickly that it seemed the sea could not consume them fast enough. Whatever enemies had sense or ability enough to see the scales had tipped away from them, dropped their sails and hoped a merciful wind would save them. Those remaining few fled and the fastest of the Kalinaw gave chase without delay.

Veadus and her fleet were defeated, but the losses were severe for all. A cry of victory rang out from every vessel on the water and likely those underneath it. The Admiral's boatswain whistle sounded.

"All vessels report in immediately," Driscol's voice commanded over the radio. "Munitions and personnel counts are priority…the dead will be mourned, but we need to assure we're prepared in the event of retaliation."

Another cheer sounded from the fleet but neither Simon nor Adger had the heart to celebrate; despite having destroyed a creature as powerful and terrifying as Veadus. Simon looked around him at the broken ships and scattered debris: hulls of vessels stuck up from the water or were impaled into others. Lifeless bodies floated in the water or hung from the tangles of tackle of abandoned vessels. He felt sick to his stomach, more than any disgust he had ever known. Without having to ask, Tortuse lowered the dome just as Simon rushed to the edge and wretched.

"This is what war brings," Simon said, wiping his mouth.

"Have you not seen death in your travels?" Tortuse asked.

"I've killed her minions and fought those fire people in Burgh—I've even thrown a few rocks in defense...but this—this is...carnage. This is merciless and needless—" he wretched again over the bulwark. He saw Adger rush to the opposite side to do the same.

Tortuse stopped wading through the mire, and extended his neck so far backwards that he was looking directly at Simon; face to beak. Simon was surprised; never had he seen a turtle's neck so long.

"Evil does not succumb to reason. Such malice is a decision contrived, not enforced through celestial manipulations. I have watched the world—this one and yours; from what they once were—and I have seen the malevolence of Aithna infect and destroy but of all his influence, none has been more effortless as that over man. You would do well to let this moment burn in your mind. Remember the revulsion you feel for it. Power begets corruption and yours will certainly be tried."

"We—we have to help them," Adger said weakly as he spit what was left in his mouth overboard.

Tortuse retracted his long neck to face forward again. "Admiral Driscol ordered—"

"Damn his report!" Simon hollered. His voice echoed off nearby ships and bounced along the placid water.

Kalinaw troops stood at the edges of the few ships that were still manned nearby. Simon felt momentarily embarrassed by his outburst and looked around at those who looked down at him from the vessels. They all looked battered and bloodied; every last one of them.

"I will help the dead," Simon said into his radio for Driscol to hear. "And I will not wait."

He stepped out of the boat and his foot was met by stone again but not that of his own control. This time it was Kapell's hand he had stepped onto. Simon looked up at his stone giant friend who smiled down at him sympathetically, with pursed lips. A single glittering stone fell from Kapell's eye and Simon caught it as it fell. It was a single ruby tear—but not one of joy or laughter as it was on that first day. It reflected the light of the giant's sword that was lashed to his back and still emitted a glow to accompany the fire of his garment.

"I too will help," the giant said, "but I need your keen eyesight by the water."

There were no more cheers that afternoon. Simon told Kapell where to scoop up the bodies and together they sifted through the mess looking for survivors. They were not alone in their efforts though. Tortuse soon followed Simon's lead and scooped up bodies in the water as they passed, sliding them down his fins onto his back. Adger and the guards helped those that still had breath in them and piled those that did not. His deck filled quickly and when it reached capacity, Kapell moved the growing numbers to Kalinaw ships that could take them.

The rest of the fleet worked through the day in a similar manner: rescuing those they could and collecting those they could not. It was an arduous task and before the sun fell towards the sea again, the fleet had gathered all those that they could find.

When all those were rescued that could be, and Kapell's ceaseless strength moved the broken remnants of enemy and ally ships, the Kalinaw congregated to mourn those who had been lost. The dead were placed in one of the spare cargo ships whose stores had been emptied and distributed. It was set on a course west, back towards the main lands and into the open sea. When it was far enough from the fleet, Kapell trudged to the outskirts of the fleet and drew his sword. He raised the rocky and fiery acquisition into the air and its formless width pulled at the light of the waning sun. The fire from the edge glowed white again until tendrils of conflagration burst forth and swirled around the blade in a cyclone. The blaze sped until it was so great that it was a singular, conical inferno. He swung it down towards the water and stopped only a hair's breadth from the sea. The fire was flung from the blade in a crescent so tall that it could have engulfed any creature in the world; even Kapell. It ignited the ship and it was soon sent to the bottom of the ocean in a hero's ceremony; worthy of every life sacrificed in the pursuit of having Etnian deposed.

23 The Invasion

The remaining ships were anchored in concentric circles with the smaller and dignitary vessels in the center. A gathering of the remaining leaders intended to ascertain what forces were left and to allow time for the crews to rest from the battle. They were in Driscol's ship, which was not small by any means, but still smaller than the warships. It made up for the difference in both speed and evasion. Simon and Adger were brought to the leaders who were gathered in a command room, much like the one in Stoikheion. Similarly, most of the same faces were there, although a bit worse for wear.

After the casual conversation had settled, Admiral Driscol called their gathering to some semblance of order by banging a stein on the table. "We need to be underway soon. Everyone has suffered from this battle, but we must reach land before the sun rises tomorrow."

"We have the enemy on the run, our crews are weary, and Veadus is dead," one man said, who looked more like a brigand than a soldier.

"Veadus may not be completely eradicated," Sid said representing Kapell again. "Do not count her out of this fight yet."

"How can she not be dead?" a sharply dressed woman questioned. "She was severed from toe to head."

"Etnian's evil reach has yet to show its darkest fingers."

"What concerns me most is where the remaining enemies have fled," Driscol said. "Our fastest warships were unable to prevent the enemy's escape. Time is, therefore, not in our favor, and Etnian will have guessed our plans by now. Word of Kynn's arrival will have reached him and we must hope his borders have not been fortified. Each moment we delay is another opportunity we give him freely."

"But we have *him*," the large mustachioed general said gesturing to

261

Simon at his side. "Without your heroics, old boy, my ship would have been lost! I will give you your heart's desire when this is over." He clapped him on the shoulder and shook him side to side.

"Power must come from the strength of an army and not the capacity of one man," Driscol said.

"Yet a hero's efforts can decide the fate of us all," one man said.

Simon interrupted their banter, feeling as if his role was being decided for him. "You're talking about me like I'm not even here. I know what my responsibilities are, and they are constantly on my mind. I have no idea what's going to happen in the coming days but, for what it's worth, I agree with Drisc—with the Admiral, this time. We need to get to Maydanok quickly, now that we've done what we can for the departed. We have allies who are waiting for us there, and we don't know if they're okay. I've been trying to reach them over the last couple of days with no success."

The group was quiet for a moment.

"Give the fleet two hours—but all ships must be ready to sail by then," Driscol said.

The group departed and went back to their ships. Driscol called after Simon and Adger.

"You cannot feel guilty, Simon."

"I could've helped," Simon said somewhat heatedly turning on him with a trenchant finger. "You saw what I'm capable of, yet you demanded I be confined?"

"I understand your frustration, and I apologize that you felt maltreated. You yourself said that you carry the only weapon able to kill Etnian. If we lose that then all the lives lost so far will have been in vain."

"Well, technically they're not dead," Adger blurted.

"That may be so, but I'm sure they would rather be," Driscol said. "Simon, I must implore you to show more restraint. Your lack of composure calls into question my capabilities and—I daresay—your own."

Simon had no response for him but was silenced in frustration.

"Think no more of it," Driscol said in his more jovial tone. "Your passion is duly noted. Focus on what is to come; we are nearly at our seaborne journey's end. If we get separated when we get to the shore, my guards will help you on your way. Please, take some time to rest here before we depart."

Driscol barely gave them an option but Simon and Adger gladly accepted his hospitality and enjoyed softer comforts than the hard deck of Tortuse's shell. He led them to a small guest's quarters, but it was so lavish that its size was overlooked. It had windows on two walls; some that looked towards the Kalinaw fleet and the rest pointed towards the looming cliffs ahead. They were glad to have a soft place to sit and lie down in addition to better food than the rations they had been hurriedly given before they set sail. Cheery conversation eluded them and their thoughts were overtaken with the recent events. Eventually they both dozed off and the sleep they had was brief but restful. They both awoke to cold drinks and hot food in their room again but they had no knowledge of being served. They ate quickly and went back onto the deck of the ship to see that the circles of ships had broken up and were heading north again.

"Just in time," Driscol said as he limped up to them. "Would you like to finish this journey with me here, or return to Tortuse's protection?"

"I thought we didn't have a choice," Simon said.

"That was before our submersibles confirmed that the Witch's body has not moved. We assumed that whatever evil gives her command of the sea would reclaim her and grant her form again. It seems that, for the moment, the sea does not pose the threat it did before."

"And what about your guards?"

"They will stay here with us but still lend their aid as needed when we arrive."

"I wouldn't mind the fresh air here," Simon said.

Adger agreed, and Tortuse followed them in the event of another attack.

The air on the deck of the ship was invigorating to them, but they were unable to blow away the scenes they had witnessed in the water. The slaughter left its mark on Simon and Adger but was insufficient enough to prepare them for what would come next.

Simon's fear diminished as the dark black cliffs gave way to the lower coastal plains of the North West lands. The dark sea lightened and became a brilliant pale turquoise as the deep seabed rose to meet the rest of the world. A dilapidated city was situated on the coast directly in the shallow water. It pushed its way through the trees inland and farther over rising hills, spreading out across the coast as far around the bend as could be seen. The short squat buildings interrupted the placidity of the water. Their foliage covered walls and roofs lent a wholesome peacefulness to the entire scene. The sea was tranquil and sloshed against the pale white structures; threatening to lull the inattentive sailor to sleep. The many buildings fought back the growth of the land but waged a losing battle as nature successfully had begun to reclaim the submerged city. Tall narrow trees lined the edge of the shore and reached their tendrils into the water to satisfy their thirst.

Boatswain whistles bounced off the water throughout the navy. The Kalinaw ships slowed in response and the soft splash of lead lines sounded across the fleet as the vessels cautioned against the rising seafloor. There was no harbor to dock in, and the buildings were so tightly packed that even the small disembarkation ships that hung from the sides of the larger craft would be slowed in their incursion.

"The port of Kamena," Driscol said, walking up behind Simon and

Adger at the prow of the ship. "It was once a home of healers and scholars but has since been abandoned out of fear for the shadow of Gorfel."

"That sounds familiar," Adger piped up with a note of his former positivity. "I think this is Orvar's home—or was, some age ago."

"So, he traded the seaside for the forest, then," Simon said. "I can't say I blame him; I do miss that forest of his."

"Cheer up, chap!" Driscol said and slapped him on the back. "It seems our assault might be without resistance; look at this place!"

"How are we supposed to get to land then; swim?"

"No, there are far too many people, and too much equipment, to risk losing them in the water; even such shallow kind. Some can ferry in the dinghies, but the rest of us will have to cross between the bridges and docks that link these old structures. See that one group of buildings there?" he said, pointing to an outcropping of crumbling structure. "With a bit of careful maneuvering, I do say we can find our way ashore there."

The buildings where he pointed were connected to the others by docks and bridges; they looked weak and worn, but there was little other option.

"There has to be another dock," Simon said. "A city this size would have a port big enough to house the whole fleet!"

"We're likely sailing above it, old boy."

"I'll bet he's right," Adger said. "Orvar told me that in the early days, Etnian broke dams and flooded the world. I always thought that was another metaphor of his. This must have been what he meant. I hope he's out there somewhere."

"Fear not, Adger; we'll find him, but please restrain your desire to call him on the communicators. I've ordered silence except for what can be said to the adjacent man."

The fleet was quiet as they dropped into the waters in small boats, or butted their vessels against the outermost buildings. They extended gangplanks and tossed out grappling hooks; lashing to any solid stone they could. The city soon crawled with the allied forces that clambered over fallen walls and crossed ancient walkways within the old city.

The Kalinaw had soon infested the outer parts of the city like an invading force of ants. Adger secretly tried to hail his brother repeatedly as he and Simon had been left behind until the metropolis could be cleared. The rest of Driscol's crew hurried across the planks and into the city. Simon was Adger's accomplice and ignored caution for the sake of their concern.

"What if they hear us?" Adger said, stopping his attempts for a moment.

"Who? Etnian's men?" Simon asked. "I guess it's possible, but at this point, if he knows we're here then looking for your brother won't change anything. Just don't say, 'We just got to Maydanok' and I think we'll be okay." He paused for a moment. "Something's wrong."

Adger's countenance dropped at the comment.

"That's not what I meant," Simon reassured. "Just because we can't get in touch with him doesn't mean anything. Where did everybody go, anyway?"

"I would guess they're making final battle plans. Driscol said something about setting up a command post again."

"Well how long should we wait if we're not allowed to call your brother on the radio? You'd think Driscol had ample time to discuss his plans already," Simon said impatiently.

"Let's just go," Adger said. "No one's out there."

Simon lingered another moment, staring out at the quiet buildings. Even with hundreds of people swarming about and preparing for their final battles, there was little sign or sound of it.

"These people really are the masters of disguise," Simon said. "Let's do our best to keep up the deception."

They both crossed over the planks and into the partially submerged city. They walked towards a section of the city that was on the land instead of in the water.

"There's no way this whole place is just abandoned," Simon said. "This is too easy."

"We did have to fight a storm and a crazy water giant to get here," Adger said.

"True, but...I don't know; something just doesn't feel right."

"Let's take advantage of the calm to find Brom. I can use Ketay."

"I want to find them too, but we need to go talk to Driscol first. I can't help but feel that we're not safe here."

The pair of them were directed through the abandoned streets by fellow soldiers who had taken up guard at various intersections. They were quickly guided towards Driscol and his assembly of leaders who had holed up in one of the buildings in better state than the others.

"Ah, there you are, Simon," Driscol said as they walked into the dusty old building.

"Driscol," Simon said, lowering his voice as Driscol walked towards them. "Something's not right here."

"This was the best arrival we could hope for," he said with a laugh.

"That's exactly what I mean; this is too easy. Has the whole city been searched?"

"That will take time; it's larger than we first assumed."

"Then I wouldn't celebrate yet."

"You're quite right," he said as he called over a trio of soldiers. "I would hope that if we were in any danger our scouts would have found it by now, but you're quite right." He turned to the soldiers he had called over, "I need you three to make your way straight to the outer most part of the city; at the peaks. We've sent a group that way, but now I worry what keeps them."

No sooner had the soldiers exited the small building than an explosion erupted. It nearly brought down the building on top of them. Chunks of the ceiling fell down on, and around them, and one of the nearby walls folded in like a partition.

Simon's ears rang and the boom of more explosions was all he could discern.

"Hey!" A muffled voice said that sounded distant. "Hey! Wake up!" the voice yelled at him again.

"Hey! Wake up!" the voice yelled at him again.

I must be asleep; he thought to himself, *I must have fallen fast asleep on the beach. Such a nice serene place to be. This is nice...I think I'll just stay asleep for a while longer listening to the soft, splashing of the waves—*

"We have to go! Now! They're coming!" the voice said, coming in clearly now.

He awoke immediately, full of fear like in the heat of the battle on the sea. The scene around him was chaotic and confusing; he could not quite make sense of it. The rubble of the room was burning and half of it had fully collapsed. People were shouting and scrambling to recover.

"What happened?" Simon asked, confused and shaky from the overload of his senses. "Wait, who are you?"

The person slapped him hard across the face. "Snap out of it, Simon!"

His delusion disappeared and he realized he was looking at Adger.

"You were right," Adger said. "All of Maydanok has come to welcome us."

After another second, Simon had fully regained his composure, despite the ringing still in his ears. The Thuaran ran into the room and rushed to Driscol and Simon; helping them to stand.

"What happened?" Driscol demanded weakly; still disoriented from the explosion with blood trickling from his forehead.

"An enemy legion to the northeast has set up mortars and cannons and are firing upon the city," one of the guards said.

"Send two brigades south and three north," Driscol said. "The rest of the infantry will reinforce them shortly."

The guard ran off to pass along the orders.

"You were right, Simon. I was careless. It seems the battle has found us faster than I had hoped," Driscol said.

"It doesn't matter," Simon said. "Even if someone discovered the artillery, I doubt that anybody would have made it back here in time for us to do anything about it. Bromle was supposed to be here too...I'm afraid to know what happened to him."

"Yes, I do wonder what has happened to our scouting battalion."

"What can we do? And don't give me that 'be safe' stuff. We need to help."

"I do need you protected, but it seems my plans need to be accelerated. There should still be another company of the Thuaran in a war vessel just at the edge of the fleet; much greater warriors than the few that accompanied you before and they can sail faster than any."

"I'm not sailing back out to sea just to avoid—"

"And I would rather not have you do that either," Driscol interrupted. "I need you to head inland and follow behind the invasion. Our forces will have made some headway north and south *around* the artillery. They will have prepared the way for you until the rest of us can rejoin you farther inland. This battle here is not yours, but your time will come. Please, save your fight for what may come next."

Simon hesitated.

"Simon, please; I'm not asking you to run this time, only save your fight for the one yet to come. One stray round will end your journey, and I would rather your talents be given a proper chance."

Simon agreed and Adger followed along with him as they ran back down the streets towards the Kalinaw ships. They covered their heads with every explosion and tried their best to stay brave enough to carry on fearlessly, but the barrage the enemy rained on the city was relentless. The percussive force of another nearby explosion knocked them both to the ground as clouds of stone and debris filled the street. It wasn't as close as the one on the command room but it was enough to knock Adger's pack from his back. When it hit the ground, the green Methatien stone that Adger carried rolled down the street.

"Una—I mean, Ketay," Adger called after it.

When the stone heard its companion's name, it took it as instruction to find Una; it picked up speed as it rolled away.

Adger didn't hesitate to pursue Ketay. He jumped up, grabbed his bag, and ran off after it.

"Adger, wait!" Simon called after him. He hesitated a moment, not totally sure what to do. He wanted to carry on with his task but couldn't turn his back on Adger either so he sprinted after his friend.

In a brief moment, he caught up to Adger who was running quickly around fallen debris. Explosions rocked the entire city and they both darted in and out of falling buildings, heading in a southeastern direction after Ketay.

"There she is," Adger said pointing. "Ketay, wait!" he called after it, but his voice was lost in the enemy's assault.

Just beyond where Ketay was heading, several impacts converged to create a super explosion that launched entire buildings into the air. The buildings around the impact lurched upward and then immediately collapsed down below the street. By the time they both realized what had happened, turning around was no longer an option.

Simon couldn't be sure at the time, but it seemed that Adger sped up once he realized a piece of the city was being sucked into the earth. Adger jumped into the open air and Simon jumped after him, hoping to use the earth or sand to catch them. He summoned what force he had on the earth and envisioned a platform beneath his feet. One began to form, and he directed it towards Adger, who had turned in midair to show his grasp on Ketay. His triumphant expression changed when he realized that Simon had followed him into the hole.

The ground had opened into a tremendous sinkhole, the bottom of which neither of them could see in the cloud of debris. A piece of earth came from behind Simon and broke the platform he was forming. He flipped backwards before he had enough sense to create another one. His mind panicked as he became disoriented in the dust cloud and chaos around him.

Something grabbed his foot and his fall was arrested. Something was rapidly pulling him back out of the hole and in another brief moment, he was free of the disaster. He looked up his leg to see Adger holding onto it with both hands.

"You're flying!" Simon said.

Great, bronze, insectival wings sprouted from his backpack just like the ones he had fixed to the desert skiff.

Adger set him down just outside of the hole and landed next to him to help him up.

"I wasn't going to let them go to waste," Adger said as the wings folded and retracted back inside the pack. "I made a few adjustments so that I can control them with a few movements of my shoulders. You shouldn't have jumped in after me."

"You should've told me that you had wings," Simon said laughing. "Did you get Ketay?"

"Yeah. Her rolling off like that tells me that Una is close and if we can find her, we'll find Bromle."

The pair of them headed towards the Thuaran ship again but had to take a less direct route due to the destruction. They were forced to climb up a pile of debris onto the third floor of a devastated building. Neither of them felt comfortable being elevated in such chaos but they had no alternatives.

When they reached the top Simon pointed at the ship. "There it is," he said.

No sooner had the words left his mouth than the ship exploded from multiple hits of the enemy's artillery. The entire area was repeatedly hit, and many of the nearby vessels sank.

"They're preventing retreat," Simon yelled over the explosions. "We'll have to move inland on our own or we're going to get hit."

They turned to retreat, but the building they were standing on was hit too. The remnants of the tower shuddered and started to slide into the earth. The building split across its width and opened like gaping jaws. They could see the underground river far below them and hoped they wouldn't be crushed by the falling debris as they started to fall along with the rest of the structure.

Simon tried again to gain a sense of direction, or spot Adger in the debris, but he quickly lost sight of him. Before he had the sense to control the chunks of earth, he landed in water and had the wind knocked out of him. He swam for the surface to see chunks of the buildings from above landing in the water around him. He held up his hand defensively and pieces of stone stopped mid-air. He struggled to breathe normally and stay afloat as more debris fell on the pile he kept elevated. He was slowly being pushed deeper into the water. He was nearly drowned as he sank lower until the water was just below his nostrils. He dug into the depths of his will to keep his head turned enough to draw breath.

Just when he couldn't stand the burning in his muscles or his incapability to inhale any longer, a large hand grabbed his coat and pulled him out of the water. The pile of debris fell when Simon lost his concentration.

"Not the best place for a swim, eh?" Bromle said, helping him to his feet on the small walkway by the water.

"Bromle," Simon gasped. "Adger—was…in there."

Bromle's beaming smile didn't change at the news. Simon looked around to see other wearied faces that stood alongside him.

"I'm here," Adger said, pushing his way through the group. "As soon as I heard the explosion, I went airborne. Are you okay?"

"I—will be," Simon said in between gasps.

"Brom, what happened to you guys?" Adger asked. "Where are Gin and Orvar…and all the soldiers that went with you?"

There were only about twenty soldiers left with Bromle and they looked like they had seen a fierce battle.

"When we got here, the place seemed abandoned," Bromle said. "We didn't meet any resistance on the river either. By the time we realized the city only *looked* abandoned, it was too late. Some of us were captured, including Gin and Orvar. She was alive when last I saw her, little brother, but we lost her in the fray; I'm sorry. I did what I could, but there were just too many of them. The ones of us that weren't captured, were lost in the first few waves. We tried to send troops to warn you before you arrived, but I guess you didn't get the message. We've tried the radios too but never heard back."

"Driscol had us turn them off," Adger said sadly. "I kept calling you too, but you never answered."

"We'll get her back, Adger," Simon reassured him.

"It was the same with us," Bromle continued trying to avoid his brother's direct stare. "We turned the radios off once we came down here. We were just heading back up to see if you arrived when the bombs started going off. This is the most cultivated part of the underground river we've seen yet and seemed as good a shelter as any. Looks more like a sewer, really. The rest of the tunnels were barely tall enough to squeeze us and the boats through with our heads bent low. Otherwise, I think we would have been here soon enough to warn you. No matter, we're here now and we need to make up for it, get back up there, and join this fight!"

Simon nodded his head in between breaths which were slowly becoming more reliable.

"When you're ready," Bromle said.

"Did you lose anything in the fall?" Adger asked him while checking his own pockets.

Simon quickly checked his belongings to ensure he hadn't dropped anything when he hit the water. He pulled out the trinkets he had from before. He put on the last two rings, remembering Sophia's words that something worn is harder to lose than something carried. Even though she seemed to fear the ring of Olim, he thought it would be better protected if he wore it. He felt unchanged and assumed that since he had been given the ring intentionally, it would do him no harm. He wondered if he was immune to whatever power it possessed.

"I think I have everything," Simon said, finally able to regain his breath. "Adger, are you okay?"

"I will be once this is over," he said a bit flatly.

The group moved down along the underground river. They stopped each time more explosions rocked the city above them so their progress was slow. Eventually they reached a spiral stairwell carved into the stone wall. It was leading back up to the city and they hoped it had not been collapsed like other stairwells they had seen.

"How do we know it's clear?" Adger asked, leaning into the archway as if he could see the peak of the stairs.

"We don't, little brother, but that's why we'll go up it," Bromle said, teasingly bumping his brother towards the dark stairwell.

"What if we get up there and then another bomb hits and then we get trapped or something?"

"Then we best be on our way before one hits." He laughed and took the lead up the stairs.

They each hurried up the winding staircase, not willing to wait for someone to ensure the way was clear. Bromle felt more confined than the rest of them but was able to ascend quickly enough. They continued their climb until the dizziness of spinning in ascending circles threatened to send them tumbling back down again. Up and up they went until they finally reached a landing that the sun was graceful enough to warm. It was a peaceful scene, if the carnage in the city beyond it could be ignored.

"Time to join the invasion," Bromle said with a subtle note of excitement.

The group moved quietly through the streets, hoping not to be seen or discovered. The explosions had become less frequent and seemed to stop altogether after a few moments of their departure from the stairs. Simon and Adger directed them back to where the command post had been, but there was no one there either; just hurriedly abandoned papers.

"Not a single person is left?" Simon thought aloud. "Adger, did he say they would all go?"

"Not that I remember—more importantly, why have the explosions stopped?"

"Would you rather they resumed?" Bromle laughed.

"We should hurry and find out what's happened then. The quiet either means they're all...dead—or captured—or successful but, either way, I think it'd be best we found out." Adger continued.

"Lead the way then, little brother."

They moved towards the edge of the city and climbed a hill to the valleys beyond. When they reached the crest of the hill, they realized why the explosions had stopped: their allies were in heated combat in the sparsely forested hills outside the city.

The enemy was a sea of black-armored warriors. Even from a distance, their dark armor could be seen flaring in spikes and blades that threatened to maim and injure, even if they missed. There were no ranks or formations in the conglomeration; just the clanging and warring of enemies.

Even through the trees, Simon could see the machines of war standing quietly instead of continuously ejecting missiles at them.

Without waiting for permission or coordination, Simon hopped up and ran towards their allies in the fields below. The group with him hesitated for a moment and then ran after him, shouting battle cries.

There was still enough open field to risk his own injury from any adept enough enemy archer but he was so caught up in the desire to participate, that he thought nothing of it. Simon saw his allies but wanted to be in the heat of it; to defend those most surrounded. He ran past the outer most edges of conflict and charged for the center of the fray. The brothers and the others were ensnared in the conflict right away while Simon had focused elsewhere: protecting the weakened, providing salvation, and—ultimately—destroying the artillery. Despite the silence of the cannons, he wanted to ensure they couldn't be lit again.

He thought of his allies, and his heart burned in sadness for those who gave their lives because of the role he was meant to fulfill. He beat the ground with his feet as his heart beat within his chest. He aided the Kalinaw that needed it and, on several occasions, raised his shield to defend those who faltered. He slashed his fiery weapon and nimbly danced around the vain attempts of vile forces to subdue him. So busily he fought that he barely had time to notice what banner the enemy flew, or what loyalty their armor might describe.

He was still the lesser part of a league from the artillery cannons. They pointed into the air amidst the trees like silent monuments of war. He spied their broad barrels that still wafted the minutest smoke from munitions recently fired. His momentary distraction nearly caused his injury as a falling axe narrowly landed beside his leg. He looked up at its wielder to see a man large enough to overtake even Bromle. The person's eyes were dark, and a wicked grin stretched across his face.

Simon glanced around him in the battlefield and thought this giant of a warrior had to be the largest of the enemies there. And in all that chaos, the beast had managed to find him and for a moment, he doubted his capability. He called for Kapell in his mind, who had long since found another path since they arrived. The thought made him wonder, almost in complete distraction, where the giant had gone. But then, he felt it! He felt the rumble of power in his chest and he stretched out his mind to strike. The ground began to quake, and the earth cracked around him in a deepening crater. Vines rose from the depths and shot towards his towering enemy and the others nearby, wrapping and choking the opponents of the Kalinaw. Mighty trunks exploded from the ground into the air and swung downwards towards the artillery. The impacts caused them to be crushed like folded paper. Simon was lifted on stilts of vines and swept down over the other enemies yet to fall. He cut them down with a fiery blade, or a pointed branch. It took effort from all, and more loss of life, but eventually the enemy was destroyed.

When the fighting had ceased and the clanging of weapons no longer filled the air, Simon sat on a broken stump, trying to catch his breath again; this time out of exhaustion. Injured and deceased soldiers from both sides were nearby. The sight sickened him but he was so tired, he couldn't find the will to vomit.

Driscol appeared next to him: battle wearied but not defeated.

"I'm not going back to the city," Simon said. "So, if you're here to take me, you can forget it. We need to keep pressing forward with what forces we have and free those who were captured or killed. I've studied the maps enough to know that Maydanok has a prison here." Simon turned his hand over and projected a map of Maydanok that his ring had captured earlier. "It's a half day's march from here, and I think that should be our next stop. We don't know how long this war could go on for, and saving me for the end of it is stupid. Whether you want to grant me your permission or not,

I'm going to get my friends back. If we're successful, that would give us more resources too."

"I'm not here to stop you—" Driscol said.

"Good." Simon stood up defiantly and started marching eastward on his own. A soldier underneath the bodies of others grabbed Simon's ankle as he passed. Simon immediately bent down, pushed the bodies off of the injured soldier, and beckoned Driscol to help him. Other soldiers nearby rushed to help him, too. The soldier was weak and looked young, even when compared to Simon's afterlife-rejuvenation. Simon knelt down and pushed the dirt and grime off of his face. When Simon touched him, a bright light shone from the man's wounds. The cuts and breaks in his body were immediately repaired and life filled the young man's body again. He looked around, confused and disoriented, but no less grateful for the revival.

Simon looked down at his hand and realized that the ring of Olim had revealed its worth. It had a subtle glow to it that waned as he stared. He forgot about his selfishness for a moment and thought about what he could do for the rest of those around him.

"But how..." the young soldier sputtered as he stood from the ground.

"It's the ring," Simon said staring at his hand, awestruck.

"It is a dark power," the soldier said fearfully. He quickly stood up and rushed away from Simon towards fellow soldiers.

"I'm not wicked!" Simon called after him. "I just saved—"

"Leave him be, Simon." Driscoll held up a hand when Simon started to go after the soldier. "He's likely scared half witless from what he just saw. The edge of death can be maddening, but you—you have the power to recall a man from that edge! How did you come by this power?"

"I had it when I arrived; it was always here with me, but I never knew what it could do until now." He was elated but his excitement was decimated when he thought of the gruesome scene on the sea. "So many people died that I could have saved."

"Well, if what my old friend Orvar believes is true, then they're not gone yet," Driscol said.

Simon looked down at the ring again. He took it off and turned it over in his fingers. "Something like this can't be evil; this is...this is a gift. What if I can heal them all?" Simon thought aloud.

"Then you best be to it, as there are many around us who still have need of your help."

Simon knew that Driscol was pleased that he now had this obligation to help and not trudge off on his own, but he also knew his brooding would have led to his own death had that soldier not grabbed his ankle. He walked over to another warrior lying nearby who was being tended to by a field medic. "May I?" he said to her.

The armored fighter had been watching what was happening and nodded her head with labored breath. She looked quite different than the Sceadwians; she didn't have the ornate armor or the lance they all carried. She had loose fitting clothing and was dressed as one of the brigands on the ships with red sails. The crews of those vessels all had similar styles of clothing: oversized boots, scarves tied around their waists, and long leather coats that hung like capes. Simon touched the buccaneer's arm and her wounds quickly disappeared. She didn't run in fear like the last one had but sat up and looked at Simon with green eyes of wonder.

She stood up and thanked him, shaking his hand vigorously. "Your healin' be much appreciated," she said with an unintelligible accent.

"The ring of life and death," Simon said to himself.

He looked at another nearby body, dead and bloodied. *I wonder...*he thought. Simon choked back the sickness that crept from his stomach but reached out anyway to touch the leg of the deceased Kalinaw. The soldier immediately sprung up with a shout but quickly quieted when he realized he had been resurrected.

Simon fell back as the soldier awakened. His eyes were wide with surprise; he didn't expect the ring to bring the soldier back but it had. Each battle they faced from that point could be easily turned; every death would not have to be wasted.

"I was in the stream—the death—there were so many there!" the soldier said frantically. "You need to help the others before they are reborn in the dark confines of the Wicked Tyrant's deakylos!" The soldier helped Simon to his feet and almost dragged him to another nearby ally. The soldier sprung up from the ground with new breath and looked around bewildered at how he had recovered from his mortal wounds. He laughed and shouted, ecstatic that he would not face Etnian's wrath after death.

Simon quickly ran from body to body touching all of them that were whole. Each fallen warrior immediately opened his eyes and gasped a breath of new life. There was a myriad of reactions, but each one stood on their own with refreshed bodies and a smile on their faces. Simon's excitement continually grew as more ranks were recovered. He had a reverent appreciation for the ring and tried to restrain the inebriation of power that came along with it. He gave without thinking, and excitedly rushed to each fallen person even when his feet became weary.

After an hour of resurrecting the Kalinaw troops, Simon looked at the hundreds walking in the battlefield and thought of the enemies that still lay at their feet. He hated war and felt guilty for being a part of it and here, he had been given an opportunity to undo it. Without giving it any more thought, he bent down and touched an enemy soldier. He silently rebuked himself for not having done so sooner. The enemy's eyes sprung open and he bellowed as if being awoken from a nightmare. He looked at Simon and widened his eyes even more when he realized what had happened. His lip quivered and streams of tears fell down his face.

"He was so angry," the soldier said. "He said he was going to make an example out of us for our failures—the worst of deaths; even worse than the plans he had for your men! He strung us up and—I can't even describe it. But you...who—are you Kynn Veyor?"

Simon nodded his head.

The soldier realized what his new life meant for him. "I am freed from the bondage of servitude. I am no longer forced to live in the service of the Oppressor Etnian if the cycle of death can be ended." The soldier wept and thanked Simon.

Thuaran rushed to Simon's side and pointed weapons at the soldier.

"It's okay," Simon said holding up his hand. "Tell me," he said turning back to the new ally when the Thuaran relaxed, "why do you serve him? He is evil."

"The wicked man is driven by blinding corruption; even to the point of belief that what he does is right," the soldier said. "He said that we were chosen ones meant to purify Dyurndale from inequality and seize what was our just deserves. I didn't believe him though, I always felt it to be wrong but I never had a choice; none of us did," the soldier said. "He tortures people into submission."

He quickly stood up and bent a knee to Simon. "Please, allow me to serve you instead. There were rumors of your arrival and I've surely seen enough to believe. If you can bring us back—keep us from the deakylos— there are others that would serve you too."

"You can't trust the enemy," Bromle said as he walked up with a few others. He was bloodied and dirty but seemed otherwise unharmed. "You can't really trust that mad-eyed Sceadwian either. He ran into the tents screaming about how you can heal people and now you're bringing them back from the dead?"

"I can offer information too," the soldier pleaded, interrupting Bromle.

"It sounds like we have an ally," Simon said. "Plus, we need all the help we can get. What else would I use this ring for but to heal the injured and free the dead?"

"We could use the power for our own people. Let Etnian's vile forces be tortured," Bromle said.

"I can't say that I would have done anything differently if I was being endlessly killed."

"I would spit in the devil's face!" Bromle said and laughed.

"It's not my place to judge them—or yours," Simon said. "We'll let them all speak for themselves. I'm sure there will be those who are still loyal to Etnian, and we can keep them tied up. If we don't help them, they're probably being resurrected right now as reinforcements that we'll just have to fight again later."

Bromle looked down at him with a frown but didn't continue the argument. He looked away at some other part of the battlefield and spit blood from his mouth.

"I hate war," Simon said as he reached down and touched another fallen enemy.

His work continued even after the sun started setting. It was tiring, but by the time he finished, no enemies were left for dead in the field or the city except for those who were so dismembered that Simon was too unsure what might happen if he touched their remnants. The majority of them joined the Kalinaw and the army was strengthened—increased two and threefold. Most of the soldiers defected from Etnian's ranks; freed from the endless cycle of death.

"You need not march to the prison alone," Driscol said to Simon later that evening.

"I'm not going by myself, but I still think that's where we should go next. I've been thinking about that, too," he said quickly. "I think we should go as prisoners; let them escort us in and then take over the place from the inside. We have hundreds of enemies that have joined us as friends, but Etnian is none the wiser."

Driscol smiled.

"What?" Simon said.

"You have a creative wit and a knack for battle."

"I'd rather have neither, and there's still plenty of fighting left."

"Indeed, there is. Rest tonight and we shall see what the morning brings."

24 The Betrayal

Simon was weary from the battle the day before and was glad to have slept so deeply. Sentries surrounded the army's encampment throughout the night which passed without incident. In the morning, the legions of troops marched east for the prison between them and Etnian's home. Several groups stayed behind to contain the resurrected enemies who stayed loyal to Etnian. Driscol agreed to Simon's plan, and the enemy escorted the Kalinaw troops as if they were prisoners.

"What if they recognize you?" Adger said to Simon as they walked. "Or, what if we didn't resurrect all the enemies and one of them is telling Etnian right now that you're here?"

"I've got my coat for that," Simon said gesturing to the changeling jacket that he still wore. At his command, it began to change colors but this time it even appeared to change shape and grow. Simon pulled the hood over his head and it too lengthened and changed. When it had finished molding, he looked no different than one of their dark escorts.

"Simon, that's fantastic!"

"Hey! You!" One of the allied troops shouted at Simon from a few rows back. "You are supposed to be escorting us not talking with us. You'll ruin the whole thing. Get back to the edge with the rest of your kind."

"Well he's rude," Adger started to say before Simon cut him off.

"This is where we part ways for the time being, but I will stay close," Simon said as he moved to the outer edge of the group he was with.

Adger moved with him and stayed close to Simon but avoided speaking with him or doing anything else that might give away his subterfuge.

They climbed one final hill to see a castle surrounded by a tall, stone wall, topped with a spiked iron fence. It was settled on a mountainous peninsula that had steep cliffs on two sides and a sloping entrance that came down to a river that flowed around the cliffs. There was no drawbridge that crossed the wide moat. Simon thought he saw the water ripple from the disturbance of a large creature beneath the surface and hoped it was just fatigue whispering illusions in his ear.

As they descended towards the structure, a portcullis that stretched the width of the sloping entrance began to disappear into the wall above it. Simon thought it was odd though that there was no bridge across the water and felt the burning desire to ask someone what was going to happen but thought better of it. His perplexity was resolved when he heard the long note from a horn being blown within the castle.

The water in the moat started to churn and a leviathan, much like the one that Simon had fought in the Vareex, came out of the water. It examined the masses as they came to the edge of the moat to wait for permission to cross. It leaned far out of the water to peer at the groups of prisoners and captors. Simon's heart raced, and he was terrified that he might be discovered by a scent or keen eye. He looked towards the ground and was grateful that his hood had formed a mask around his face like that of the other enemy forces. Still driven and overwhelmed with curiosity, he stole a glance up at the creature. He wondered if there was only one great leviathan in the world or if this was yet another great beast to be feared. He waited for the confirmation and tried to avoid making eye contact with the serpent. Then, he saw the creature's eye crossed with a fresh red scar from Simon's attack. It was the same creature that he had fought before; this beast was Saipere! His heart pounded with anger at the remembrance of Lazuli's death.

Simon thought of the capabilities he had not had when they first met. He considered striking out at the creature in vengeance.

"What say you, Saipere?" one of the guards said in the front of the formation. The voice interrupted Simon's fury, and he quickly turned his gaze back towards the ground.

"I say you reek of the enemy's stench," Saipere said. "And there is a foul smell that..."

The leviathan moved near to where Simon was standing. Gusts of air blew into the ground from the creature's breath. Simon stood as motionless as he could manage and channeled the familiar power of the earth below him. He slowly moved his hand to his sword and quietly pulled the hilt from his belt. He felt the warmth of the handle and readied himself for the attack. He even managed to get his shield dislodged and was ready to defend himself if it was him that Saipere was after.

"I cannot tell what that familiar smell is," Saipere said. "There is too much wretched filth in your ranks." He retracted his body back into the water, and just before his serpent face disappeared beneath the water, he hissed, "You may pass."

The space between the land and the castle churned as wide pieces of earth rose from the water. The stones were dry by the time they had stopped moving and they created a flat road to walk across.

"That's right worm," one of the guards said up front. "You best let us pass."

The water exploded as Saipere quickly emerged and snapped his jaws around the guard; swallowing him whole. He growled at the other guards and constantly huffed breaths on them as he smelled them when they passed.

"I should eat the rest of you as recompense or, at least, twenty of the captured," he said. "It's only fair."

The creature opened his jaws wide and moved towards the prisoners. The stench was so awful that one of them actually vomited. Several guards nearest to him laughed.

"Your breath is punishment enough, Saipere," one of the guards said laughing.

The thousands of troops were marched into the castle. The gates swallowed them like the gaping mouth of a hungry creature. Guards were poised on the ramparts, aiming weapons down at them; all dressed in dark armor like the other Etnian guards. The prisoners were ushered by rows of enemies and every additional regiment Simon saw made his hope diminish a little more. They were continually dragged and shoved along and into a massive field that could have held the entire Kalinaw fleet with room to spare. They were all faced the same direction and were ordered to silence. After the masses settled, they stood in silence just long enough to become uncomfortable. A horn blow sounded like the one at the gates, and even the guards quieted for what came next. Simon looked around with just his eyes but saw no indication of what was to happen.

"Welcome to Deakylos Gulta!" a voice boomed.

Simon looked around and spied a man standing on a balcony on one of the surrounding walls. His features were indistinguishable but his importance was no less lost by it.

"I am Warden Daudi, your rehabilitator and guide through this deakylos; although your arrival is less than customary. Soon you will all understand the wisdom of our leader, Lord Etnian de Aithna!"

The guards cheered at the mention of their King, and Simon—as disgusted as he felt to do so—cheered along with them so as to maintain his ruse. Simon feared whatever the plans were for his friends and even more so did he worry that the plan would be enacted too late.

The people were soon split into multiple, smaller, and more manageable groups. Simon followed along with the group closest to him and kept quiet. He had stowed his weapons again, but the clanging alarm in his mind told him to strike. He had an eye on Adger but not his brother; he felt that Bromle could handle himself if the need arose. Despite the success that the Kalinaw had so far, he became increasingly nervous about Driscol's plan that had been laid out earlier that morning. It remained to be seen whether they could successfully coordinate the attacks of all the allies and the defected enemies. Attacking from within seemed the most logical thing to do, especially when considering that access to Maydanok was only granted by the leviathan, Saipere.

The evening was full of celebration by the enemy. The trust that was being burdened on the defectors nearly consumed Simon as he sat amongst the revelers. He was sitting with fellow guards in an open dining area of the fortress that was large enough to hold about half of the Kalinaw fleet. The enormity of the enemy masses gave him a meager peace in that he hoped he would be easily overlooked.

He avoided drinking but welcomed the food. He refused to make eye contact with any of those around him and ate quickly so as to get his mask back on. He sat on the outer edge of the hall so that he was not entirely beset with enemies. When it seemed he could slip away quietly, he did and went to find Adger.

The prisoners were kept in roofless cells that, on their own, were entire wings of the buildings. The prisoners were contained by little more than a cell door and only guarded by a few soldiers that patrolled the walls above. Simon eyed the patrols and hoped they had either been convinced to join the coup or had not noticed him. After some quiet questioning of the prisoners he managed to find Adger amongst them.

"Do you think the defectors are convinced enough to help?" Adger asked.

"I hope so," Simon whispered. "If not, I'll be all alone in a prison where torture and indoctrination are standard practices."

Their conversation was interrupted when several of the guards fell from the wall and landed in the groups of Kalinaw troops. Troops quickly rushed to the fallen bodies and took what weapons they could and dragged the bodies to dark corners. Driscol's plan had begun.

Before Simon could open the door and cut away any cuffs, enemy guards rushed in from hallways leading to the cell. Simon pulled out his sword and shield and ignited them in defense. His coat changed to a dark mix of colors and he pushed back his hood so that any of his allies would know not to attack him in the middle of a skirmish. The guards that rushed towards him held up their hands to show a lack of aggression once they saw who he was.

"We're on your side," the closest one said. "The other groups are being released as we speak and their weapons returned to them."

The soldiers opened the cell doors and the Kalinaw troops rushed out whispering orders and making barely a sound. They split up in different directions, grabbing weapons and blue scarves as they ran past the carts the guards had brought. They all knew their assigned tasks and quietly moved in coordinated groups to implement the takeover.

The defectors had tied blue scarves around their arms and nodded at their new allies as they passed. Most of them split off with the Kalinaw while a few stayed behind to help direct them. Simon waited for all the Kalinaw to exit the cell and pointed at the defectors' armbands with a confused expression.

"Your High General Driscol recommended it," one of them said. "Hopefully it will decrease the likelihood we will be killed by Kalinaw soldiers."

Simon and Adger rushed off with the last group to leave the cell. Their task was to capture or kill Warden Daudi. At first, they met no resistance. As the group quietly rushed through the halls the tension steadily grew.

"Where is everybody?" Simon asked the lead defector that ran alongside him.

"Most of them should still be enjoying the feast; they'll either be passed out, or too satiated to fight effectively. Our groups feigned the indulgence as best they could so our wits should be as sharp as our blades."

After a few more turns, they were back at the feast halls. A hallway went around the entire circumference of the room which gave them protection from being completely exposed unless they walked out into the hall. Long rows of empty tables were the only thing there; not a single enemy was in sight. Even the stars in the sky started to fade as the sun washed them away.

"Who is going to the barracks?" Simon asked.

"Brom went," Adger said. "He wanted to catch them while they were sleeping."

"We rarely sleep on a day of victory," the lead defector said. "Something is wrong."

He walked out into the banquet hall looking up towards the long open balconies that lined the vast room on upper floors.

"I do not understand," he said.

His sentence was interrupted by a cloud of arrows that pierced him from multiple directions. His body fell to the floor.

Swarms of arrows shot towards the outskirts of the room where the allies were standing. Before they could react, many of them fell to the floor dead. Those that had shields, or were farther back, were fortunate enough not to be killed in the first or second barrage. Simon had the wisdom enough to extend his shield when he realized what had happened.

"Not all of your defectors are allied," Simon said to the closest of guards.

"You are right," he said. "Not everyone believes in you." And with his last word, he stabbed Simon in the side with a short dagger.

Without hesitation, Adger cut the man's head off with his wooden sword. He dragged Simon to a wall where they wouldn't be hit by the arrows and were able to keep the defectors to their front. Kalinaw soldiers rushed to defend them. Only Adger had seen the guard stab him and both groups were now uncertain of allegiances. The enemies were all around them, and it wasn't clear if every defector had been truthful in their conversion.

The arrows stopped and silence hung in the air. Neither the defectors nor the few Kalinaw surrounding Simon and Adger knew how to proceed. A group of the defectors reached up and pulled the blue cloths from their shoulders. They quickly moved into the enormous banquet hall for the protection of their archers. The ones that stayed looked towards the Kalinaw with expressions of surprise and alarm.

"We knew nothing of this," several of them said.

"You cannot win this, Kynn," one of the guards said from out in the banquet hall. "You are surrounded by enemies."

Several other groups of defectors walked into the center with their blue scarves held high. They threw them down on the ground as they joined the growing betrayers.

Before every armband had hit the ground, the earth beneath them exploded upwards as bodies, rocks, and dirt flew into the air. A creature crawled out of the hole that seemed large even when compared to the enormous hall. Its skin looked like ancient bark and in some places, it looked like the pattern of fallen leaves on a neglected forest floor. Its back was covered with foliage that ran in a ridge up to its enormous head. Each detail of it was indicative of a terrene origin. It was certainly the fourth dragon from the statues of Stoikheion but was more akin to an enormous pogona bearded dragon than the more serpentine expectations that Simon might have had for a traditional dragon. It stomped on the guards as it climbed out of the hole and was undeterred by the arrows the enemy archers shot at it. The arrows bounced of its skin, unable to pierce its tough hide.

Simon was breathing heavily and had suffered greatly from the stab wound. He wanted to see the battle through to the end but began to worry he would be pulled to some other deakylos when his life expired. He looked to Adger, but his senses became muddied and it was hard to tell what he was doing. Adger had enough sense to pull the black and white ring from Simon's finger, put it on, and touch the wound. All the while, Simon was fading from consciousness. The wound shone a light from within and a moment later, Simon was renewed. He jumped to his feet and ignited his sword and shield; full of life.

"I guess it works for you too," Simon said. "Keep it for now; we'll have need of it soon enough."

From around a small window looking out into the banquet hall, Simon peered at the creature that was decimating the disloyal defectors.

"It's the last creature from Orvar's frame, Jortho" Simon said.

"I hope he's on our side," Adger said.

It was unclear at the time of Jortho's intentions, but the Kalinaw were glad that he was set on distracting their enemies. Loyal defectors took aim with their ranks towards the balconies and started firing towards enemy archers, or those who fled from Jortho.

The soldiers that escaped from Jortho's destruction had no other choice but to charge towards allies on the outer edges of the room. They were readily received and swords clashed and soldiers fell. Simon and Adger both joined the fray and fought their way out of the room. Finding the Warden would be more of a challenge with the betrayal of the defectors.

A group of the enemy was launched into the banquet hall as a large part of the wall was blown inward. Bromle stepped through the hole with his gloves smoking from the orbs he had used. He rushed over to his brother and smashed the guards together that he and Simon were fighting.

"The barracks are empty," he said to them. "Not many of them were there; seems like you found the rest of them," he said gesturing to the balconies. "What can you do, Simon?"

Simon closed his eyes and the brothers provided him protection while he concentrated. With his mind, he reached into the earth and stretched out his hands after he quickly stowed his weapons. He could hear the shifting of sand and scuffling feet around him but it was deeper than just what his ears were gathering. He felt the crawling life in the dirt below and the vibrations of Jortho's stomping. He wanted to move the earth and throw it towards the archers but something even deeper felt as if it was calling him. He felt the chill of the river deep below the ground and a shiver ran up his spine. He thought of Saipere and his fight with Lazuli, and he wondered if she was still in that river somewhere, or if she really had perished at the leviathan's hand.

He was reminded of the small metal frog in his pocket and with little pause, he reached into his pocket, pulled it out, and threw it towards the hole Jortho had emerged from. The object was well-aimed and disappeared down the hole. The battle raged around him, but Simon still felt connected to the water below them. He felt it surge and spurt. A moment later, a geyser spewed from the hole in the banquet hall with Lazuli at its top in all her armored splendor.

"Lazuli is alive!" Simon shouted gleefully.

He ran towards her without waiting for protection or coordination. He extended his weapons again and deflected arrows or cut down enemies as he went. He jumped towards the geyser, and the water twisted and reached out to catch him. He rode the wave up to where Lazuli stood with a sharpened, golden trident that had jewels at the base of each barb.

"My, you've come so far from that panicked boy in the boat," she said to him as he joined her. "I see Jortho has joined you, too," she said, gesturing to the forest-dragon.

"I'm sorry I was so useless in the Vareex," he said to her quickly. He felt so ready to apologize, he thought of little else to say.

"You're not so useless now, are you? *This* is not my doing," she said gesturing to the water.

"Far from it," he said. "Even still, I am so glad to see you're alive. Thank you for saving my life."

"There will be time for all that later. Now, come! Let us fight together!"

He projected the water in stretching waves towards the balconies and picked up earth as he flew and threw it into the archers. He simultaneously used his weapons to either protect them as they surfed, or strike those that the pieces of stone missed. The battle there was fierce, but the advantage had begun to shift in their favor, especially with Jortho's aid.

The enemy soldiers fled from the banquet hall and all the allies pursued them. Jortho smashed through walls as he followed; barreling along as if the stone were nothing more than paper. The fortress' legions converged in the field that the Kalinaw army was first brought to. Other groups of defectors and allies were pushing their way into the field as well; the enemy was being boxed in from all sides in the center. Even still, their ferocity was no less diminished, and many Kalinaw fell that day.

Simon's water supply continually funneled through the hole in the banquet hall. Whether from his expenditure of the water or something else, the speed and supply of water on which he moved started to diminish. Eventually it was insufficient enough to support him and Lazuli, and they both rolled to the ground.

"What happened to the water?" Lazuli asked him.

"I don't know," Simon said. "I can still feel it, but something is blocking it."

The something was immediately revealed as Saipere smashed through the hole that Jortho had made. He slithered along, pursuing the allies and swiveling his head in search of the forest dragon. A surge of water followed along behind him and flooded the field nearby. Jortho turned to face him in the field and charged him with as much ferocity as he had when he blew holes in the walls. Simon realized that Saipere had managed to dam the hole somehow and try as he might, he could not produce any manipulation of the water. Saipere and Jortho slammed into each other and became entangled in a rolling struggle for power. Each one of them savagely tore and scratched at each other. Simon wanted to help Jortho but knew his efforts would be ineffective. Instead, he turned his attention to the dwindling enemy forces.

Now that he was in the thick of the battle, he had lost sight of the brothers. His heart skipped a beat when he wondered if they had fallen. He looked back and forth for them and even shouted their names. Simon felt a pang of regret for having given Adger the ring of Olim; not out of selfishness, but because he worried a severe wound would prevent Adger from using it on himself. To lose his friends now would have devastated him, but he resigned his fears and focused on the battle.

"Have you seen the brothers?" he shouted to Lazuli when he wasn't deflecting an enemy swing, or striking in response.

"How can anyone—" Lazuli said before struggling to push back an enemy. "You must stay focused! If you fall this will have all been for nothing."

Simon hated the thought of carrying on without being able to defend his friends, but he knew that Lazuli was right. He grit his teeth and charged into the next enemy. A couple of the Thuaran ran up next to him and stopped a pair of converging swords that would have otherwise ended Simon's efforts in a second. The clashing weapons made him thrust his blazing sword in defense. He incinerated the enemy and nodded to his saviors.

He continued the fight alongside his comrades but was unable to fling chunks of earth or masses of sand like before due to how mingled the crowd had become. Before, he was able to focus on a color or variation that isolated the enemy from allies. The bedlam was too overwhelming for Simon to effectively use his abilities, but his sword and shield were put to good use. He longed to do more; ever looking for a lapse in the enemy or an opportunity to save another ally. Etnian's forces were continually pushing them in from all sides.

Jortho and Saipere continued to wrestle in the open field behind him and rolled in a tangled mess of dragon fury, smashing into the outer walls. When Simon turned his attention back forward again, he saw the outline of a creature in the sky that was flying through the dissipating clouds of the dawn. The shape was familiar to him, and he hoped his assumption was wrong. The creature burst from the clouds and came straight at the battlefield. It was a crimson dragon with every detail like the one towering over Stoikheion. It flew below the tops of the walls and indiscriminately incinerated a group of allies and enemies. Simon vainly cried out for the loss and was glad Tortuse was not there to feel the same pain of betrayal again.

When the smoke cleared from Cineris' attack, Simon saw that the dragon had a rider who wore a dark fluttering cloak which masked his features. His robes, however, were so close to the color of the dragon that he seemed to be an extension of the creature. They flew high into the air and turned as if to blast the field again. Before it spewed another stream of fire, a second winged creature slammed into its side. The red dragon spun wildly in the air and released the fire in a chaotic arch and landed in the field, sliding across the earth.

"Cineris and Hekaze," Lazuli said running up next to Simon. "The dragon of fire and the serpent of wind."

"I have met Cineris before, and I recognize that the blue one—" Simon said as he cut another enemy that charged them. "It was in Canton and tried to kill us!"

"You must be mistaken. She is an ally and kind unless provoked. Did she truly attack you?"

"Come to think about it, no; her people were actually attacking the Canton guards."

"We will ask her if we come through this but know she is a friend."

"And who is Cineris' rider?"

"I fear, Simon, that you are about to meet your true enemy. I have never seen him, but I can only imagine that he would not shy from this battle...especially not with you here."

Simon didn't need her to explain who *he* was; the fearful realization had come to him clearly enough: Etnian de Aithna had arrived.

The long note of a deep battle horn sounded across the field and a flash of flame jumped from the very skin of Cineris.

The fighting closest to Etnian subsided as he stood from behind the fallen dragon who stayed still, dazed from Hekaze's attack. Etnian stood in a flurry of long, scarlet robes. He wore a helmet that encased a menacing scowl he directed towards Simon. His skin was black, like the creatures Simon had battled in the arena and outside Kamena. He was as big—if not, bigger—than even the largest of his forces Simon had seen in the battlefield. It was obvious that his size was not simply a cause of clunky armor either. He unfastened the cloak from around his neck to reveal two hilts sticking up from his back. The armor Etnian wore was covered in a mixture of spiked scales and glittering designs.

Flashes of the stained glass doors in Sophia's library filled Simon's mind. His need for gallantry was ever present in the evil land of the enemy, but here, under the gaze of his diametric nemesis, the need was greatest. The sight of the foe ached Simon to his core as if fear was not oppressive enough.

The sky above the battle scene turned dark even though the sun was much higher than it was before. Black clouds rolled in and darkened the day as if the sun was too fearful to shine. The darkness made Etnian's evil more overwhelming; enveloping, sharp, and piercing. Simon was almost grateful that he was momentarily distracted by the attack of several enemies around him as he pushed them back with his fiery blade.

"Kynn Veyor!" Etnian bellowed. His voice was deep like rolling thunder. It was enough to strike fear in any and all who heard it. "Kynn Veyor! Your death is at hand!" Etnian roared.

Etnian's followers dropped to their knees when they saw him; even some of the defectors groveled when he walked by.

The whole of the armies had not ceased their battle; even the dragons had not lessened their skirmish. Their bellowing and grunting immediately drowned out any remnants of fighting in their proximity. Jortho and Saipere wrestled back through an adjacent wall, and their crashing sounds quieted as they distanced their battle.

Etnian ignored the armies until one Kalinaw soldier jumped up and charged him. Etnian whipped out a ghostly pale blade and shoved it through the man's chest. The soldier shuddered and fell to the ground, gray and shriveled.

"You see that Kynn?" Etnian said. "Because you've created delusions in these fine people, that man will never know life again."

Simon didn't understand, which must have been an obvious expression on his face.

"This sword does not take life, it kills the *soul*," Etnian said. "To fall by its edge means to fall a final time, never to rise again."

"I'm not afraid of you," Simon said as he got closer.

"Foolishness is often mistaken for bravery. Tell me, child, what can you provide these people that I cannot?"

"A freedom from endless death," Simon said angrily. "You've ruined this world, and I'm here to undo your corruption."

"Ah, yes; the Gate of Naru, right? Don't you need this?" Etnian held up the ring-key.

Simon panicked and looked down at this hand but the ring was still there. He felt a moment of relief and nearly laughed because he believed Etnian foolish enough to assume he had the ring. Simon simply held up his hand and smirked while pointing at his ring. A long moment went by, and Simon was unsure of what to do next. He had the ring felt no threat of failure besides the obvious risk of being slain by Etnian's wicked blade.

"Where is Filch?" Simon heard himself demand.

"Who? Ah, yes; she mentioned what others had become accustomed to call her."

The gears turned slowly in Simon's mind; he assumed what the statement implied but was in such disbelief that he refused to acknowledge it. He started to wonder if the ring he had was the right one and his confidence was destroyed when Filch sheepishly stepped out from behind Etnian.

"Filch!" Adger said from close by, shoving his way through allies next to

Simon. "Are you okay? Did he hurt you?"

Simon was grateful to see him again; it was a wave of relief but was insufficient to outweigh the implications of Filch's return.

Etnian let go an evil and involuntary laugh. "You stupid, fat, boy," Etnian said. "She will never redeem her disloyalty, but I would not harm my own wife."

A moment of silence passed as Etnian's words hung in the air like the dark clouds in the sky.

"You rotten thief!" Bromle shouted from another crowd close by. "We trusted you!" He plowed through the battling he was amidst, reached out to an ally near him, and grabbed the spear he held. He quickly hurled it at Filch. In the last second before skewering her, Etnian deflected the spear with his sword and a flick of his wrist.

"I am...I'm sorry," she said quietly.

"We would have given you our *lives!*" Bromle shouted again, so passionately that he nearly came off the ground.

"You don't understand," she said as a single tear rolled down her cheek like a small crystal bead. Her eyes met Adger's and several more tears chased the first.

"You were our friend," Adger pleaded; desperate for understanding, his own eyes welling up with sadness.

She hung her head, unable to bear the weight of her guilt.

"You owe them nothing!" Etnian interrupted, shoving her back behind him again. "So, what will it be, hero?"

"I will never submit to you," Simon said.

"Neither will I!" Adger shouted.

"Nor I," Bromle said.

Others voiced similar refusals throughout the crowd.

"How touching," Etnian said sarcastically. "Sentiment is always the companion of delusion."

Etnian thrust his hand straight out into the open air, but his hand and most of his arm disappeared like he had thrust it into a dark lake. When he retracted his hand, it was wrapped around a woman's neck who dangled from his grip as he pulled her the rest of the way from whatever portal he controlled.

She was dressed as a warrior from another time. She wore clothes with plates of armor sewn underneath the cloth. Over her pants was a thick tasset of leather and across her chest was a breastplate of metal. Her armor and clothes were scarred and dirtied from battle. She carried a sword in one hand that dripped with black blood, and in her other hand, she held the freshly hewn head of an enemy creature.

"Hello, sweetie," she said, smiling despite having Etnian's hand squeezing her throat. "I wondered if I'd find you."

When she spoke, Simon realized who she was.

"Anna," he said.

When the word left his mouth, he was immediately overwhelmed with love and nostalgia. He became sick to his stomach with joy and sadness, simultaneously. His heart felt as if it might burst with a fire that would have been hot enough to melt the hardest steel. Flashes of his previous life filled his mind and brought him to his knees. His hands fell to his sides, and his weapons clattered onto the ground, returning to their stagnant, harmless forms, but he cared not. He recalled memories of first kisses and nervous young hands, holding each other tightly. He remembered joyous tears shed for the birth of new life: children, and children's children. He thought fondly of warm embraces and late night conversations over candlelight. The same love he felt for her for a lifetime poured forth from his very soul and the deepest of his emotional rivers. It felt like his compassion was being ripped from him; as if it was being taken without his will. Hot tears streamed down Simon's face at the realization that Etnian had somehow found his wife.

"You have one final chance to submit. Give me your life for hers," Etnian said.

Simon looked up at his wife. She smiled at him with her eyes in that way that only she knew how. He knew what she would have him do, but it tortured him to do it. He thought about giving in right there; throwing himself at the mercy of the enemy for the sake of sparing her soul. He looked at her again, peering into the deepest parts of her eyes. He inhaled deeply to steel his nerves and picked his weapons back up, squeezing his sword even more tightly.

"Don't listen to him, Simon," Anna said hurriedly as Etnian tightened his grip. "I couldn't be more proud of who you are."

Simon knew that to be his queue and blazed his weapons to charge Etnian. Before Simon could make a swing, Etnian quickly raised his pale sword and swung it downward towards Simon's wife. His attack was interrupted when a shot rang out over the sounds of battle. The bullet that followed tore through Etnian's shoulder. He stumbled backwards and lost his grip on Anna but not enough to avoid pulling her down with him. She quickly jumped up with a smile and ran towards Simon. He dropped his weapons again and knew he was being haphazard, but nothing was going to stop him from holding her again. He smiled and for the briefest of moments, he forgot what he was there to do. They were steps away from each other when Anna stopped short as Etnian's sword violently thrust from her chest. She grabbed at the blade and looked towards her husband with a withering gasp.

Simon was immediately overcome with a rage so savage that the world around him became silent and all he could hear was the beating of his own heart. The loud roar that escaped his lips seemed muffled and distant to him, but it was enough to instill terror in every soldier on the field; madness, unbridled, and unapologetic. His lungs were so full of air, it was as if the bellow would never stop. His eyes and throat burned with emotion and the blood boiled in his veins. Simon felt the same oneness to the world around him that he did in the stadium and the desert. It was as if the land mourned alongside him. He pulled up pieces of the ground around them, larger than he ever had before. He rose above Etnian on a wave of sand and earth while his frenzied utterances were fueled by what had happened. His sword and shield both blazed on their own and hovered into the air. They rose to his height and rushed to Simon's open hands and his command.

Etnian callously threw Anna's body to the side. She landed with a crude thud as the surrounding forces fled from Simon's elemental storm. Kalinaw soldiers picked her up from where she fell and laid her back down as respectfully as they could. And it was just as well they did because the brunt of Simon's fury was immediately released when she was out of the way. He charged forth like a tsunami of earth. His sword spewed a geyser of flame to rival the greatest of volcanic eruptions and his shield spun with slashing, fiery blades on the edge. He directed every iota of his wrath towards Etnian, sending rock, sand, and fire to intercept him. Simon rode the wave of raw energy that slammed into his enemy with a devastating force that sent Etnian all the way to the outer most wall of the fortress. When he impacted with it, it exploded like a tremendous bomb. Huge chunks of the wall went flying into the air and countless people were knocked to the ground from the shockwave.

Simon dropped to the ground as his wrathful reaction dwindled into empty horror. The masses of soldiers knocked down from the blast stood up as he ran past them. Even those who were kneeling to Etnian stood up. He rushed to his wife's side and carefully picked her up in his arms. She smiled with blood running down her cheek from her mouth.

"I've missed you so much," she said to Simon as he cradled her in his arms.

"Where have you been?" Simon asked her. He turned and screamed for Adger before she could answer.

"Hoping to find you," she said in between coughs. "You're so beautiful," she said reaching up and touching his face.

"Adger!" Simon shouted hysterically.

Adger ran up as he was shouting and Simon hurriedly put on the ring. He touched his wife's injury but no light shone from the seeping wound.

"Why isn't this working?" Simon said through frustration and tears. He repeatedly tried the ring.

Orvar ran up with Gin holding her long rifle.

"I tried to stop him, Simon," Gin apologized.

Simon tried again and again, each time concentrating with every bit of focus he had.

"Gin! Orvar!" Adger said excitedly running to embrace Gin. "Where were you?"

"Up there," Gin said pointing to a tower. "We went up there so I could use this," she said holding up her rifle.

"Some good it did," Bromle said sadly as he walked up too.

Ignoring them, Orvar spoke to Simon, placing a hand over his which frantically pressed against his wife's wound repeatedly.

"The ring can give life to those who need it, and those who are beyond its power can have their soul restored with the sacrifice of another," he said.

"Then I give it gladly! Just tell me what to do!" Simon said.

"It cannot be you. Your path lies elsewhere." Orvar took the ring from Simon and broke it in half, separating the black and white parts.

"What are you doing?" Simon asked frantically.

Orvar put on the black part of the ring and slid the white one over Anna's finger. He picked up her hand and touched the portions of the rings together. A small whirlwind encircled them up to their knees. Orvar immediately started to age and the color in Anna's face began to return.

"No, Orvar!" Adger cried rushing forward. Tears immediately streamed down his face. "Orvar, you can't go! Let *me* go, please."

Bromle restrained him and kept him from intersecting the whirlwind.

"Take faith, my dear friend," Orvar said reaching a flaking hand towards the saddened younger brother. "There is need of you yet."

"But what about…" Adger struggled to find an excuse to prevent his friend from disappearing. "—your books, Orvar; who will look after…" Adger was unable to finish his meager pleas. "Please don't go; I still have so many questions!"

"My home is yours now; you have always loved its stories. You will look after it well."

Adger's sadness overwhelmed him and his knees weakened. Bromle held him tightly to support him and to keep him from preventing what Orvar was doing.

"I have been given many years," Orvar said as more of his skin started to crack and chip like old pages in an ancient tome. "I will not return here like your wife will, Simon, but I may not be altogether lost."

With those last words, the rest of his body disappeared in the wind. The small storm settled just as quickly as it started. Simon looked down at Anna who was still smiling.

"I'll see you again," she said as she slowly disappeared like the light of the dusk. Simon's hands were left empty.

"She will return," Lazuli said placing a hand on his shoulder. "And we will find her—you have my solemn promise that I will personally find the deakylos she emerges from—but...right now...we need to stop Etnian from reaching Naru."

Simon stood up with concrete resolution. As terrifying and monstrous as Etnian was, Simon had no fear of him. He rose himself up on a platform of stone so that everyone in the massive courtyard could see him. He raised his sword and made it burn so intensely that it reached the dark clouds above. When the flames touched the clouds, they were blown away like a leaf in the wind. The raging battle had stopped on both sides in response to the change. Simon shouted loud enough for the furthest corners of the deakylos to hear him. He wasn't sure they would, but he spoke with as much vigor as he could muster and his voice carried to every ear.

"You have all fought with me and died alongside me. For those of you who have fought against me: know that you've been deceived! Etnian may be powerful, but only because you allow yourselves to live in fear of him. Through strength and the unity of numbers, we can overthrow him, but we must move now and make for the Gate of Naru."

Shouts and cheers of support rang out across the crowd but it was unclear how many of Etnian's followers were swayed by what he said. Simon lowered himself to the ground and walked up to his three remaining companions. Filch was being held with them by two guards.

"What should we do with her?" one of the guards asked.

"Let me kill her," Bromle said.

"I was going to give it back, Simon," she pleaded. "The fake one was harmless. But then I was caught and...you don't understand who he is."

"My wife died because of you!" he said as he got close to her face. "And your betrayal may mean the end of everyone here—*everyone*—if we don't stop him! That blood will be on your hands."

Simon grabbed her hands and wiped some of his wife's blood on them. "You might as well have killed her yourself. Lock her in a small cell with plenty of guards to keep her there. Do not kill her; that will only give her a chance to escape."

A bestial roar echoed across the field as Cineris flew into the air with Etnian on his back. Hekaze flew towards him but the fiery dragon turned and shot fire towards her and swatted her to the ground. Hekaze landed in the field and lay still, unable to continue.

Soldiers encircled Simon to defend him and they all readied for Etnian's attack. Instead of incinerating them, Etnian circled the field and Cineris roared one final time. He flew away to the east and as he turned his back on the field, all his loyal soldiers turned to embers and were drawn to form a cloud behind him. Etnian and all his allies were gone in an instant.

"We need to get there *now*," Simon said. "Where is Kapell when I need him?"

The remaining troops quickly organized into groups and prepared to start the long march to Naru. Simon checked his own belongings but was still unsure how to catch up with Etnian before he made it to the gate.

"What about Hekaze?" Simon asked Lazuli.

They both ran over to her. The beast was still breathing quietly in the field but appeared unconscious.

"She's in no shape to be burdened by us," Simon said. His ring of life was gone and he could only hope she would recover on her own.

"What other option do we have?" Adger asked as he walked up.

"Kapell, where are you?" Simon shouted out of frustration more than actually hoping Kapell would hear him.

Simon felt the ground tremor slightly and was hopeful that he had been heard. The vibrations became more intense and Kapell showed up on the other side of the wall carrying something in his hands. "He has the key to Naru, Kapell," Simon said hurriedly. "We need your help. Can you get us there?"

"That is why I have brought you gifts," the giant said as he kneeled down and opened his hands. "I would have brought more but could only find a few in such a short time."

Out of Kapell's hands walked a sable antelope, a wildebeest, a blackbuck, and a lion. Each one of them wore varying saddles and armor crafted for them individually. They were calm as if they knew what their purpose was. Simon, however, was not completely clear on the gift Kapell had brought.

"These are the fastest animals of their kind," Kapell said. "You must go ahead, and I will bring the army behind you."

Simon, Adger, Bromle, and Gin approached the animals, each mounting the one that kneeled for them to climb aboard.

"I will help them here, and I will see you soon," Lazuli said.

"I've never ridden a lion before," Bromle said excitedly.

"Just do not spur him very hard or you may become a meal," Kapell said to him.

"Please don't delay," Simon said. "I have no idea what we'll be riding into."

"Good luck, Simon," Kapell said.

With a final farewell, Kapell lifted them over the moat and the four of them rode east as fast as the animals would take them. They could only hope that they would get there before Etnian did.

25 The Duel

The four of them spurred their mounts and the animals ran without exhaustion. They nimbly leapt over obstacles and uneven terrain without slowing down or tiring. They rode for several hours. The sun reached its apex before they stopped for water, or food, and even that was brief.

"Can you tell how close we are, Simon?" Adger asked.

Simon opened his hand to look at the map of Maydanok.

"I'm guessing," Simon said, "but it looks like we're about an hour away from this field in front of the gate. If he brought his army, it'll be impossible to get through."

"What about a way around?" Adger suggested.

"It looks like there is a ridge that surrounds the area, but if we walked along it, that would take us hours out of the way."

"Let's hope there aren't many troops then," Bromle said.

After a short time they reached the edge of the valley before the gate. They climbed a steep hill bordering the land beyond, and with the help of the animals, it didn't take very long. They were on the crest of a bluff overlooking the valley below that was filled with trees.

"At least we'll have some cover," Simon said.

To the south, off to their right, a wicked storm was coming from the sea. To their left and north a dark dust cloud was moving in the converse direction. Both storms looked like they would converge in the valley.

"Do you think that's—"

"Sammos and Veadus?" Simon said. "Yeah, I'd bet it is. That explains where Sammos is but not where he went. As for Veadus, I thought she was dead."

"Death is a relative term around here," Adger said.

The sun darkened slightly as a hazy cloud blocked its light. The group looked up only just in time to realize it was the shadow of a volley of arrows.

Simon pulled out his shield and extended it wide enough to block all four of them. The arrows clattered on the extended range of the shield and sank into the ground around it. The four of them retreated back down the hill to avoid the archers' range.

"They must've been waiting for us," Simon thought aloud. "Did anyone get a look at how many there were?"

His companions shook their heads.

"How are we going to get down? Oh, I've got it," Simon exclaimed.

After he explained his plan, they dismounted and prepared to release the animals to their homes. Bromle kept a firm grip on the lion's reins.

"We could use them," Bromle said.

"The forest below is too dense for them to be effective and using them might go against Kapell's expectations," Simon said.

"This is war, not a dinner party where we retain our manners."

"Aye, it is a war, but I'd rather not be on the angry side of a beast such as yours when he'd rather be on his way home," Gin chimed in.

Bromle hesitated another moment and then let go of the bridle, and his mount rushed off the way they had come.

"Is everyone ready?" Simon asked. "Bromle, why don't you get us started?"

They all nodded and Bromle charged up some orbs in his gloves. He launched them towards the crest of the hill and it ruptured into huge pieces of earth. The four of them ran at the cracks that formed in the ground and, when they reached the top of the hill again, Simon ripped up the ground beneath them in a flat slab for them to stand on together. The hill shuddered and then collapsed down towards the valley in a landslide with the great slab at its top. Simon directed the chunk of earth down from the crest of the hill and onto the landslide like a giant sled. Gin fired her weapon into the trees, creating a barrage that would kill any enemy unlucky enough to be caught in it. Bromle continued firing orbs of air and fire into the trees while Simon tried to protect them with his shield as much as possible. Adger had his bow, which transformed rocks he dragged across it like the stick he did so long ago outside Orvar's cabin.

The enemy continued firing volleys of arrows as the group slid down the steep bluff. When the mound of earth had been filled with the black shafts of enemies' arrows, the landslide had neared the bottom of the hill. The earth crashed into the trees and swallowed archers indiscriminately. As the slab finished its fall, they all jumped and Simon launched the stone sled from beneath them towards the trees like a giant discus. It cut through the forest like a saw, leaving stumps of trees and soldiers in its wake. It wasn't sufficient enough to destroy all remnants of the enemy; plenty more stood up, firing arrows from the broken and cut trees.

More enemies emerged from the undamaged forest around them and the four of them were immediately engaged in a heated battle. Adger pulled out his sword which provided a concussive blast every time he struck with it like it had a gale within it, waiting to be released. Bromle used both his strength and gloves to smash enemies or launch debris towards them. Gin made easy work of the enemies, but her purely offensive capabilities required her frequent retreat or intervention from the others. Simon's weapons and capabilities created an unequivocal advantage, but the mass of enemies leveled the imbalance. Their enemies were relentless and fearless, despite the ferocity the small band of warriors had. It seemed the recurring waves of black-armored enemies would never stop charging them.

They fought well, but their progress was slow, and they needed to hasten if they hoped to reach the gate in time. All of their bodies wearied from the constant flood of enemies. The bodies of their opponents were trampled underfoot by both ally and foe and made the terrain nearly impassable.

"We'll never make it there before him," Bromle said as he launched another orb with one hand and hurled an enemy with the other.

"Your optimism," Adger said as he struggled with an enemy, "is just the motivation this team needs." Gin shot the enemy Adger was struggling with. "Thanks," he said, grinning.

The ground began to tremor again as it always did when Kapell was on his way.

"I think help is nearly here," Simon said pointing towards an opening in the bluffs behind them.

Through the narrow opening in the hills, a giant's silhouette could be seen carrying what looked like a proportionally sized platter. He bounded through the terrain and jumped over the hills to land in the valley. He set down the platter he carried right on top of the trees. It was a massive slab of earth that created an expanse of open ground in the forest. On the plateau was every troop from Deakylos Gulta. They rushed to Simon's aid, overrunning the enemy as they went. Kapell went in the other direction, stomping the ground and the enemies upon it.

"Kapell!" Simon shouted up at him, hoping that he would hear him.

Kapell stopped and looked in Simon's direction. He had heard him indeed.

"We need to get to the gate. Please, help us," Simon shouted as loud as he could.

Kapell gestured for Simon to come to him and he stepped carefully through the forest to avoid crushing his friends.

Simon and the others fought their way towards Kapell and with the help of the reinforcements they came within his arm's reach. He knelt down and opened his hand for Simon and the others to climb in. The enemy relentlessly fired arrows at Kapell that he paid no attention to. The four adventurers were moments away from his rescue when a massive tidal wave slammed into him, sending Kapell flying. Simon and the others were momentarily caught up in the torrent and were battered against trees in the surging waters. Simon reached out and steadied himself on a tree as the waters shifted direction towards where Kapell had been pushed.

Through the trees, Simon saw the twisted body of Veadus standing triumphantly over Kapell far to his north. She was no longer the beautiful specimen of before. She was misshapen, like she had been pieced back together hurriedly. Simon was shocked; he thought about the way she had died and shook his head in disbelief that she could have any life left in her.

Bromle crashed through the trees, fighting an enemy his own size with minimal armor and bare, blackened skin, cracked and craggy like Kapell. A red fire burned in the creature's eyes and Simon worried he might overcome Bromle. He rolled onto his back and kicked his opponent towards Simon who swung his blazing sword and cleaved the enemy.

"What does it take to kill that giant, watery ghalla?" Bromle said, standing up and brushing himself off as he looked up towards Veadus.

The northern dust cloud overwhelmed Veadus and forced her to the ground. Through the haze Simon thought he saw Sammos' form but as large as his brother's; distinguishable by the shape of his royal armor. Simon had no more time to consider it because another group of enemies attacked Simon and Bromle, rushing in from the trees around them. They were surrounded on every side, but before the enemy converged on them, Adger and Gin crashed through their ranks with slashes and blinding bullets from Gin's gun. The group erupted into battle again.

Despite missing the opportunity to expedite their pursuit, the four heroes did not relent. They fought with even more ferocity as they knew that their time was running out. Their attacks were repeatedly coordinated like a ballet. The enemies pushed and the allies pushed harder. With the aid of the newly arrived Kalinaw, the relentless tide of the enemy was pushed back.

The sky darkened again from the storm that had accompanied Veadus.

"I hear the sea again," Gin called out to the others. "Everyone grab on to something!"

Another wave crashed through the trees. Sea-born enemies washed in from the south and shifted the battle in their favor. Even Bromle took a few cuts from the strengthened army. Amidst the battle, Simon felt something familiar despite the chaos—the same shifting influence he had in the desert—but it was beyond his control even after his repeated attempts to call it forth. Pillars of sand shot through the trees and crashed into the naga and scaly warriors of Veadus. Simon was bewildered in that he had not been the one to summon the sands. The enemies slowed and darkened as the sand filled the inside of their watery bodies with shifting seabed until they cracked like parched earth and were petrified in place.

Simon and the three others pushed their way through to a hill that rose out of the valley and from it, they could see the battle was being waged everywhere. Sand warriors from the desert rushed in from the north and more sea creatures charged from the south. The two armies smashed into each other, creating another battle group for Simon to pass through. He could see the three giants battling away to the north and felt a moment of debilitating panic; his only hope was to have Kapell carry them over it all, but he was fiercely engaged with Veadus.

"Adger!" Simon yelled to his friend with one last desperate idea. "I need your wings! It's the only way I can hope to stop Etnian in time."

Adger fought his way to him and quickly stripped his backpack off. He handed it to Simon, who threw it on his back and tightened the straps.

"It's made for me, so I don't know how well you'll be able to control it," Adger said. "You hold your hands out in front of you to go forward—"

Simon cut down an enemy that ran towards them as Adger tried to demonstrate how to use the wings.

"—and you tilt your arms to turn," Adger continued.

"I just don't know what other option we have," Simon said.

"Good luck, Simon. Don't forget, I believe in you; all of us do." Adger clasped his hand around Simon's forearm and Simon did the same. They patted each other on the back and let go.

"I'm sorry to leave you guys here."

"We'll be fine, hero!" Bromle shouted as he launched an orb into an enemy that was coming up behind Simon.

Simon was fearful to fly into the air where he could easily be shot by an arrow, but he was ready to risk it in order to end Etnian. Simon stuck his hands up in the air and the wings jumped from the pack. They immediately roared to life and he was airborne in an instant. Simon turned his arms as Adger had instructed, and the wings took him the direction he needed to go. He avoided getting too high as it seemed Veadus had brought a raging storm with her. Lightning flashed above the ceiling of the clouds. Below him, arrows arched in single apexes that failed to reach him. Nevertheless, they were still another threat he had to avoid.

He aimed for the cliffs on the opposite side of the valley where he remembered his journal outlining Naru. He kept the cliffs to his right and the battle to his left. He saw no openings on the cliff face, nor anything that looked like a gate. The enemy seemed more focused on the larger groups of Simon's allies so he felt slightly more at ease about his search. He was ever-aware that each second spent was another moment Etnian might find Naru first.

If it's a small gate, he thought, *then Etnian might've already found it and this has all been for nothing.*

A thunderous crack interrupted Simon's search and was so loud, it made Simon lose his concentration and caused his wings to shudder and falter for a moment. Simon was nearly overwhelmed with fear as he dropped in the air, but he closed his eyes tightly and the wings fluttered to life again. The ground to his left had split open and revealed a hellish chasm filled with fire and bright orange light. Simon could feel the heat from it, even as high as he was. The trees around the edge of the chasm sparked up in flame and quickly withered, leaving nothing but blackened landscape. He expected to see a volcanic eruption or a cloud of ash, but instead he saw giant, long fingers reaching out of the ground at the edge of the crevice. They ignited anything they touched. They flared brightly with burning fires that glowed through its skin. A fiery giant as big and wide as Kapell leapt from the crevice and out into the valley. It was more terrifying than Cineris or even Etnian, largely in part from its size.

Simon would rather have faced Etnian than his fiery giant. Its skin was constantly moving; a flowing river of fire and magma. It carried no weapons, but Simon gained the distinct perception that it did not need any. It was bipedal but had no other similarities to a man. It balanced with a tail bigger than the four dragons bound together which was likely to compensate for the wings on its back. Each one was big enough to wrap around one of the other giants twice. Its fingers were long and thick like the redwoods from around Orvar's cabin. Simon hoped that Kapell and Sammos could handle the creature because he was sure his efforts would do little to deter it. This was even more apparent when he noticed the thick plates of armor that covered its legs and arms; they were enormous hulls of metal ships with thick lashings to keep them in place.

"Simon," said a voice coming in through his communicator. He had managed to keep the new one quiet and hidden throughout his allies' capture and had nearly forgotten about it.

"Gin?" Simon asked. "Is that you?"

"Aye. Simon, that's Aryfel; he is Etnian's 'darkest conjuration,' as Orvar put it. He warned me about it in case he didn't—you know…make it."

"How am I supposed to find Etnian *and* avoid that?"

"If you kill Etnian, the evil he controls will go with him and that includes—" Her voice was interrupted and the communicator was silent.

Fortunately, Aryfel had not initially seen Simon flying through the air as his back was turned to Simon, but as if the terrifying creature could hear his fearful thoughts, the wicked giant spun his head. Simon now needed Kapell and Sammos more than ever. Getting their attention would be difficult since they were struggling with Veadus on the opposite side of Aryfel.

Simon called for Kapell, but he couldn't hear him over the distance in the way he had so many times before. Simon doubted they had not noticed Aryfel whose entrance was less than subtle.

Aryfel started stomping towards Simon and he darted down into the trees to hopefully avoid him. The fiery giant's feet kicked groves of trees aside like they were toothpicks in the sand. Simon could only hope to avoid the beast for a short time. Meanwhile, Veadus managed to keep the giant brothers at bay and prevent any aid they hoped to give Simon. She was twice her lithely form; misshapen and contorted similarly to when she called the water to her body in the early hours of Simon's adventure. Her face was an awful reminder of what Kapell had done to her and her vengeful rage was obvious in the way she fought the giant brothers back so easily.

"Call your servant," Kapell shouted to Sammos as they wrestled with Veadus.

"If I do then the Kalinaw will be without my warriors."

"If you don't, then they will likely be without a master just the same."

"No conjuration you call will help you," Veadus yelled in a broken and twisted voice; all feminism gone from her tone.

A roar sounded across the valley and Rykos, much larger than he had been before, sprinted to the brothers with a war hammer raised above his head. Rykos slammed the maul into Veadus' side and her form shuddered as masses of her water fell to the ground. She quickly gathered it back up and charged back at him with a wicked curved blade she had pulled from her side. The three giants converged on her and easily subdued her. Sammos and Rykos held Veadus down as Kapell raised his dark sword to cleave her again. Aryfel abandoned his pursuit of Simon and turned to aid his ally.

Aryfel sprinted towards Rykos and the brother, and Simon used the distraction to try and find Etnian. He hoped that Etnian would be close to where Aryfel emerged, since it was his conjuration after all. Simon hoped his propensity for serendipity had not disappeared yet. He scoured the land below him for any signs of Etnian, but all he saw was the mass of his forces running to engage Simon's allies on the eastern side of the volcanic chasm. The crevice prevented any help Simon could hope for. He could only hope that Etnian saw the chasm as enough of a barrier to keep him from harm and not expect an attack from above.

In a small clearing amongst the trees, Simon finally spotted him. There stood Etnian; his focus centered on controlling and directing Aryfel; his minion required consistent direction. Without really developing a plan, Simon dove with all the strength he could manage to force through his wings. He mustered all the heat his blade could blaze and directed it downward at Etnian, hoping to catch him off guard and end the evil that he had been so generous to share with Dyurndale.

Simon landed on top of Etnian and his blade sunk deep into his shoulder.

"What color do you bleed?" Simon whispered in his ear. It was a bit morbid of a thing for him to say, but he was furious for all the death Etnian had caused. He wanted to savor the moment with a bit of arrogance.

Etnian bellowed and Aryfel reacted to Simon's attack. The fiery giant turned from the gigantic brothers to protect his puppeteer. The change in Aryfel's determination spurred Kapell and Sammos to strengthen their efforts in making their way to him. Kapell swung his sword downward across one of Veadus' shoulder, across her torso, and back upward again to cleave the other limb. Rykos and Sammos stumbled back with her watery, severed arms in their hands. She didn't scream that time but laughed instead. Before her body fell apart, the water around her evisceration reunited the skin. New arms formed at her shoulders and she punched Kapell hard enough to make him stumble. Rykos and Sammos pushed Veadus harder yet somehow, her rejuvenated form was even stronger. Rykos dropped into a formless sea of sand and rematerialized behind Veadus. The sand giant grabbed her, dropped to his back, and bucked her in the air. Sammos and Kapell jumped over Rykos and simultaneously kicked her in the chest, sending her flying towards Aryfel. Her body knocked the burning giant back down into the crevice he was birthed from. When her watery form slammed into him, tremendous plumes of vapor filled the valley.

Veadus screamed more dreadfully than she had before as her form began to disappear in the cloud of steam that reached towards the black clouds in the sky. Aryfel tried to get up, but the water that Veadus released when she hit the heat of his skin slowed him down. His brightly glowing skin darkened like the rapid cooling of molten metal. The foul creature cracked and his limbs broke. His remnants, along with the ghostly portions of Veadus' contorted deathly expression, fell into the crevice that Aryfel's arrival had created. A towering cloud of vapor erupted from the hole in the earth as whatever moisture that Veadus retained was finally evaporated. The land around the crevice was plunged into a palpable fog of vapor, eliminating any reasonable amount of visibility.

As soon as the moment of victory was won, Sammos and Rykos fell into formless masses of sand and flowed towards the raging battle of the Kalinaw. Kapell rushed to the crevice and smashed the ground around where Veadus and Aryfel fell in their twisted form. He hoped to seal them beneath the ground and provide aid to Simon. He continued beating the ground until no red light crept through the earth. Once he finished demolishing the fissure, he put his hands on his knees and peered through the fog.

"Where are you, little hero?" he said, waving his hand through the mist to attempt to clear it.

Kapell could not find him, but Simon saw him swinging through the haze. He was not overly concerned for the giant's help after unbelievably scoring the first strike though; assuming his victory was imminent. Simon's arrogance allowed Etnian an opportunity, and with a flourish of robes and blades, he knocked Simon backward through the trunks of several trees. Simon felt as if his body was being broken repeatedly as each trunk slowed his flight. An entire portion of the forest was cleared from Etnian's retaliatory strike, and the shockwave from Simon's impact bent any tree that hadn't snapped entirely.

Simon was tangled in a heap of trees and branches. He felt foolish to have used such a vital opportunity for an insult but was glad that his body could handle more abuse than he would have assumed. He was hurt but not eliminated from the fight. He blazed his sword again and burned a hole through the knotted mess above him. The smoke made him cough, but he released himself from the devastation so quickly that he wasn't affected for long. Simon crawled from the intertwined destruction and scanned the trees for his aggressor.

I'm lucky that I found him, and now he's probably on his way to the Gate, Simon thought.

"You have a choice, Coward," Simon yelled, hoping to goad his enemy instead of drive him further towards the objective. "Either face me and prove you are the almighty power you claim to be, or give me the ring and give yourself up."

Etnian's evil laugh echoed through the otherwise tranquil forest. Simon walked along with his sword and shield, ready to defend himself. He entered a small clearing and moved to its center to hopefully have a clear view of Etnian's strike.

"What worth do you have that would justify my submission, boy?" Etnian said followed by another laugh.

"You rule in threat and instill fear for control! How is that righteous?"

"Fear is righteousness!" Etnian roared with anger. "I have no desire for such frivolity as benevolence. It softens the mind and creates such placidity that can never be relied upon. What boldness you have only comes from the gifts you've been given and not some inward power. Strength is created in force."

Simon felt uneasy with the banter. All the while they spoke he had no visibility or assumption of where Etnian might strike from. The mist that Veadus' demise had created obscured everything around him. He no longer had the surety of his first strike on Etnian and wished Kapell could intervene.

"The boldness I have is from the kindness of others, and the gifts I have are extensions of that grace. Your tyranny only exemplifies your weakness;

you are alone!" Simon felt pleased with his rhetoric, considering the circumstances.

His pleasure was interrupted by a rapid separation of the fog at the edge of the clearing, caused by the enemy's charge and the fluttering of his red cloak. It trailed behind him and added to his intimidating size. He wielded the ghostly white blade high above his head, ready to strike. He bellowed so loudly that Simon's momentary confidence vanished.

Simon raised his shield just as Etnian hit it hard enough to push Simon back, sliding on both his feet. The trees nearest them buckled and the dirt at their feet rippled outward from the force of their fight. They were locked in a moment of impasse where neither one wanted to relent: Simon had the defense, and Etnian had the destroyer of souls.

Simon thrust his sword over his shield and grazed the side of Etnian's face, leaving a searing wound in his flesh. It healed almost immediately, leaving no traces of the cut.

"You don't understand who you're fighting!" Etnian said with another laugh.

"And you don't seem to grasp who is about to kill you," Simon said out of intoxicating fear.

Without waiting for additional commentary, Simon shoved Etnian back with his shield. He quickly lifted the earth beneath Etnian's feet and turned it in the air to crush him back down into the ground between two massive protuberances. When Etnian started his descent, he sheathed his sword and pulled out the two smaller blades he kept on his back. He shredded the stones as if they were decrepit bark. He stood proudly as the pieces of the stone fell around him.

"Try as you will but you cannot win this fight," Etnian provoked.

He stretched out a hand towards Simon and thoughts of Simon's past life filled his mind. Simon tried to resist what he knew was coming, yet when he saw the faces of his children and relived the birthdays of his grandchildren, he could not control his response. He fell to his knees and the overwhelming emotion of the images threatened to consume him more than the bouts of nostalgia he had experienced before. His heart felt as if it might burst with longing as he saw his dying wife in his arms again; so fresh was the memory that it seemed the most powerful. Again he saw the children he left behind and the sadness constricted his throat when he replayed hearing them first call him, "Daddy" and say, "I love you." A burning blindness filled the bottom of his eyes as an outpouring of tears threatened to obscure whatever clarity he still had.

His thoughts drifted to the beyond; to Adger, Bromle, Orvar, Gin, and even Filch, and what they had done for him over the past few weeks. He felt sympathy in that moment for Filch and truly forgave her. He knew it was Etnian's evil that had corrupted her; not a darkness in her own heart.

She was a fearful mouse, caught in a serpent's jaws. It was as if a switch had been flipped in his mind. Simon decided to turn the sadness into power. Instead of being stricken by the longing he had for his loved ones, he used it to fuel his aggression. He thought of all the people who had suffered in Dyurndale for so long and considered what it would mean if he succumbed to Etnian's curse of reminiscence. Instead of being burdened by his responsibility, as he had in his early moments in the world, Simon felt empowered by it. His success would mean his friends' freedom and his own. He knew if he could succeed and overcome this evil, they could pass on after him. He thought one last time of his wife's smile and that she would live again to fight the evil left after Etnian was gone. Without Simon's success, she would be tortured forever. And that was all the motivation Simon needed to finish the fight.

"This is for you, Anna," Simon said quietly to himself.

"What did you say, boy?" Etnian derided.

Without another word or gesture, Simon rushed towards Etnian who was surprised that his affliction had failed. Simon swung his blade as fast and furiously as the sinews of his muscles would allow. Again and again he beat Etnian back with each strike. In a flurry of movements, Simon stowed his shield and used his free hand to hurl stones and trees too. Etnian did not expect Simon's sudden tenacity and his expression showed it. Simon struggled with the arrogance that came with his successful attacks but combated it by focusing on his friends who needed him to be successful. He continued pushing Etnian back towards the scarred landscape and was gaining ground with every single blow. Even with two weapons, Etnian had insufficient time to properly retaliate.

The battle around the trees in the forest left a wake of burning stumps and severed landscape caused by Simon's fiery weapons. Still he struggled against Etnian's obvious years of experience. Nonetheless, Simon never relented and gave everything he could into each strike. At one momentary lapse of Simon's onslaught, when Etnian had darted behind a particularly dark sprout of saplings, Etnian managed to stow his two weapons and draw out his pale sword. Simon realized that even a glancing blow from it could leave him withered like his wife had been. He knew that whatever would end the fight needed to be done soon; time was waning fast. He successfully blocked Etnian's retaliatory attacks, but knew that his inexperience would eventually be his downfall.

The tyrant looked to the skies for a brief moment and caught glimpses of what he perceived to be his momentary advantage: Cineris was flying in his direction. The dragon would be able to provide the incineration that Etnian so desperately required. Simon's peripheral vision caught sight of the creature too. He would be unable to react to any attack from Cineris amidst Etnian's forceful strikes. He feared that any momentary lapse in aggression would give his opponent adequate time to strike him down.

Simon couldn't have been more relieved to see swarms of his allies rush in from the mist and cross the scarred landscape of Aryfel's emergence. Some rushed at Etnian while others took aim at Cineris with bows and guns. It was the distraction that Simon needed, but before he could utilize the advantage and smite his opponent, Etnian rushed off to kill the marksmen aiming at his mount. He swung madly to prevent the death of his dragon; slashing, and hacking at the Kalinaw.

Despite the archers and gunmen, Cineris focused on Simon and opened his mouth to fire. Simon had no other choice but to defend himself and abandon his opportune moment to strike out at Etnian. The dragon spewed a stream of hell that was incomparable to its fire before. Simon ducked behind his shield and its diameter extended to block the inferno. It took what waning strength he had not to collapse from the sheer force of the dragon's viscous fire. It burned the world around him and blackened the densest of stones at his feet. His legs buckled and he dropped to one knee. Sweat poured down his face and his hands became slippery on the handle of the shield.

Etnian noticed the tipping scales and stopped his slaughter of the Kalinaw archers and soldiers to rush back towards where Simon hopelessly defended against Cineris. Amidst the fiery torrent, he walked up to Simon's side and was unaffected by the fire that splashed off his skin as harmlessly as tepid water.

"Now, you die," Etnian said, raising his white blade.

Simon could not move. The force of the fire he defended against required both his hands, yet on his exposed side stood Etnian with the weapon that could not only kill him but extinguish the mysterious soul that fueled his being. Simon felt his death lingering more closely than the heat that caused perspiration to soak his brow.

Etnian turned his blade to skewer Simon and thrust it towards his side. Simon knew that Death had found him in this life like in the last. He recounted his adventures in such rapidity that he finally understood how an entire lifetime could be recollected in a moment. He thought of all the experiences that he had gone through in Dyurndale and couldn't avoid the guilt he felt for failing the story he was meant to fulfill. He felt so foolish for working himself into the vulnerable position that he had, rushing into battle on his own without support. A momentary breath of knowledge was infinitesimal compared to the experience that he realized Etnian had. Time seemed to slow and Simon watched the sword drift down towards his side. He expected the pain of the fatal blow but before the weapon pierced him, it stopped in mid-air. It was only a hair's width from his skin. There it hung in empty space as if Etnian had decided to destroy him in some other merciless manner. Dark blood dripped from the tip of the sword but Simon felt no pain and was sure it was not his own

"I'm sorry, Simon," said a soft and pleading voice.

A shimmering apparition appeared at the end of Etnian's sword and after an unfastening of her cloak, Filch appeared with the sword jutting from her sternum.

Simon felt mortified. He assumed he would have had time to forgive her in another conversation, but there she was, sacrificing herself without reconciliation. He was speechless and could only consider the selflessness as a cause of his inability to impart forgiveness at the time of the offense.

He reached up with shaky hand, still struggling against Cineris' inferno, and touched her face. "*I'm* sorry too," Simon said.

She smiled for one of the first times Simon had seen. "Thank you," she said as the rest of her last breath left her.

Simon spun out of the path of Cineris' blast and quickly looked for a way to kill the creature. He spied a fallen branch and hoped it was not as burned as the woods around it. He reached out with his mind and hurled it towards the dragon. Cineris reeled and darted, but the spear found him and skewered him as ferociously as Etnian pierced Anna. The beast fell to the ground and crashed into the trees without another sound.

Simon turned to face Etnian on his knees who held Filch in his arms.

"This blood is on your hands," Etnian said to Simon.

"All the blood spilled in this world is on yours!" Simon screamed back at him. "You have ruled with such merciless dictatorship that the mere mention of your name struck fear in those who heard it. How can you possibly have compassion for her when none has ever existed in you?"

"I deserved more than this," Etnian said as if thinking aloud. "It was my idea, after all."

The whole of the Kalinaw army walked up to him and surrounded Etnian.

"Your army is defeated," Driscol said to Cineris as he limped up next to Simon. His arm was in a sling and obvious signs of battle marred his uniform but his demeanor was resolute.

"It's over, Etnian," Simon said to him.

With a final effort, Etnian screamed and charged at Simon with his deathly blade. Simon stepped to the side and swung down at the edge of his enemy's blade. Etnian's sword shattered like an icicle on stone. Simon pivoted and sank his blade deep into Etnian's chest.

The two nemeses were inches from each other's faces.

"This could have ended differently," Simon said to him quietly through gritted teeth with some sadness in his voice.

"You're right," Etnian said between labored breaths. "It should have ended in your death and so it may still, but I pass that responsibility to my brother. He sends the population of hell in vengeance. My death…is only the beginning."

Etnian's life left him with those final words. Simon pulled the ring from Etnian's finger and cast his own forgery aside. When the ring was fully seated on Simon's finger, the ground began to quake.

"What now?" Bromle complained. "Can't we just win, already?"

The ground between the allied forces began to split and crack. Nightmarish creatures emerged amidst the Kalinaw and from the lands around them. They were so far from the form of mankind that it was obvious what their demonic heritage was.

"The forces of Etnian weren't enough; now we must battle the forces of hell, too?" Bromle exclaimed.

The quaking and cracking continued, splitting the earth in a spider web of fissures. One of the splits reached all the way to the cliffs in the east and up their face to the plateau far above. Light shone from it so brightly that it made them all squint. The gap in the stone widened near the bottom until it was wide enough to easily allow several men to pass through. An archway way reached across the expanse like vines of gold; it hung down and formed two doors that seemed as if it might not hold up to the most deliberate of assaults.

"That must be it!" Simon said. "Driscol, that's the gate!" He shouted.

Driscol's voice amplified above the disaster, "To me, Kalinaw! All arms to me!"

The whole army converged on Simon and surrounded him like a thick dam. When cracks in the ground formed and sucked portions of the allies down, more troops filled the gaps. They steadily moved towards the crack in the cliffs; all of them hoping beyond hope that Simon was right.

The creatures that emerged from the fissures in the earth emitted evil cackling calls, and cries of bloodlust. Without command, the vile demons attacked the shifting huddle that so desperately protected their hero. They pushed the enemy back and pushed Simon forward towards the last hope of salvation for Dyurndale. This was the end; be it the end of them or the evil, the Kalinaw did not know, but they were willing to sacrifice life or soul to defend Simon.

Clanging swords ignited all around Simon and it was not without his involvement. Involuntary battle cries echoed across the valley from the lips of the valiant survivors. The good was beset by evil more foul than a single one of them could have imagined. Many fell by dark blade, and Simon prayed that their existence would not be lost on his account.

No man is worthy of this sacrifice, Simon thought. *Let them not end for me.*

Creatures of all size poured from the gaps in the ground: some small and others more formidable, requiring the attention of several men to defeat. Kapell aided them as best he could, but in such battles, it was impossible for him to pick out the enemies amidst his allies. His brother was helping push back the tide of Veadus' last remaining forces and also could do little more than hope Simon was well protected. Sid came barreling into the fray to help, and Lazuli's brilliant reflective armor was easily spied amongst the blackened demons, but Simon could not determine the allies' outcomes by the end of things.

The group was creeping ever closer to the looming cliffs. They were nearly at a point where the eastern most flanks could open the way for him. He was so close to the gate and whatever final adventure his soul was destined to be on. As the allied huddle moved to the crevice, the ground around them ruptured and a reinvigorated mass of evil vomited onto the landscape around them.

"Simon," Driscol panted breathlessly pushing his way to the innermost circle. "We can't...we're losing."

For the first time in Simon's whole adventure, Simon begged for intervention.

A trumpet sounded above all the noise of battle. A light shone from beyond the top of the cliff face, but it was greater than that of the sun creeping its way past its zenith. Creatures appeared in droves at the top of the cliff. Their robes were made from the purest white that reflected the sun in a blinding brilliance. The outer garments were hemmed with gold cord, and surrounded polished armor made of silvers, gold, and copper. They wore chest plates covered in gem stones from every color that could be envisioned in the finite limitations of imagination; rainbows of refraction poured from them like streams of water. On their heads were helms with metal feathers that swooped backwards into points that held singular and flawless orbs of crystal. They raised their hands to reveal a myriad of weapons that were all as ornate and ordained as the rest of their armor.

One of the soldiers of light walked out from the gate of Naru; calmly opening the gate and striding towards the warring masses of Kalinaw. On his back were magnificent feathered wings that stretched out once he passed through. He was so tall and wide that he even made Bromle look small. His hands were like slender talons that gave him a likeness to a bird. Simon remembered the statue outside the gate where he first arrived in Dyurndale. He wondered if this was the last of the four giants. This winged man was indeed a giant but not nearly the size of Kapell, Aryfel, or Veadus. The winged man raised a sword that was as clear as the crystal in his helm. When he dropped his arm and pointed it towards the enemy, his warriors fell from the tops of the cliffs. They streamed down the walls like a waterfall and screamed joyous cries of battle. Their shouts were fearless as they ran straight down the face of the cliffs as if they sprinted on flat land.

The dark evil creatures that encircled the allies seemed to know what the new warriors were, but Simon only had the faintest of inclinations. As they came closer, the Kalinaw army prepared for an attack on both fronts but the white soldiers flew over or between them like a breeze.

The angelic troops ran towards the enemies around them and, without an order, the entire Kalinaw army rushed to join them. The cries of the enemy were drowned out by the clashing of metal and the trampling of the charge. The enemy was not yet defeated but was severely outnumbered. Even with the reinforcements, victory was not secured. The emergence of an ally gave the Kalinaw hope, and they fought with every bit of strength they had left in them.

"Simon," Bromle said as he rushed to Simon and grabbed his arm. "It's time for you to go. GO! We'll hold them back!"

"Come with me!" Simon shouted over the battle. "You and your brother both; you've done enough to earn your way."

"No; our place is here! We were brought here to help you fulfill this task and you've done it. Now, go! We'll get our chance to follow you."

"I can help you win this battle; you know I'm capable enough," Simon pleaded.

"Little brother, you cannot turn the tides of this war. It will continue until evil's candle is snuffed out."

Bromle escorted Simon towards the cliff, and he went reluctantly. After several close calls and a final few enemies, Bromle and Simon made it to the crevice of Naru. The gate sat open and was one final step away.

Simon desperately clutched Bromle's sleeve. "Where is Adger?" he said, filled with the sadness of leaving his friends behind.

Adger pushed his way through the soldiers closest to them. He rushed to Simon and hugged him tightly.

"I now have two brothers," Adger said. "I will miss you greatly." Tears filled his eyes.

"Thank you for your guidance," Simon said to him. "You were the map when I lost my way." Simon handed Adger the green journal and Adger nodded his head.

"Littlest brother, we must let him go," Bromle said to Adger with a hand on his shoulder.

Adger reluctantly released his hug and shook Simon's hand more vigorously than when they had first met.

"I don't think I'll need all this where I'm going," Simon said, beaming. He handed him his bag of trinkets and rings (beside the ring of Naru), and doffed the wings Adger had engineered. "Goodbye, my dear friends."

"Goodbye, Simon; Kynn Veyor," Bromle said smiling.

"Goodbye, Simon," Adger said as he wiped tears from his eyes.

Simon turned and rushed through the gate. As he passed through the metal fence, a rumbling started in the ground around him. He glanced back at Adger who waved at him with a smile still on his face. A tear rolled down Simon's cheek; he was saddened from the finality his journey had reached.

Death was the beginning of his adventure and now that his quest was complete, he feared he might miss it. The rumbling continued and Simon saw its source: Kapell was running towards the gate with his black sword held high.

Sid leaned his head around the corner of the gate and made Simon jump. "Stay back from the gate, Simon. Master dun Shan must seal it for now. Please, step back. And good luck on the other side."

Simon's eyes widened as he quickly backed away from the opening. Kapell leapt and spun over the remaining Kalinaw forces and stuck to the towering cliffs with the flats of his feet.

"Goodbye, my young adventurer," Kapell said, looking down through his legs at Simon.

Before Simon could wish him well and thank him for all he too had done, Kapell dun Shan stabbed the ground in front of the gate, effectively sealing Simon off inside the pass.

A flash of green light shot up towards the sky from the other side of the sealed gate. Simon could feel the life that the light was pouring back into the world, but he did not have the privilege to witness the change that spread across all the realms. The world of Dyurndale was being restored and Simon had become Kynn Veyor in its fullest promise.

He heard a soft voice from either within him or on the other side of the dark sword. Only one word came through with enough impression to give him action: "Go." And so, he began to move forward, down the narrow ravine, on to answer the greatest mystery of all.

Simon was, as when he had entered the world of Dyurndale, completely alone.

26 The End

Simon was in a narrow passage filled with thorns and brush, as if neither time, nor caretaker, had the thought to maintain it. He spent the afternoon pushing his way through the brush and getting scrapes and cuts enough to make a casual walk painful. Eventually he exited the suffocating ravine into a wide open field that stretched away for endless miles. The rolling fields were full of plush grass, and endless rows of cultivation, reaching far out into the distance to the foot of cascading purple mountains.

The mountains went on infinitely, and Simon thought he could stare at them for an age if not for the other things that ensnared his attention. The temperature was perfect, like the cool breeze before autumn's grasp. The air carried scents of jasmine and honeysuckle, and made him forget any injuries he sustained from his journey.

A peaceful vigor filled his lungs so greatly that he forgot the pain of every awful moment he had endured both in that existence and the one before it. The overwhelming nostalgia that Etnian had inflicted on him disappeared. The memories were still there but not so full of anguish as they had been before. Instead of the rage he felt for Anna's end, he thought of how she had likely already been resurrected. Instead of paranoia that she would awake within a deakylos, he knew—truly believed—that Etnian's evil influence had fallen along with him. He obviously had no method to confirm his suspicions, but there was still a serenity about it. He envisioned Anna's smiling face as she stepped out of the stream in her warrior's splendor. He wondered what her new story was but knew he would see her there soon enough to ask her.

He recalled the guilt he felt for his cowardice in the Vareex with Lazuli, but he didn't feel the guilt; he was simply aware of it. He did experience the excitement of seeing her again, though. Every laugh he shared with Adger and Bromle was on the tip of his tongue, and he found laughter rumble out of him involuntarily. He thought of Adger's love for food and, for a brief moment, could still taste that first meal of mystery meat they had eaten together.

Newly uncovered, forgotten memories filled his mind too. He remembered joyous moments of his childhood; things that had long since been lost to him. He perfectly recalled his descendants' first steps and first utterances. He remembered the smallest things as if they had just happened, but through it all, there was no sadness.

His eyes filled with tears, but the ones he shed were out of such happiness that no gift could ever replace them. Indeed, they were a gift all on their own. A lifetime of memories filled his mind in complete recollection. He could have sat there for weeks replaying them, if not for his need to press on and come to know this new end.

A city far in the distance shone a light from its center as if the sun had set in its midst. He was drawn to it and felt compelled to move his feet despite the thoughts for the friends he left behind. He looked back towards the overgrown pass of Naru and felt confident that they were well-equipped to survive the battle he left them in. He did hope they would not suffer, but the worry didn't consume him like it might have in days past. The splendor of the new environment was a pleasant distraction and impressed a tranquility on him that washed away his qualms. There was so much life in that place compared to the world on the other side of Naru.

Beasts of stunning size and variety roamed in between the trees and flew through the air; reptiles, mammals, and avian beauties filled the land. Simon thought he may have become delusional, but some of them stared at him from amidst the trees with such intensity that it felt as if they might know him. He tried to remain timid and nonthreatening, but just coming out of a battle with the evil he had faced made him unsightly. He kept his weapons stowed and tried to seem as peaceable as a filthy, bloodied, and injured person could. Simon stayed completely composed even when a cobalt tiger walked up to sniff his hand. Its fur was a blue hue, and it was so large it nearly came up to Simon's shoulder. He felt the impulse to pet it, so he did. He knew it was a dangerous creature, but he felt no fear and received no aggression in return for his affections.

"I'm not accustomed to a human's touch," the tiger said in a deep but pleasant female voice.

"You talk!" Simon exclaimed.

"So do you," she said with a laugh.

"You're not the first talking animal I've met, but you are the most beautiful."

"Many thanks to you. Pray tell, where did you come from?"

"The Gate of Naru," Simon said, turning and pointing back to the dark ravine.

"No one comes that way any longer," she said circling in front of him but keeping her eyes fixed on him.

"Oh yes—of course—I have the weapons, here." Simon quickly fumbled with his belt.

The tiger growled and Simon froze out of fear; a feeling that felt unnatural in that land. "There is no need of those here; we know who you are quite well."

Simon steadied his nerves and felt the familiar peace quickly return. "What is that city there?"

"I have the feeling you know well where you are.

"I have an idea of what it is." Simon watched as the tiger circled around him again and sat beside him to stare at the city. "What of my friends? Kapell closed the gate, and I doubt anyone can find another way in." He looked at the gate ring still on his finger. He felt no worry for them, but he still burned with curiosity.

"Fear not for your friends. Their story will end in its own time but in a different manner. The way is not lost; just sealed for a time. It will stay that way long enough for them to finish what you started."

"And what now?"

"The path lies before you but you cannot be made to take it."

"Well, then take it, I shall," he said trying to sound formal. "Good day," Simon said bowing slightly.

"You humans are quite strange." The tiger chuckled and walked into a nearby grove to disappear amongst the trees.

Simon stood there for a few moments longer then looked back at the dark ravine one last time. He turned away from it and steeled himself for whatever life came next.

The closer he walked to the city, he realized that animal eyes were not the only ones that watched him. The faces of young and rejuvenated people stared out at him from the sides of the road. He was uncomfortably aware that none of them stood on the road itself, and so he worried that he should not be walking on it either. Some of them were frozen in place to stare at him; reaching up to pick fruits, or bending to pull vegetables from the ground. The people at work in the fields carried baskets of food or were in the midst of placing them on carts pulled by animals that idly swung their tails.

"Hello," Simon said as kindly as he could to those he would pass.

Not a single person returned the gesture or the greetings he provided, and it made him apprehensive; he would've rather had the enormous tiger at his side than walk alone.

After an exorbitant amount of that awkward procession, Simon took a final turn on the crest of a hill and could see the city in its fullest splendor. Tiered walls carried waterfalls that filled places in the city with majestic plumes of mist. Simon thought it would be pleasant to get lost in those plumes and be refreshed by them. The walls that weren't masked with water seemed to be constantly ablaze with sparks of a welder's craft. The designs being etched across the city were too far to see, but he was excited to discover them. The outermost wall was interrupted by a single massive gate at the front of the city; its doors were open wide. As difficult as the city's intricacy was to see from the distance away he still was, Simon could tell that every detail of it was immaculately created. No one artisan could spend an infinity crafting it on his own.

The city was a feat of architecture but the world around it was a wonder all its own. Millions of people roamed in open flat land outside the gates and inside the open archways. More people wandered the plains around the city than Simon had ever collectively imagined or seen in his few years of previous existence. There were innumerable carts and booths that surrounded the city and they were all filled with food, wares, gifts, and all manner of craftsmen. Rows upon rows of people were showcasing their amazing things in the world, either made or discovered by them.

Simon's feet continued to carry him like he was stuck in a pleasant dream that he never wished to wake from. Despite all the people he saw, not a single one gave him anything more than blank stares as he walked past them. He continued to greet them, feeling less threatened but no less confused. He slowly descended the hill towards the city, assuming that eventually someone might return his greeting or tell him where he was.

When he walked past the booths, he noticed that people would take freely without payment, or excitedly give something in exchange. Not once did he see any currency or bargaining that might denote a semblance of confrontation. People ceased their activities so readily upon their notice of him that he couldn't be certain. Nevertheless, the tranquility was encouraging; whatever their reasons for silence, Simon did not feel threatened by the people there.

There were booths for bugs, birds, and animals of all shapes and sizes; all of which were also still and quiet when he walked by them. People were on the backs of bears, rhinoceros, and even a giraffe. Some of them carried eagles on their shoulders, or had fruit bats hanging from an extended arm. Others were followed by mammals that, in any other setting, might seem dangerous. Everything in that exotic place seemed like it was there to be shared and enjoyed by all. Children were laughing and playing; trailing ribbons and kites in their wake—until they took notice of him, and their toys fluttered to the ground.

No matter how long he walked, the city never seemed to grow close enough to examine it in better detail. The sense of urgency he felt over the past weeks was gone from the forefront of his mind.

He continued to greet people but they remained stoic—not threatening but not responsive. He didn't think they feared him, but Simon started to think he did not belong there. He even tried varying tactics of reassurances but all his words seemed to fall on deaf ears. He thought he caught the murmur of hushed whispers but when he would turn to the noise, people were quiet and still.

After turning another corner in the myriad of booths, he started on the final approach to the city gates. He assumed that if he could obtain no answers outside the city, maybe there was someone inside that could help him. He wondered if this was his end or if there was yet another journey he had to make.

The dark archway of the gates disappeared and shone a bright light, even though it still seemed to be miles away. Simon could see a singular blot blocking a small part of the light. All the people to the sides of the path turned their attention towards the gates and their unanimous movement startled Simon. The people seemed to stiffen and straighten their stances. The blot became a shape and the shape became a person.

The whole crowd stayed still and silent all the while; only turning to face the figure as it passed. Having turned their attention towards the gates, the people took no more notice of Simon on the path.

"What's going on here?" Simon asked completely exasperated at being ignored. "Please, what is this place?" he said as he ran to the closest person, trying to break their attention.

Simon eventually gave up his efforts and focused on the small blot walking towards him. A long time seemed to pass as the silhouette became more of a person than before. The man had discernible and simple features.

"Hi...hello," Simon said. "Can you tell me what this place is? I was told I was supposed to come here."

"We've been waiting for you. Welcome home, Simon."

The crowd erupted into cheers and applause. Waves of joy seemed to wash over them and up and into the fields beyond. Simon smiled and felt his face warm as the blood rushed to it. He was excited, even though he wasn't sure what might come next.

The man stepped next to Simon and wrapped his arm around his shoulders. He walked with Simon towards the gates of the city and smiled down at him.

"Come, I have prepared a place for you at my table."

ABOUT THE AUTHOR

Dylan Marquis is an American author of fantasy fiction. He currently lives in Charleston, South Carolina with his wife and children where he works in the aerospace industry. The excitement of reading and imagining great stories is a passion of his that started at a young age; writing and drawing illegible tales and imagining other worlds. He has long had the desire to publish the stories growing in his mind but only recently harnessed the true meaning of writing for the sake of the story.

His drive comes from his family, and he loves spending time with them more than anything. When not going on adventures with his kids, exploring the backyard or the wonderful streets of downtown Charleston, he enjoys gratuitous amounts of streaming media and video games.

Writing has always been a delight of his; it just took a while to focus it into the pages of his first novel; a life-long dream finally achieved.

If you like what you've read, make sure to check out the Dyurndale Facebook page to stay up to date on signings, sales, and news for upcoming books. If you enjoyed the book, and can spare a moment, please don't forget to leave a review on Amazon, Goodreads, or whatever other site you'd like to! Let me know your thoughts or send me a personal message at dyurndale@gmail.com. Thanks for reading!

Dyurndale: www.facebook.com/dyurndale

56787099R00195

Made in the USA
Charleston, SC
28 May 2016